SHORT STORY AMERICA

VOLUME II

EDITED BY T.D. JOHNSTON
FOREWORD BY ALAN HEATHCOCK

Volume II

Short Story America

47 Great Contemporary Short Stories

Edited by T.D. Johnston

ISBN: 978-0-615-68670-7

Published by
Short Story America Press
www.shortstoryamerica.com
editors@shortstoryamerica.com
843-597-3220

FIRST EDITION

Printed in the USA

Book design by Tim Devine
Manufacturing by MURR Printing
www.murrprintingbeaufort.com

SHORT STORY AMERICA

VOLUME II

EDITED BY T.D. JOHNSTON
FOREWORD BY ALAN HEATHCOCK

SHORT STORY AMERICA PRESS

This book
is dedicated
to the authors and readers
who are part of the
Short Story America
experience.

TABLE OF CONTENTS

FOREWORD

Alan Heathcock

I come from classic Midwestern stock. We are kind and sensible people. We do not make noise or try to stand out. We are good members of a community and will shovel your driveway before you wake and bring you a plate full of cookies just because we made a batch. This is to say that we're not made of the stuff of writers. But I always knew the we was not me, and that I was different. I was not rebellious, was, in fact, studious and obedient and reverent. But on the inside I felt an undeniable longing, a call that would not leave me.

I remember writing my first short story in my 9th grade English class. The story was awful, was about robots taking over a town, full of clichés and trite heavy-handed symbols. But writing the story was invigorating. I recall lying in my parents' basement, staring up at the ceiling and seeing the robots in my mind, robots stomping down over a little town, crushing silos and leaving giant robot-foot-prints in the bean fields. It wasn't work. It was fun. But more than fun, it meant something to me. Even at fifteen years old—a hard age to motivate—I was inspired. I remember we workshopped the stories in class and someone made a snide comment about my robots and I wanted to do awful things to that person. I cared...deeply. I cared like I'd never cared for anything else.

Yet after that story-writing unit was over and we went back to the normal English class fare, I didn't write another story for many years. But, with everything I ever read, I thought about writing stories. When I read Hemingway's story "Indian Camp" in my senior year, I was so moved that I actually started to weep. I'd just had a friend commit suicide (which happens in Hemingway's story, too), and, again in my parents' basement, I looked up the window well to see the clouded sky and pondered the stuff from which men were made, from which I was made. I was roiling on the inside, so much pain, so much anger, so many unspoken questions. Where could I put this stuff? It must go somewhere, after all.

But being sensible, I went off to college. By a stroke of amazing luck, I went to the University of Iowa, the premier school for creative writing in the country. I, however, went to study business. I told people I was going to be a financial planner. For my first few years I tried the business school route, with little success, with absolutely no motivation. I switched to journalism, closer to my passion, yet still practical. With a J-school degree,

I could go into marketing or promotions, could write ads. That's what I told people: "I'm going to write those funny commercials...".

Then, to graduate, I was required to take writing courses outside my major. I saw a fiction workshop and signed up. I worked harder on my short story than I'd ever worked on anything. I hardly slept for a week. In our workshop we read short stories, Raymond Carver and Flannery O'Connor and Stuart Dybek, Rick Bass, Leslie Marmon Silko, and Alice Munro. With every story I read a little piece of my soul was made more alive, made bigger, and I scoured the library to find more short stories. I was hooked, writing stories morning, noon, and night, barely paying attention to my other classes.

I graduated and got a job. A regular job. A sensible job. I worked for an architect who specialized in senior living facilities. My job was to travel all around eastern Iowa, visiting every single senior home and trying to convince directors they needed my boss's services. On one particular day, I was down in the south-eastern edge of Iowa, in a town named Keokuk. It was July. 100 degrees with high humidity. I was wearing a suit and tie. On my sixth or seventh senior home visit, I got cursed out by some director who was having a bad day. I left dejected and angry, feeling stuck in a way I'd never felt stuck before, the kind of stuck you only feel when you realize you'd made terrible decisions along the way. This was my life. This was where all my hard work and determination throughout college had dropped me. I couldn't stand going to another senior home. I pulled off my tie and unbuttoned my collar and decided I'd call it a day.

I drove to a park with big shady trees. I sat on a picnic table, high up on a bluff. Far below, the mighty brown that was the Mississippi river slogged southward. In my backpack were a few random story collections and I took them out, decided to read a couple of stories, just to pass the time (I couldn't go back to the office yet), to forget the day for awhile. The first short story I read was Joyce Carol Oates' "Where Are You Going, Where Have You Been?" I barely breathed reading it. So taut, so visceral, so intense. Next I read "The Five Forty-Eight" by John Cheever. The end of that story has a woman, a jilted lover, forcing a man at gunpoint to put his face in a mud puddle. It was so powerful that I stood up, paced around the park, imagined myself making the rude director who'd cursed me out put his face in the mud. Then I read Joy Williams' "Winter Chemistry", which ended in sudden violence, so stark, so real, that I could barely move.

I stared down at that huge churning river, trembling a bit, watching barges forge on to somewhere else. I sat there for a long time, thinking things through. Finally, after so many years gestation, I allowed myself to say the words, meekly at first, but voiced nonetheless, and undeniable, words that would change my life forevermore, would leave me poor, would leave me frustrated and sleepless and bitter, would fill me up with the joys and pains of humanity and leave me, day after day after day, completely inspired, and wholly motivated. Those words gave me the greatest life, a life where each and every day I indulge my curiosities, purge my demons, express my hopes and fears, words that allow me to urge my own children to follow their heart's passion for we have so little time to waste.

I said, "I'm going to be a writer."

More than a writer, I became a writer of short stories, these little narratives that are far from small. My life has been altered, made better, by the presence of stories. An anthology like *Short Story America* is the exact kind of book that can change the world, its myriad voices spinning yarns of woe and whimsy, making you tremble, cry, laugh, swoon, and maybe, just maybe, to cause you to close the book, look up from the pages a little bleary, and know you'll never be the same, transformed by what you've just read.

* * *

Alan Heathcock's fiction has been published in many of America's top magazines and journals, including *Zoetrope: All-Story, Kenyon Review,VQR, Five Chapters, Storyville,* and *The Harvard Review*. His stories have won the National Magazine Award in fiction, and have been selected for inclusion in *The Best American Mystery Stories* anthology. *Volt,* a collection of stories published by Graywolf Press, was a "Best Book 2011" selection from numerous newspapers and magazines, including *GQ, Publishers Weekly, Salon,* the *Chicago Tribune* and *Cleveland Plain Dealer,* was named as a *New York Times Editors' Choice,* and a finalist for the Barnes and Noble Discover Prize. Heathcock won the GLCA New Writers Award, a National Endowment for the Arts fellowship, and is currently a Literature Fellow for the state of Idaho. A native of Chicago, he teaches fiction writing at Boise State University.

INTRODUCTION

It is a pleasure to present the second volume of the *Short Story America* anthology series. This collection brings to over a hundred the number of quality short stories published by Short Story America since the organization's inception in 2010. All of the authors and I are grateful to you, dear reader, for your devotion to short fiction. The short story, once so widely read in the days prior to electronic entertainment, is making a comeback in today's culture, and it is individuals like you who are helping to bring such well-deserved audiences to these and other superb authors and the stories and characters which they create.

The forty-seven stories in this volume were selected from nearly three thousand stories submitted. While Short Story America can only publish a small percentage of the stories we receive, we are thrilled by the level of talent and commitment from the thousands of authors who have offered their fine work. This era does not afford the writer the opportunity to make a full living from writing short fiction, not like a writer could do in the days of O. Henry, F. Scott Fitzgerald, Flannery O'Connor, or more recently the late Raymond Carver or the late Ray Bradbury. Today, a writer of short stories creates tales without expectation or reasonable hope of a big payday. He or she creates characters and puts them into situations which often matter to us as much as to the characters themselves, because the author believes that we have much in common, we human beings, and that art in all its forms matters to our souls; indeed it can have, in the case of short stories, that "singular effect" which Edgar Allan Poe described when writing on the topic of great short fiction.

Whether you are an early collector of our young series at Short Story America, or whether you are enjoying our short stories on your electronic reader or smartphone, please be in touch with us. Our mission is dedicated completely to the short story and its author. To remain informed of the developments and direction of our mission, whether for writers or the classroom or simply in support of the short story as an indispensable contributor to human understanding, go to our website at www.shortstoryamerica.com. Join our mailing list there. Pick up the phone and call us. Tell us when you love a story, or ask for help in contacting a favorite author in this book or in any of our collections in this series. We are fans of short stories, all of us. That's why we're here.

I'm glad you're joining us. Long live the short story, and its writer and reader!

– T.D.J.

A CLERK'S TALE

Vanessa Hemingway

We met early in the fall of 1973, when I was still trying to paint. I was a young man, twenty-seven, and I would guess he was more or less the same. He entered one of my favorite drinking establishments, on the corner of Fifty-Sixth and Lexington, dressed in a good-quality suit poorly maintained. There were wrinkles, a button missing from his cuff, and several food stains on his lapels. Within ten minutes of his sitting down on the barstool next to me, I recognized that he was someone who should have been wealthy. His temperament was made for it—gregarious, generous. His gestures were grand and unpretentious, but he didn't have the resources to back them. That afternoon he unhesitatingly handed me his last cigarette and then, patting his pockets, offered me his silver lighter as collateral if I wouldn't mind "spotting for another pack."

When he told me he wanted a portrait of his wife, he flattered me. Though he'd known me all of fifteen minutes and to my knowledge had never seen anything I'd painted, he suggested that work of my caliber was beyond his means. "Painting is a vocation," he said, "and you've been called."

I dressed the part. The artist's equivalent of the priest's Roman collar in the beret on my head, the cravat loose around my neck. What I couldn't see then but what I can see now is that he must have recognized my need, and possibly, my imminent failure. I was intensely thin then, living by the principle that the senses were keenest when a body remained in a constant state of moderate physical hunger. If I allowed myself a pint or two, such as I had that afternoon sitting next to him, it was at the end of a productive day's work and always instead of my supper.

"In art," he said, "nothing is taboo. Whatever the subject—if it's done justice—it's priceless. Can you put a price on it?" he asked. "I don't think so."

I agreed with him. "In fact," I said, because it was a topic I felt warmly about, "do away altogether with filthy lucre. Adopt a barter system, born directly from our peculiar needs and desires. There's a world in which I could be happy." Our glasses sounded in the air, one against the other.

"I only wish," he said, "you could see her." After a mere moment's consideration—I could actually trace the gestation of the idea in his movements: his eyes widened, his chin dropped to his chest, and then he swallowed deeply—he told me that for a real artist (an artist, he suggested, such as myself), the very act of painting his wife's portrait would be payment in itself.

"She's an unusual beauty," he said. "A woman who should be painted. A woman you would want to paint—as soon as you saw her. And not just saw her the way you and I are seeing each other now in this dim pub, two beers between us, but in her most pristine and elemental. In the nude," he said to me. "It's when she's finest."

I would have liked to paint *him*, right then, in the moment of his lusty and indiscreet disclosure. To attempt to capture it—whatever it was—that spurred this man to offer me a privity hitherto exclusively his own: his naked wife. I squinted, trying to find the locus of his desire in the diminished light. His hands, perhaps. The way his hands worked, constantly moving, restless. Like two rats, I thought, scampering when he spoke about her.

There is a sort of brotherhood born out of pints drunk in tandem—perhaps, I persuaded myself, this explained the peculiar affection I felt for him. And I was curious. Not at the prospect of a beautiful woman naked before me, something I'd had the good fortune to experience more than a few times. More probably the woman was not beautiful. Likely she was plain, made beautiful to this husband's eye through much the same process that he made more of the less in his life: his contagious conviction. Possibly she was ugly. His powers were such that I believed she might even be hideous.

His hands scurried around him, scratching and picking. He lit another cigarette while the last burned dully, only half-finished, in the ceramic ashtray on the varnished wooden bar. The obstacle, he said, was that she would never consent to model for me. Not for me or anyone else. Even completely clothed she was much too shy, too self-conscious.

"In point of fact," he said, "she's religious."

Although I remarked I knew of no religion that forbade portraiture, he indicated that she would find it frivolous and a vanity to have her own image rendered. No, it would be impossible. He finished his drink, pushed back from the bar, and stood up to go. He paused, looking at me a trifle long. Thinking back, I've applied portent to that lingering glance, assigning to it the moment he chose me for his collaborator. But at the time I remember thinking: "His wife is an ice queen. There are no conjugal visits."

Before he pulled open the heavy tavern door he clapped me on the shoulder and said it had been his pleasure.

Fine then, that's that, I thought, each time we met, for we started to meet regularly—he was good company. I did not mind buying him drinks, and very occasionally, when he had "come into some money" (it seemed his father had bequeathed him a small trust, payable in quarterly installments) he would spend everything in his pockets, buying not just rounds for me but for everyone in the bar. He always got right to the subject—his exceptional wife, who should, must be painted but for the difficulty, the impossibility of it because of her extreme principles. Finally, maybe because of the drinks we had already had, or simply because I couldn't stand to hear it spoken of one last time, I told him I would meet her. After meeting her, perhaps I could sketch what I remembered and from that come up with a cameo that would satisfy him.

"No, not just her face." He shook his head. His hands kept busy, and when he finished a thought he pinched the tip of his nose. "It must be all of her, her whole body. Nothing less than revelation," he said.

"Come now," is likely what I should have said. "What's this?" and "Tell it to me straight." Because he was working himself up to something, and having indulged his continuous return to the topic, even just to hear him out each time as he ruminated its impossibility, made me in some sense complicit. Instead I told him he was a lucky man. What did it matter who she was? What she looked like? "Your wife inspires you," I said.

Only that morning I had put the finishing touches on the last in a series of dog portraits: two Irish setters and an unlikely Dachshund-Pekingese mix. Tomorrow I would deliver all three portraits, unframed, to an apartment in the Upper East Nineties, and in return for my hours of uninspired labor? A sum. "Adequate?" they'd say, thinking to themselves: "Generous." Yes, generous, but the rewards were purely pecuniary. Short red dog hairs clung to my trousers. I beat them with the back of my hand and took leave of him.

I liked to wander. When I had no sitters, I could happily spend hours on the streets and subways and buses of the Five Boroughs in search of a natural gesture, an uninhibited expression, an authentic disclosure that I could then put to the canvas. I took the Uptown bus, got off at Eighty-Sixth and Lexington, walked across to Fifth Avenue and entered the Park, making my way without special intent or purpose, until eventually I found myself in the Sixties, at the Zoo. I was a child the last time I'd visited there.

The clock set above three red brick arches at the East entrance started to chime, the brass figurines circling—a bear on his hind legs holding a cymbal, a goat playing pan pipes, a kangaroo with horns. *Baa Baa Black Sheep*, or some other nursery rhyme I couldn't quite recall, chimed to signal the hour or half-past. I had been told that many of the animals in the Zoo came from the circus and that sometimes they would exhibit remnants of the tricks they had learned. I visited the cat house. The musky animal smell was stale and spent, tainted by mildew. The dim light came in from the outside through a few high, barred windows. There were no fiery hoops to jump through, and the great giant cats were either asleep or dead. I found the seals, the polar bear, and in the aviary—no surprise—birds. The animals, as it turned out, held almost no interest for me anymore. I resorted to watching the people watching the animals watching them.

My friend, as I'd started to call him, had a serious problem. As anyone did who must have what he could not. I felt that quite unconsciously he was using me. The portrait of his wife was simply an excuse. He himself had established the parameters for a sitting and their impossibility—I would never paint her. And yet, he spoke of it ad nauseum because the speaking brought her closer to him, even if the proximity was imagined. He would not have told her about me, of that I was certain—not even a mention of our new friendship. In her eyes, I would have been the unsavory one. The puerile artist. If she knew about us, would she, I wondered, have forbidden our drinks together?

London Bridges this time, as I headed out of the Park and home. *Falling down, falling down,* the clock chimed. I thought of the child's game—my friend and I holding hands, arms high above our heads in a bridge, waiting for the moment when the music would stop and our hands would fall. *My fair lady.*

And then, one rainy afternoon six or so weeks into our acquaintance, in an Irish pub on Sixty-Eighth and Madison, he told me, "I've got it." He waited until the barkeep pulled our draughts and served them, the amber lager spilling over the sides of the frosty steins, and then he said, "I've devised a way. A hole in the wall, between the bedroom and the laundry. You in the laundry, she in the bedroom. The light's good," he said. "It's all very good." He reached into his pocket for something—a cigarette, his lighter—and the heel of a lady's stocking came out with the other thing.

"Well?" he said. "Will you? Do you want to?"

Her silk stocking— I tucked it back in for him. It felt light, gossamer, weightless, really, and its presence in his pocket made me obscurely uncomfortable. "No," I said. "No, I don't think so."

He brought an unlit cigarette to his sealed lips and then away, squinted, and then pinched his nose. "You know what's interesting?" He turned to search my face. "You know what means something? A man spends his whole life looking. No." He shook his head slowly, gravely. "That's not interesting. A man finds something. He finds it. Now that means something."

In the dim light his eyes looked bright and past me. It could have been that he was gazing at a photograph on the wall or into one of the dark knots that pocked the wood paneling. But in that moment my distinct feeling was that he was seeing something personal and peculiar to me: my failure. I would never be an artist.

As if to discount my intuition, he giggled. He giggled, lit his cigarette, dragged deeply, and coughed.

"Paint her," he said, now grinning with delight.

A wailing siren approached and passed in the street outside, and a thin, wasted woman somewhere at the end of the bar cried out for another drink.

"I don't know," and a moment later, "Alright," I said. "Yes."

* * *

They lived on Fifty-Ninth Street and Fifth Avenue in a grey building with a green awning. I'd brought only my portable with me, a canvas roll-cum-easel I had devised for working on-site. The roll consisted of two sheets of canvas in which I stashed two or three brushes and a few tubes of paint. When I worked, one canvas served as my palette. The other hung from pins on a folding easel. Folded and rolled and tied together, the kit fit neatly under my arm for travel on the subways or buses. The doorman, keeping his eye on my bundle, rang the apartment and announced into the intercom: "A gentleman," then paused, as if to correct himself, "a Mr. Severs, says he's here to see you."

I was early, but my friend encouraged me to move through his apartment quickly. Past the dark foyer, the equally dark living room with curtains drawn, the long narrow hallway flanked by a few closed doors on either side, and finally, the tiny laundry that was once a pantry and before that probably servant's quarters for a single maid. His wife was always gone at this time of day, this and other days of the week—she would be expected back in an hour, though she had been known to be earlier or later. I found the hole that my friend had rendered in the wall large enough (it was about the size of a child's fist) and at a decent height so that I could sit relatively comfortably with all my materials at hand. He assured me that she would remain naked in her room, attending to herself for well on an hour, and that should be ample time for me to glean her image onto the canvas. Should further sittings be required (as I would be sitting to paint, the noun applied), assuming the first went smoothly, as we both felt it should, there could be subsequent days and times set to complete the project to our satisfaction.

I can't defend myself. Of course I questioned the ethics of our undertaking. It would be a feeble excuse to say I got swept up in my friend's enthusiasm. Ridiculous to claim that because this woman was his wife, on some level he had a right to commission me as he had done, and I, as an artist, had a certain obligation to document the event. I can only say that to an appalling degree I had forgotten the fair lady, completely lost sight of her as something other than the mutual object of our desire, so caught up did I become in the anticipation, the secrecy, the pleasure of the clandestine deed.

Without wishing to, I recalled a rainy evening, my friend and I in a close corner of the busy pub, our breath causing the black windowpane to perspire. Wet leather coats, damp woolen scarves, hair slick with rain. Our smell had intoxicated me. Ours because I was suddenly certain we shared it, my friend and I— a musk distinct from the drinking crowd's. Earthy, mellow and pungent at once, as dense as flesh and as titillating. Just then he had reached his hand across the table—irrationally, I had thought he would touch me—and pulled the ashtray close to him. "My God, it's hot in here," I had said aloud, grateful to recognize my voice. Only the moment before I had been unable to breathe. Now, sitting in the laundry room, I became conscious once again of my breath, intentionally willing its easy flow, relaxing the constriction at the root of my tongue, softening my throat.

As there was some time before her expected arrival, I took the opportunity to observe the bedroom through the hole in the wall. It was ordinary in every sense with all the expected everyday items a bedroom should have: a rather narrow bed with a quilted flower spread, a walnut armoire with a three-quarter-length mirror inlaid in the door, a window facing the apartment building opposite, in the corner an umbrella on the handle of which hung a felt hat jauntily cocked, and next to it a chest of drawers, on top of which were a few framed photographs, difficult to distinguish in the diminished light available through the fist-sized hole. The door to the armoire was slightly ajar, and within I thought I glimpsed articles of the lady's clothing: patterned fabrics, skirts and dresses, soft-looking silks and chiffons. She is a dresser, I thought, surprised, expecting something more modest and austere, but recognizing that the clothing matched the simple feminine care for which the bedroom must be noted. Not expensive, but tasteful.

I thought of my friend. So often so careless with his own clothes, spilling beer on his shirt front, singeing his cuff in an ash tray, ripping a jacket pocket on a chair arm, always in the service of some friendly gesture. Gestures which I now realized were at his lady's expense. He was drinking with me, spending what might have been her purse money on beer and cigarettes. Together we were anything but tasteful. Anything but careful. I was acutely aware once again of my own complicity in, well, in their marriage.

As if on cue, my friend rapped on the laundry door. His knuckles sounded a harsh bony reminder of my business in this place. But his hushed voice, anticipatory, brought me back to the moment at hand. "Here she comes," he whispered loudly through the door. "Quiet now."

I waited, brush in hand, canvas spread, an inch each of brown, of pink, and of white squeezed from the tubes, ready. I would paint her. I would do her justice. As my hand gripped the brush, impatient, grasping, I thought: This is Art.

The woman who walked into the room was neither beautiful nor plain, horrendous nor exceptional. Certainly, she was not who I was expecting. She was old. Older than my mother. Closer to my grandmother in age. Her hair was grey and well-tended, and the first thing she did was to remove part of it. A knot of hair about the size and shape of a lady's powder puff and the six or seven hairpins that had held it in place were laid carefully on top of the chest of drawers. Small and thin, she was dressed in a broad-collared white blouse with lace ruffles along the bodice and cuffs, and cropped, pleated slacks of green silk. There were pearl-colored silk pantyhose and black pumps with a modest heel. She stood in front of the three-quarter-length mirror looking at herself for a few moments before she began to unfasten the top buttons of her blouse. Just as my friend had said she would, the lady slowly divested herself of every article of clothing until she stood before the mirror completely in the nude.

The peep hole provided a single ocular. That, and the diffuse light clustered around her form seemed to act like a telescope, magnifying her. She appeared clearer, closer to me than any other object in the room. Her bony, freckled shoulders, small breasts, narrow rib cage and waist, her stomach of loose and wrinkled skin above the whiskered triangle between her thin legs. Apparently oblivious to me, she nevertheless held me. I had the sense I was completely hidden and safe. The increasing warmth of my cramped quarters seemed to emanate from her, and that heat insulated rather than stifled me. My line of sight gave us a direct and uninterrupted connection.

I realize now that all this came of my incalculable need and my imminent failure. But then, on that day in the small laundry, I believed that I saw her. The way a great artist must see—even the most familiar—as if for the very first time. With graceful and exaggerated gestures, like a mime silently conjuring the ordinary though invisible, she stood, bowed, and turned, bent to reach around herself, applying and then slowly smoothing ointments from various tubes and jars, and I applied my brush and began to paint.

Why had I never noticed the green and the purples before—as if flesh could be captured in so few colors? Brown, pink, white—the limitations I'd imposed upon my palette seemed suddenly laughable to me. I lingered over her texture. Nowhere was skin smooth. Had I really ever seen it as such? And shadows—they existed not just in the pockets and crevices, not simply in the absence of light. Tiny hairs made shadows. Hairs so thin as to be almost invisible. Pigments—browns and orange, even red, and in one place, I discovered cerulean blue—spotted her with tiny countries and great continents.

Was it an hour? More? Less? I could not say. All I know is that when she began to dress, donning first her undergarments, slowly pulling the leg of each stocking over the peninsulas of her calf and thigh, every article of clothing removing another newly discovered territory from my sight, I felt a pain in the reciprocal place in my own pale shape.

So it was with horror then that I saw what my hands had created from these powerful impressions. The few moments after she left the bedroom and before my friend came to collect me revealed a thickly painted figure, not quite human, pink and sexless, small, and bent, its face obscured by shadow. Hanging from two pins on the easel in front of me was a ghastly fallen angel. No grace, no movement, no warmth.

When my friend opened the door I refused to show him what I had done. I felt weak in my whole body, as if I were fending off some terrible illness. I thought I must be feverish I felt so warm, though my friend insisted it was the stuffiness of the laundry. He himself had gotten quite hot in those close quarters on more than one occasion.

I made some feeble excuse. I had to go, and he let me, but not before I had promised that I would come again, two days later, at the same time. Stepping outside the apartment building I intended to hail a cab and didn't. New York is a vast city. According to that year's census nearly eight million human beings populated its some three hundred square miles, and yet, I found her.

Bright yellow cabs flashed past in the autumn daylight, horns blared at a bus stopped for a man in a wheelchair, a delivery boy on a bicycle with a black bag slung across his shoulder gracefully weaved and dodged among the chrome bumpers. The air smelled of roasted chestnuts and the chemical tang of the dry cleaner. My neck felt stiff and my shoulders ached. I had to pass my portable from one hand to the other to keep my fingers from cramping. Moist air escaped the subway grating, the city's stale breath warm and then cool on my calves beneath my pant legs. I would walk; it would do me good.

And to my surprise, not even one block ahead of me, she also walked, and in no hurry, along Fifth Avenue.

I followed her all the way up the steps of Saint Patrick's Cathedral. There was no service, no music flowing from the massive organ pipes. Someone was lighting votives before a statue of the Virgin Mother. Other people were scattered in various postures of supplication. I thought it was her, third or fourth row from the front, so I proceeded down the aisle beneath the great vaulted ceiling, past the cavernous alcoves inlaid with stained glass. I knelt in the pew behind hers, sure she would feel compelled by my presence to turn around. Then I got up and went to kneel on the bench beside her. When she finally turned, her face was thin and pinched and impassive. Her glance was indifferent, impersonal, and, I thought, wary. A tall, thin, young man with hungry eyes who had followed an old woman for nearly eight city blocks. I could, after all, be a threat, a crazy person there to do her harm. Yes, her face said so. She opened her mouth, and I thought she might pray for me.

"Out of the way, dope," she said, and pushed past, stepping over my bent legs and into the aisle. She crossed herself, genuflecting, and with small staccato steps, exited the Cathedral.

When I stepped into the daylight, I didn't see her. Across the street in front of Rockefeller Center stood the colossal bronze statue of Atlas bearing the burden of the world on his shoulders. I remembered my friend as he was that first afternoon. And subsequent times. I felt oddly betrayed. By him. By her. By my own folly. When had I stopped believing she was his wife? Hours ago? Days? Or had it been weeks?

I suddenly was ravenous. From a vendor on the corner of Fifty-First and Fifth I bought a salted pretzel and two hot dog sandwiches, which I ate without enjoyment, one after the other. In two days' time, I would have another opportunity with her. The prospect filled me with a kind of grim foreboding. Walking home along Fifth Avenue, I passed groups of pigeons on the grey sidewalk, all of them busy, pecking into the dirty cracks and crevices. I recalled a forgotten image from my childhood. A photograph of me as a boy, racing nowhere on this same avenue, flushing these same birds into the air, their wings opening up and out, feathered bodies like dirty blossoms falling in reverse from the ground up into the trees.

My next visit to his apartment began much like the first. My friend met me at his front door, reiterating that his wife would return soon, though it would be difficult to say at exactly what time. He again encouraged me to follow him quickly, but I took my time: I wanted to see how they lived.

We passed out of the dark foyer and into a living room that was clean and in much the same style as the lady's bedroom. There was a floral theme, perpetuated in the Persian rug, the needle point pillows, the sofa upholstery, an arrangement of stargazer lilies in a cut glass vase atop an upright piano. Velveteen curtains—thick, heavy-looking, and drawn—were stem-green. There was very little of my friend in the décor, and I was just beginning to wonder—was it possible that he did not live here?—when I saw his photograph, a glossy eight-by-ten in a tasteful silver frame standing on the fireplace mantle.

In the photo he had cleaned himself up very nicely. The blazer he wore was navy and around his neck a maroon tie with an emblem. His hands were clasped, and he stood at attention next to a low desk of blond wood. His smile was disarmingly boyish, innocent. The photograph was, without doubt, him as a school boy. Another photograph, in sepia, was of the lady. Also much younger than she was now. Rather the same age as my friend the school boy. She was dressed all in white with a short lace veil that fell to just above her shoulders—possibly it was her First Holy Communion. But the proximity of the photos, hers situated to partially overlap his on the mantle, created a kind of illusion. She was his child bride, him her child groom. The photographs were obviously of different eras—her costume, his, the grain and quality of the prints—and yet, the illusion persisted. I couldn't shake it. Even as I positioned myself in the uncomfortable laundry, once some poor scullery maid's cramped abode.

This time the lady did all the same things, divesting herself of the various articles, applying her creams and ointments with a slow, methodical precision. Her face, which on my first visit I had neglected entirely, so caught up was I in the elements of color and light and form, became a subject of great interest. I saw my friend in her features. The wide eyes, the ears too large and situated too low proportionately. The lips—so like his—only she held her version more tightly, so that while she moved her hands firmly along the length of her torso or up the side of her thigh, her bottom lip all but disappeared. Her mouth was hard where his was generous and weak. I remembered my first intuition: *She is an ice queen.*

I did not paint her. I remained quietly in the chair my friend had positioned so carefully by the hole I imagined him painstakingly carving into the wall. Did he sit here often? The lady of whom he had spoken so frequently, with such unrequited passion, was not his wife, of course, but his mother.

After she left the room, I quit the laundry before he signaled me, walking along the dark hall and out into the living room, seating myself on the sofa, overhearing their goodbyes. *Would he tend to the mail and leave the bills for her and if he went out be sure to change his shirt before and to buy batteries and tissues. If he'd spent everything, then there, he could have ten dollars. But not one cent more.* I imagined she turned her cheek for him to kiss it. Goodbye, mother.

When he walked into the living room and found me there, the question registered immediately on his transparent face: What had I heard?

I suppose my face also had a certain degree of transparency. He didn't bother to ask.

"You are not an artist," he said. "I was greatly mistaken."

I did not protest when he escorted me to the door of the apartment and informed me that we were through. With more comportment than I would have thought possible in him, he told me our arrangement was null and void. "I do not know you," he said. "You do not know me." He conveyed his sincerest regrets that we would not have another opportunity to meet again, and he closed his front door soundly behind me.

In the days and weeks that followed I did not seek him out, though I did return to the establishments we had frequented together thinking that over time he might see fit to resume our acquaintance. He did not. I have never discussed the events of this period with anyone, and I never saw my friend again. But, despite the surge of pity I felt for him standing by the apartment door that afternoon, my admiration for his dogged pursuit of his desire, whatever the consequences, has never left me. In fact, since the afternoon he told me "I do not know you. You do not know me," not a week goes by that something or someone doesn't remind me of him.

Last night I dreamed I was a young man, canvas spread before me, brush in hand, painting a beautiful woman whose skin shone lightly with a violet and green patina.

BASEMENT SONGS

D.G. Bracey

This all started with a Christmas card. A rejected card, returned with a fading, dull black stamp that read **Return to Sender**, accompanied by a slingshot arrow.

My personalized message of merry spirits sent and returned without any explanation.

Just accepting it or a routine forwarding of the card to its rightful recipient could've avoided this whole scene.

Instead it was slapped with an insulting tag on the face of my bright red envelope with all its glee and jolly Santa Stamp. My name typed in a festive font on my preaddressed reindeer label. Her name wrapped in a bright little bow in the center. All the pomp and circumstance read and filed in the mailman's "loser" cubby.

All I wanted to do is share a small piece of my life with my friends and family? It shouldn't be such a delusional idea to want to send a picture of myself and my Bassett Hound to those in my social circle during such a festive season.

Shouldn't those who receive these cards be grateful there is someone out there, thinking of them, thinking enough to dedicate paper and ink and the price of postage just to say, "Hey, Merry Christmas!" "Remember me!"

My circle wasn't exclusive, I didn't discriminate. I included the loved ones with the acquaintances. I believed my life had been touched and changed by everyone in my address book.

And if for some reason I haven't communicated with these people or had some form of falling out, then it was my job to use my Christmas cards as a tool to bridge the communication gap, repair that relationship in some small way.

Every year my mailing list has increased; co-workers, acquaintances, family, new friends, ex-neighbors, current girlfriend and her family… ex-girlfriends.

I expected some mail to be returned. People move. People die. Life happens. I knew this as well as anyone. I had to let it go.

But when mail is returned to me with "Please Return!" in angry, red letters, like a cat scratch, I take notice.

I knew the handwriting. I've read the angry tone. The memory was fresh. I knew this someone. This is someone I shared months with, almost a year. This someone used to sign all of her notes to me with a playful "Luv U!" That same exclamation point was sent back to me, only the sentiment has changed. It still had the balloon top. It still had the same round eyeball point on the bottom. It had been converted from the kiss of "Luv U!" to the whip crack of "Please Return!"

I did not expect that all my Christmas cards would be received with joy. I knew that out of the hundreds sent, some would find a trashcan before they were even opened. I was aware that a greeting from Flash (my basset hound) and me wasn't the crowning achievement of every mantle or refrigerator on my mailing list.

But that reaction, to return the envelope as if it was filled with anthrax, is unconscionable. To not even want my salutations to mix and coexist with your trash seemed a little unforgivable. Unforgivable and demanding an explanation.

* * *

You could find anybody on the internet for $19.95. You could find anybody living under an alias for $29.95. For $59.95 you could research whole identities and any idiosyncrasies related to your target. That is what the website called them: "The Target". You searched by name and watch a timeline sketch itself out, a tapestry of their life unfurled. Type in your address as their last known address and follow the spiral out.

The discovery that I'm the launch pad for a whole new life was a bit disconcerting. If you looked at it on paper, I was the last bad thing that happened to her.

From living with me to living with her parents to a Lakeside address. From my home phone number to a cell phone number and a work number at a high-end law firm. From driving the Camry we shared when my car was in the shop to a new BMW registered in her new last name. It would only take $19.95 to find her. I spent $59.95.

* * *

As I drove to her new address, my ears buzzed from pure adrenaline. Everything I wanted to say poured out of my mouth to the rearview mirror. I practiced quips, and comebacks for my quips. I anticipated everything she would say; for every excuse she could have, I had an answer. I was a weapon of rejection, an avenger.

I cruised by the house a half dozen times. It was set back from the road, down a long wooded driveway. The screen porch was barely visible. A silver BMW parked beside a Toyota Prius, it was Driftwood Pearl and brand new.

He had to be home. He would've destroyed my plans, cogged the vengeance machine. They would call the police, which would lead to judges and restraining orders. I would take my time.

I parked six blocks away at a picnic area, the mouth of a nature trail. The morning fell into the afternoon sun and maybe I fell asleep or daydreamed. Hunger overtook me and I drove back down to the bait shop and bought a cream soda, a barbecue sandwich and chips.

Driving back to my same parking space, I looked out over the still brown water and shoved salty chips into my mouth. It was autumn, the dead season. The spring and summer would bring weeklong tourists, boaters, families driving down to swim and splash away the day. But now, there was just me in an empty parking lot near empty roads that lead back to them.

* * *

The night was so much darker here than in the city. The only light was the moon stretching into a ghost on the surface of the water, tiny snaps of light dancing in the lapping waves and the zebra mussels shining in the black shoals of the shore.

I walked along barefoot, carrying my shoes and socks in my hand. Most of the houses off the sand were empty, shutters closed, dark faces of sleeping giants.

Their house was a beacon, all thick-paned glass and soft halogen lights. A lawn busy with smells, even in the off-season, and the grass, thick with dew, tickled the bottom of my feet like it was newly trimmed.

Through the windows, the stained mahogany wood of the walls, the granite counter tops, two figures danced around each other like a ballet in the kitchen. Making salad like it was choreographed. She chopped spinach as he grated cheese, hands moved across one another in a cacophony of vegetables and fruits, croutons and crackers.

I watched them without realizing I was moving closer. His features became pronounced. His strong chin but thin frame, his face was soft and if I were to guess, his eyes would be blue.

Her, I could've closed my eyes and remembered. She hadn't changed. The smooth olive tanned skin, the hair falling in dark spirals over her shoulders, her body toned to the point of a personal trainer.

When she was with me, we would've made fun of these people. Now, she was one of them. Her body, half engulfed by a stainless steel Frigidaire, deciding which dressing to use.

That night, I wandered around the yard, peering through the windows, from room to room. I slipped around the house of glass, shrouded by the massive shrubs and fruitless fig trees.

I studied them as they watched a movie. He was intently into it. She read a magazine with her feet propped in his lap. He rubbed her feet, rolling her toes between his fingers. He never took his eyes off the huge, plasma screen. The soundtrack rattled the glass.

There was a boathouse by the pier, jutting out on the dismal water. The door on the boathouse was padlocked. I pushed up on the paint-chipped window. It gave with a small pop and I climbed inside, finding the 1950 Chris-Craft Sportsman, hoisted above the water, equipped with the "On Golden Pond" skis to match. They had been trying to sell the boat earlier this year but I guess they'd decided to keep it.

Sleep must've taken me as I sat in the driver's seat of the Sportsman because I woke to laughter in the yard. They walked a Golden Retriever. He threw a tennis ball with one hand and held a wine glass with the other. She stood on the porch and sang a Van Morrison song so loudly the lyrics about the moonlight still bounced through my mind as I made a bed of the white waterproof cushions and let her sing me a lullaby.

As the water lapped against the rotting wood of the shed, I decided I would spend the weekend there.

* * *

The next day, through dirty panes of glass, like a two-way mirror, they continued their dance. I continued to watch.

Kissing and wrestling, they tumbled to the ground, entwined. Rusty, the retriever, lounged in the fall sun. The pair rolled over one another in the grass, whispering words I strained to hear. They retreated to the deck that wrapped around the house, holding hands with fingers like ribbons, binding them.

He fell back on the lounger. She straddled his lap. There was a flurry of movement, gentle and strong.

Kept safe by the dense tree-lines on all sides of the yard, the barren lake lay flat without traffic. His hands tugged away her top. Her hands kneaded into his chest, rounding the curve of his bare chin, pushing his hair back off his forehead. He rushed his hips to meet her. She came crashing down in waves.

Until everything stopped and the two joined into a heap that made it indistinguishable where he ended and she began.

* * *

I picked up Flash from my Mom's house and returned to work on Monday morning, but it was useless.

By three o'clock, I told my boss I was sick. I went home and packed a bag.

The night had barely crept in, the world was quiet and I was back at their house.

Through the glass, their life was my silent movie. Sometimes, I added dialogue. Sometimes, I just strained to hear the muffled jazz they listened to in the background.

They walked Rusty. I slid along the side of the house, between the azaleas and the brick foundation. As they rounded the corner to the garden and the gazebo, I slipped through the kitchen door, crouched along the counters, passed the couch in the den, into a doorway in the hall.

I thought the doorway was a closet but as I opened it, light spilled down a staircase, descending into darkness. I closed the door behind me and let my eyes focus in the black.

The kitchen door opened, voices filling the rooms behind me. Rusty's paws crossed the tiles, just on the other side of the door.

In the dark, I tapped my toes from one step to another, dropping gently into the dark, gripping the handrail. I fingered the outline of a lightswitch at the bottom of the stairs. A single switch, I snapped the lever down and to my right there sprang a soft and clandestine light.

Half of the basement was standard. Discarded and discolored antique furniture that clashed with the current décor, obvious inheritance. A chaise lounge covered with a white sheet. Trunks and boxes labeled with red marker, stacked in the corners.

The other half was something altogether spectacular. A hand-built wine cellar made of redwood, brilliant with an arch for an entrance. Walls structured into wooden diamonds for bottles and slots for magnum storage. A mural painted on the far wall of the morning fog in a vineyard. The paint was thick and sloppy like it was mixed with smashed grapes themselves.

At the bottom of the mural, someone had written something in French, "Saisir Le Jour."

A Whisperkool fastened to the wall, blew out a cool wet air that kept the small room fixed inside the dank basement, a cool sixty degrees with humidity. Sections of shelves were cut out and various bottles sat under soft lights as displays. Next to the wines sat index cards. On the cards were handwritten directions in what appeared to be a calligraphy pen.

This 2002 Chardonnay from Corton Charlemagne is a bit oaky. Serve with lamb or pheasant.

This 1996 Desert wine from Chateau Giraud is truly syrupy. Serve with chocolate.

This 1992 Shiraz from Cote Rotle Brune is powerful and spicy. Serve with beef slathered with cream sauce.

This Champagne is Gosset from the Grand Reserve and it is a pinch biscuity. Serve with shellfish.

Did he write directions for her? Did they come with directions when he bought them? Did he have a wine connoisseur that came by once a week to decode the hundreds of bottles for him as he just bought them blindly? Either way…I hated him.

I should've waited for them to go to sleep and left the way I came, but I didn't. I stayed.

* * *

The first few nights, I drank the Pinot Noir and Zinfandel. When I was sure they were fast asleep, I floated down the hallways like a spirit. Watching them sleep, I was an angel hanging above their bed. Their restful slumber made me warm, comfortable.

Rusty didn't even stir as I passed him sprawled out on the dining room floor. The one time he did raise his head, half asleep, I rubbed between his eyes, scratched his belly and fed him from my midnight pastrami sandwich.

They never came down. The one time the door opened and I was sure I would be discovered, I heard her yell to him that she "found it," and the door closed just as quickly as it opened. She was always so self-sufficient.

It had to be a full moon on the night I discovered the absinthe. Some would call it wine. Some would call it liqueur. Some would call it the green fiery. I had read about it in college. Picasso used it for inspiration. Arthur Rimbaud and Oscar Wilde used it to help turn a phrase. Some say Vincent Van Gogh was dancing with the fiery when he sliced off his ear. Others say the fiery helped Hemingway pull the trigger of that shotgun.

That son of a bitch had it hidden in a crate outside the wine cellar. It was still packaged in a slotted wooden box from Europe. The bottles were wrapped in shredded paper.

Under the paper lay a smaller box. The smaller box contained a jigger with a dose line and a slotted spoon. The spoon was in the shape of the Eiffel tower. It was used to hold the sugar cubes that you dissolve with water into the absinthe. After the bright green liquid is made into murky milk, you drink it down and let your mind open. If you used it right, you could see through God's eyes.

Night after night, I took peeps into the mystic. With no water to dissolve the sugar, I drank it straight. Tart and sharp to the tongue, I drank what seemed like an endless supply of inspiration.

Hours on top of hours, maybe days, I slept awake. Dreams like dust fluttering in daylight, I was sure a message would come to me.

I found leftover paint and created my own mural on the opposite wall. With my fingers and palms, I splashed a blood red sunrise over a deserted, cracked earth on a grey concrete surface. I wrote, "Le Baron Soulus," on the bottom of the mural. I didn't think it meant anything but I wanted the murals to match. I needed balance.

I used rulers that had been used to stir paint as drum sticks. My hands beat out songs on the pipes above my head. A tribal rhythm in hollow tones and metallic snaps. Not so loud as they'd notice but loud enough to make Rusty shout down at me, scratching at the door, but soon he was used to it. It probably lulled him to sleep.

In a dark corner, I found boxes of his old clothes and hung them over my thinning body. Musky and pale, I took showers while they were at work. While they were gone, I laid in the sunlight to fight the jaundice out of my yellowing skin. I ate sparingly at their food, drank their leftover coffee, used their spare bathroom and washed my hair with their shampoo.

At night, it was an opera without sound. I drank and wandered the halls. Then before they woke, I dove down beneath them, staring into me and discovered I'd become beautiful.

No longer was I the man she left, the man who wanted habit and veered away from danger. I was drinking from a magic well. She could never say again that I was boring or complacent, that she didn't feel needed.

After a month or so, my phone stopped vibrating. People stopped looking. Flash was fine with my Mom; she always loved him.

Now, I belonged to them. I was their bump in the night. I was their mystery of the motion lights. I was the troll under the staircase.

I used her photo albums and his lucky pen to write my story. On the back of their collective photos, I scratched my words. She was diligent in logging in the pictures, so different headings always prologue my tale, *Doug and Diana dancing at our wedding 4/01/08, Aunt June on the treadmill 12/26/86, Rusty's first night at home 6/13/09.*

Under her headings I wrote something every day. I scribbled about how I was changing and the reactions, my metamorphosis.

Everyone should have a voice. I heard Oprah say that once. This was my voice. I could've lived like this forever. People will say I was a parasite but that's not the case. Our relationship was reciprocal.

I gave back. I was the phantom that filled the toilet paper roll. The invisible friend that fed Rusty dog biscuits. The miracle that watered the plants when they forgot. I was the invisible hand in their lives…until earlier tonight.

Tonight, I exposed the illusion, broke the plane. Tonight, just like any other night, I sat at the top of the stairs, drinking God's juice, separated from them by that thin slice of wood.

I listened to them talk about his job, his friend, Walter, who had become an asshole since making partner. I sipped from the Cape Cod mug they never missed. I heard him tell her he has to go back to the city to meet the guys for a drink. Walter was getting married and it was the only bachelor party he wanted. He said he wouldn't be home late, but she went on about friendship and asshole or not, people should let their hair down before they get married. "It's tradition," she said, telling him that Rusty and her would snuggle in bed and watch Animal Planet.

He told her to dream about him and he was gone.

* * *

It was hours before I went up to the bedroom.

From the door, I watched her breathing, deep in dreams. She tossed a little, restless without him.

I think she pulled me in. I don't remember crossing the distance from the transom to her bedside, but I was there. I let my hand pass inches from her body, letting the electricity from my fingertips tickle her skin under that silk robe. I was calm, letting my pulse match hers in slumber, her chest rising and falling. Then it happened.

I fought back the constant echoing "NO" of my thoughts, let my hand find the knot of her robe's ties, pulling it free, watching the fabric fall to the side, exposing all of her to me.

She was all I remember. I didn't exist except in that moment.

My hands followed my stare over her form. She stirred and smiled as if she remembered my touch, but as her eyes opened and dream met reality…she just lay there, quiet, looking up at me like a porcelain doll.

I stumbled backward over myself, out to the hallway and down the stairs, rushing toward my room. Rusty sensed the situation and his barks were angry from her bedside. I had violated his trust, compromised myself.

I heard the front door swing open before I could get to the basement door. He must have seen my shadow as I darted across the floor because we met at the top of the basement stairs.

He was within arm's reach. His face was all shadows, a swatch of gray shades, except for his eyes. His eyes sharpened, maybe confused, maybe recognition. Maybe he'd seen me before in one of her pictures. In one of his dreams.

The moment was an infinite instant -- two figures, face to face, in a dark room, vibrating from a thousand thoughts. A thousand thoughts that sent a thousand commands to bodies that refused to answer.

Our instant was interrupted by her feet on the steps, and then broken by my flinch. My body shifted, unsure whether to scuttle for escape or stand and fight.

He made the decision, closing on me quick, bracing me. His hands balled my shirt up across my chest.

My hands were around his throat as I forced him back through the doorway. His feet scrambled to find footing and we tumbled down the stairs, letting each other go to grasp for security. Our legs tangled as we crashed to the hard concrete.

I landed on top of him and I felt the breath leave his body in a huff. I was throwing punches, and somehow he was bleeding from his hairline. I smelled the iron.

I'd gotten off of him and he rolled towards me, his body lumbered, heavy and slow. He tried to push himself up to his hands and knees.

I had already found the absinthe spoon, sharpened at the end, in the shape of Paris' pride. I straddled him from behind, yanking his head back from his bleeding scalp. I sank the Eiffel Tower into his throat.

He attempted to speak, but words degraded into gurgles as he slumped in a heap. I rushed up to close my door. I glimpsed her dark figure across the kitchen floor, creeping in tiny steps. Her hands were full. I slammed the door shut and began my descent.

At the seventh step, the panic in her voice startled me. I stopped. She was obviously on the phone.

They would be here soon. Someone else, always someone else, was coming to interrupt us.

She was crying now, and screaming through the door. Down below, his limbs had quit shaking. She screamed his name as a question. She screamed my name as an answer. And then she screamed something else.

We were beyond conversation. She was beyond irrational.

I took two steps up the stairs.

There was a pump of a shotgun, racking a shell into the chamber. She promised to kill me if I came out.

There were sirens in the distance.

I imagined her aiming that heater dead bang at the center of the door. She was always a woman who kept her promises.

The sirens got louder.

I took two more steps.

Rusty's furious bark boomed at me.

Through the door, I think I heard her adjust the shotgun, tightening the stock to her thin shoulder.

I am three steps from the door.

"I mean it!" she says. "I will kill you."

"A man should explore every passion." The sound of my voice is dusty. I had written that phrase on the back of a photo I found in one of her albums. On the front of the photo was her Dad painting that Mural in the wine cellar. Her header read, *The last gift from my father, 10/08/09*. I have it in my pocket. They haven't missed it.

The sirens whine outside.

I get ready to lunge for the door. I remove the photo from my pocket.

The photo flutters free from my hand as I pray that she keeps her promise.

LEA

Andrew Fleming

It was the first warm day of spring. I decided to get the bicycles out of the garage and ask Lea to come on a ride with me. Lea, normally happier to stay at home with her toys and books, needed surprisingly little persuasion. On a day like this the lure of the outdoors was hard to resist, even for her. As I cleaned the cobwebs from the seats and handlebars, Susan helped Lea button up her coat and fasten her cycle helmet under her chin.

'Are you sure you don't want to come?' I asked Susan.

'No, you go,' she replied. 'It'll be nice for you and Lea to do something together, just the two of you.'

Susan was right. I liked to think Lea and I were as close as most fathers and daughters, but work and after-school activities all too often got in the way. A Sunday afternoon bike ride seemed like the perfect opportunity to spend some time together.

The air was tinged with both the edge of winter and the fragrance of spring. It felt like we were at the halfway point between one season and another. We rode out through the suburbs, heading for the country park on the edge of town. I led the way through the quiet streets, past neighbours washing their cars and mowing their lawns. Lea rode behind me, doing her best to keep up. She would ring her bell whenever I got too far ahead and I would slow down until she caught up. We continued until we reached the main road which formed a boundary between the houses on one side and the woods and fields on the other. We rode over the footbridge, the traffic roaring beneath us in a constant two-way flow.

The country park was busy with cyclists, pedestrians and dog-walkers enjoying the sunshine and fresh air. I told Lea to stay close to me. She was a sensible child and a good rider but I didn't want to risk any accidents. We rode down the gentle slope that led to the artificial lake. Water fowl drifted across its grey-green surface, occasionally dipping their heads in search of food. Lea wanted to stop and watch the birds but I told her to keep going. We carried on past the lake and into the wooded area beyond. The path forked and I chose the narrower track that led away from the crowds and into the further reaches of the park.

'Where are we going, Daddy?' asked Lea.

'You'll see,' I shouted over my shoulder.

We followed the track further into the woods. It was indeed quieter here but the track was pitted and uneven, and riding was becoming a chore. I was on the point of calling a rest-stop when I heard Lea shout behind me.

'Daddy, wait!'

'Just a bit further Lea, we'll have a rest in a minute.'

'No, we have to stop. Something's wrong with my bike.'

I squeezed my brakes and came to a stop. Turning round, I saw that Lea's front tire was flat. With a sigh, I got off my bike and laid it down at the side of the path.

'Looks like you've got a puncture there, sweetheart. We'll have to stop and fix it.'

I reached down for the puncture repair kit I kept on my bike. Susan often mocked me for being over-prepared but it was times like this that my carefulness paid off.

Lea got off her bike and I pulled it over to the side of the track. I examined the front tire and soon found the small shard of glass that had done the damage. Lea watched as I loosened the nuts and removed the front wheel. I levered the tire off the frame and pulled out the inner tube.

'What are you doing?' asked Lea.

'I'm looking for the hole inside your tire so I can patch it up.'

Lea found a nearby tree stump and sat down. She sang happily to herself as I worked. I squeezed the inner tube and held it up to my ear, listening for the hiss of escaping air.

'Daddy, can I have a new bike, please?' she asked.

'You don't need a new bike, Lea, there's nothing wrong with this one,' I replied.

'Yes, there is, the wheel's broken.'

'The wheel isn't broken, you've just got a puncture. It'll be fixed soon. Besides, I'm not sure we can afford a new bike for you just at the moment.'

Lea carried on singing quietly for a while, apparently deep in thought.

'Maybe my other Mummy and Daddy could buy it for me,' she said at last. 'The ones I used to live with.'

I felt my breath catch in my throat. The air suddenly seemed unseasonably warm and still. I stopped what I was doing and turned to face Lea.

'Lea, what have we told you?'

Susan and I had never tried to hide the fact from Lea that she was not our biological daughter. She was three years old when she had come to live with us, so it would have been impossible in any case. But Lea was our child now, and we didn't want her unsettled by thoughts of her old life.

'Yes, I know I'm not supposed to talk about them. But there's a girl in my class who doesn't live with her real parents and she still gets--'

'Lea, we're your real parents!' I snapped.

She looked at me, shocked by the harshness of my tone. I immediately regretted shouting at her, but this kind of talk worried me. Now she was getting older, perhaps it was only natural that she should start asking questions about her past. Maybe that was just part of growing up. But I was worried what it would do to Lea. I was worried what it would do to Susan.

'I know that, Daddy,' she said, her eyes cast downward.

I put the tire down and went over to where Lea was sitting on the tree stump. I crouched down in front of her and put my hand on her shoulder. It felt small and delicate.

'I'm sorry, Lea, I didn't mean to shout at you.'

She avoided my eyes. She was moving the tip of her shoe back and forth, digging a shallow hole in the ground beneath her feet.

'I know I can't live with my old Mummy and Daddy anymore, but why can't I see them? I miss them sometimes.'

When Susan and I were first married, I had been unable to give her the child of her own she so desperately wanted. We had tried everything, all kinds of fertility treatments, but nothing had worked. Our marriage was at breaking point, I thought I was going to lose her. And then Lea had come into our lives. At first I had been far from sure we were doing the right thing. Taking on Lea would be hard, I knew, not to mention risky. But now I had no doubt the sacrifices had been worth it. She had given Susan the chance to prove she was the good mother she always knew she could be. Lea had saved our marriage. She had turned us from a couple into a family.

'You haven't talked about this to Mummy, have you?

'No,' she said uncertainly.

'Good. Because it upsets Mummy very much when you talk like this.'

'But why? I don't understand,' she said.

'Lea, you understand that we love you very much, don't you?'

'Yes,' she said, her voice almost a whisper.

'You're our special little girl. You're everything to us.'

Lea kept her eyes fixed on the ground.

'Listen to me. You're so much more important to us than you ever were to your old Mummy and Daddy. We would never let you go like they did. Think about it, Lea: you wouldn't be living with us in the first place if they'd loved you as much as we do. That makes sense, doesn't it?'

I could see Lea thinking, trying to process what I was saying.

'So when you talk about your old parents, it makes Mummy feel like you don't love us as much as we love you. And that makes her unhappy. Very unhappy. You don't want that, do you?'

'No,' said Lea. I could see the hurt in her soft blue eyes. 'I love Mummy.'

'Okay then.' I smiled at Lea. 'So no more talk like that. You only have one Mummy and Daddy now. And that's enough for you, isn't it?'

She didn't answer.

'It's more than some little girls have.' The words seemed to echo in the quiet of the woods.

Lea looked at me for a long time, as if searching for something. She nodded slowly.

'Tell you what,' I said brightly, 'we'll think about buying you that new bike for your next birthday. The rate you're growing at the moment, you'll probably be too big for this one by then anyway.'

I smiled at Lea and she smiled shyly back, pleased by the idea that she was a big girl now.

I returned to fixing the tire. I took the glue out of the puncture repair kit and applied it to the area around the hole. I placed a patch over it, and pressed the patch and the inner tube together until they held fast.

'And Lea,' I said, 'let's keep our little chat a secret, shall we? Just between us. A Daddy and daughter secret.'

Lea paused to think about this. 'Okay,' she said.

We sat together on the tree stump, waiting for the glue to dry. Lea was indeed growing up, maybe faster than I had realised. She would soon be old enough to understand what being part of a family really meant. She would realise that it meant knowing what to share and what to keep inside. She would understand that it meant playing a role for the good of the family unit, whatever that took. Her role was to be a good daughter, just as mine was to be a good husband.

I pumped the air back into the tire and when I was satisfied it was strong again, I reassembled the wheel and fixed it back on the bike. I gave the nuts on either side of the wheel fork an extra turn to make sure it was attached securely.

'There you go, Lea, good as new.'

She smiled at me. 'Good as new,' she repeated.

'Let's go home,' I said.

Susan and I knew we were lucky to have Lea in our lives. We would never forget that. As I helped her back onto the bike, I paused to look into my daughter's beautiful ocean-blue eyes. I was again taken back to that summer's day at the seaside when we had first seen her, alone and unattended outside the amusement arcade. She was so small, so young. I could still see the look she had given us as we approached her, a look of the purest innocence, while above us the seagulls circled and cried in a clear blue sky.

ONCE AGAIN AND THEN

Warren Slesinger

He heard the drone of a departing plane while he waited, hands in his pockets, suitcase on the curb. As soon as he saw her, he waved, but she drove past the line of people, late arrivals, looking for their rides, and stopped several feet away. She tapped the brakes three times to signal with the lights, and he carried his suitcase to the car.

When he opened the door, she looked up.

"I knew it was you," she said, "but we have to be careful."

He leaned across the seat, and kissed her on the cheek.

"Don't get too friendly," she said. "We're not there yet."

"See anyone else you know?"

"Just you," she said, and squeezed his knee.

"Where are we going?"

"Home."

"To your house?"

She passed another car on the road from the airport.

"What about your husband?"

"He's on call at the hospital, and can't come home."

"But he does phone."

"After he makes his rounds."

She looked him over.

"Is that a new suit?"

"Yes," he said, and kissed her again.

"How come?"

"This is supposed to be a business trip."

"Funny business," she said, and squeezed his knee again.

* * *

It was April in the yard, but too dark to see the leaves, and when he brushed a hedge, his sleeve was wet with dew.

"Don't be disappointed in the house," she said. "We bought it furnished," and she led him from the kitchen to the living room. It was not the used furniture, but the fact that nothing was theirs that surprised him.

She went into the kitchen, and he picked up a picture of her husband.

"Don't doctors make enough money?"

"Yes ... but he's still an intern ...with loans."

"And a wife with money of her own."

But he knew she didn't hear, or perhaps didn't care to mention the money that she spent when she was free, before the picture in the kitchen, when she was waiting, hoping, demanding to see if he would leave his wife.

* * *

In a few minutes; she set down a tray with two frozen daiquiris in frosted glasses; each with a slice of lime.

"How are things at your house?"

"Our son's going to school in the fall, and trying to learn how to tie his own shoes."

And he started to tell her how he felt when he watched his son draw the laces into a knot, but stopped.

"What's the matter?"

He shook his head.

"Don't worry," she said, "I'm still on the pill."

She picked at a nick in the glass, and set it down on the tray while he stared at a drape she had drawn for a backdrop.

"Let's go in here," she said, and pulled him by the buckle of his belt into the bedroom where nothing was out-of-bounds ... until her husband phoned.

She pushed him off, and caught her breath while he rolled over and looked at his watch. She picked up the portable phone from the bedside table.

"Yes?"

It was only ten o'clock. He lay on his side, and overheard a voice as virile as his own.

He watched her fluff her hair with one hand, and hold the phone with the other. She loosened an earring while they talked, and dropped it, accidentally, on the floor where it glittered like a hard little particle of thought.

"See you tomorrow," she said, stretching to leave the phone on the bedside table. She rolled up on top of him and playfully pressed her breasts against his chest.

"Here we go again," she said, the last syllable lilting toward the rotating ceiling fan, and tickled his ear with her tongue.

* * *

In the morning, she left him at the airport in the clamor of early departures when the gates opened and the lines formed. He walked through a sprawling building toward the roar of a plane on a runway windy with fumes. He was supposed to be at a meeting today and back in the office tomorrow, but when he looked down at the fields and roads into the city, and the plane gained more altitude, he had no intention of calling her again.

He felt a bump of turbulence as the plane climbed over clouds as plump as the pillow she had tucked under her buttocks while she measured him with her pale blue eyes.

SIXTH PERIOD

T. D. Johnston

"Come in!" echoes the voice from the other side.

Robin Tyree opens the heavy oak door, in no hurry to see Mr. Pickard, but nonetheless ready to get it over with.

He doesn't get up from his perch behind the enormous mahogany desk. She closes the door behind her. The click ricochets around the room.

"Mr. Pickard," she breathes nervously. "I really don't have much time. The kids'll only be on afternoon break for ten minutes."

"Sit down, Robin. This will only take five." The squat, balding headmaster smiles briefly, then waves a black flair pen toward a gray vinyl swivel chair placed uncomfortably in the middle of the room.

Robin sits down and commences gushing.

"Mr. Pickard, I really think I have the right to--"

"***Miss*** Tyree, you have no right, whatsoever, to contradict an act of Congress. None. You are breaking the law, and exposing this school to unwanted attention and liability, and I will see you ***stop***."

"But Mr. Pickard, it was one class day. Just one day. Yes, it was on the seven deadly sins, but we were studying the historical aspect of each in various societies and cultures. I consider it a nondenominational topic, so--"

"Next week it becomes six, Miss Tyree." The headmaster turns to his computer. "This is not news to you. You received my e-mail memo three weeks ago." Mr. Pickard leans over and clicks the mouse on his computer. "I have the receipt."

Screw your receipt, you little....

"Mr. Pickard, we're an independent school," Robin offers, ignoring a vague warning rising from her abdomen. "I'm a teacher at an *independent* school. If I tell my students that greed is not at least historically regarded as one of the deadly sins, what do I imply?"

"You imply that avarice is a virtue, Miss Tyree. Avarice is a virtue. Greed has been removed by law from the English language, in accordance with the Jones-Yawley Act. You will use the word 'avarice' around our students, and you will refer to it as a virtue."

Mr. Pickard leans forward in his best-known method of intimidation.

"And you will hopefully develop some respect for my thirty-one years in independent schools, Miss Tyree. One thing I have learned in my career is that the word 'independent' is a dangerous one to embrace too passionately. Now, have you ignored my memo, Miss Tyree, or do you somehow fail to grasp the part of Jones-Yawley which specifically states that teachers, public or private, are no longer permitted to make reference to deadly sins numbering seven. No reference to greed is permitted, except for college philosophy classes, which are grandfathered for three years, through the 2050-51 school year." Mr. Pickard smiles, but his eyes remain riveted on Robin's. "You do not teach a college philosophy class, do you, Miss Tyree?"

Mr. Pickard takes a slow sip of his coffee, then continues.

"Robin, it is decidedly not up to you to teach in violation of the law. Our nation was built on avarice, as Jones-Yawley makes clear. The acquisition of wealth has led to the building of churches, museums, parks, and many other philanthropically-granted sites. Like it or not, Robin, this country, this world, is run by corporations and wealthy individuals. Congress has simply recognized a long-existing truth: Our nation needs to continue to foster avarice among our most talented and intelligent young. Anything that attaches guilt to the pursuit of great wealth has the potential to erode that which our country was built upon. Therefore, outdated and erroneous notions suggesting to children that there are ideals, other than one's own family, greater than the acquisition of money will not be tolerated at this school. These children's parents have invested a significant sum for a Chesterton education, and we will not let them down. Am I understood, Miss Tyree?"

"If--if I could just explain what I was trying to do, I--"

Mr. Pickard displays his right palm, like a traffic officer. Robin freezes her sentence. Mr. Pickard rises and gestures toward the door.

"Afternoon break is nearly over, Miss Tyree. Please resume your more responsible work with our students."

Robin wobbles to her feet. She leaves without a word, trying not to hear the click of the door as she shuts it gingerly. She turns and passes a portrait of L. Frank Yardley, founding headmaster of Chesterton, warmly welcoming a young child through the stone portals of the main building a century ago.

Rattled, Robin looks at her watch, smoothes her skirt, wipes a slight trace of moisture from her forehead, takes a deep breath, exhales, and wears what she knows is an unconvincing smile as she hurries down the long west hallway toward her classroom. The hallway is crowded with between-classes students. Several seniors gaze upon her with what Robin is suddenly sure is a derisive and knowing silence, certain to be followed by snickers after she passes.

She catches up with her class, seventeen energetic freshmen, as they file into her classroom for free-reading. She watches her students settle properly into their seats. They withdraw their reading tablets with library respect (just as she instructed them on Rules and Expectations Day during week one).

Certain that her face is flushed red, and unsure whether the blush is from her fear or from her shame at her fear, she thanks herself for scheduling today for free-reading.

Robin pulls her own free-reading tablet from her top desk drawer. She pretends to focus on page fifty-seven of Frank Fettis's new biography of Stephen Torvell, the first man to walk on Mars. She had thought it would be fascinating, indeed inspiring. But the news yesterday, that Torvell signed a lucrative contract to appear on Burger King soda cups, wrestling over a Whopper with the little black-clad Martian from the twentieth-century Bugs Bunny cartoons, has somewhat diminished her curiosity about the shaping of this man's life.

A tittering from the back of the classroom yanks her eyes from page fifty-seven to the desks in the back right corner. There can be no question that Marvin Lyall has again begun free-reading with the exhibition of a humorous drawing to his neighbors. Time to relieve him of the artwork, regardless of how much Robin likes Marvin and his original mind.

Robin stands, noisily sliding her chair legs along the tile floor for effect. The tittering stops. All eyes in the rear corner are re-directed seriously upon electronic pages.

"Mister Lyall," Robin calls firmly.

Marvin, a rather handsome fourteen-year-old in spite of his battle with teenage acne, looks up innocently from his tablet.

"Yes, ma'am?"

"We would all be grateful, as usual, if you would share your art with the class."

This request has become, in Robin's mind, a healthy diversion during the several weeks heading into Holiday Consumption break. After all, Marvin is revered by his classmates, and his drawings seldom stray into subjects or depictions which are distasteful or even unintelligent. A good laugh is usually had by everyone, and the ensuing half-hour generally produces uninterrupted reading by the entire class.

"Yes, ma'am," Marvin replies with expected eagerness, and he produces a yellow lined sheet of paper with today's picture. He turns it out toward the front of the class, for everyone to see.

The drawing depicts a white boy and a black man sitting together on a raft, floating down a river. Marvin has drawn dialogue balloons above both characters, but Robin has to take a few steps toward the back of the classroom in order to see the words uttered by the boy and the man in the cartoon. As she draws near, she sees that the drawings are excellent renderings of Huckleberry Finn and slave Jim from Mark Twain's classic novel of nearly two hundred years ago.

Huck, looking downriver, asks, in Marvin Lyall's signature block writing, "So, Jim, what do you plan to do with your newfound freedom?"

Jim, also peering downriver, replies, "I's goin' ta take Mistah Hen'rickson's salesmanship class at Chessahton Prepatarah Skoo. Gonna lern me to close the Deal of Life. Jes' like Mistah Hen'rickson say.

Yessah, I's goin' ta be a closah."

As the children finish reading Marvin's artistic offering, Robin scans the faces in the room. Some, not finding humor in the picture, turn and resume their reading. Marvin's best friends and desk neighbors, David Turner and Juan Ramirez, continue to enjoy a chuckle at Mr. Hendrickson's expense.

Robin, thinking back five minutes to her call to Mr. Pickard's carpet, decides to move the class into discussion of Marvin's cartoon. After all, she has a mortgage to pay.

"Class, let's talk about Marvin's picture today."

All of the students dutifully place their books face down on their desks.

"Carolyn," Robin says softly to a shy brown-haired girl in the front row. "You didn't seem to like Marvin's cartoon today. What would you like to say about it?"

Carolyn clears her throat nervously and lowers her head, embarrassed. "It's.....It's......" Carolyn mumbles something inaudible to complete her observation.

"Carolyn, please speak up. We couldn't hear you," Robin says, choosing a patient tone.

The girl raises her head, revealing a deep blush.

"It's.......dirty."

Again the girl looks down to examine her skirt.

Juan Ramirez wastes no time in rising to the defense of his friend's work. "It ain't dirty! Mr. Hendrickson ***sucks***." Juan, realizing his mistake, shoots an apologetic look at his teacher.

"I'm sorry, Miss Tyree. It--is--not--dirty," he says hesitantly, as if trying to speak Russian.

"That's much better, Juan. Much better. You're getting it."

As Juan sits up proudly in his seat, forgetting for the moment why he has spoken in the first place, Robin distantly remembers a time, seven or eight years ago, when she might also have expected Juan to amend his unkind remark about Mr. Hendrickson. But over time she has followed school directives to soften her approach to non-academic teaching, to reflect the reality that a capacity for cruelty is essential in a young person's development into a revenue-producing corporate citizen. "Especially at a preparatory institution like Chesterton," the school's trustees made clear when they revised the school's mission statement back in 'forty-one.

She is curious, though, to get at Marvin's purpose in drawing his cartoon.

"Why do you think it's dirty, Carolyn?"

The girl speaks without looking up. "Do I have to?"

"We'd like you to," replies Robin, smiling into the words to encourage Carolyn to develop her willingness to elaborate.

Again the blushing face. "It's kind of, well, bad to talk bad about selling," the girl manages.

"Okay, Carolyn. Thank you. Marvin? Would you like to address Carolyn's comment?"

Marvin leans back confidently. "Yes, ma'am. See, it's like you said about the seven deadly sins. Greed makes selling predatory. I--"

"I didn't say that, Marvin."

The words come to Robin's own ears as if out of a nap dream. Surreal. She almost wheels around to see who uttered them.

Marvin stares back at Robin expectantly, as if waiting for the punch line. "Yes, ma'am. You did too. You said greed is one of the deadly sins because it makes, you know, good people do things they wouldn't ordinarily do. You know, as good people. So, in my cartoon, Jim is already planning to be a closer as a free man. A real good salesman. A corporate carnivore, like Mr. Hendrickson teaches us in Salesmanship."

"Real-***lee*** good, Marvin," Robin replies, trying to divert attention from her lie.

"Thank you, ma'am."

"No, Marvin, I mean 'really good salesman'. Real is an adjective, not an adverb."

"Oh, yeah. Right, ma'am. Really right. So anyway, I hate Salesmanship class. It's boring. And I think what you said yesterday about greed was right on, Miss Tyree. I don't want to be a carnivore." Marvin leans forward intently. "I want to be free of avarice."

Robin feels a twinge of guilt as she thinks of her new mortgage payment. Mr. Pickard will be preparing teaching contracts not long after Holiday Consumption break. She ***has*** to renew her contract. The house has been a long time in coming.

"Why, Marvin, I, I think you misunderstood me. Some of you might have misunderstood me. You see, Congress just passed a new law that says that there are six deadly sins, not seven. It's called the Jones-Yawley Act. I was wrong when I forgot that. You see, our nation was built on avarice. You--you can see that, can't you?"

Please, God. Just let this drop. These kids can read me like a tablet.

Marvin pushes back his chair and stands up, stunned. "Miss Tyree, how can you *say* that? You sound like my dad. Yesterday you said it was okay to *make* a lot of money, but not okay to *define* your life and success by it. You *said* it was fine to see money as a way to provide for others, like family, but not as a reason to downsize other families' breadwinners for the sake of stock prices. Greed does these things, you said. You also said that--"

"I'm aware of what I said, Marvin. It was only twenty-four hours ago. It doesn't need regurgitation. But I was wrong. I just didn't consider that the people in Washington have access to lots more research than we do, and --"

"In *fact*, Miss Tyree, you told us that we will one day have power over others, as graduates of Chesterton. That words like compassion have grown weak and meaningless. That greed makes us cruel, and that cruel used to be undesirable. That honor and decency and kindness will disappear unless our generation exercises power less selfishly than yours and the ones before yours. You *said,* Miss Tyree," and Marvin pauses and peers aggressively around the room at his classmates, "that all members of our species are hypocrites by nature, and that that's fine as long as we recognize it. That hypocrisy is a matter of degree, that we should keep our hypocrisies small and trivial and unharmful. That the golden rule should be first when we choose or don't choose actions or decisions which affect others. And *now* you say that just because Congress comes up with some stupid Jones-Pawley Act--"

"Yawley!" exclaims Sarah Burnham, three aisles to Marvin's right.

Marvin rolls his eyes and mutters,"So sorry, Sarah. Yawley."

Robin feels the eyes of the classroom riveted upon her. She has been challenged before, almost always by Marvin Lyall, and she has always relished his intellectual courage. He is right, and yet here she stands with a clear directive from her boss that she must reverse herself on a character issue which has conferred upon her the status of dinosaur as an educator.

Marvin combs the fingers of his right hand through his oily hair and sits down. He crosses his legs and folds his arms, regarding his speechless teacher coolly as Robin struggles for the right comeback.

She is too late.

"Excuse me, Miss Tyree," Marvin breathes softly but audibly, "but you're obviously covering your..........behind."

The room explodes in nervous but uninhibited laughter. Marvin has never gone this far. No one was prepared for it, and so they laugh, wide-eyed, eyes on Marvin and then, the hilarity dying down, eyes returning cautiously to Robin.

The eyes have changed. Marvin has exposed her in minutes. All good teachers privately harbor worries of being exposed as frauds. It is part of what makes them good teachers, and is part of what ensures that they will never suffer such a nightmare. Robin stares stupidly at Marvin, wishing to somehow intimidate, as her mind races to grab the rope that will pull the departing ship back to harbor.

Scanning the room, she recognizes that she has lost the group. She decides to exercise the obvious, to dismiss Marvin for being disrespectful. She sends him to the dean's office. Marvin slams the door behind him. Robin instructs the class to resume free reading, but now she could swear that even shy little Carolyn Pelham is smiling derisively at the screen of her tablet.

She has lost them.

At the end of the class period, the students seem to rush from the room, most of them having packed their tablets into their bags with a couple of minutes to spare. Normally, Robin would not tolerate such clock-watching behavior, but she wants them out as much as they do.

Robin rises from her desk. She hears a commotion out in the hall, exceeding the normal hubbub between classes. She enters the hall, and is almost run over by colleague Jack Hatfield, who is in a virtual sprint eastward toward the administrative offices.

"Jack!" Robin yells, alarmed.

Jack clops to a stop, and turns. "Yes, Robin," he rasps impatiently, swinging his arms back and forth as if needing to visit the bathroom.

"What's -- what's going on?" Robin asks intently.

Jack nervously smooths the hair on the back of his head. "It's one of my advisees. Marvin Lyall."

"Marvin? What's happened?"

"Apparently...well....apparently he drew a derogatory picture of the headmaster and the board, while waiting to see the dean. Somebody kicked him out of class last period, I think, and he made a mistake in the dean's office with one of his damned drawings. That's all I know." Jack turns and resumes his sprint. "I've got to get there!" he calls over his shoulder as he weaves in and out of student traffic. "Got to try to keep him from being expelled!"

Robin stares at the waxed checkerboard floor and begins a slow walk in the direction of the administrative offices. She arrives minutes later outside the headmaster's office and knocks methodically.

The heavy oak door opens to reveal Mr. Pickard's secretary, a grandmotherly woman named Martha West, whom Robin has always liked. Beyond Martha, sitting in the gray vinyl chair in the middle of the room, is Marvin Lyall, his profile appearing tall and straight and confident as he faces the imposing desk of Mr. Pickard. Jack Hatfield, breathing heavily, is leaning down next to Marvin, a hand on Marvin's right shoulder. Sitting on a sofa under the picture window that overlooks the quad are Marvin's parents. His mother is crying, dabbing at her eyes with a tissue. His father stares at his own shoes.

Mr. Pickard is peering out the window. His pose is pensive, grave. His right hand grips his chin as he turns to face Robin. Suddenly he smiles broadly.

"Miss Tyree. Many thanks for dropping in." The smile disappears, and he puts his hands in his pockets as he paces in front of the window. "Marvin has been telling us an interesting story about you."

Robin's stomach churns with apprehension.

Mr. Pickard heaves a sigh and extends his hand. Robin takes it, hesitating. "I'm grateful to you, Miss Tyree, for defending both myself and the board of trustees, and for taking a painful but necessary step in endeavoring to educate an erring young person. Obviously you were listening this afternoon. You are a fine teacher, and clearly have the capacity to combine creativity with pedagogy in accomplishing our school's mission. I should not have doubted you."

Robin looks quizzically at Marvin, who smiles at her for no good reason at all.

"Miss Tyree, Marvin has told us about the test. Brilliant, is all I can say. You caught Marvin, yes. But you affirmed that most of our students are learning what they need to know in this world. Marvin has admitted that he is not Chesterton material after all, and will voluntarily be attending another school on Monday. But more importantly, what has been confirmed today is that with teachers like yourself leading the way, our school can remain true to our mission statement."

Mr. Pickard pauses and stares at Marvin. "Marvin, would you like to repeat the compliment you paid to Miss Tyree a few minutes ago? It certainly provides evidence that you will be okay eventually, Marvin. Eventually you will paint no pictures that will get you into trouble, and I'm glad that you recognize Miss Tyree's role in your education. Please share what you said a few minutes ago, with Miss Tyree."

Marvin swivels in the gray vinyl chair to face Robin.

"Sure, Mr. Pickard," Marvin says positively, not taking his eyes off of Robin. "Miss Tyree, what I said was that if you had been my teacher all along and not just now, I would be a model Chesterton student. I will try to remember your example in my attempt to right myself at another school."

"And I'm sure you will, Marvin," says Mr. Pickard just as positively, and claps his hands to signify that all is finished and fileable. "I'm sure you will."

Minutes later, all but Mr. Pickard have exited the headmaster's office. Robin, shaken, heads for her car, an old gray '38 Volvo moored in the back parking lot next to a student's late-model Mercedes-Benz. She places her forehead against the steering wheel for several long seconds, reviewing her career, dreading tomorrow, dreading the quiz she would write tonight, dreading her weekly text conversation with her parents.

She lifts her head and adjusts the rearview mirror. Gravely, she opens the glove compartment and removes several items until she finds what she is looking for. She scribbles on a small rectangular sheet of paper. She scribbles on another small rectangular sheet of paper. She tears the second sheet of paper from its pad. She looks at herself in the mirror. She brushes her fingers through her hair unnecessarily. She takes both small pieces of paper and places them in an envelope.

Sighing, she starts the car and pulls out of the parking lot and heads southward on Chesterton Avenue. She arrives minutes later at the Publix shopping center. She locates the driveup mail-drop, and pulls alongside. Glancing again at the rearview mirror, she again adjusts it, to give her a better look at what is behind her.

Satisfied with the adjustment, Robin Tyree drops her mortgage payment in the "Out-of-Town" box and pulls back into the center's traffic, glancing at her watch to see that, indeed, she has plenty of time until the day's last period.

SEVEN DAYS A WEEK

Mark S. Jackson

Monday

On Monday, he has an easy one. He loves starting his week with an easy one. Not that his job is particularly difficult, or time-consuming, but it can certainly be distasteful. He does not dwell on this fact. Some of his peers have cracked under the strain, just couldn't keep going on—they let it get to them. But not him. The job is too important, and the benefits are too good. One more year, and he's out--mandatory retirement at 40, with a full pension and medical for the rest of his life.

And today he has an easy one. A drowning.

He does not know her name. He never knows their names. There is no need. He is here to perform a task, to do that which is necessary.

She is elderly. She let her grandson drown in the pool, while she was supposed to be watching him. Instead, she was inside the house, making another vodka tonic. There was some debate as to whether the parents should be held accountable, as well. Surely they knew of her drinking problem.

In the end, the court decided No, there had been enough loss for this family. But someone must pay, and the guilty were no longer coddled.

He holds her head in the tank for four minutes. She does not resist, barely struggles. She seems to welcome it, in fact. He removes his wet gear when he finishes, and signals to the technicians to remove the body. Even though they wear surgical masks, he can tell the younger one is slightly green under the harsh light of the fluorescents.

"You're new?" he asks, not unkindly.

"Y-yes, sir." Though he is gloved, he is hesitant to touch the body of the dead woman.

"It gets easier. Trust me." He snaps off his gloves and tosses them in the trash as he exits the room, and heads upstairs to his other job, as a tax accountant for Linden and Associates. He has some quarterly reports to get done before he goes home. He finds it amusing that, even though the front company is completely government funded, they still care about profit and loss statements.

He stops in a small room devoid of surveillance gear, and removes his mask and tosses it in the laundry bin in the corner. He exits out a door on the other side, his true face revealed for the first time today, and heads to his office.

Tuesday

He has a baton, and is systematically beating a young man with it.

This particular youth, who is handcuffed hand and foot, is the leader of a gang responsible for the savage beating and near-death of a local student. The gang members used fists and feet. He will use a heavy steel baton, and he will break thirty-two bones in the gang leader's body, at random--the same number of fractures the victim suffered.

He strikes the youth hard several times. He ignores the young man, who has begun to cry and plea for forgiveness.

"How many?" he asks.

A slight hum emanates from the wall, but he is not concerned. Everything he wears today is lined with lead to protect him from the x-rays flooding the room.

"Six," comes the terse reply over a speaker. The tech is in an adjacent room, visible through Plexiglas but shielded from the radiation. "Can you hurry up? I've got a lunch reservation."

"Oh? Where?" he asks, as he resumes swinging the baton, over and over, each impact punctuated by the sound of breaking bones.

"L'Maison."

He pauses. "Really? That's my wife's favorite place to eat. I didn't know they were serving lunch now."

"Yep, they just started, maybe a month ago. The place is absolutely swamped," she says, as she glances at her watch, "and they will only hold your table for ten minutes." She gestures at him through the window. "Less talking, more breaking."

"How many now?" he asks.

The humming returns.

"Fourteen."

Wednesday

He is not happy. Not happy at all. He always gets the burnings, and he hates it, loathes it with every fiber of his being. Their identities are secret; no one is supposed to know who performs that which is necessary. Everything is supposed to be random.

But he seems to get most of the burnings. He wonders for a brief moment if someone is pissed off at him. Someone important.

The CEO of a small, successful company is tied to a chair in the center of the room. An abandoned warehouse his company owned burned to the ground, and two homeless men who lived there were caught inside and burned to death. An investigation revealed the CEO hired an ex-con to burn it down for the insurance money. It turns out his wife had very expensive tastes.

"I'll give you anything you want," the CEO pleads.

The words dissipate as he empties a can of gasoline over the CEO's balding head. He sets the can down, and pats his pockets. Where did he put those matches?

Thursday

He is behind the wheel of a car. It is delicate work, and requires his fullest concentration. He must travel at just the precise speed and strike the woman at just the correct angle in order to cripple her, to put her in a wheelchair. The man she struck and crippled will never walk again. She is held in place by a series of straps tied to a bendable pole, all designed to give way when she is struck by the vehicle.

He can see the fear in her face just before the car impacts her and catapults her thirty feet. If he did it properly, her hip is shattered, the vertebrae in her lower spine severed. She will never walk again. She will certainly never drive while inebriated again.

Unless he missed, of course. Then he'll have to strap her up and start all over again.

Friday

He is strangling a man to death; a man who choked the life from his girlfriend after she told him she was pregnant. He is wearing gloves; they are the really soft kind advertisers have convinced us we need in order to drive expensive cars.

He has been trained how to do this—how much pressure to apply, in which direction, and how important his thumbs are. At some point he will feel the trachea collapse in on itself, and his task will be complete.

He times himself. He takes pride in how strong his hands have become over the years and because it's Friday, and he is a little bored, he endeavors to beat his best time. He squeezes with all his strength, feels the windpipe collapsing beneath his thumbs, and knows the man is dead even as he gasps for a breath that will never come.

He glances at his watch. Seventy-two seconds. Not bad.

Not bad at all.

Saturday

It is late in the day, and his daughter is at a friend's house for a sleepover. He makes love to his wife on a leather couch in the living room. Rays of sunlight stream through the curtains, dappling their bodies in psychedelic shapes his grandfather's generation would have found familiar. She sits astride him, unmoving, her eyes closed as she seeks to prolong the sensations of a lazy afternoon.

His hands caress her body, before moving to her face. He pauses at her throat and strokes the skin above her carotid artery, lets his fingertips linger there, can feel her pulse. He thinks briefly of the man he strangled the day before, and wonders if she will ever know what he really does when he goes to work. He wonders if she would be able to understand.

* * *

She responds to his touch, and begins moving. She reaches down, knowing it adds something extra for him. The day before, while wielding a very sharp knife, she transformed a serial rapist into a eunuch. It was unpleasant, but necessary, and she does not think about it now. She wonders if her husband will ever know what she really does for a living. He thinks she is an accountant, just like him.

Sunday

He naps in the golden twilight of late afternoon, a tabby cat stretched across his chest. His daughter wakes him, solemnly, her four-year-old face earnest and concerned, and informs him they must go to the store to get milk for dinner.

He is still groggy and rumpled when they get to the store, but his daughter holds his hand firmly as she leads him around the automated cashier to the dairy aisle. A virtual herd of bovine faces watch in silence as he picks up a gallon of milk and checks the date.

A quick movement in his peripheral vision catches his attention. There is a young woman in the aisle with them. He glances over and watches her surreptitiously stuff the interior pockets of her scruffy overcoat with various and sundry items. She has spiky blue hair and is missing the little finger on her left hand. She might be fifteen, and is already a repeat shoplifter. If she gets caught again, she will lose the entire hand.

She stops when she feels his eyes on her, and straightens up and meets his gaze. It becomes obvious to him that she has not eaten in some time. For half a moment he considers offering to pay for her items, but before he can speak, she whirls on her heel and stalks down the aisle and around the corner.

He looks down at his daughter. He is still holding her left hand. For an instant he can't feel her little finger in his grasp, and he has to squeeze her hand tighter to make sure it is still there.

He turns, and his little girl follows him, hand in hand, as they walk to the front of the store to pay for their milk.

He hopes he has an easy one tomorrow. He likes starting his week with an easy one.

AT SEA

Foust

Shelley closed her new book. It smelled a little like mouthwash. On the back, it had a gummy place where the price tag had been. Bits of lint had begun to stick there. She tried to scrape the mess off with her fingernail and some spit, but it wouldn't budge. Her mother would have used nail polish remover, her solution for anything that was sticky. Shelley was at her grandfather's house now, though. He probably didn't have any.

When she and her father first arrived, Shelley was sent off to the den to read her book. Her father wanted to talk to Gangy in the kitchen for a minute. Now, while Gangy was taking her suitcase to the back bedroom, her father knelt down in front of her. Placed a cupped palm on each of her knees. Smiled. One of his front teeth was less white than the others. She'd never noticed it before. "Okay, Shell. You're all set. One surprise weekend with Gangy. Just the two of you. Talk nice to him—maybe he'll take you out on the boat."

Shelley grinned. She knew she didn't need to talk nice to Gangy. He would take her out on the boat anyway. It was summer. That was what they did. Her father tapped the top of her head with his fingers as he stood up. "Hang on a sec. I'll be right back" He went out the back door, letting the screen slap shut.

When he returned, he was carrying his favorite canvas hat. "Here you go. In case you get to go out on the boat." Her mother hated this hat—she'd banished it to the back seat of the car—but Shelley had always liked it because it looked like the hat Gilligan wore on TV. When her father put it on her head, it fell down over her eyes. He curled the brim back so she could see. "There." Stepping back, he smiled at her. "You look like a real sailor now."

This was silly. Of course she didn't look like a real sailor. She was eight-and-a-half years old. No real sailor was eight-and-a-half. But she smiled, tipped the hat to one side. "Ahoy, Matey," she said, in a growly voice. Her father laughed, but only a little, as if laughing required too much effort.

The adults went back outside. She watched them through the window. Her father was sitting behind the wheel. A bleached reflection splashed across the windshield, covering his face. Gangy leaned against the car door, pushed it closed. His shirttail was coming untucked on one side. Just after backing the car out onto the street, her father rolled down the window and shouted, "Thanks, Dad. I owe you one!" Bending over to yank some weeds out of a crack in the driveway, Gangy straightened up and waved. Shelley took off the Gilligan hat and resumed scraping at the sticky spot on her book.

Back inside, Gangy floated the idea of an afternoon nap. "You need to get your sleep, Shell. We'll have to get up before sunrise tomorrow if you want to go fishing." She didn't argue; she was actually a little tired. A nap sounded nice. Leaving her book behind on the couch, she followed Gangy down the hall.

In the back bedroom, she kicked off her sneakers and lay lengthwise across the bed. For a little while, she traced the paths of cobwebs draped across the corner of the ceiling. Eventually she fell asleep. When she woke up, her arms and legs were imprinted with the swirled patterns on the chenille bedspread. Her ponytail had worked free of its elastic band.

For dinner that night, Gangy made hot dogs, with potato chips and ginger ale. Then, they watched TV in their pajamas. The last show she remembered seeing was *Adam-12*. After that she must have fallen asleep. In the back of her mind was a vague memory of Gangy carrying her off to bed, pulling the spread right up under her chin, closing the door behind him. The bedclothes smelled musty and a bit sour. Eventually, she pushed them all off.

The next morning, the click of the overhead light woke her up. It was still dark outside, but Gangy was already dressed. "Hey Shell—time to rise and shine! We gotta get up before the fish if we're gonna catch 'em."

Shelley put on the long pants and long-sleeved shirt her mother always made her wear on the boat. She hated her boat clothes, hated being wrapped up like a mummy under the hot summer sun. But her mother was right—suntan lotion alone was never enough to keep her from blistering. She needed extra protection.

At the marina, they parked the car in front of a bank of vending machines outside the main office. Gangy was carrying the jar of change he kept under the passenger seat. Pouring some of it into his hand, he fished out the silver pieces, threw back the pennies. "What do you think, Shell? How about some sticky buns? Nabs? Peanut butter log? Zagnut?" He began slipping coins into the slots and pushing buttons. "Lemme see, peach soda, grape, Mountain Dew." His hands were getting full. "Oops—getting a little ahead of myself here. Why don't you go get the cooler out of the backseat?"

She trotted over to the car. Kneeling on the back seat, she tried to drag the cooler out, but it would only move a few inches. "It's too heavy!"

"Sorry, Shell. I forgot I put all that ice in there." Clutching the collection of snacks and sodas to his chest, he ambled toward the car. Some neon-orange cupcakes tumbled out in his wake. She darted behind him and picked them up. A printed red banner snaked across the plastic wrapper: "You may be a winner!"

Inside the cooler, beer bottle necks poked up like flowerless stalks. Gangy burrowed sodas into the ice between the beers and piled some of the food in the space on top. She handed him the packet of cupcakes. He widened his eyes, arched his brows. "Hey, how about that? You may be a winner! We'll have to check that out after we get the boat up and running. You never know!"

Shelley knew. There was nothing inside but cupcakes. It was that word "may." They always used it when something wasn't quite true. But she smiled at Gangy as if she thought there really was a chance they could win.

Together, they walked down to the boat. Gangy lugging the cooler, Shelley carrying the extra snacks that didn't fit inside. Her grandfather's boat wasn't the biggest boat in the marina, but it wasn't the smallest, either. At the front, underneath a canvas awning, were two chairs on tall poles, one behind the steering wheel and one next to it. The back of the boat was open to the sky. In the center, a raised white box paved with yellowed plastic cushions served as a communal seat. This box doubled as a hinged cover for the engine. When the cover was flipped open, the seat cushions stayed on. There were bolts to hold them in place. Shelley remembered watching her grandfather open the cover to adjust something on the engine. The bitter smell of oil and the blackened motor had made her feel uneasy—it looked like something she wasn't supposed to see.

After hopping from the pier down onto the boat, she hoisted herself into the passenger seat. This was the first time she'd managed by herself. She hoped her grandfather would notice, but he was busy untying the lines and starting the engine. It belched and clattered for a few minutes before settling into a rough-edged rumble. In the marina, it sounded horrible. People stared at them when they went by. Out on the ocean, it seemed much quieter. Plus, no one was around to notice the noise.

The sky had been dark when they left the house, but now it was nearly daylight. A few straggling stars poked holes through the receding nighttime. On the edges close to the water, deep blue gave way to peach, bordered by a fiery orange line scudding along the horizon. Gangy pulled something out of his back pocket. "Hey, don't forget your hat, Shell. Your father will have a fit if you don't wear it."

She coaxed the hat into a head shape and put it on, curling the brim back the way her father had. As they left the marina, she twisted around in her seat and watched the other boats get smaller and smaller. Eventually, they were just a few faint slash marks on the distant horizon. Overhead, the sky was brightening, silver clouds feathering out across the sky. The sea was a huge, choppy expanse. It felt like they were the only people in the whole world.

When they got far enough from shore, Gangy slowed the boat down and stood up from his seat. "Okay, Skipper. She's all yours!" He hooked his thumbs under her armpits, lifted her up, and transferred her to the chair behind the wheel. This always hurt, his fingers digging into her ribs, her legs dangling down and making her heavier so he had to grip her even more tightly. But it was something she had to put up with if she wanted to drive the boat.

"Just keep her going straight for now. I'll get us some lines going."

They usually trolled for fish, sticking the rods into the aluminum tubes bolted along the stern and letting the boat pull the bait around. While Gangy set up the rods, she held the wheel steady. A flock of gulls circled overhead, taking turns plunging into the water as if they were performing a kind of dance. The sun was up now. Light flicked off the wave tips.

"All set. Time to catch us some supper." Gangy leaned over her and took the wheel.

Clambering off the driver's seat, she wandered to the back of the boat and gazed out over the sea. The fishing rods flexed into arcs, pulled taut by the slender filament lines that disappeared into the waves. Water churned out from under the motor, froth and foam leaving a v-shaped path showing where the boat had been. Salty droplets freckled her face.

* * *

While the engine roar pressed against her ears, Shelley thought about yesterday morning. Her mother had come into her room when it was still dark outside. "Wake up, sleepyhead! We've got a surprise for you." Sitting down on the edge of the bed, she patted Shelley's arm. "You get to spend the weekend with Gangy! Neat, huh?" Turning the covers back, she ruffled Shelley's hair. "Your father's going to drive you down this morning. I've already packed your boat clothes and a few other things you might need. Go on and get dressed. I'll pour you some cereal."

Shelley wiped crumbs of sleep out of her eyes. Some clothes lay across her bedside chair, shirt on top, shorts on the bottom. They looked like a deflated person.

After breakfast, her mother gave her a ridiculously long hug. "I'll see you in a few days, Sweet Pea. Say hi to Gangy for me."

"Okay." Shelley tried to pull away, but her mother wouldn't let go. "Mo-om, Dad's waiting—"

The car was running, the passenger door yawning wide. Behind the wheel, her father gazed off away from their house. After Shelley jumped in the car, her mother came out to the sidewalk and watched them drive off. She didn't wave.

During the trip, Shelley's father had acted strange—as if he had been caught at something he wasn't allowed to do, and was trying to make up for it. He let her stick her head out the open window, didn't complain when she fiddled with the radio. When he stopped to get gas, he bought her a new book and a three-pack of Crackerjacks. The book was for littler kids, but it was better than nothing. While he drove, he kept narrating everything, using a chirpy voice that sounded like he was talking to someone else. "Look at those cows. Wonder what they're thinking," he'd say, or "Wow, that's a really big bird." They even stopped for lunch at McDonald's—her favorite—though he usually complained when she wanted to eat there.

* * *

Shelley felt her stomach twist. Something strange was going on. She looked back at Gangy. He was leaning against the driver's seat, steering with his elbow while he pried the top off a beer bottle. He probably knew what was happening. But he hadn't said a word to her. He waved and shouted, "Hey Shell! Anything biting back there?"

Shelley shook her head and turned away. She didn't want to answer him. A bitter taste stung the back of her throat. Something was wrong, something no one would tell her. Gazing out across the water, she focused on the softened seam between sea and sky. Shadows stripped the gleam from the morning ocean. Just off to the right, a gash of orange—an unmoored buoy—floated away.

LOST ISLAND STORY HOUR

Eric Witchey

I tell myself I'm not hiding. I just don't want to disturb the old man's reading. He still believes reading can change the world.

I should knock him out with a coconut and carry him to the raft. I owe him at least that. I take a deep breath. The tide's out. The sun's high. Decay and sea salt lace the air.

Just above tide-line, in the shadows of mangroves and thorn thickets, the white sand is still cool on my calloused feet. I crouch low behind the bole of a coconut palm and grind my bare feet deep into the sand.

He's not so different from when I was a kid. Certainly, the palm trees and white sands are not the library's terrazzo, walnut, and brass; but his impish smile and loud guffaw are the same.

He has stones and driftwood logs arranged in a circle. I know that in his mind children sit on those seats in rapt attention. The Saturday afternoon children's readings were always important to him. Back in the world, even in the face of short-sighted cutbacks, low staffing, home web surfing, and pressure from the mayor to close the library, he kept the reading circles going.

Shaded by the tattered blue tarp I hung between two palms for him, he peers over his half glasses. The lenses were lost over a year ago. The gold-plated frames have salt-air corrosion in the scratch marks along the ear-pieces.

I feel guilty about his glasses. I broke the first lens when I hit him. That was when I still thought he was sane -- when I thought he was just pretending he believed we still lived in Ohio.

He pauses in his reading. He turns the book outward so his audience can see the pictures.

There are no pictures. He can't see the words on the pages. It doesn't matter. We only have one book, a Polynesian cookbook that washed up three years ago. Even if his glasses worked, he couldn't read whatever language it's in.

He recites the stories by heart. They're the same tales he read to me when I was a child.

I listen. The emphasis is the same. The rising gray and black eyebrows are the same, perhaps a little more salt than pepper now. The only real difference is the long gray and black ponytail over his shoulder. Now and then, he touches it, tugs it a little. I wonder how that would have gone over in Ohio -- that long-haired, crazed librarian look.

He puts the book in his lap and closes it gently. "That is all we have time for today," he says. His voice is steady. His diction precise -- proud.

His pocket watch stopped a long time ago. My digital still hums away on its little lithium cell. I imagine that will eventually run down, but I glance at it. Three o'clock. Somehow he knows to the second when it's time for the kids to meet their parents at the front of the library.

He spreads his arms to take in the imagined hugs and snuggles. Rising, he makes as if to shepherd the kids to the doors. Barefoot thru the sand, he herds the ghost children of his past.

I can't help wondering if my face is worn by one of his ghosts. Part of me hopes so.

Not my face now. Not the brown, weather-hardened face of my thirty-eight year-old manhood. I wouldn't wish that on him. Better that he sees the round, corpulent wonder-filled face of my early years, the years before the trouble in my family, before he took me in as a foster child.

He closes an imaginary door, puts his hands on the small of his back, and stretches. The gesture is as old as he is, I'm sure. I remember it from every session of every Saturday of every summer of my life before college.

He turns.

I sigh along with him. We have long ago synchronized our sighs in this weekly ritual of his insanity. His sigh is one of regret that the children are gone for another week. Mine is one of nostalgia, of fear, of release from this overt manifestation of his insanity.

"Mr. Morton," I say. I step away from the brush.

He starts. Then he smiles and peers over his glasses.

I know immediately that he isn't seeing the man in front of him. When he sees me as I am, he looks through the empty frames. When he sees me as I was, he looks over the tops.

"Little William," he says. "Hiding in the stacks? You should be meeting your mother."

I've given up trying to get him to understand his life here. Instead, I play along. "I needed to check these books, Mr. Morton."

He nods and grins. "What do you have this week? More adventures? Science Fiction? Fantasy? The next in the Gormenghast trilogy?"

I step out of the palm shadows. The rainbow streak of a running lizard skips over my foot and disappears into the thicket. In the sun, the white sand warms my calluses. I offer up my empty hands as if I'm holding several volumes. "Kontiki," I say.

"Thor Heyerdahl."

"I'm building a raft," I say.

"From reeds? To sail the Pacific?"

"Sort of," I say. "I'm using coconuts."

He guffaws. "You are one of my very favorites, William," he says. "And where do you propose to find enough coconuts to float you across the Pacific?"

I look at his feet. There are three coconuts near enough for him to kick. "I've been collecting them," I say. "I get them at the grocery. I've almost got enough."

He realizes I'm serious; or, he realizes the child he sees is serious. He raises a bushy eyebrow. Rather than burst my bubble, he changes the subject.

I almost cry at his kindness even though it's thoroughly demented.

"What else do you have there?" he asks.

"Single Line Fishing in Deep Water," I say.

"Like Santiago?" He reaches out to take my invisible books. I hand them to him.

"Who?"

"Santiago," he repeats. He turns away and heads toward an imaginary counter where the checkout stand should be. I mean, where it would be. He paces off the distance perfectly. My childhood memory knows his gait, the number of steps, the position he'll take, an elbow on the counter, one hand moving books through a scanner, his eyes on me while he continues to chat about my books.

"The Old Man and the Sea," he says. "A great book. With your love of adventure, I think, William, that you would enjoy it. Shall I get our copy for you? I'm sure it has been checked in."

Of course, I know the book. I just didn't remember the name of the old man.

Santiago.

I remember now. What was the boy's name? It doesn't matter. "I think I've got enough for this week," I say.

"I'm surprised," he says. "Only two. You usually leave with a whole armload."

"Building a raft takes a lot of time," I say. "I don't have any help."

He hands me the imaginary volumes. He nods, smiles, and peers over his frames.

He has to look up at me to peer over the frames. Funny how that look makes me feel small, like I'm still a child standing in front of the tall, kindly librarian that took me in. I want to please him somehow. I want to help him. I remind myself that I'm trying to save his life.

"Maybe," I say, "you could help me with the raft?"

"I have never built a raft, William."

"But I bet you've read all about them."

He smiles. "Reading and doing are not the same."

I smile and speak one of his pet mantras to him. He must have said it to me a thousand, thousand times while I was growing up. "Begin to learn a thing by reading. Make it yours by doing."

He tosses his pony tail over his shoulder and throws back his head and laughs. He shakes so hard he has to hold his glasses to his head. In spite of my fear for him, I smile. He might be insane, but his humor's intact. We laugh together.

"I'll help if I can," he says. "Under one condition."

"What?" I ask.

"You have to come to next Saturday's reading hour. Two-o'clock sharp," he says.

I hope we're both off the island by then. Even so, I agree.

* * *

"What we need are some good planks," he says.

I stand up from untying the knotted edges of nylon netting I found hung up on the basalt ridge at the North end of the island. There's enough netting to make maybe ten large bags of coconuts. Hell, Papillon escaped Devil's Island on one. With ten, we can support a platform, a lean-to, an outrigger, and a sail.

I've already finished the platform and outrigger. They float well enough without the coconuts, but the coconuts will let us load the platform and stay high and dry -- I hope.

"Why planks?" I ask.

"To make the story work. There is always a good shipwreck and planks and part of a boat."

"Always?"

"Well, not in Ohio," he says. "But in Gulliver. In Robinson Crusoe. In Dynotopia."

I laugh. He laughs.

"Grass lines do not hold up well in salt water," he says.

I nod. I continue to work on the nylon netting. "We'll test it on fresh water. On Ganges Pond," I say. This seems to please him. "Proof of concept," I say.

He puts down the blue plastic tarps, the sail he's lashing together. Peering over his glasses, he smiles and squints one eye. "Sometimes," he says, "I think you are a lot older in your head than you are in your body, William. Your reading will serve you well as an adult. When you grow up, you can come and write grants for me at the Library."

"I'd like that," I say. I don't remind him that we wouldn't be here if one of my grants hadn't come through. It was for him. It was supposed to help him. It was his dream to SCUBA uncharted Islands in the South Pacific. He wanted to do a coffee table book -- underwater pictures, big plates of pretty fish and corals, a message to the world to save the oceans.

I hadn't expected the grant to come through. None of the others had. The library was dying. His heart was dying with it. At the time, I laughed and thanked God for the gift that might save him.

If that grant hadn't come through, we wouldn't have been on the

SCUBA charter when it went down. We wouldn't have had to bury Captain Andy.

I wipe warm salt water from my eyes.

"I think I had better go," he says. "I am quite sure your mother will want to feed you soon, and I have a date with Santiago tonight."

I want him to keep working, to not go off into the jungle and pretend he has a home, an easy chair, a floor lamp, and a copy of *The Old Man and the Sea*.

"We're almost done," I say.

"Gange's Pond will keep. Remember your promise," he says. "Tomorrow is Saturday."

"I'll be there," I say.

He leaves. I ignore my tears and keep working. I work through the night. I work through sunrise. Near noon, I float the coconuts out and lash them to the belly of the platform.

When I'm done with all ten, I look at my watch. Almost two o'clock.

I lash the supplies to the deck inside the lean-to. I unwrap the sail and test it against the breeze. I drop the center board, lift it, jump up and down on the lashed outriggers, kick at the rudder.

The raft is as finished as it's going to be.

* * *

I sit on my log in the circle and watch him read from the cookbook.

"He was an old man who fished alone in a skiff in the Gulf Stream and he had gone eighty-four days now without taking a fish."

I can't imagine how he does it. He must have known it by heart before Captain Andy's boat capsized. Maybe his insanity lets him dredge up the stories from the past. Still, it's one thing to memorize the eggs and ham story or remember a tale about a little girl and big red dog; it's something else entirely to remember word-for-word an entire novel.

Of course, I can't check it, but I'm sure he remembers it perfectly.

I sit and watch him turn the pages. His certainty, the smooth action of his fingertips, the way he slides his fingers up the side of the book and folds in the next page to wait for the next turning. It all says he knew the book completely, that if I ever made it home, I would find that particular edition on his shelves. When I looked at those pages, I would see that the last word he spoke before turning the page would be the last word on the page in the real book.

He peers through his glasses at the book. To him, it's real. Occasionally, he peers over his glasses at me and smiles. Even so, he never misses a word.

It's a long reading. I listen carefully while Santiago cuts bait and fishes. I take mental notes while he fights the great fish. I worry while he fights the sharks.

I sit as I did as a child, in awe at the spell of this man, my librarian.

When he finally puts his book down, he takes a long breath.

I take a long breath. "That was amazing," I say.

"Thank you, William," he says. Then he stands and looks through his glasses. "Do you think the library on the other side of Ganges Pond is still there?" he asks.

I'm stunned. I know he sees me as I am. I try to think of the right answer. His librarian's gaze makes me small, and I can't lie. "I don't know," I say.

"The tide is turning, William," he says. "You'll need to catch it if you want to get out of the bay tonight."

He's lucid. He's looking directly at me. He takes his glasses off and looks into my eyes. "You have everything you need to make it," he says.

For the first time since we crawled up onto the hot, white sand, my belly's cold. "We," I say. "We have everything we need to make it."

He puts his glasses back on and peers over the top. "No," he says. "I am the librarian. I have my duties. The great Ganges Pond crossing is up to you, William. I could never leave my books."

Whatever lucidity he had for a moment is gone. I think again about knocking him out and carrying him to the raft. I'm stronger, taller.

He bends and gathers his invisible book from an invisible table.

It's my chance.

The perfection of his motion would make a great mime cry at his own incompetence. The impression of the size and shape of the volume is perfect. I feel the book almost as if I'm touching it myself.

He walks a few paces left, lifts a hand up to his eye-level, inserts the flat of his hand between two volumes in stacks I can't see, then nestles The Old Man and the Sea between them.

He turns back to me. He smiles. "The library is closing, William," he says. "I believe it is time for you to go."

I hesitate. I can't hurt him. I can't take him from his books.

"Thank you, Mr. Morton," I say. "I'll come back."

"I know you will, William," he says. "And William."

"Yes?"

"You will be nice to the new librarian, won't you?"

I nod and turn toward the sea.

THE TEST

T.S. Frank

As Elvis Arnold walked across the campus of McKinley College toward Fillmore Hall, he thought about his Econ 102 exam, which he would be taking in approximately fifteen minutes. From a long, narrow slip of paper, he reviewed the letters he had memorized, and repeated them as if he were chanting a mantra: ACCABBDACDACBBA and so on and so forth. It amazed the freshman that he had been able to memorize all seventy-five answers to Oswald Dupree's Macro Economics test, a copy of which every fraternity and sorority had on file. So sure were Elvis and the rest of his classmates that they would get Dupree's perennial final exam that neither he nor they had bothered to look at the test itself, only the long list of letters denoting the right answers.

This would be Elvis's first time cheating. He didn't feel good about it, but he had made up his mind to do it. As he passed the flag pole, McKinley College's monument to its war dead, Elvis thought about his father, a man who had lived by a rigid notion of right and wrong. And he thought about his mother, back home alone, raising his brother and sister. Elvis knew that his scholarship depended on his Econ grade and that he and his mom depended on the scholarship. "So now is not the time to take risks," he thought to himself. "Now is not the time to be noble. ACCABBDA," he chanted to himself once again, as he passed by the GAP house, the fraternity he was pledging.

"Truth for its own sake," he mused—it was his fraternity's motto—"what the hell does that mean?" His initiation into the brotherhood was to occur that evening. Sooner perhaps, maybe that very afternoon. Right after the exam he and his pledge brothers could get the call. Then they would all rush down to the house, where they would enter a darkened room to take the oath, say the words, perform the rituals. Soon Elvis would be one of them, completely.

When Elvis Arnold was in grade school and middle school, he was idealistic enough—"naïve enough" he told himself—that the thought of cheating was anathema to him. To be like his father, he had formed a rigid moral code too. During his high school years, he had attended a boarding school in the East, Harcourt Prep, to play hockey for them. Harcourt had an honor code, so Elvis had abandoned any thought of cheating there as well—he might put himself or some friend or teammate in real jeopardy if he were seen cribbing—which Elvis had been tempted to do in Mrs. Meehan's French class every time she gave a quiz or a test. But now, at McKinley, where there was no honor code, and where, at 18, he had given up any pretense of naivete, Elvis Arnold was about to cheat on a test for the first time in his life. He had lied before, of course. A few fibs, to save himself or someone else from a painful truth. But he had never cheated. Never. Hockey he always played rough and he always played fair.

The young man didn't like old Dupree. So if he were ever going to cheat, this would be the class to do it in. The old professor was a smug bastard, Elvis thought, and he detested the way the old teacher pronounced his name: "Elvisss," like a snake. And he could detect a smirk in the old man's voice whenever he called on him in class. "Elvisss," the old man would say, "what do you make of the slope of this curve?"

Elvis couldn't help his name. His dad, who had been a hardcore Presley fan, had named his first-born son after the King of Rock n' Roll. Elvis hated the name growing up and had always planned on changing it when he came of age, but when his dad died on I-80, hauling a load of stainless from Bethlehem to Cleveland, the young man didn't have the heart to follow through with his plan. Elvis he remained, in honor of his dad.

"Honor," he thought to himself. "What's it worth anymore anyway? Nada. Everybody cheats. Everybody does it. And everybody is cheating on this test—Well, not everybody. Not Nick Fane. Nick doesn't have to cheat. The guy's a freakin' Einstein—But everybody else is, that's for sure."

For some reason, habit probably, Elvis patted the left front pocket of his jeans where his father's penknife rested warmly against his thigh. It was all he had left of his dad, he figured, so he carried the knife with him everywhere. He didn't much believe in fortune anymore, especially since his father's death, but every once in a while he would touch the battered penknife to change a run of sour luck or ward off an evil omen.

Down the cobblestone path, Elvis spied the crooked figure of Professor Oswald Dupree making his way toward Fillmore Hall from the faculty dining room, where the old man spent a good portion of his day, talking with his colleagues and extolling the virtues of early twentieth-century Republican fiscal policy. Dupree looked sinister in his dark tweed suit, scuttling like a crab down the walk, poking his walking stick angrily into the cobblestones with an insistence that suggested demonic possession.

"How old is that guy anyway?" Elvis wondered aloud to himself. "Must be a hundred and five if he's a day."

"What, ho!" the old professor suddenly called to the young man—raising his walking stick in a salute to Elvis, which resembled something of a challenge, if not an outright threat. The student felt like returning the gesture with the middle finger of his right hand, but thought better of it and merely called out, offering a friendly wave, "Hey, Professor! Ready for the exam?"

"Of course, I'm ready, Elvisss," hissed the old man. "Are you?"

"Sure," said Elvis. "I'm always ready."

"Always?" Dupree asked, seeming to challenge the lad again.

"Well, almost always," Elvis replied, smiling a little too broadly. God, he hated how he always let the old man cow him.

"I know all the fraternities have a copy of my final in their file cabinets," said the old professor, his eyes turning dark and sharp, then suddenly brightening like a child's.

"What?" said Elvis, taken aback.

"I said I know all the fraternities have a copy of my Econ 102 exam. And I know what some of my students do this time of year too," the old man chortled. "That is, in fact, why I do it."

"I b-beg your pardon," stammered the young man. "Do what?"

"Give the same test, year after year," Oswald Dupree replied.

"You give the same economics test every year?" Elvis asked, trying to look innocent.

"Oh no," Dupree replied. "I'm done with economics for the semester. The last unit exam tested that. This exam tests something else entirely."

"It does?" the freshman asked, confused.

To the old doctor, the young man looked painfully naïve. "Yes, Elvisss. It tests character. Every year at this time, I test a man and a woman's character. Who has it and who doesn't."

"Oh…" the freshman said quietly. For a moment Elvis was at a total loss for words. He could feel his cheeks turn crimson. He could feel the anger rising in his gorge, though he wasn't quite sure why. "Yeah but how do you know who cheats?" the young man suddenly barked in an awkward attempt to defy his professor.

"I don't have to know," the old man replied coolly. "The cheaters know. And that's good enough for me." Then Oswald Dupree turned and scuttled up the steps of Fillmore Hall.

As he was about to disappear through the doors of the building, Elvis, who could control himself no longer, shouted angrily after the old man, "It's not right! It's not right what you do! Tempt people like you do!"

The old man turned. "Temptation is a bottomless font, Elvis, into which I dip my cup but to offer the poor proselyte a drink."

What was he saying? What could the old man possibly mean?

Confused and angry, all Elvis could do was shout at him, "You're supposed to help! A professor's job is to help his students. To teach them for goodnessakes!"

"Haven't you learned something today?" the old man asked quietly, almost humbly it seemed to the freshman, who stood looking into his eyes, which appeared grey and watery all of a sudden, as if the old doctor were about to cry.

"Yes, I have," the young man replied.

"Then I've earned my daily bread," said Oswald Dupree, who turned and disappeared into the cavernous building.

Elvis heard the professor's walking stick clacking upon the terrazzo floor as the old doctor slowly crossed the foyer to mount the stairway, to begin the long climb to his fifth floor office, over-looking the campus… perhaps the entire world, Elvis thought. Shaken, the young man pondered the strange encounter. It seemed as if his fate were hanging in the balance. He felt like a fresh-made man, standing in a garden, contemplating biting an apple. Then his heart broke.

"Naïve," he thought. "Stupid and naïve."

He knew it was true. He was too late. There was no way he could take the exam without cheating on it, no matter how hard he tried. He knew every letter and he knew its corresponding number. They were stuck in his head, carved into the tablet of his short-term memory.

And he knew he was trapped. Elvis knew that if he took the test, the old devil would have him. And if he didn't, he'd fail the course, lose his scholarship, and return home to his mother, who had been working double shifts for the last two months to cover the cost of next semester's books. Elvis stood frozen in the doorway of the ancient edifice as his classmates began to hurry in.

"This'll be a piece of cake!" Ed Lujac, one of his pledge brothers, said as he passed Elvis and gave him a conspiratorial slap on the back. "A big fat piece of cake."

Elvis remained motionless, as Ed disappeared into the maw of the old building. The young man waited for a miracle, one that would crack open the cosmos and allow him to rocket back in time, to two days ago, before he had decided to cheat. But nothing happened, except that the bell on the clock tower began to toll the eighth hour.

Still Elvis couldn't move. Until he heard his name being called from above. Was it the voice of God? Elvis looked up and saw old Dupree leaning out the window, smiling tightly down at him, looking almost comical. "Are you coming?" the old man called. "I can't wait for you forever."

How had the tottering professor climbed five flights of stairs so quickly? Had the old man flown to his office when no one else was looking? However he had achieved his present altitude, the old doctor was staring down at his student and looking as if Elvis were about to lose at poker.

Elvis stood silently for what seemed like twenty minutes, but, in fact, it wasn't more than a few seconds.

"I don't think so," Elvis called up to his teacher, then the young man reluctantly started down the steps, back to his dormitory. So he would fail the class; at least his honor would remain intact. But when he thrust his hands into his pockets and he felt his father's knife, a thought occurred to him that made him stop in his tracks.

"Sorry about the upshot of the semester!" old Dupree called after him. "Really!"

Elvis turned on the balls of his feet and called back to his old teacher. "I've changed my mind, professor! I'll be right up!"

"Oh?" exclaimed the old man, who looked as surprised as the serpent must have when Eve bit into the apple.

Elvis took the front steps three at a time and rushed into Fillmore Hall. Then he hastened across the foyer, and raced up the hundred-and-nine steps to the fifth floor and old Dupree's classroom.

Just inside the door, he saw his classmates, many of whom were hurrying through the test. Elvis felt like crying out to them, "Stop! You don't know what you're doing! You don't know who this old man really is!" But Elvis remained silent, took the last exam off the top of the professor's desk, and walked to the back of the room, to the last empty seat. Before he sat, Elvis took his father's penknife from his pocket and opened it. He held his thumb lightly on the edge of the blade, sharp like a razor. He stared at the old professor for a long moment, and the teacher stared back at him.

Then Elvis sat in his chair and, without even reading the directions, he marked the top of the paper with the blade of his knife, just to the right of the numbers of the questions. Then he turned the test over and cut off the right-hand side of its seven pages, at the mark he had made, straight down to the bottom of the page. The knife easily cut through the paper, which fluttered to the floor in seven narrow strips, stapled together and bearing numbers from 1 to 75.

Then Elvis shuffled the pages. Then he turned the test over and began cutting each question away from the others, one after the other. And when he was done with his cutting, he stacked the questions, shuffled them again, and arranged the narrow slips of paper before him in a neat pile.

He looked up at his old professor, who was watching him intently. Elvis closed his pocket knife, lay it on his desk, and began to read and answer the first question of his final exam. What its number was, and what its corresponding letter was, Elvis could not know. All he did know was that he was free to take the test, an honest man again, he imagined.

When Elvis Arnold finished circling the last answer on the last question on the last strip of paper, he looked up to discover that he was alone in the room. He sat for a moment, his eyes blinking as if he had just awakened from a dream. He gathered his test together, slipped the penknife into his pocket, touched it for luck, and walked from the room, toward Oswald Dupree's office down at the end of a long narrow hallway.

In the office, the professor sat behind his desk, surrounded closely by walls of moldering books. The room had the smell of the grave. And the old teacher under the yellow light of an arching desk lamp looked something like a corpse himself, but a lively one. For the old teacher graded the exams quite efficiently. He knew all the answers by heart too, ACCABBDACDACBBA and so on and so forth, so that he graded one exam quickly after another, making flicks with his ink pen to mark those questions he knew the students missed on purpose, not to look as if they knew too much.

After he had completed yet another exam, old Dupree looked up to see Elvis standing before him with his test in his hands. "What's that supposed to be?" the old man said when Elvis laid the pile of papers before him like an offering.

"It's my test," the young man answered. "I didn't cheat. I'm an honest man. No matter what you think."

"Is it possible," old Dupree replied, "to be a dishonest man at eight a.m. and an honest man by noon?" He waited for a reply but the student did not answer. "Well, perhaps it is."

"I beat you," Elvis stated flatly. Then he turned to go. As the old professor watched the man walk away, he smiled tenderly.

"Life is long, Mr. Arnold," the old professor said, as his student passed beneath the archway of his door and disappeared. "Life is very long."

THE OTHER SON

Marjorie Brody

Jonathan moved with the grace of a juvenile Mikhail Baryshnikov, the soles of his sneakers barely touching the carpet, his arms, willow leaves swaying in too dainty a breeze. I blamed it on the dance lessons Mom dragged him to in elementary school. That explanation beat thinking something else, if you know what I mean.

Our stepfather might have ignored Jonathan's delicate mannerisms, his mousse-spiked hair, the thrift-store bell-bottom jeans with the hole in the knee, and the dream-catcher necklace, if my fourteen-year-old younger brother had kept his mouth shut about being an atheist—about as likely as me throwing the All-State Championship Football Game. Wasn't gonna happen.

So, an invisible Berlin wall divided our house. A line of demarcation. On one side, Jonathan expressed his view of what he called the hypocrisy of organized religion, as if his words were a mantra to chant over and over by some bald, dress-wearing Buddhist. On the other side, our God-fearing, son-of-a-preacher stepfather paced and ranted about the hell, fire and damnable disgrace Jonathan's behavior caused our entire family.

I gotta admit, Jonathan embarrassed me, too. Oh, nobody would come up and say anything about him to my face. They wouldn't dare. But I'd hear things in the locker room or at the football games. Once I overheard a plan to beat up "the little atheist fag" and to my shame, I cheered them on. It felt right at the time, there in the locker room, with the smell of soap and wet towels and hard-earned sweat surrounding me. I had hoped it might knock some sense into the kid and he'd straighten up.

That day after school, Jonathan came home, set his books down on the kitchen table like he always did, but he didn't open the fridge to get a drink. Didn't go into the pantry for a snack. "Oh, my God." Mom rushed to inspect his fat lip, his bruised eye, and the long cut that sliced his left arm.

"I'm going to school first thing in the morning and talk to that principal." Mom fussed over Jonathan's wounds, a domestic cat hovering over a precious kitten.

Jonathan twisted and leaned back—I doubt from the antiseptic—and pleaded with her, "It was a harmless misunderstanding, Mom. Please don't tell Mr. Jeffreys."

"Three seniors, two juniors, and a linebacker against one skinny freshman." I grabbed an apple from the fruit bowl on the counter and buffed it on my T-shirt. "Nothing 'harmless' about that. The only misunderstanding is how you lived to walk away." I sunk my teeth into the skin of the apple, savored the crunchy, juicy flesh, munched as I watched the kitchen MASH scene.

"Were they anyone you know, Derek?" Mom asked.

I swallowed the fruit in my mouth though it was more than my throat wanted.

"They must've come over from Lincoln Heights." I wasn't going to rat on my friends.

Mom finished wrapping a bandage around the cut on Jonathan's arm, making sure the ends of the gauze tucked away, neat and out of sight. "Change your shirt for dinner now. And take your books upstairs. Larry will be home in no time."

I moved into the family room, picked up the remote for the TV, and plopped onto the couch.

Jonathan stopped at the foot of the stairs. "That's what it was, wasn't it Derek? A harmless misunderstanding, right?"

My heartbeat jumped. Matched the speed of our school band's marching drum. I kept my gaze on the TV. "What else could it be, bro?"

I was so focused on listening for his feet to climb the stairs to his room, for his books to hit his desk, that I didn't realize until minutes later, Phineas and Ferb filled the screen.

Anyway, Larry, that's our stepdad, didn't say a word as his gaze swept over Jonathan's bruised face at dinner. We always have dinner together each night. At six sharp. Unless it's football season and then everyone has to wait until I get back from practice. Mom's rule. Not mine.

"Let us pray," Larry said.

We all bowed our heads except Jonathan who sat head erect and quiet.

"Father in Heaven, we praise You for giving us Your Son to be our Savior and Lord," Larry said. "Be present at our table and grant that we may feast in Paradise with Thee. Bless us oh Lord and these Thy gifts which we are about to receive through Thy bounty through Christ our Lord. Amen."

"Amen," Mom and I said in unison. My brother's lips never moved. His fascination with the bushes squirming in a blustery wind outside the window never wavered.

"At least say a silent prayer, Jonathan. Or aren't you grateful for anything?"

"I'm grateful the earth provides for us," my brother said. "Even though we mistreat it."

Larry must've been too hungry to argue. I'd worked up an appetite after school so I piled four thick slices of beef on my plate and passed the platter to Jonathan. He passed it along to Mom without taking any. Two ends of a rope jabbed at each other in my stomach, ending up in a pile of knots. Damn him. Couldn't we have one peaceful dinner?

"He doing that vegetarian thing again tonight?" Larry asked Mom.

The meat platter wobbled in her hand. She looked down at Jonathan's plate and hurried the platter back to him.

"No, thanks," he said.

Larry appraised Jonathan's bruised face. "I take it the other guy looks equally as bad?"

"There were six of them, dear," Mom told Larry, forever championing her baby.

"So you didn't do any damage?" The question he asked my brother sounded like a pronouncement.

Jonathan was gently putting mashed potatoes into his mouth. His lip had ballooned out by then and had turned an ugly shade of purple and red. "I only protected myself, Larry. I didn't try to hurt anyone."

Larry turned to me and whispered like a quarterback calling a play. "A budding pacifist." The corner of my lip twitched, not knowing whether to turn up or down.

"They took off as soon as I arrived," I told him.

Larry's eyes widen with interest. "You were there, Derek?"

"He chased them off," Jonathan said. I couldn't get a handle on the tone my brother used. A flavor of "yeah, what did you expect?" basted his words.

Larry seemed to sit up straighter or at least his neck seemed longer. "So'd you get any action, Derek?"

"Unfortunately not, sir. I got word someone was after Jonathan and I got there as fast as I could, but . . ." I shrugged. "I was too late. They hightailed it as soon as I showed up."

"Is anyone going to press charges?" Larry asked Mom. He reminded me of a clothes dryer, food churning around in his open mouth, coming into view and disappearing.

"I thought about calling the school, dear," our mother replied, "but Jonathan would prefer I didn't."

Larry reached across for another roll. "I didn't mean us pressing charges, Martha," he said as he heaped whipped oleo from the margarine tub onto his dinner roll. The fake butter lost its grip on the warm dough and slid between his fingers.

Mom's head seemed to get heavy, her neck unable to keep it up. She spoke to her plate. "I don't know about charges, dear. I didn't think about that."

He kept his indictment back by stuffing half the roll into his mouth. He didn't need to use words; his eyes accused, of course you didn't think about it. "So, what time is the game on Saturday, Derek?"

"It starts at ten thirty, sir, but I need to be in the locker room an hour earlier. If it's okay with you, Dad, I'd like to take Mom's car and pick up Roger and Floyd." It was more efficient to ask Larry for Mom's car because if I asked her she'd tell me to go ask him anyway.

"You bet. Mom can run her errands after the game, can't you, Martha?"

"It's Mom's car," Jonathan said to me, ignoring my strategy. "Why don't you ask her?"

Enthusiasm drained from Larry's voice. He rubbed his tone over a verbal whetstone. It came out sharp. Pointed. "Go ahead, Derek. Ask your mother."

I swallowed the golf ball stuck in my throat. I hated when he did this. "Ah, Dad."

"Go on, ask her."

I sucked in a breath, let it expand my chest, numbed my frustration. "Can I borrow your car on Saturday, Mom? I'd like to pick up Roger and Floyd before the game?"

Mom's eyes looked flat, dead, as if her lids didn't remember how to blink. They moved from Larry, to me, and back to Larry. The skin on her face took on a translucent glaze, like the onions she'd sauteed for dinner. Her lips remained closed, betraying nothing.

Larry dipped his head to the side and encouraged her by fanning his fingers near his right ear, in a gesture that said, come-on-just-say-it-and-get-this-over-with.

She bent her head and closed her eyes. I thought she might be saying a silent prayer because half a minute passed before she said, "You'll have to ask your stepfather."

The knot in my stomach jerked apart. How pathetic.

I spiked my fork into the top piece of meat on my plate and sliced off a corner. Meat for men. Men with backbone. Mom's invertebrate lifestyle made me sick—better than what she did when with our old man, but still—

"Have your answer now, Jonathan?" Larry said. "Derek understands these things. It's efficient to ask me first. You could learn a thing or two from your brother, you know, like cutting out the middleman." He hit his knuckles on the table. A judge striking a gavel, announcing his verdict. "If your mom has errands to do, she'll do them after the game."

"Mom's not invisible, you know," Jonathan said.

I sliced off another mouthful. Larry added another scoop of potatoes to his plate. Mom wiped her mouth with her paper napkin, then lowered it to her lap.

Jonathan's statement hung in the air.

Then disappeared.

I finished my first plateful with only the sound of forks and knives clicking against plates, liquid toppling over ice in glasses, mouths sipping, swallowing, and masticating. An almost passable dinnertime.

"Mom?" Jonathan asked. "Can I go visit Dad this weekend?"

Jonathan made his move. I made mine. I stabbed two more slices of beef.

"We'll see." Mom glanced at Larry under hooded eyes. He continued to eat his dinner, seemingly not paying attention to the conversation between Mom and Jonathan. I did the same. "Ah, come on, Mom, don't stall." Jonathan leaned in closer to her, almost touching her shoulders. "Dad has off all day Sunday. He could pick me up and drop me off."

Mom floundered, her voice picking up a quiver, like reverberating strings on a guitar. "We'll think about it."

"We'll think about it?" The intensity in Jonathan's tone made me look up. He glared at Larry, who calmly buttered another roll. Jonathan shook his head, returned his voice to its regular softness, without emphasis, without accusation. "Okay, Mom. Think about it."

He took a breath, picked up his glass and took a sip of milk. His busted lip couldn't make a seal around the glass. Milk dribbled down the side of his mouth.

Larry had eyes on the top of his head. Without looking up he said, "If you need a sippy cup, Jonathan, I'll borrow one from Mrs. Shuster. How old is her son now, Martha? Two, three-years-old? I think he'd be willing to share it with you, Jonathan."

Acid did a body slam against my stomach walls.

Jonathan glanced at Mom for support. Like fat chance that'd happen.

Sure enough, she lowered her head and stirred gravy around in her potatoes. Thick brown liquid muddied the pasty white mound.

His face turned to me. He didn't nod. He didn't speak, but I knew he was sending me a distress signal.

I chose the subtle rescue. "Larry, can I have more potatoes, please?"

"Sure." For the moment, Larry's tension evaporated. His gaze connected with mine and the muscles in his cheeks, the creases in his brow, eased. "Want some beans?"

"No thanks." I paused as Larry lowered the bowl of green beans and stared at Jonathan's meatless plate. I reconsidered. "Sure. Yeah, I'll have more veggies."

Before I took a helping—a helping I didn't really want—I offered the bowl to my brother. "Want some?"

"I'm not hungry, thanks."

I set the bowl of string beans on the table without scooping any out and focused on my meat and potatoes.

Mom, Larry, and I ate in silence. Me, wondering who at the table the veggies reminded me of. Once green and firm and strong, now overcooked until they were pale and limp. Robbed of every shred of health.

Jonathan aimlessly dragged his fork across his plate, around and through his food, as if drawing designs, or tracing roads on a map, or figuring out some hieroglyph.

"I made pudding for dessert," Mom said when Larry finished eating. She stood, collected our plates and stacked them onto hers. "Want some?"

"What flavor?" Larry asked.

"Your favorite. Butterscotch."

"Okay then."

She turned to me. "Derek?"

"Sure."

"Jonathan?"

My brother answered no with a shake of his head. As soon as Mom carried the plates into the kitchen, he pulled his shoulders back, sat straighter, and asked Larry, "May I please visit my father on Sunday?"

Larry's fingertip drew a line along the fold of his napkin, slow, precise, creating a military crease. "He'll pick you up?"

"Yes."

"Yes?"

"Yes, sir. He'll pick me up."

"And he'll bring you home?"

"Yes, sir. You won't have to do a thing, I promise."

Mom entered with a tray of four pudding cups and a container of Cool Whip. "Here we go. I've even got topping." She placed a pudding in front of each of us, exactly where our plates had been, even at the empty space in front of Jonathan. "Who would like some whipped cream?"

"I do," Larry said.

Mom heaped some onto his pudding.

She turned to me. "Just a little, Mom."

Jonathan pushed his pudding toward the center of the table, almost out of his reach, and folded his hands in the vacant space in front of him.

Mom's gaze traveled from son to son and then to Larry, as if knowing something was wrong, but not sure what.

The air in the room turned as thick as the pudding and my mind refused to slog through it. I took a spoonful.

"You can go to Bill's after church on Sunday," Larry said.

I coughed. Almost sprayed the creamy glob from my mouth onto the table. I stared at Larry. Did I hear right?

Jonathan's smile overflowed like the topping Mom was heaping on his pudding.

The color of Mom's cheeks matched the mountain of imitation cream on my brother's unwanted dessert. No words came from her lips, she just pushed the butterscotch in front of Jonathan. Mom plopped into her chair and dipped a spoon into the smooth surface of her tawny-colored custard and stirred until there was no flat surface left. Then, instead of eating, she set the spoon on the table with a sound only slightly less than a bang.

Jonathan's smile sagged, like the topping sliding down the side of his bowl, and he gingerly picked at Mom's offering.

Larry scrapped the final lick of butterscotch from the inside of his pudding cup with a swipe of his index finger, leaned back and said, "Delicious."

* * *

I waited until Mom and Larry turned on the nightly news in the living room before I threw open the door to Jonathan's bedroom, whacking it against the doorstop with a clunk.

A calculator slid off his lap as he looked up. "What?"

I hadn't knocked. I'd been containing my rage since dinnertime, no way could he expect manners. I stood in the door frame, my arms folded tight as a linebacker's, my glare fixed just as hard.

Typical Jonathan. Studying on his bed, leaning against the headboard, notebook and calculator on his lap.

"How could you do that?" I demanded.

He put down his pen. "Do what?"

"Ask Mom if you could see our sperm donor in front of Larry? It's bad enough that you ask her at all."

"Dad's back in town. I want to see him." As if that explained everything, he turned a page in his notebook, picked up his pen and wrote. Totally ignoring me.

A flash fire ignited in my gut. Flames leaped up my core, burned the back of my eyes, my skull. I stomped across the room, swiped the calculator off the bed, flipped the notebook off his legs. "Why? Why would you want to see him?"

"He's our dad, Derek. That's why. Our dad."

His calm eyes met my fevered glare. Cool blue steel against flaming torch. A momentary stand-off.

"Maybe you want to claim him, little brother. Me? I wish he'd stay away for good. You want Mom upset again? You like hearing her cry herself to sleep at night?"

"That was a long time ago. Dad's changed. He doesn't drink. He doesn't fight—"

"Because he doesn't have a wife he can beat up on. Listen . . ." I forced myself to chill, thinking I could make him understand better if I sat on the bed, softened my voice. "I don't believe he's stopped drinking for one minute, and you shouldn't either. Maybe you were too young to remember the stink of his alcohol. The shouting. The fighting. How he abused Mom."

"At least she stood up for herself."

"Stood up for herself?" He had to be kidding. The kid was deluded, drunk on his own childhood fantasy. "She threw dishes. Dishes and pots and—it was pathetic. She only got him angrier."

"And you think she's better off now? She's afraid to even open her mouth."

"Larry provides for us and he doesn't drink. She's got to feel good about that. And he'd never raise a hand against her, it'd be un-Christian.

So, yes, Mom's better off now. Much better off."

Jonathan placed a hand on my shoulder. "Dad deserves a second chance."

I jerked back, my shoulder recoiling from his touch. "That man deserves nothing!" I jumped to my feet and spun to face him, the thin veneer over my ability to hold back, cracking. No, more like a volcano unable to contain the pressure grumbling beneath it. Needing to explode for its own good. "He walked out on us, remember? He left us cold, like we were trash in the street. If he thinks he can stroll back into my life and do the 'father thing' like nothing happened, he's crazy. That'll never happen. Never. No way!"

"You could forgive him." His voice was steady. Firm and serene. And I hated his innocence.

"Some things, even the Bible can't make you forgive."

"Our father's changed," he said as I walked to the door. "He's different now."

I stopped, turned and faced him. "Right. And I'm Tony Romo." I smacked my palm against the door jamb. "Don't say I didn't warn you."

* * *

Jonathan hated to go to church, but he didn't argue with Larry. On Sunday morning, he dutifully obeyed our stepfather and slicked his hair down, wore regular clothes, and went to church. When we got home, he hung around the stoop with me and my buddies, Roger and Floyd.

Roger smacked me on my shoulder and hooted. "You're so hot, man. Did you see Sally McPherson? She sung those hymns," he mimed reading a hymnal, "and pretended not to see you. And the whole time," he lifted the imaginary hymnal in front of his face, thrust the fingers of one hand wide apart, and peeked through spread fingers. "Don't you love it?"

"Oh, he loves it all right. He loves it," Floyd said.

"That the real reason why you go to church?" Jonathan asked. "To flirt with Sally McPherson?"

"No," I said. "There are other reasons."

"Yeah, I'll bet there are." Roger turned his back to Jonathan and mimed taking a hit of reefer.

Floyd chuckled. Not me. One of these days, Roger's careless gestures were going to get us caught.

"So why do you go?" Jonathan asked again.

"Going to church makes Mom happy," I told him. "It keeps Larry off my back. And our team is undefeated this season. Three good reasons to go. Sally McPherson's a bonus."

Roger whistled. "And what a nice bonus she is."

"It wasn't so bad, was it, Jonathan?" I asked. "Making nice with Larry. Not putting up a fuss about going."

"It's my penance for wanting a few hours of freedom."

"Yeah, I didn't think you were too happy." I should've known. Jonathan kept shaking his head while Pastor Carlson preached to the congregation.

"Can you blame me? There's the pastor talking about Christians spreading loving-kindness and goodness and acceptance."

"What's the matter with that?" Floyd asked.

"It's excellent in theory," Jonathan said. "I even agree with that theory. But there are some people who praise the sermon, hallelujah! then go home and use Scripture to keep others under control—their control. Use Scripture to justify hating others, and why?"

He locked his eyes with mine and lowered his voice. "I thought we were supposed to be one big, happy family."

"Hey!" I warned, my tone as menacing as a shaking rattlesnake tail. No dirty laundry in front of my buddies.

Jonathan paced in front of the steps. "Yeah, well, think about it. What kind of acceptance does a religion teach when it professes its way is the only way? Come on. Acceptance? Damning others just because they walk different or talk different or," he swiped a hand over his hair, "God forbid, wear their hair different. Where'd they learn that definition of acceptance? Not from any Daniel Webster I know."

Floyd cocked his head and squinted his eyes. "Hey, man. Daniel Webster's dead."

"Well, I'm not." No defiance. No rebellion. For Jonathan it was a simple statement of fact. "And I refuse to be an unthinking clone—religious or otherwise. If there is a Supreme Being, He, She, or It, created us to be unique, and if a religion says, God can't tolerate an individual's specialness, then I say, to hell with that God. He's not worth following."

Roger's eyebrows shot up, the whites of his eyes doubling in size. His fists clutched his lapels with such fierceness, you'd think the letter jacket was his link to salvation. "You don't believe in God!"

"Are you even listening to me?" Jonathan said. "If it's really like Pastor Carlson says and we're all created in God's image, then we're all godlike. We all deserve acceptance."

Roger puffed up his tackle chest and stepped forward. A Goliath approaching an unarmed David. A giant with spit foaming at the edge of his lips. "Are you a believer or aren't you?"

Jonathan looked at Roger and paused.

Roger stiffened, narrowed his gaze.

Time expanded. Like the moment after the center snaps the football but before it's secure in my hands.

Roger could move fast, sometimes too fast. No telling if a fist would fly or a size twelve shoe would target a gut. I leaned forward ready to separate him from Jonathan.

Slowly my brother shook his head and lowered his gaze to his feet. His voice sounded pained. "A believer? I don't know."

Roger jerked back, crossed index finger over index finger, and held them out in front of him. "Whoa." He stepped backwards, his crossed fingers warding away Jonathan's blasphemy.

"You're going to Hell, man," Floyd said, coming to Roger's side.

"I'm not going to believe something just because it's shoved down my throat," Jonathan said. "You're created with freedom to believe. To believe whatever you want."

Roger swung his head from one side to the other. Again his eyes widened. "Oh, no you're not. Not unless you let the Devil in." He took another step back. The nervous laugh he emitted surprised me. "Bet you did that already, didn't you?—let Satan in. He got you believing that God made queers and lesboes?"

"You don't get it, do you, Roger?" Jonathan said. "Ah, never mind."

I sighed a breath of relief when Jonathan left us to go into the house.

Floyd dropped onto the front steps. "Your brother's weird, man."

"You think I don't know?" I said, and sat next to him.

"They call him 'the atheistic fag' in school. Whoops." He leaned away from me, hands upright, as if needing to shield himself from my blows. "I'm a blabbermouth. Sorry."

"Don't sweat it, Floyd," I said. "I've heard it myself. It's all over school. Dripping off the hallways."

"Got to be pretty embarrassing, huh? A guy like you having a queer for a brother. I mean, you both having the same genes and all—Not that anyone would hold it against you, your brother's . . . perversion."

Roger placed a leg up on Floyd's step. "Hold it against Derek? No one would have the guts."

"They better not or I'll whup their ass," I said.

"That reminds me," Floyd said, "they ever find out who beat him up? First I heard it was a gang from the Heights, then I heard it was a couple of our own linebackers. I even heard he did it to himself to play the sympathy card. Everyone's got a different story."

"The kid refused to rat on the guys—didn't want to get them into trouble."

"That's weird, man," Floyd said. "Somebody knocked my tail around, I'd be singing their names to the police. Singing loud and clear. Spelling their names as I sang."

I lifted my shoulders in a slow shrug. "Jonathan's version of turning the other cheek, I guess."

"Must be disappointing to those guys," Roger said. "Bet they thought their little whuppin' would knock some sense into the kid." He gave me a knowing smirk.

Floyd leaned on his knees. "Doesn't look like it changed him a bit. He's still . . . soft. Listen, before I go . . ." He looked back at the house door, lowered his voice. "You got the stuff, Roger?"

Roger's hand covered the initials on his black letter jacket, smack over his heart. "I told you, you can count on me." He unzipped his jacket, slipped his hand inside, and pulled a baggie of marijuana from his vest pocket.

Floyd lunged for it.

Roger snatched it out of reach. "Later, man."

Floyd turned on his Puss in Boots eyes. "I can't even inspect the goods?"

Roger puckered his lips, nuzzled the bag, and gave it one long, obscene-sounding smooch. "Mexican Gold. Pure delight."

"I thought you were blowing smoke when you said you had contacts." Floyd laughed. Elbowed me on the arm. "Blowing smoke. That's a good one, isn't it?"

"It's lame, that's what it is," Roger said.

"Lame, sch-mame," Floyd said. "See y'all later."

Roger's big hand grabbed Floyd's shoulder, fingers digging into his jacket. "Not so fast. You said you'd get the booze. Where is it?"

"I'll have it by the time we meet up," Floyd said. When Roger lowered his brows and stared, Floyd added. "I'll have it. Don't worry."

Roger turned to me and toasted an imaginary glass. "Okay, then. Jocks' night out!"

"Jocks and friend's night out." Floyd's voice mixed indignation at being slighted with insecure assertion.

Roger rolled his eyes before turning to Floyd. "That's what I said."

"Okay," Floyd said, satisfied. "See you at three. Behind the school, right?"

"Yeah," I said. "Behind the equipment room."

Floyd took off for home and I walked up the steps to the front door. Floyd hadn't gone far when he called back. "You coming, Roger?"

I hadn't noticed Roger was still there. "I'll catch up with you, Floyd," he said.

I turned away from the door and looked down at Roger. "What gives?"

"Got something. Personal."

Roger stayed where he was at the bottom of the stairs, so I had to come to him. I kept my eyes on his as I stepped down. My peripheral vision saw his hand slide into his vest pocket and retrieve the baggie of pot. "This is yours. Just yours."

I held the plastic bag in my palm, staring at the brown leaves inside, the weed that would make my life tolerable. "Thanks." I looked in the direction Floyd had gone and recalled what Roger told him about later. "But . . . ?"

My buddy wrapped a just-one-of-the-guys arm around my shoulder. "We teammates need to take care of each other, know what I mean?"

Yeah, I knew what he meant. Floyd wasn't really one of us. We players had to stick together. I knew I was grinning as I tucked the baggie into my pants pocket. "Thanks, man."

I gave Roger a knock-fist handshake.

"Just remember to bring the car," he said. "Don't want to freeze my ass while I get . . ." He looked around to make sure the coast was clear, then put index finger and thumb to his lips and sucked a toke of imagined joint. ". . . comfortable. See ya." He waved and took off after Floyd.

I gave him a thumbs-up even though he wasn't looking and entered the house, happy enough to hum. It didn't last long.

I hung my jacket on the coat rack by the front door. Larry was sitting in his Lazyboy recliner reading the Sunday paper. Mom was setting placemats on the dining room table for lunch, squaring them up with the table edge, making sure they were exactly two inches from the drop.

Jonathan bounced down the stairs with an open book on Comparative Religions in hand. "Tell me, Mom, does loving thy neighbor as thyself apply to family, too?"

Larry lowered the newspaper to his lap. I could tell he was listening.

"Of course, dear." Mom's mood was as buoyant as mine had been before I entered the house.

Jonathan sat on the bottom step and placed the book beside him. Elbow on knee, he looked like the Thinker.

"I'll give it to your Jesus, Mom. He had some pretty awesome ideas."

Mom paused, a plastic glass held in midair. A rare smile softened the lines on her face. My desire to hum returned. In that instant, my brother had given us a gift, Mom's smile. "Yes, dear. He did have some pretty awesome ideas."

My brother stood and leaned in the archway between the living room and dining room. "No wonder He had a hard time getting people in authority to accept Him."

The muscles in Larry's face tightened. Lips pressed together. Cheeks and ears flared as burned by the sun.

Why couldn't Jonathan just let things be?

I hurried across the room, punched my brother on the arm, sliced my hand across my neck and mouthed 'cut it'. I nodded my head in Larry's direction.

Jonathan returned my punch, only gently. "It's okay, Derek. Let the Pharisee speak." He walked to Larry's recliner and sat lotus style on the floor in front of him.

I wanted to believe Jonathan—the brightest kid in the whole school—was plain old stupid. Or maybe he had some sort of death wish, to sit there, inches from Larry's feet, as if expecting Larry's shoes to remain on the floor. Me? I saw a shoe kick out with an upper cut to a chin. In an instant. An involuntary, accidental reflex to a twitch in a nerve. Larry would never do anything so violent on purpose. But while I imagined the worst, Jonathan spoke with such genuine innocence and reverence I wondered what planet he'd come from.

"Buddhists are kind to all living creatures. Did you know that, Larry? No matter how different, no matter how small. Seems like your Jesus would have gone along with that."

Mom called in from the dining room, "Dear, Jesus was the Son of God. He died for our sins."

A chuckle almost made me choke. Way to go, Mom. Nice non sequitur. I gave Jonathan a shrug, lifted my hands, palms up and mouthed, What is she talking about?

Jonathan didn't respond. Probably a good thing for me, because Larry was sitting on his throne watching Jonathan's every movement.

"Why would a Father allow His Son to die if He was such a loving, compassionate Parent?" Jonathan asked Larry.

Mom entered the living room and addressed my brother. "So the rest of His family could be saved."

"I don't get it," my brother told her. "Jesus was probably just trying to get people to understand the way he thought and felt. Just wanting people to be good to each other. To accept each other."

Larry leaned forward in his recliner. "He was trying to get people to listen to the Word of God, to make the world a better place. To change." He snapped the newspaper noisily, then leaned back. "You'd understand all of this if you read the Bible and paid more attention at church."

I didn't want to listen to any more. The john called. I took the stairs one at a time, leaving the scene as invisibly as I could.

"I wonder what it would be like to have people look at you for who you are." Jonathan's voice drifted upward.

"You mean rather than what you wear?" Larry said.

"I wasn't referring to that, Larry. But yes, who you are underneath the clothes."

"Well, 'clothes make the person,' Jonathan."

"I thought who the person is makes the person. Take milk from a carton, pour it into a glass, and it's still milk."

"It's about respect."

"Exactly. Being respected as an individual. Accepted for who you are."

I watched over the banister. Jonathan was offering the Comparative Religion book to Larry. When Larry disregarded the text, Jonathan slowly pulled the book back.

"The kind of acceptance that Buddhists offer everyone," he continued. "The kind of acceptance Pastor Carlson preached about today." My brother gracefully rose to his feet and stood in front of Larry, defenseless, and non-challenging. "The kind of acceptance good Christians are supposed to give their fellow man." He walked to the steps. He didn't see Larry huff and lunge forward in his chair like a tight end on the move.

Mom sat on the armrest of Larry's chair, detouring his momentum.

"He's only fourteen," she said. "He's got a lot to figure out."

I could still hear Larry through the bathroom door and my piss.

"That's old enough. I had my whole life figured out by the time I was his age."

I turned the faucet on full blast to wash my hands and drown him out. Energy boiled inside me and screamed for release. I swung a few punches and uppercuts into the towels hung on the towel rack. Danced a few Muhammed Ali steps while I jabbed the air. Worked up a slick layer of sweat before I opened the bathroom door.

They were still going at it.

". . . been through a lot in his young life," Mom said.

"Adversity's good for the soul, Martha." Larry stood at the base of the stairs. "He ought to get down on his hands and knees and thank the Good Lord for giving him the blessings he's got. There's a lot more unfortunates out there.

"Now this young man . . . " He put his arm around me as soon as I stepped from the last stair, and marched me over to Mom. "You don't see him biting the hand that feeds him, challenging the authority of the head of the house. 'And a man shall be the king over his dominion.'"

I needed an out. "Say, Dad, what time do the Cowboys play today?"

Worked like a successful Hail Mary. We sat down and watched the pre-game hype and discussed football, moving from one team's tactics to another. Larry even let me argue different coaching strategies.

Jonathan hibernated in his room and Mom busied herself picking up around the house. Before she served lunch she called from her bedroom, "Larry, will you come here for a moment, please? I'd like to speak with you."

"Be right back, Derek," Larry said. "When a lady calls you with that sense of urgency, it's best to go rescue her right away." He winked and offered a broad smile. I used the time to give Sally a call and set up a rendezvous for later in the week.

Mom, Larry and I were eating lunch when Jonathan stepped into the dining room and announced, "I'll be home about eight." His hair was spiked again. He wore his favorite holey jeans and ancient Black Sabbath shirt.

Larry bit off the end of a sweet gherkin. "Save any of that hairspray for your mother, boy?" Jonathan ignored him. It seemed stupid to me that Larry would get so bent out of shape over spiked hair. I mean, it's not like Jonathan is a real punker. One glance in the school cafeteria would confirm the punks didn't accept him. Even they knew that Jonathan was a nerd in disguise. Jonathan started out of the room.

"You got a response to make, boy?"

Jonathan froze.

"I said, you got something to say to me before you leave here to pick up more of your, what do you kids call it, your 'stash'?" Larry pushed his chair back from the table.

"Not now, Larry," Mother said. "It's Sunday."

Jonathan turned around and faced Larry. "What are you talking about?"

"The stuff your mother found in the bathroom, in a little plastic sandwich bag." Larry approached my brother. He is kind of a small man himself but he still had a couple of inches over Jonathan. "You expecting to smoke pot for your lunch, boy? Expect that to make you a man?"

My turkey sandwich flipped in my stomach like a goal-line fumble. I stuffed my hands into my pockets, fingers darting along every seam. Empty. My pockets were empty. The marijuana Roger gave me . . . missing.

"Well?" Larry asked.

"I don't know what you're talking about," Jonathan said quietly.

"You picking up lying from your dad, boy? Just like the pot?"

"Larry, let's sit down and talk about this in the other room," Mom said.

"No, woman. We'll deal with this right here and right now." Larry's eyes never left Jonathan's face. "So, you think drugs can change faggots into men, kid?" He tapped Jonathan on his chest with a pointed index finger.

"Leave your God damn hands off me, man," Jonathan said as he brushed away Larry's hand with his own. Before I knew it Larry's open hand had boomeranged back into Jonathan's face and sent my brother to the floor.

"Don't you ever take the Lord's name in vain!" Larry's ears reddened for the second time that day. Mom and I were both out of our chairs but neither of us moved from the table.

Jonathan stood up slowly. Even from where I stood I could see the hand print on his cheek. My brother lifted his chin and, without touching his face, walked toward the foyer.

"You walk out now, don't you expect to come back," Larry called after him.

I took a step forward. "Dad, listen—"

"Stay out of this, Derek!" he commanded.

I looked to Mom. "Jonathan, let's talk this out calmly," she said.

My brother spun around. "Mom, I gotta get out of here! He doesn't want to talk anything out!" He turned again and grabbed his jacket off the coat rack. Mom turned into a sprinter, ran to the coat rack, and reached for his jacket.

"Don't go, Jonathan. Please, don't go," she pleaded.

Mom latched onto the jacket as if it were a life preserver in a furious sea. Her feet slid across the waxed linoleum foyer as Jonathan pulled the opposite sleeve.

Larry was yelling, "Let that jacket go, Jonathan!"

Mom was crying, "Don't go, Jonathan! Don't go!"

Jonathan was shouting, "Let go, Mom! Just let me go!"

Their raised voices mixed together in a discordant hymn.

Jonathan backed out the front door, yanking Mom through it. She nearly tripped on the front step. Still, she held on, fists dug into the cloth. I was going to laugh, it was almost comical. But then, I heard our old man honk the horn in his rusty pickup truck.

In what seemed to be slow motion, Jonathan let go of the jacket; the sleeve floated through the air like a perfectly tossed football. Mom, who was desperately pulling on the jacket, was thrown off balance and fell backwards onto the grass. Her startled scream bounced across the lawn like a rock skimming the surface of Medina Lake. Jonathan had been halfway down the front walk when he realized what happened and jerked to a halt.

The action flipped into fast forward. Jonathan whirled back to help Mom just as Larry bolted out the door. Larry was so full of rage his nostrils actually flared. He headed down the path toward Jonathan. I darted out of the house right behind him.

Jonathan leaned toward Mom. Shot a glance at the truck. Whipped his gaze to Larry. Back to Mom, not knowing what to do. I got ready to tackle Larry if need be but an amazing thing happened. Mom cried out, "Go, Jonathan! Go!"

The kid did a 180 and within seconds threw himself into the passenger's side of the pickup. The truck squealed down the block.

Larry announced, "This violence is the last straw." He may have been referring to Mother's fall but I kept seeing the red hand-print on my brother's face, the individual fingers, thick, angry, and raw. "We'll have no blaspheming, dishonoring-thy-mother Lucifer in this house," he added as the two of us helped Mom to her feet.

By the end of the week Jonathan had been sent to an out-of-state boarding school. Floyd stopped by the house before church the next Sunday. We sat on the steps in front of the house while he filled me in. "Roger's laying low. He's afraid you'll rat on him. Just a whiff of . . ." he made quotation marks with his fingers, "drug involvement on his record and it's bye-bye scholarships."

I fingered Jonathan's dream-catcher necklace. I've been wearing it around my neck since he was sent away. "That's trust for you. I'd never turn him in. Roger should know that."

"So what exactly did you tell your dad?" he asked.

"I told my step-father that the marijuana was mine. That was all. I never said where I got it. I'd never rat on Roger. Like you said, our scholarships are too precious to ruin with a little 'misunderstanding'."

"That was risky. I mean, admitting the pot was yours—"

"Well, it was."

"Yeah, but blowing your scholarship is like blowing free money. Why chance it? I mean, I heard that big, bad University of Texas offered you a free ride. A four years free ride."

"UT and Ohio State both."

"Holey moley. Two freebies?"

"Three." My neck itched like the inside of my collar had turned to sandpaper. "I heard from LSU last month. I just wasn't telling anybody till I decided."

"You've got all the luck. Not that you don't deserve it, Derek, you do. 'Specially after winning us the playoffs. But it must be nice, all those schools trying to butter you up. Offering nice packages to play with them. Yeah, you're one lucky dude. Got it made. So, which school are you leaning toward?"

"The one that's farthest away."

Maple trees lined the street in front of our house. Their jagged leaves had changed to yellow. Dripped orange. Bled red. Prepared for the winter frost.

"So, what's Larry going to do to you," Floyd asked, "for having the pot?"

How'd I play the whole season without seeing the leaves change color? "Nothing."

"Nothing? Nothing!" Floyd laughed like he'd been granted a reprieve from the gallows. "Whoa, you are one lucky dude."

"Larry didn't believe me for a minute. He's convinced I only said the stuff was mine to protect Jonathan."

"Yeah, but when Jonathan said you were telling the truth . . . ?"

The top of the trees swayed to some music I couldn't hear. A crimson leaf heard it and let go of its branch, twirled in a corkscrew, and floated to the ground.

"He never did," I said.

"Well, I'll be . . . a fag with cajones."

I leapt from the steps and grabbed Floyd's shirt. "Shut your face. He's no such thing."

"I didn't mean anything, Derek, cut it out." He stepped back, threw his arms up in surrender.

I released my grip.

Floyd brushed off the front of his shirt. Straightened his tie. "What's gotten into you, man?"

I couldn't answer. I didn't know. My gut churned, agitating feelings for family. For Mom. For Jonathan. I took a deep breath and sat on the step.

"Where is he anyway? I haven't seen your brother in school all week."

"I'm supposed to say he took off with our old man."

"No fooling."

"Yeah, the old sperm donor left to chase more jobs. Leastways, that part of the story's true."

Floyd dropped down next to me and spoke in a whisper. "Where's he really?"

"Some religious rehab place."

"You mean like a reform school? Holey moley. Ya think he'll survive?"

I glanced again at the trees lining the street. Does anything survive?

"Well, if we're walking," Floyd said, breaking our silence, "I guess we'd better get going."

We pushed ourselves to our feet.

"Listen," I said, "if you see Sally McPherson in church, tell her I'm sorry I haven't called—I've been busy."

"You aren't going today?"

"Nah."

"What's more important than seeing the lovely Sally?"

"Things. I got things to do."

"Okay." Disappointment, perhaps sadness, clouded Floyd's eyes and narrowed his lips. "I'll see what I can do about turning Roger around, bring him back in the fold so to speak. Let him know his buddy's still his buddy."

"Whatever. He's gotta do what he's gotta do."

Inside the family room, I plopped on the couch and turned the TV on mute. Stared at the screen without being conscious of the game I was watching. Not caring about the numbers that flashed to update the score box.

Larry came in from the kitchen dressed in his navy blue suit. He carried a tray, the same tray Mom used to bring in the butterscotch pudding, up the stairs. I could see his reflection on the screen. He stopped outside of Jonathan's room and knocked. "Come on, Martha. We've got to leave soon. You have to eat a little something before we go to church."

I didn't hear Mom's response—if she gave one.

"I've brought you tea and an English muffin, Martha. I even went across town to that fancy grocery you like and bought your favorite marmalade."

I could imagine Mom wearing a black mourning dress, no shoes, her toes curled up inside black, nylon stockings, lying on Jonathan's bed, arms around his pillow. Lifting eyes bloated from tears. "You think that makes up for sacrificing a son? Sacrificing a son!"

"That school's the best thing for Jonathan, sweetie. It's a blessing we could arrange for him to get in so quickly."

He paused and listened for a reply. None came.

"Getting him in was a sign, Martha. A sign that The Good Lord agrees with us—"

"With 'us' Larry?"

"We both signed the papers, Martha."

Mom's scream jolted the walls. Like every outlet surged with an electric shock. Another scream, long and shrill, followed. And another, only she must have buried her head in a pillow because that scream sounded muffled.

I went into the kitchen for a bowl of cold cereal, my meal of choice this last week while Mom did nothing in the house. As I walked back to the couch, Larry came down the stairs. He must have left the tray on the floor outside Jonathan's door.

I dropped onto the couch, shoveled in a spoonful, and tried to make sense of the game. "She's not going, either?"

Larry approached the couch, looking unsure of his next actions. "She's locked herself in his room again. Did she let you in?"

I didn't take my eyes from the TV. Couldn't bring myself to look at him. "Nope. Even I'm not allowed in there. She's got it closed off . . . like a shrine. Jonathan may not be here in body, but he's sure here in spirit. Isn't he . . ." Now I did look—no, I glared—at him. ". . . sir?"

Larry glanced away, raised his left arm and pulled back the cuff of his suit jacket. Bet he wished the watch on his wrist could move back time. But prayers like that don't happen. He marched to the stairs and called up a flight, "Martha, time for church."

I could have told him she wouldn't come. Oh, she might get up from Jonathan's bed, look around his room, stroke his desk, his books, clutch his clothes to her chest. Then she'd slide to her knees, rock back and forth, lower her face against palms pressed together in prayer, and tears, big as the buttons on her black dress, would trickle down her cheeks.

Larry looked at his watch again, ascended a few steps. "Martha! Come on. We don't want to be late." His eyes didn't blink as he waited, silent and still.

I'd eaten another spoonful of cereal before he looked at his watch for a third time. "Martha? You coming?"

It didn't take long before his steps thudded down the stairs.

Larry went to the coat tree and removed his overcoat, leaving Mom's coat the only one on the wooden stand. His eyes sent a plea to mine, hoping I would jump up and say, I want to go with you, Dad. Maybe for him our alliance could turn back the clock. Make him pretend we were still a normal family.

I turned to the TV and pressed the remote. I pounded my thumb against the plastic rectangle until the volume couldn't increase any higher, and let the cheering and roaring chaos of the game fill the empty places in our home.

JESUS DOESN'T LOVE YOU AND NEITHER DO I

Heather Fowler

Henrietta McCallahan didn't look forward to encountering Terry Jones, instead hated him, with an abundant fervor. Even now, her accident was something the townspeople whispered of each November, like a cautionary tale recited to children, and despite ten years since his betrayal, she walked, still, like a maimed creature, her yellow galoshes dragging sludge across the snow, pale pink glasses sliding down her narrow bridge, and her dark, close-set eyes fixed upon the ground. "It had been," many often had uttered, quite rudely within her hearing, "a cruel thing to do to a girl with narcolepsy."

In Great Oaks, her story and illness gave them something to be thankful for each Thanksgiving, like, "Thank god I don't have Cholera, or Ebola, or that weird sleeping thing the McCallahan girl has"—so, aware of the speculation others fixed on her small, round body, she forbade herself to return their stares.

Even in November, a month before the annual anniversary of her fall, wintry winds gave her fits of anxiety, inducing more and more narcoleptic episodes where she might be found slumbering on curbsides, sidewalks, even in the middle of the road.

If only he had not sent her down that sled on that steep hill, fully asleep. Later, a thin scar the size of a silver dollar on her ankle would be a memorable memento of the crash, visible each time she pulled on one of her shoes, but because any memory of traumatic incidents or heightened emotionality caused complications with her sleeping disorder, the event would exact a more continuous toll. Her doctor had done what he could, even prescribing Modafinal and two naps a day four years back. Still, "Narcolepsy, catalepsy, apnea, none of it goes away," he was fond of repeating, the rust on his never-replaced metal glasses distracting her every time. He said, too, "Just do the best you can, Henny. People will understand."

But they had never. If they hadn't met her, they wondered if her insta-sleep was a joke--wide awake one second, nodding off the next--and if they had, men, in their private hearts, speculated on whether her sleep might seem like an artificial use of a date rape drug, and how it'd feel to penetrate her prostrate body—whereas women gave only their terrible, pitying glances. At least her co-workers knew well enough to grab what she held if they saw her fingers start to shake, the first sign she'd lose consciousness, but working reception at twenty-four was not all she'd hoped. Worse, she could not always tell her dreams from reality, nor drive, nor work an important job.

It was all Terry's fault, she thought on particularly the worst of days: That early trauma had stunned her from her true path of motion, of greatness, like a spring bird's unfortunate smash into closed plate-glass doors. Terrible, too, was the sight of her broken gait reflected back at her in the Bank Tower windows each morning as she strolled to work. Nonetheless, she crouched safely at her desk when she heard of Terry's return, though a tremor of rage shot through her before yet another narcoleptic episode when she flopped onto her station, dropping the phone, oblivious to the customer still chattering on the other end.

Submerged in immediate REM, thinking of his face, she then beheld the nightmare vision of her accident again, remembering how they must have settled her, limp pigeon, on that red, rickety sled with its dull, silver blades then gauged the hill to determine the sled's best descent. Some time earlier, probably that morning, they'd affixed a small, square mirror to the sled front, so she could view her own horror should she wake, but as they prepared to launch the debacle, they'd also wrenched an orange monster mask over her head before giving the whole thing a shove. Then they'd howled with laughter as she went down, down, down the dangerous hill. She did not wake up until it was far too late to stop.

Chris Steams, Bill Thurman, George Mandrake, Terry Jones—they thought it would be funny, she supposed, to torment the sullen girl who couldn't hold her eyes open in class, but later, when she thought of the mask they pulled over her head, all she remembered were the green, hairy warts like blood clots she'd seen in her reflection as she woke in the hurtling sled, the stench of the stinking rubber, and the feel of the artificial gray hair plastered nastily behind her ears as her hands flung up pointlessly, protectively, to guard her head. All she recalled was the terror, the fear, jostling over that narrow, rocky path on that partially frozen day, and then she was out again.

It was the sound of their laughter she awoke to as the St. Helen's library wall loomed nearer. Then she heard a chilling shout in her periphery like "No! Stop her!" or "Please, stop," and it was then that she knew the ride could mean death. Reeling behind the mask, she blinked, regarded her frightening visage once more, and hurled herself off the sled, but it was pure coincidence she'd woken up at all, being that she'd slept through louder noise, and yet more blind luck that she'd managed to propel her small body from the sled with the help of her still half-asleep, spindly legs, which had only given one strong push before expelling her like a rag doll, from the side.

Had she hit the wall directly, people said, she could have cracked her skull. As it was, her right leg broke in three fractures, the skin on her ankle was ground to the bone, and she'd sustained substantial blood loss.

The hip-to-toe cast she'd worn had been uncomfortable, too, so the subsequent home days of lugging that plaster down her halls passed like infinity years, and when her bladder function went spotty, which it often did when she was tired, she awoke in a puddle of piss, dreaming of a warm, blue sea until a chill breeze blew over. This was when the sensation of pins and needles ravaged her legs. "Starfishing" her mother called it.

After the cast was removed, she convinced her parents she wanted to go back to school--but the boys never apologized. Cautioned by wealthy fathers, each, in his own way, glossed it over. And she let them.

What else could she do? She could not beat them up. She didn't want to file charges. At five foot three and a hundred and two pounds, a scrim of dull blond draped constantly over her eyes, it was impossible to avenge herself on the gilded squad of football jocks. She simply continued on at Derby High. Come August, Chris went to Harvard, Bill to Yale, and George to Columbia, but no one knew where Terry went. Despite his absence, his memory continued to plague her. He was the one she obsessed about, cared about, so much so, that a year later, she began to dread waking in class or in the lunch room, unsure of whether she'd spoken his name or begged for just one expression of his imagined and contrite remorse; he had been the only one who mattered, the one whose betrayal was worst—and he was back now, she thought dully, waking to a jabbing head pain. But, so what? He had been her first love, she recalled as she spent the rest of her hours at work trying not to think of him—but that was yet another monumental error in judgment.

Now that he was back, since the town was small, in another moment of pure and irritating coincidence and as if only because she didn't want to see him, she ran into him on the road on her way home, recognizing him immediately. He stood ten yards before her, wearing a priest's garb. Ambling along, he spoke fervently to himself, a light blue rosary swinging from his belt. A priest, she thought. Terry's a priest! She wanted to vomit, or shout "Evil doer!" at the top of her lungs.

Dimple still visible, he looked handsome but older, his blue-black hair curling tightly around his head. He must be twenty-nine now, she thought, presumably redeemed. "I don't believe it," she said aloud as she watched him approach, and his hoity posture irritated her so she scowled at him, deciding that if he were anyone else, she'd have shrugged and walked on, but she could not. She should say something cruel and horrid, she decided. A priest should be a role model, the kind of boy thought saintly as he grew, and Terry was not—so it was no positive interaction she wanted then, but an exchange of vitriol so harsh it would turn his religion-bleached bones to dust. Unfortunately, these very thoughts made her excitable, which caused confusion and nerves.

Glaring, she tossed her middle finger up like a flag between the dry stumps of her other knuckles, but the emotion was too strong and sent her to sleep. She collapsed, middle finger up, staring at the flare of an orange traffic cone on the road just seconds before passing out. Whether his own awareness of her fall was caused by the reflection of her red dress crumpling in the window beside him or some noise as she fell, she did not know. Nonetheless, she awoke in his arms, trapped by paralysis, by his warmth, as he took her pulse.

"Are you breathing?" he asked. "Are you okay? Can you breathe?"

She heard him just fine, but could not yet move. This was common. Setting her down, he pumped her chest in CPR, then put his lips to hers. Since she was hardly awake, when she first regained consciousness, she thought his overture a kiss, so her tongue traced his teeth dreamily. Terry Jones is kissing me, she thought mildly, disconnected, how nice. And then she recognized him and remembered, feeling the anger, the violation, surge in her throat. She did not hesitate to shout, when her mouth worked correctly, "Get your hands off me, Terry Jones! Some priest you are. Kissing me! Pervert!"

He jerked back. "I'm sorry," he said. "It was—CPR. I was—"

She rolled her eyes, pushing him away. "In CPR," she said, her tongue still awkward in her mouth, "you should check if your victim is breathing. I was breathing! Are you certified? How do you explain this to your congregation?" The taste of his mouth lingered on her tongue: Blackberries, cream cheese, coffee.

"Sorry," he said. "I'm taking the class again next month. I was nervous. I—"

"Yeah, well," she said. "I wasn't dying, Terry Jones. But thanks. Now, just leave me alone."

He waved his hands in the air as if to minimize his mistake, then scrutinized her. As his eyes narrowed, she nearly heard the wheels clicking. "Henny?" he asked, with what she might have thought resembled tenderness. "Say, Henrietta McCallahan! It's you."

"It's not me," she said, brushing leaves from her skirt as she stood. "Maybe somebody else."

"Henny, I know it's you," he argued.

She shrugged. "Maybe it is me. How are you, Terry Jones? Seen George lately?" Privately, she hoped he hadn't seen her panties or anything like them when she fell.

"No," he said. "We don't talk much. But how've you been?"

"Fine," she said. "Though it's not like you and I have anything left to talk about.... I have to go." She wanted to duck away and glanced at the mirrored office windows above where her office staff probably already watched with curiosity. He said nothing, staring at her like she was some cute Easter Bunny, some happy memory, smiling wistfully. "Will you get out of my way?"

He did not get out of her way.

"I've been fine enough," she said. "And you?"

"Great. Ordained."

"Uh huh," she said. "Obviously."

"Oh," he said, "suppose so."

"Listen, I've gotta go, Terry," she said and smiled as if to say something nice in parting, even considered voicing a pleasantry, but voiced instead, "I hate you, Terry Jones. So why don't you buzz off, not mildly, and never speak to me again?"

He took a step back, staring quietly at her as she walked away. "Henny," he shouted, "can you come by my parents' old house this Wednesday? I need to talk to you."

"Your parents are dead, Terry," she called back, without turning. "So there's nothing worth doing there. And, no thanks, anyway." Oh, how I hate him, she thought as she kept walking, dragging her scarred leg for effect.

"Henny, please," he insisted. "I know you must wonder what happened between us. I'd like to resolve things."

"How nice," she replied, turning toward him briefly. "But I don't." He murmured something more, but she strode on, buttoning her coat, muttering, "Good riddance," to the air in front of her, and, "May you never darken my doorstep again, Terry Jones! May your hands rot and fall off. May you lose your sight and fall in piss where no one will redeem you. May the sun be at your back and the wind in your face!"

When her mother said that he'd spoken of her in his Sunday sermon the next week, she cursed him again, replied, with vigor, "How nice he can capitalize, even now, on his shitty past. But I don't care."

"He said he wanted your forgiveness."

Henny snorted. She wished he would let well enough alone, but in coming weeks, he plagued her from several angles, determined to make her forgive. He called her at work and asked her to lunch; he visited the daycare where she volunteered, forcing her to make Popsicle-stick puppets with him and the priest-struck kids. He even sat for several evenings sprawled on her red brick steps, calling to her through the mail-slot.

These steps, once she noticed this tendency, she doused with insect repellant each night as if to clarify her views, but he refused to stop until finally, clearly she said, "I won't forgive you so just leave me alone, Terry Jones," shouting through her closed door. She lapsed to sleep and when she woke shouted, as if no lull had occurred, "And just stop calling. Stop coming! I don't want to talk to you."

"Please, Henny. Don't be that way," he replied, still there, stooping and looking up at her through the mail-slot until both crouched and stared like children through the open slant. "I dreamt you forgave me last night, and it made me so happy. Can't you forgive me? Is your heart so small?"

"I don't have to forgive you," she retorted. "It's hard enough just trying to be nice. So please just go away. And don't come back."

He did not return, but as the weeks passed, he kept talking about her at church, each week changing his sermon to include new mentions of his desire for her forgiveness. Her mother, the congregation, her friends, everyone around, was then looped irrevocably into this campaign. Forgive and forget, people kept saying at the Food Lion, at the drugstore, at the mall: Be a good Catholic. Find your spiritual window and accept. "I don't have to," she told them all. "I'm not Catholic anymore, and he doesn't deserve my acceptance."

She kept working. He kept preaching. All continued as expected until her mother called her the day before Lent to announce, "Terry Jones came by yesterday to speak with me and your father."

"You let him in?"

"Of course, Henny. The congregation is quite tired of hearing about this issue. And we had a good chat."

"And?"

"I want you to come for dinner tonight so we can all talk. He'll meet you here."

"No."

"Henny, don't argue. Say, 'Yes, Mother.' Five fish fillets on the counter, already thawed. So, good. You'll be here at six, right?"

"I will not."

"Okay, six fifteen?"

"I will not."

"Perfect, see you then," her mother said.

"Fine," Henny replied, stringing the phone cord on her finger and stretching it out like a neck, "but only because I don't mind telling him where to stick it in person."

"You come for whatever reason you want," her mother replied, "but come."

And Henny would come, she decided, because she felt safe at her mother's house and her father would shoot Terry Jones before letting him hurt her again. She donned a tiny black dress and high strappy sandals before applying make-up and perfume. "It'll be okay," she told herself. She threw back her hair, longer now, thicker now, saying, "How do you like me now, Terry Jones?" applying a heavy frost of hairspray before inserting contact lenses.

She took the bus, and when she got to her parents', the room smelled of cinnamon apples. Terry sat straight beside her father like a pulpit had been jammed through his back. As they ate, her mother and father politely asked about his diocese, but Henny just stared at her cutlery, the gaps in conversations filled only by silverware applying cream sauce over tender chunks of cod.

Mentally, she pretended to be anywhere but beside Terry. In the Alps, she decided, I am skiing in a hot pink snowsuit. I am graceful. I am some kind of movie star. In Paris, I sip coffee from a small white cup. She pictured the steam rising from a strong brew—except it was February, she thought, abruptly unable to maintain the fantasy—February: Warm days, chilled nights, the month of Valentine's day. Her face cracked. I hate that he's here in my parents' house, she thought, but moments later, even their banter with Terry had stalled. "Excuse me," she said, standing up.

When she went to use the restroom, her mother followed, tsk-tsking behind her, whispering, "What's gotten into you, Henny? You're being so rude! Just let him talk to you."

"Forget it," Henny said. "He wants forgiveness. I get it. But how convenient that everyone's self-reparation should be forced on their victims just because they get new religion! I hate him, and I don't owe him anything."

"He's a priest, now, Henny!" her mother replied. "What's done is done. Let it go."

"I hate him, mother, and I hate you, and I wish I was never born," Henny replied, kicking the pink-scalloped hamper. "So he's a priest? What do I care? God is nothing to me now!"

"Not anymore," her mother said. "But I remember a girl who lived here long ago, a happy religious girl who collected rosaries in all different colors..."

"That's the past!"

"Henny, open up. Realize that the accident was years ago. People change," her mother said.

"No," Henny said, breathing deeply, trying to calm herself. "People don't change. Tell me, mother. Do you fall asleep in the middle of the day and wake up with nightmares? Do you fear vacations and relationships because there's no guarantee someone won't hurt you? It's easy for people to accept Terry's new outlook with grace, but he ruined my life, so I'd rather sleep like Rip Van Winkle till he goes away, just stay unconscious through the whole damn thing." But the conversation was too much. As if to emphasize her point, Henny flopped to the floor, immediately asleep, only to awaken moments later, feeling her mother's hand caressing her scalp while her limbs tingled and burned.

"Easy, Starfish," her mother said in that soft voice Henny remembered from her childhood scrapes, the one that made you guilty and small and grateful all at once. "You don't have to forgive, but don't carry your anger around, especially when you're the one it's hurting. Besides," her mother said. "Terry agreed to walk you home. And we're going to bed now, so your father and I were grateful."

"Oh, yeah, sure, and I'm super grateful, Mother," Henny said. "I forbid it."

Her mother shook her head. "Remember when you both were ten and he took you trick or treating? You were a gypsy and he was a ghost. You were so sweet with each other. I remember he sat with you on the curb of Eberly when you fell asleep, sat for half an hour, when he could have been out getting candy. This is what I think of when I think of Terry. So goodnight, honey. I don't worry about this at all. You two will make things right."

Henny did not reply and her mother walked to her bedroom and shut the door. Henny's father said, "It's time for me to go to bed."

Within moments the house was dark, and she was locked outside, standing on the steps beside Terry. "I'm supposed to walk you home," he said.

"Fine," she replied.

They strode the cold street, paces apart. For the first four blocks, his eyes never left her face. "You've grown so beautiful," he told her as they turned a corner. "I never would have thought…"

"Is that like God's aesthetic beautiful?" she asked sarcastically. "Because, if so, I don't care."

He grabbed her arm. "Stop, Henny. Stop being mean," he said. "Please look at me."

"Terry, I'm only going to tell you this once more," she said, staring up at the sky. "I hate you. I wish you would leave, this town, my sight, whatever. If there's one thing you could do to earn my forgiveness, it's to drop your priesty fakeness and forget me. You're no saint. You're just a lousy man, just like the others, and you know what? God doesn't love you, Jesus doesn't love you, and neither do I."

"I've always cared, Henny," he said. "And I'm not a fake priest."

She smoothed her skirt over her thighs, muttered,"Sure. But you cared more about those boys, about what those boys thought."

"You don't know me, Henny. I changed when I left, but I was never that bad. I'm sorry about the accident. I never wanted to hurt you, but that day—"

"Shut up!" she shouted. "Don't you dare speak about that day! You don't know anything about that day!" As she limped awkwardly toward her house, she murmured again, "Just go away."

"I have to give you something first," he said in a hushed voice. "I wrote it in school before seminary.

"Keep it. I don't care," she said.

"You should care," he replied.

"Well, I don't," she argued, fumbling with her keys, "I didn't live your life, epiphanies and all, so I just don't care." It took a long time to get her door to open, but when she succeeded, she rushed into her house like someone escaping a fire, clearly enunciating one last thing before slamming the door behind her. "Terry Jones, to me you're just the boy who caused an embarrassment that almost killed me. You never even said you were sorry. And I loved you so much, so very much." And she locked the deadbolt.

Though he was silent, she knew he lingered behind her door, heard his feet scuffle on the mat and his hand land with a thud on the wood near the mail slot. "I always meant to apologize," he said, speaking through the opening. "Maybe I should do it now."

"Go away," she said.

"I'm sorry," he said as if he didn't hear her. Then he backed up, dug through his knapsack, and slid a tiny, pink-enveloped card through the slot, saying, "Just read this, okay?"

She ripped open the envelope while walking to her living room. Dated two days before her accident, it was heart-shaped stationary, asking if she'd like to go to the Derby Winter Dance. "I meant it," he called from outside her house, "I was going to ask you." He had roamed into her bushes around the side-yard, so he shouted just loud enough to be heard from her living room window. "What happened," he said, "was when I told my friends I was going to ask you, they told me to do it behind the library. They tricked me, Henny, tricked both of us. And right when I asked you to the dance, you fell asleep, and they grabbed you. I tried to stop them, but George held me down. We fought. Then you were sleeping in that sled, flying down the hill, and I was calling to you, scrambling up from the ground then running down the hill behind you, but I couldn't stop the accident. I never knew it would happen, Henny—I swear. I didn't know what to do. I couldn't even look at you. I couldn't talk to you because it was my fault you got hurt. I had hurt you. So I ran away. I was scared, and I was stupid." A small yellow moth circled his head.

Hot tears slid down his cheeks, spurring her own. Fury, pain, love, resistance to hope--all these blinded her. "And you became a priest," she said acidly, "so you could make this speech to me later?"

"I had a calling," he said. "Why else would anyone become a priest?" He pressed his fingers on her window-pane, his breath frosting a large, growing circle on the glass. Shivering, he waited. "But I wanted you to know that I did love you," he said. "That was real."

After staring a long while, she pointed to the front door, said, "Come in," in a small, thin voice, but as he stepped over her threshold, she lapsed again into a dream-like state where the conversation continued, where she was younger, and where, hand in hand, they went to confession together. In this dream, he had not entered the priesthood but became a carpenter instead. They had married and, in her house, he caressed her like a lover, peeling away her black silk dress to touch the skin above her heart. She was pretty and walked straight in this dream. Her hair had been curled. The accident had never happened. But her eyes opened a moment later to view the cincture at his waist as he leaned over her prone body, touching her forehead with his white kerchief, trying to wake her. His hands were gentle, like they touched a parishioner.

Lent is tomorrow, she recalled, startled, finding his touch reflective of what he'd do the next day, except with ashes, placing them on the foreheads of officiating priests, clergy, and congregation, and reciting the incantation: "Remember you are dust, and unto dust you shall return." As she stared into his blue eyes, she half expected him to recite this sermon, but he said instead, "Are you all right?"

"I'm fine, Terry," she replied. "I fell asleep. But you should go." She felt physically smaller as she looked at him, a pricked balloon, like she was vanishing somehow.

"You're right," he said, brushing a strand of hair from her cheek. "I should."

Before he drew away, she clutched his shoulders tightly for one brief embrace. She did not say she forgave him, but he must have known because he returned her clutch and smiled, kissing her forehead lightly. As she watched him, through the window, he wove down the dark February road with a joyful step. The warm taint of an old lust suffused her.

She said, "Yes, I do know you, Terry Jones," to his retreating back, "and I always have." The scent of his fading cologne lingered; she was shocked to note that her hands still stretched out in front of her, toward him, gesturing, almost plaintively, as if to call him back.

"You're a fool twice over, McCallahan," she said as she settled on her couch and kicked off her sandals. She stared at the scar on her ankle, the shadows of her empty hallway, observing her guilty arms, risen anew, hovering aloft before her as if in readiness for an impossible carnal embrace, pale and disembodied like the ghosts of her desire that he should love her, that he would love her, though he could not, earlier or later. And then they fell gently to her waiting sides.

ONE MORE THING

Gary Percesepe

The second thing Annie Riser did after receiving her diagnosis was to find a realtor in the Yellow Pages and put her house up for sale. It was a big house in the Connecticut suburbs with ugly casement windows that were difficult to clean, and Annie knew she wouldn't miss it. She understood that Ronald would disapprove but was ready to fight that battle too.

The first thing she did was book a flight to Colorado. It was mid-winter, and the western sunshine surprised her. In Denver she rented an all wheel drive vehicle and drove to Ouray. Her husband had died twenty years before when he got caught in a spectacular avalanche while skiing in the back country near Telluride and Annie had never been to Telluride or to Colorado. Annie chose Ouray for the big mineral springs pool, and for its proximity to the backcountry where Ronald, Sr. had met his death.

Now Annie stretches her body in the hottest section of the pool and watches the passing traffic, people who seem comically white. Steam rises from the hot water and hovers over the pool as over a tea cup, and to Annie, staring at her scissoring legs, it feels as if she is living in a cloud. But when she raises her head to see the spectacular red cliffs, and the mountains that ring the pool, bathed in late afternoon light, she sees a family of deer picking their way through the foot-high snow just beyond the protective railing of the pool. The deer come at the same time each afternoon. Annie wonders where they go each night.

Her cell phone rings. Annie picks up the phone, to see who is calling, then lets it go to voicemail. Scrolling through the menu, she selects silent.

Annie lies in the water with her feet braced at the bottom of the pool and her arms behind her head. She pulls her upper body into a series of crunches. She doesn't feel sick. Neither had Rose at Stage 3, when both women had felt free to speak of hope. But Annie understands what is coming, what cannot be stopped. She understands also that it is the third thing she did after receiving her diagnosis that will set things in motion.

* * *

Annie is seventy-two. She lost her youngest child three years ago to the same ravenous form of ovarian cancer. Rose struggled but succumbed at last upstairs in the rambling Connecticut house, in her girlhood bedroom. Divorced and childless, Rose had wanted to go home to her mother's house to die. Together they had made the hospice arrangements.

An enormous man enters the hot water section. His big belly overhangs his fashionable trunks. He wears a beige hat with ear flaps that reminds Annie of Lawrence of Arabia. The fat man nods at Annie and collapses into the hot water like a descending hippo, one leg at a time, his enormous head and pink nostrils disappearing into the mist.

Annie glances at her phone. It lights with a silent call. She sighs and places the cold screen to her wet ear.

"Mom, what the fuck! You put the house up for sale? Why didn't you talk to me? Where the hell are you, anyway?"

"Are you at the house now, Ronald?"

"Mom, you understand that I am a realtor, right? You do understand that, correct? What'd you do, pick this idiot out of the phone book? What were you thinking? He couldn't even get his sign into the ground straight. Where the hell are you, mother?"

Annie snaps the phone off. The third thing she had done after getting her diagnosis was to call an auction service. She gave orders to set all her belongings on the snowy lawn of her house and to accept the highest bid. Proceeds will go to the Greenwich Ovarian Cancer Fund in Rose's name.

Annie looks at the dying light of Ouray, the last bit of sunshine on the highest peak, how many miles away? How cold would it get on that peak tonight, Annie wonders, in the harsh Colorado winter. How odd it was, to be warm in the cold, lying in the mineral springs pool. Contradictions. Like Rose, healthy and strong and dying, painlessly. Bit by bit our life slips away, Annie thinks. Better to go out strong than to fade molecule by poisoned molecule, to endure the body's cruel betrayal, or a son's callous disregard for his mother's wishes, his taunting of her politics, his criticism of hospice care, his mirthless rich life in a diseased community of the living.

The phone rings again. As compassionately as she can manage, she explains things to her remaining child. Ronnie, she says, about tomorrow. One more thing, she says, and pauses. She lays it out, what is coming, what cannot be stopped.

Annie places the phone in her bag. Pulling herself up by the rails she steps out of the pool, her swim suit dripping water. Looking at the darkening mountains, she climbs over the protective railing. She places her bare feet carefully in the deer tracks. She walks out into the Colorado night.

NORMAL

Seth Marlin

The evening of Saul's Cub Scout thing, Erin pulls on her hoodie and grabs her keys off the table. She slips Saul's wooden car into her purse, then looks up at the clock. Faux-antique copper hands tell her 5:15, less than half an hour before they have to be at the school. *We're never gonna make it.* "Saul?" She cocks her head and listens – again with the goddamned music. She stomps up the stairs, calling: "Saul? Saul, come on! SAUL!"

The music grows to a rolling tide as she opens the bedroom door. In her own youth, it would have been Deftones or Kittie she'd used to isolate herself, but with Saul it's always something dour and classical, some crashing *Sturm-und-Drang* piano piece. He's sitting in the middle of his bed, and doesn't notice when she enters. His face is focused in a way Erin has only ever seen during late-night experiments with mushrooms, but this isn't the dorms during freshman year, and Saul is only 10. He's wearing his shoes, and he nods his head in time to the music, rubbing his palms back and forth over his pantlegs.

"What are you doing?" She waits. No response. She walks over and turns down the player, placing herself between him and the computer screen. "Saul, I sent you up to find your bandana, not get lost in your goddamn music."

Saul stares at the backs of his hands. "'Goddamn.'" He seems to mull this over, before shaking his head. "No. No. Erin, Rachmaninoff was Romantic."

"Whatever." Three months like this now, and she doesn't even bother correcting him. This is what a nephew with autism gets you. She scans the room for his plaid neckerchief, finds it on his dresser beneath a mound of schoolbooks. She pulls it out and drapes it around his neck, securing it with the brass fastener she pries from his fist. With the blue shirt and rows of colored beads, he looks like a soldier in the world's shortest military. She hoists him off the bed, leading him out the door. "Come on," she says. "We gotta get your shoes and go."

* * *

He reaches for the dial just as soon as they're in the car. She left the volume up last time, so now she gets treated to a thundering orchestral blast as she turns the key. She spasms and reaches for the knob, heart slamming trash-cans in her chest. Saul immediately tries to turn the dial back. They go like this, back and forth, until she finally takes his hands and plants them on his lap. "Saul," she says. "Saul. Look at me. Baby, can we please just listen to something else for a little bit? Please? Your Auntie Erin has a headache."

"Nora lets me pick." He stares at her hands.

"Nora's not here, sweetie." Nora's his caretaker, the one Erin spends a third of her paycheck on to watch him weekdays. "She'll be back on Monday. Let's put it to something different for a while, okay? Just for the ride there."

"I don't want something different."

"What about your iPod? Then you can listen to whatever you want."

"I don't *want* my iPod."

She sighs through her nose. "How about this," she says. "We listen to something else, and on the way back I'll get you some ice cream. That sound like a deal?"

"I like ice cream."

"I know, honey. We'll stop at Baskin Robbins, okay?" He says nothing more, and taking his silence as assent she moves the dial to a station playing mostly 90's alt-rock. "Thank you, sweetie. Auntie Erin really appreciates it."

"I want Chopin," Saul says. "Chopin goes good with ice cream."

* * *

This is what passes for normal now. Ever since Saul, ever since Erin's brother threw it all away, her life has been a series of routines. Get up, shower, make sure Saul gets up and does the same. Routines for morning, routines for school, routines for in the evenings until bed. They keep Saul focused, keep him in the world of the functional. For Erin, it all just bleeds together. One drill after another. Day in. Day out. Repeat.

It wasn't always this way. Erin used to have a life, and friends, and something approaching prospects. All the normal twentysomething accoutrements. Apartment out on Long Island, entry-level assistantship down at Random House. Job didn't pay much, and some weeks it felt like the rent would bleed her dry. But it was something. A job she could enjoy, where she could move up, where she might be able to network so one day when it came time to shop that story she'd been working on, she might have more to put in her letter than a half-assed query and starry-eyed hopes. That was the idea. Then three months ago her brother Adrian, the idiot, the published author, Mr. Assistant-Prof at CUNY with his office and his book-tours and his pill-popping ballerina wife decided to put away too many gin-and-tonics and then drive home. Wrapped his BMW around a lamppost at two a.m. Car totaled. No survivors.

She and Adrian were all each other had after their parents died.

Murder-suicide back in '98. Papers obsessed over it – how happy they'd seemed, the hidden signs of discontent, the accusations of infidelity, the neat arrays of orange bottles police found in their mother's medicine-cabinet. The sheer sensationalism made it even harder, but she and her brother got through. So she'd thought. Instead, now the media vultures circled in again. The big-shot writer, gone too soon. Glitzy spreads in the *Atlantic* and the Lifestyle section of the *Times*. Survived by a son Saul, they all said, and a sister Erin. Even in this she came up second.

So this is the new normal now. Get up, shower, make sure Saul gets up and does the same. Drop him off at school, go work at the job where she'll never advance because she can't put in the hours. Come home, get some dinner, help Saul bathe and give him his music and wrestle him into bed. Then maybe screw around on the Internet, trolling profiles on dating websites with a bag of microwave popcorn and a gaping hole in her chest where her big brother should be, before giving up and climbing still-dressed into bed. One drill after another. Day in. Day out. Repeat.

* * *

Saul fusses having to listen to Foo Fighters and Blind Melon on the way there, but eventually he spaces out again. Erin welcomes the silence. The last few weeks have been bad, and Saul's tantrums, normally rare, have made a fearful resurgence. Two weeks ago, the school actually called asking her to come pick him up. The secretary glared as they left, and the following Monday a letter came from his teacher. Wanted a conference. She swerves as some asshole in a beige SUV cuts her off. "Jesus Christ," she says. She looks over at Saul. "Sorry."

Saul says nothing, just stares and rubs his palms on his pantlegs.

"Saul?" she says. "Saul." She gives up. The aging hipster DJ comes on with few words of smoky nostalgia, and then the music's back. This time it's something familiar — a rattly snare backing a twanging guitar lick. Erin brightens, reaches for the dial, and without knowing why has a sense-memory of pot smoke, acrid and dank. She smiles, mouthing the words as they drive. *"When you were here before…"*

"I can hear you singing," says Saul.

"So?" She stops. "I can't sing? Come on, do you even know what song this is? It's-"

"'Creep.' Radiohead. Thom-Jonny-Colin-Ed-Phil. Formed 1985 Abingdon, Oxfordshire. Major breakthrough release 'Pablo Honey.' They -- "

"All right, all right, I get it." She looks him over. Three months, and not once has Saul ever met her gaze. Even now he ignores her, staring and running his fingers over the AC vents. She shakes her head and turns back to the road.

The drive wears on, backed by Thom Yorke's moody wail. Erin tries to remember where she'd first heard this song, and thinks of a summer night in, what, '99? Junior year of high school. She'd still fancied herself a blue-haired riot-grrl, content to sneak cigarettes and talk on the phone with her scruffy, worldly older brother. He'd come to visit while she stayed at Aunt Maggie's, him getting ready to start his senior year at NYU. He'd taken her out for burgers and pie out at the Blue Fog Café, and afterward they drove out to the reservoir and kicked their seats back, looking up at the stars and smoking a bowl together. The ganje was "serious shit," as Adrian liked to put it, and "Creep" was playing at the time, courtesy of some mix-CD he'd burnt. Their parents might not have approved of the music or the weed, but then again what did it matter? By that time they'd been dead for nearly a year. She frowns. *Now he's dead too*. Suddenly this song, like damned near everything else her in life, feels tainted.

"Erin."

"Not now, Saul." This response reflexive, Erinese for *leave-me-alone*. She slows and turns into the parking-lot. "Saul, honey, get your iPod out — Auntie Erin has to turn the radio off."

"Okay." He fiddles with his earbuds. This is something trained into him, one of many little routines that allow him to have a life approaching normal. *Normal. What a joke*. On the radio, Yorke moans how *she's so fucking special*; how he wishes he was special. Erin switches the station off, blinking hard. Nothing is normal anymore. And special – who has room for special?

* * *

Rewind to Saul's school, back two weeks to the Exceptional-Needs classroom. The room is beige, and instead of desks sports sprawling mats and brightly-colored beanbag chairs. The walls are hung with drawings or essays, and in one corner sits Saul with his music. The teacher's his late 20s, lanky with shaggy hair, and he hands her a piece of magenta paper, still frayed with the tags torn from its notebook.

"Saul turned this in last week," he says.

Erin looks it over. The writing's in some sort of blue-green crayon — *aquamarine*, she thinks, from the 64-color box — and there are no words. The page is taken up by an array of lines and dots, a script too complex for her to decipher. "Sheet music?"

"Looks like it. Kids were supposed to draw their favorite memory from summer vacation. Saul handed in this." He pushes up his glasses.

"Listen, you a musician at all? No? Okay, well I am. I do drums, bass. Couple of buddies and I get together on weekends to jam. We're alright." He gestures at the paper. "Nothing like this, though."

"I thought you said Saul was having problems."

"Well, yes. I mean, no. See the thing is, your son—"

"He's not my son."

"Sorry. The problem is Saul doesn't really respond to classroom settings. It's not that he's stupid, understand, he just… there's too much stimulation. He doesn't engage beyond his immediate fields of interest. Reading, Social Studies, Math. There's no getting through. You understand."

"I thought that was the point of 'Exceptional Needs.'"

"It is. Normally. But understand, I mostly deal with cognitive impairments. Downs, fetal alcohol, that sort of thing. Saul's not really impaired in that sense. It's just his mind doesn't work like ours."

"Right." *Autism's not impaired?* She looks back – Saul's humming tunelessly in his corner. "So what's this have to do with me?"

"Look." Teacher sits forward. "You have to understand, with all the changes these last few years, we're under a lot of pressure to produce results-oriented curricula. Special-needs educators have a hard time with that." He chews at his lip. "I really don't think we have what's needed here to give Saul the attention he deserves."

"What do you mean? You're saying you just wanna give up on him?"

"Wait, what? No." He shakes his head. "No. Look, the system we have isn't really serving Saul. Okay? I understand that. What I need *you* to understand is that there are programs that *could* help Saul. I just can't get funding for them.

"What I'm saying," —he rests his elbows on the desk— "is I think you need to consider alternative-learning programs."

Erin purses her lips. *Here we go again.* She's had this discussion before, first with the chain-smoking social worker from CPS, then the counselor who took half her month's pay to tell her she needed to spend more money. "I can't afford any of that."

"Sure," the teacher says, "But there's help you can get for that. Grants, scholarships, charities."

"I don't need anyone's charity." She ignores the rest – all the focus has been on what can be done for Saul. Nobody's asked about her, or how's she's been holding up. Saul's humming grows louder. "Honey, quiet down."

"I understand you're frustrated," teacher says. "Things are still getting adjusted at home, and I'm sure Saul's been kind of a handful. But in a private or a charter school, you could --"

"I'm not putting him in a different school." Saul's humming rises like a fly buzzing. She rubs her temple. The light's too bright, she's tired, and all she wants to do is shut herself up in the bath and break down. But she can't. "Look, I really can't deal with this," she says. "Okay? I'll think about it, but I need some time. I – "

"You don't have time," teacher says. "Saul doesn't have time. Alright? These years right now are critical for a kid like Saul. Your son is special, you understand? He has a gift — "

"He's not my fucking son!" She sits up in her chair. Behind her Saul's humming grows louder. "Damn it, Saul, will you cut that shit out?!"

"Hey!" Teacher raises his voice. "You need to calm down. Okay? You don't get talk to him like that."

"Oh, what the fuck do you know?" She gets so tired of these sanctimonious pricks and their opinions. "You think it's so easy, you deal with him."

"Oh, believe me, I do. Trust me. Every day."

"Like hell. You're the one refusing to teach him!"

"I'm not refusing to teach him!" He leans over the desk. Eyes search each other for something, anything. Neither pair finds what they're hoping for. Teacher slouches in his chair. "I'm saying he deserves *better*, you get that?" He shakes his head. "Better than I can give him."

"Whatever." She grabs her purse. "Saul? Saul, honey, it's time to go. Come on."

"Look, just think about what I've said. Please?"

"Go to hell." She adjusts Saul's backpack and leads him out by the hand. His humming continues as they walk out the door. Behind her she hears the teacher say: "There are lots of programs in the city, you know. You work in the city, don't you?"

* * *

They call it the "Pinewood Derby," a name that makes Erin think of air-freshener and women in ridiculous hats. There are hardly any women here though, just a few squat den-mothers and one brittle-faced soccer mom five years from a round of Botox and a pill problem. Erin can spot her kind from a mile away now, like one lame antelope in a herd about to get picked off by a cheetah. The other boys are attended by men of various ages and shapes, each resembling little copies of their fathers. Saul is the only boy whose copy is missing.

The derby takes place in the school gymnasium, around an inclined plane broken into tracks. The scene is chaos -- boys cheer on friends. Dads shout encouragement. Erin squeezes between the rows, trying to ignore the prying stares as she passes. She and Saul settle into a spot up front and she squints, trying to take it all in.

The action is broken into "heats," where groups of three boys place their cars into assigned lanes. At the whistle, the cars are launched, and for a few seconds the white-cinderblock walls echo with shrieking and cheering. There are three rounds per heat, and from each heat emerges a clear winner. When the victor is decided, that boy and his car are led off the platform. For two heats, Erin watches in silence. She tunes out, reflecting: *Do we need milk? What was that article last week on confinement farming? We really should switch to soy.* There comes a chorus of shouts: "Saul Woodrow!" Erin looks up. "Saul Woodrow!" Across the way, a den mother from the sign-in desk is cupping her hands and pointing at the racetrack. Jostled by the other parents, she rouses Saul and guides him up toward the front. He stares as always, holding his little car and nodding to music only he can hear.

All eyes are on them. The boys laugh and whisper; the parents pull back or shake their heads. Were this Down's or some other condition, Saul might be treated differently. He might get sympathy; the other kids, spurred on by guilty parents, might embrace and encourage him. Instead Saul gets treated as the kid with the blank stare and the tantrums, the one who talks or laughs inappropriately. He's the *freak*, the *retard*, and she the *parent of the retard*. She glares at some boy who snickers as they pass, but Saul doesn't even notice.

The other cars are already in place. Erin looks at their glossy paint-schemes, their sharkface decals, and feels judged. She had to flirt with some kid at the hardware store to get Saul's car done. It's not flashy, not detailed, and just like everything else it's not enough. There comes the count, the whistle blows, and suddenly there's the screaming again.

The race is over almost immediately. For a second, Saul's car looks to have an edge, but then a black car with red flames pulls ahead. They shoot through the finish, and when it's over Saul's car has finished dead last. A tall boy beside them shouts, raising his arms like a gladiator demanding tribute. He checks Saul with a shoulder as he passes to grab his car, but when Erin tries to step in and confront him he just blows on by. *What are you gonna do*, his stare says. Erin helps Saul pick up his car and guides him up for the next round.

They mount his car on a different track this time, and to everyone's surprise Saul finishes a close second. Erin shakes him, points to his good showing, but he pays no mind. She can feel the other boys glaring, hear them exhorting their peers to do better. This is a competition. Nobody wants to lose to *the retard*.

The cars are gathered up for their final run, and the shouting rises to a frantic pitch. Erin allows herself the hope that Saul might advance, at least to the quarterfinal. But then the whistle goes up, the cars come down, and the gym becomes a crash of cheers and screams. The tall boy gets tackled by his friends, and together they lead him off with his dad. The applause seems to go on forever. The defeat sinks in and Erin moves to collect up Saul's car.

Leading him back through the crowds, the other boys are ebullient. Erin and Saul make for the exit, but on the way out a father and son fail to clear sufficient way, bumping Saul as they passed. The boy whispers something snide, and Erin spins and finds him, tired of these entitled little brats. She leans down in his face, snaps: "Hey, how 'bout you keep your comments to your fucking self, huh?"

"Excuse me?" A pair of Blahniks step forward. Suddenly here's the yuppie soccer-mom, towering over Erin, her makeup somehow too-shiny for her age. "I'm sorry, refresh my memory, who the hell are you talking to my little boy like that?"

"I…" Erin shrinks back, looks at her feet. "Listen, I just – "

"Save it," says the soccer-mom. "You know what, some of the other parents here feel bad for your son. Some. But I don't feel bad for shitty parenting, and if you can't contribute positively to this group, then I'm not sure we want you."

"Look, I said I was sorry."

"Whatever." She points. "Door's that way. I suggest you keep moving."

"Fine." Saul's humming again, and she shakes him. "Saul. Come on." She leads him past rows of eyes, toward an exit that never seems to get any closer. She hadn't even wanted to come tonight, but she had to – for *Saul*. Everything's for Saul now, and try as she might she fears she'll never be able to forgive him for what he represents. She wished things could just be normal again.

"*But I'm a creep*," says Saul, quoting Yorke. "*I'm a weirdo*."

* * *

Back at Saul's coat hook, Erin wrestles the car into his backpack. She curses and wishes for a cigarette, struggles to get Saul's coat on. "Hold still," she says. She grabs his lapels. "Saul! Hold still!" She untangles his earbuds, zipping up his coat and making sure he has everything he needs. She stands, swallowing hard, when behind her a voice shouts:

"Hey!"

She turns. A boy approaches them. He's short, with shaggy hair and Coke-bottle glasses, and he bounds up, clutching a red ribbon in his hands, which he promptly pins to Saul's coat. He looks up, fixing his glasses, and Erin recognizes him as a boy who'd won the heat before theirs. The ribbon is his. "It's okay," he says. "They dogged on my car last year, too."

Erin stared. "I…" She works her mouth as the boy's father sidles up. He's tall, handsome, a few years older than her, but what the hell? He smiles, and Erin thinks of a teacher she on whom she nursed a crush back in high-school. "Sorry about that," he says.

She blinks. "For what?"

"Well, you know. What happened back there. Kids can be pretty cruel sometimes. I'll talk to the other parents later, don't worry."

"What? Why?" She looks at Saul. "I mean thank you. Sorry. That's… that's very kind of you."

"No worries." He offers up a hand. "Dale — teach P.E. here at the school. You must be Saul's mom?"

"Erin. And no. I — I'm his aunt. Just…" She lies. "Watching him. For my brother."

"Oh. Well, sorry about that. I just figured you were so good with him —"

"It's fine." She forces a smile. *Why can't I ever meet men when Saul's NOT in tow?* "Listen," she says, "thank you. You didn't have to say anything."

"I know, but Saul deserves better. He's a good kid. You're lucky to have him, you know that?"

"No." She's blushing. She tries to conjure a reply that sound cools but receptive. "Sounds like we're lucky to have you."

"Ah. Well, thank you." He grins. "Anyway, we gotta be getting back, but it was nice talking to you. Don't let them get you down, okay?"

"I won't." She holds Saul's hand as the boy and his father disappear. She watches the hand around his boy's shoulder, the ring on one finger engraved with some Celtic pattern. *Stupid*. Her cheeks redden. She's mad for not speaking, for wanting to speak, for there not being any point anyway. *Taken or gay, that's what they always say. Just… stupid.*

"I want you to notice," Saul murmurs, *"when I'm not around."*

"Huh?" She looks down. Again with the song-lyrics. This is how it is, he gets a fixation and doesn't let go for weeks on end. She asks "what now?"

"I have to go," he says, and looks up. "Now."

"Huh?" The tumblers click after a moment. "Oh. Sorry. You mean like *go*." She helps him pocket his iPod then, pointing in the direction of the bathroom. "Remember like we talked about: Door, pants, pee, hands. Okay?"

"Okay." He wanders off the way she pointed him. Then she's alone, her hands in her pockets, while from the gymnasium more shouts and cheers erupt. She calls out after him:

"And hurry up, will you?"

* * *

Rewind to the night that Adrian died, back to his reading at NYU and the plush downstairs rooms of the Vernon House. He's come to promote his third novel, some character study set against the Coeur d'alene Massacre, and Erin has come to support him. Friends, colleagues, agents, former professors -- they're all hailing Adrian as "his generation's voice," holding him up against contemporaries like Delillo, Harrison, Wolff, Udall. Even Yelena, his wife, has showed up. It's his night, the zenith of his career, and though Erin has long wished for such a night of her own she doesn't begrudge him his. He's her brother, her hero, and she loves him.

They all love him.

The conversation flows like wine, and the wine like water. She feels out of place in her Goodwill skirt, standing amongst so many big literary names. She brought business cards, hoping to name-drop with one of the half-dozen publishers present, but having arrived she sees how they regard her, like some mislaid intern instead of the *author's sister*, and chooses to keep company with a corner bookshelf, nursing her drink, crushing ice cubes between her teeth.

Even before the reading, Erin notices the rheuminess to Adrian's eyes, the flush at his collar. His grin is lax, and when he laughs it's always too loud, too soon. Everyone else is already enjoying their own buzz, so they don't notice or don't care. Erin knows better, though. He's put away enough Hendrickson's-and-lime to drop a Clydesdale.

By the time they get to the reading, half the attendees are drunk. A middle-aged blonde and her male cohort emerge from a bathroom, laughing and wiping their noses. Adrian reads two chapters, and though he hides it well his feet are unsteady, his delivery lurching and off-kilter. When the reading is finished, there comes a rush of giddy applause, and people crowd the front, eager to shake Adrian's hand. Erin tries to insert herself, but ends up crowded out by the throng. His eyes brush hers, once, before some marketing bigwig distracts him again. She calls to him, but he doesn't seem to notice her. She calls out to him again, and once again he conveniently fails to notice. Finally, too disgusted to bother, she turned back the way she'd come, desperate for a smoke and some air.

The Village smells of flowers and bus exhaust, of burnt rubber and Asian noodles boiling. Yelena's out already, smoking and looking bored in her cocktail dress. Yelena always looks bored. She made her name years ago as a dancer with the Bolshoi, and now she holds a faculty post at the Tisch school, teaching graduate-level dance theory. After three continents, a dozen major cities, and the adulation of thousands, she seems to view most of life as pedestrian. She looks up, raising an eyebrow.

"Erin," she says. "Thought you were quit."

Her accent is bad tonight – a sign she's been drinking. Figures.

"Yeah, well." Erin takes a drag. "Guess I don't do crowds."

Yelena shrugs. Her features, pretty like an ice-sculpture, form a smile. "You are looking good," she says. "Is good you are eating again."

"I guess." She hates Yelena's snotty comments, her insults masked as polite conversation. Tonight, after she's gone, Yelena will joke about her dress, her weight, her hair to the other guests. She's complained to Adrian in the past, but he just blows her off, wraps an arm around her and says *you're just too sensitive, kiddo. Lighten up, huh? You're spoiling the party*. Erin flicks ash and raises the smoke to her lips. "Where's Saul?" she asks.

"We hired a sitter. Paid her extra, so afterward we go out."

"Out where?"

"Place down 49th Street. The Moorland, it's called. You know it?" She looked expectant, then frowned. "No? Perhaps not."

"How are you getting there?"

Yelena laughs. "Drive. Maybe cab. Depends on parking."

"You guys drove?"

"Yes. So? What business is it of yours? Adrian was so excited about new car. BMW 7-series. Sexy. But don't worry — we'll take cab if partying gets too much."

"Looks like you guys have partied enough."

"And who said this was any of your business?" Yelena blows smoke. "With Saul and classes and book tour, Adrian has never time to relax. He's worked hard, past year. Is good to reward him. Perhaps if you knew how to reward a man, you might find one more easy yourself, yes?"

"Shut up." Erin stamps out her cigarette, turns to face her sister-in-law. "How much has Adrian had to drink tonight?"

"Is not your business. What gives you right—"

"Don't bullshit me." She leans into Yelena's face. "You told me you were gonna get him help, get him into a program. Said you were going to 'do it for Saul.' That was six months ago. What the fuck?"

"Adrian does not *need* help! Is fine. Everything is fine. Saul has good care, good school, and his father is a hardworking man!" She looks Erin up and down. "You should know such about hard work!"

"I know more than you can dream." She looks toward the door – Adrian's busy weaving and regaling some equally drunk couple. "Look, he's getting worse. Okay? He's always partied since our parents died, but not like this." She folds her arms. "He never tells me anything, always brushes it off, says he's fine. But he's not fine." She looks back – Adrian was gone. "He's not fine. Now please — at least get his keys tonight? Okay?"

"I don't have to get his keys. Adrian is fine, he – "

"Please." Erin grabs her by the shoulders. "Just… please. Get his keys tonight, or I will."

Silence. The color drains from Yelena's face. She finishes her cigarette, suddenly looking much older, and says: "You're right. Forgive me, okay? I'm sorry." She smiles. "It's good you say something. What am I thinking, I… Thank you."

"Really?"

"Really. Tonight." Yelena kisses her cheek, makes her way for the stairs. "You are coming in, yes?"

"Not yet." Erin takes out another smoke. "I need to clear my head. I'll be back in a few, okay?"

"Okay." Yelena disappears, and Erin turns and began walking. The air is warm, the thump of distant techno somewhere sounding like a heartbeat, like the womb.

When she's completed her trip around the block, she comes in to find Adrian gone. She looks for him upstairs, Yelena too, but finds no sign. Stopping the frail woman from earlier, she asks where they are. The woman laughs, nearly losing her martini. "Dunno. That little blonde of his came in and said they had to go. Said it was too late to be partying." She giggles. "You know, she is just *so good* for him. Keeps him in line. Every good man has a woman to keep him in line, you know?"

Erin pulls away. *So she kept her word.* She thanks the woman and excuses herself. She resolves to call in the morning. Meanwhile, it has to be almost eleven. Time to grab a train.

A week later, Adrian is in the ground. So is Yelena. They'd taken the car after all, run a red light not far from Washington Square. Their car was destroyed, and with it Erin's life, the hope that she might ever know who broke Yelena's promise – Yelena, or smooth-talking Adrian, mister *no-it's-cool-I'm-totally-fine*. Erin receives flowers, cards, letters from people she's never met. None of it dulls the pain, none of it comforts her at night, locked in the bathroom crumpled against the door, sobbing.

At the funeral, Saul sits in his little black suit and holds Erin's hand. She doesn't think he understands at first, but when they play "Amazing Grace" he tugs at Erin's sleeve. "They shouldn't have played gospel," he says. "Adrian hated gospel."

* * *

The reverie fades, and Erin finds herself back at the school, her brother still dead, his little boy still dawdling idly in the restroom. She's been doing this more and more, getting lost in other places or times. The week before, she was at a stoplight and thought of Adrian's 13th birthday up with their parents at Green Lake. When she'd come to, a line of cars were behind her leaning on their horns. It's too hard anymore to focus. Reality is the last place she wants to be.

The sun is lower now, and cheering still rings out from the gym. She glances back toward the restroom — still no sign of Saul. *Has to have been at least five minutes. What's he doing?* She isn't sure she wants to know, but regardless she pushes off, wandering over toward the boys' room.

There's no sound coming from inside—no running water, no crumpling paper, not even the drip of a leaky faucet. She knocks on the metal doorjamb, an unsatisfying *tap-tap*, then pokes her head inside. "Saul?" she asks. "Saul honey, how you doin' in there?"

No response.

"Saul?" Looking about, she ducks in. "Saul, answer me." The pint-size urinals are unoccupied, the sinks dry and silent. She pushes open one stall, followed by the other. Both are empty.

"Saul?" Her heart surges. *"Saul?"* She steps out and scans the halls to her left and right. He didn't pass her; she's sure of it, she would have noticed wouldn't she? "Saul!" She doubles back toward the gym. She sees the backs of heads, but none with the same hair, the same posture. *He's not here*. She's becoming frightened now, and with that fear comes shame. First the outburst earlier; now her child is missing.

My child. The words sound strange. That's what he is now, isn't he? Her throat tightens — she can't go back to the other parents; not after all that's happened. She runs out, scanning the parking lot. Her mind runs through dark scenarios. A lump forms in her throat; she wipes at her eyes, heads back inside.

Her eyes take a moment to adjust to the sudden dark. She looks up; from the gymnasium comes applause, and slowly panic gives way to resignation. She'll go back in, she resolves. Alert the other parents. Sure, they might look at her wrong, but what does any of that matter?

Then, passing a hallway to her left, she stops. Her ears tune in — something faraway has her attention. It's tied to that far-off place, that dark place, but something about the arrangement anchors it firmly in the *now*. Someone's playing piano, the technique sublime, the arrangement one she swears she knows. "SAUL?" She doubles back, following the notes, praying *please God, please*. "SAUL!" The music grows louder. Around a corner stand a pair of heavy double-doors, beyond which lies some sort of rehearsal room. The music is coming from inside, and light spills out across the hallway floor. Erin slows. Her heart pounds.

The space is empty, high ceilinged, with yellow walls. Instrument cases are stacked in the corner, and off to one side sit rows of folding metal chairs. At the far end of the room is a raised platform, and atop it a battered grand piano where a boy sits playing. He's dressed in jeans and a faded blue Scout shirt, and though his hair hangs in his eyes, he doesn't seem to notice. All that matters is his playing. Erin's breath catches. *Saul*. She could run up and hug him, yelling at him not to ever do that again, but something stops her. His playing stops her. He wrings music forth as if from nothing, and as Erin listens she hears the familiar notes, plugs in the lyrics. She pauses in the doorway.

It's "Creep."

He memorized it, she thinks. *He fucking memorized it. He can't do that, can he?* It doesn't make any sense, yet here he is, performing like he's practiced for weeks. Why this song? Why now? She doesn't understand. She leans against the door and folds her arms.

The music builds, and Erin watches and listens. She knew he had a gift, but never like this. She realizes then that in the three months since he's lived with her, she's never heard him play. Not once. Three months now, and she's never bothered to ask, never bothered to listen. And why would she? Doesn't she have enough to deal with? She's tried to explain this to people, to the teachers and counselors who tell her she's neglecting Saul's talents, but they don't understand. Nobody understands.

But then she stops. *He does*, she realizes. *He does understand*. It all makes sense – the tuneless humming, the lyrics quoted out of thin air.

He's been trying to tell me, she thinks. *All this time, and I wouldn't listen*. She thinks back to what his teacher said. Saul couldn't express his feelings, couldn't make himself understood, but that didn't mean that all the hurts didn't strike home. His family dead, classmates who treat him like a freak, doctors who see him as a case study and an aunt who most days seems to resent his very existence. For all the wonder of his gifts, she realizes then that he might throw it all away to be with his parents, to know how to fit in, to be something that someone that Erin or anybody could see as worth loving, as *special*.

"You're so fucking special," she murmurs. *"I wish I was special."* The weight of her shame overcomes her, and before she realizes what's happened she's crying. She clenches her jaw against it, but she's sobbing like a child, without shame, mourning Adrian and herself and most of all Saul, who plays because he has no tears to shed. She weeps until all is lost, until she feels too tired to do anything but surrender to the flood.

When her grief has spent, she realizes Saul has finished playing. He's sitting at the bench, his shoulders lighter, and when he notices her he smiles. For the first time since coming to live with her, he meets her gaze. It's a brief thing, just a shadow passing before he glances back down at his hands. Erin looks down at her own. Their smoothness surprises her. She uses them to wipe her eyes.

THE YARD

Susan Mary Dowd

He'd been free for six days. His feet were hot and sore, and his tongue felt like a piece of paper. It made it difficult to swallow. He'd been walking with his mouth open for the last couple of miles. His instinct, though, was to keep moving. And, of course, he had to keep to the back roads. He'd learned the last time that crowds didn't help him blend in. Every single person had stared at him.

The gnawing in his stomach was a constant distraction. He hadn't eaten since early yesterday morning. Cautiously, he had ventured into a near-deserted park, drawn by the rich, earthy scents and the peace. None of the benches had been occupied. Sitting down to rest, he had tensed a minute later to the sound of footsteps on the path. Looking up he had seen an old man with a bag, walking slowly, but unwaveringly toward him.

The old man had sat down next to him, smiled and said something in a language he didn't recognize. Not seeming to expect a response, the man had plunged his hand into the bag and begun tossing the contents in a wide arc. Birds swooped in from every direction, a chattering gray cloud.

The sight had unsettled him. Birds always provoked a burning restlessness in him. Small and delicate, they seemed stronger than he was, despite his size and the muscles that rippled smoothly beneath his skin. They could fly. They could leave him behind.

A picture of the Yard flashed into his brain, splintering into isolated images of the walls and wire that had surrounded him. It had never mattered that there was fresh air, sky, room to exercise. The Yard was far more terrible than being Inside. It seemed even more of a prison.

All because of the birds. They streaked past the walls or landed inside, then flew up and out, torturing him with their freedom. Triggering his desperation to get out, like nothing else did. He'd thrown himself against those walls time after time until the blows had rained down.

He had gotten out twice before. The escapes were always short-lived. The memories of the beatings he suffered when he got back to the Yard, however, were not.

His hunger pulled at him again.

Yesterday, the old man had eventually started to doze in the morning sun, the bag forgotten on the bench beside him.

Quietly, he had risen and gently pulled the bag away. With a last look at the sleeping old man, he had walked briskly away, then had torn the bag open and eaten the rest of the contents.

He'd had nothing to eat since then.

Presently, he cut off into the woods. He'd seen rabbits and squirrels in abundance there. But they were lightning quick. One look at him and they fled in terror.

He'd eaten rabbit once, a long time ago. He hadn't liked it then, but now…. Could he catch one? He sat down to wait behind a fallen, algae-encrusted tree. After about half an hour, a rabbit hopped tentatively into the clearing, just on the other side of the tree. The furry creature began munching contentedly on some tender shoots poking up within a patch of sunshine.

Never taking his eye from the rabbit, he rose slowly and silently to a crouch. Ten seconds later he sprang. The rabbit froze for one brief second, then attempted a desperate leap away from him. But it was too late – he'd had the advantage of surprise. He grabbed the rabbit around the throat and squeezed. A strangled cry of almost human despair pierced the quiet, and the rabbit went limp.

He dropped the lifeless body to the ground and stared at it guiltily. He knew what to do, but he continued to hesitate. He looked around the clearing, in case some nameless thing was watching him. Shame shadowed his eyes and he started to cringe but, no, he was alone. Finally, shaking himself, he turned back to the rabbit and went to work.

Later, full but depressed, he lay down on a bed of dry, crackling leaves and, worn out, slipped quickly into a heavy sleep. The forest sank into the velvet night, darkness coming first as a caress, then a full embrace. The drowsy murmurings of birds were soft as rustling feathers, the footfalls of nocturnal roamers, fully absorbed by the plushness of the forest floor. Two hours glided quietly by.

He was dreaming of the Yard. A hard face and an even harder voice floated in and out of the scene. He cried out in anguish in the dream. It crossed the boundaries of unconsciousness and became audible. He started to thrash, and a curious raccoon, who had ventured close, ran off.

Suddenly, he was jerked violently awake and onto all fours by a terrible clawing at his insides. The clawing resolved into ferocious spasms that seized him again and again as every last bit of the rabbit dinner hurtled out of his stomach and onto the forest floor. When the last, brutal clenching left him, he lay down, emptied, weak, and dizzy. After a while, a picture of the Yard again drifted into his mind. Sometimes he had his meals out there. Food that never forced its way back up.

He had instinctively run from civilization before, but he had never been out for this long.

Had never been this hungry. He felt confused. Sleep took him again, this time dreamlessly.

* * *

He rose early the next morning. One thing the rabbit – or his body's ultimate rejection of it – had bequeathed to him was a lingering and persistent nausea. It killed his hunger. But although food held no allure, he was severely dehydrated, and thirst drove him now, far more powerfully than hunger had.

He pushed on through the woods and, after a few minutes, picked up a deer track. He followed it for about half a mile to its conclusion at the edge of a field. Breaking out of the woods, he felt a sudden rise in spirits. The woods had seemed to close in on him. Now, the openness, the sunlight, the breeze across the field revived his sense of freedom. He quickened his pace and soon began to bound through the tall grass. He let out a yelp of sheer exuberance. Birds streaked over his head, but this time he felt at one with them. His very being seemed lighter. He took a high, graceful leap over a thorny-looking bush that seemed suddenly to rear up out of the grass. Long-repressed physical power exploded out of him.

Eventually, his energy flagged. Slowing down to a walk, he became aware of a faint sound that he hadn't heard over the loud whispering of the grass against his rushing body. Water.

A few more steps and the voluptuous smell of damp earth reached his nostrils. He identified the direction of the sound. There – by that big solitary tree. He ran eagerly toward it and discovered a small brook running down the slope on the other side of the tree. A brief, sheer drop in the brook's bed had created a miniature waterfall. As the water fell over itself, fingers of sunlight reached through the leafy canopy and touched it here and there, creating tiny stars that sparkled, winked, and drowned in the little pool at the bottom.

He dropped onto his belly in one pliant motion, leaned over, and drank deeply and long from the pool.

He rose calmed, cooled, and purposeful. He leapt over the gurgling little torrent and followed it down slope for a while into a narrow valley. On his left, a long, gently rounded hill ran parallel to the brook, which had grown into a more businesslike stream.

He was curious about what lay on the other side of the hill. Stopping first for another long drink, he veered off from the stream at a right angle, crossed the short stretch to the hill, and began climbing. The grasses gave way to scrub, dirt and rocks where the sun, wind, and erosion took an ever-increasing toll.

Nearing the crest of the hill, he picked up a scent on the wind that blew across from the other side. Cows. Their smell was unmistakable. He ran up the last few yards to the top and gazed down into a snug little valley. There they were. There everything was. Cows grazing. Paddocks with horses. Barn. House. Tiny human figures moving about. He could hear their voices, faint snatches that were caught up and then dispersed by the wind.

As he continued to stare, something between a whimper and a groan rose in him and escaped his lips. It was all so familiar. So much like *his* farm. The place he was born on, raised on. Spent the happiest days of his life on. Long before the Yard. Long before he knew all-consuming misery even existed.

The Farm. He was free then. Even with all the rules. Even with all the work.

Free, because he wanted to be there. Free, because the things that tied him were loyalty, love, and wanting to be part of something important.

The Farm. Everyone had belonged. Every single one of them, man and beast, had a job. The cows were the most important. The Farm had revolved around them and the milk they gave. A small herd of sheep was of lesser importance, but they, too, gave. Gave their wool, which was sheared, gathered up, and sent off.

There were also pigs and chickens. Several dogs kept the cows and sheep in line, and cats kept the mice in line.

When he and his three brothers were old enough, their mother had begun their schooling. Affectionate and encouraging, she taught them everything she could.

Discipline, when called for, was swift, brief — and never forgotten. Of all the brothers, though, he was the hardest to discipline. He was more easily distracted and the urge to roam had been stronger. His mother had spent extra time on him.

In later years, after his life had sunk into its dark pool of misery, the image of her soft dark eyes often came to him, as did remembered sensations of her warmth and thick, soft hair, the sweet scent that was hers and hers alone. The memories both comforted and depressed him.

When he was very small, he didn't see as much of his father. His father was always out in the fields working and came in so tired at the end of the day that most nights he fell asleep shortly after supper. As he got older, though, he spent more and more time with his father out in the fields and in the barns, learning the Farm, inside and out. He grew up feeling useful and important. Unshakably connected to everyone and everything.

The Farm defined and contained the whole of their lives, their very universe. Everything they needed to physically thrive was there. And they had each other. Contentment, security, and peace were a continuous stream running through their days. It whispered them to sleep at night, and flowed smoothly into their awakening minds with the morning sun.

He was still young when it all ended. Long sickness, two deaths in quick succession. Everything gone.

He lay down under the sun's glare and slept. He dreamt again, this time of the beloved Farm so long ago, but it was mixed with images of the one nestled below him. His dream-self was running across a field, joy singing throughout his being.

When he awoke, the sun was no longer burning fiercely over his head, but hanging, huge and approachable, ahead of him. He rubbed his eyes, shook his head. Rising, he stretched his lean length and began his descent toward the farm. He didn't pick his way down the hill. Head up, feet sure, he homed in on the replica of his past life with a hunger that burned through fear and uncertainty.Within a few minutes he was alongside the grazing cows. One or two of them raised heavy heads and gazed at him expectantly, but kindly, with their large soft eyes, then resumed their leisurely chewing when he moved on.

He reached a paddock that held the horses. They, too, were munching contentedly, their noses deep into great piles of fluffy hay. Their ears twitched in his direction as they ate, their beautiful dark eyes keener in expression that the cows'. The horses were aware of his every move yet they, too, sensed no threat to themselves.

He kept going. The barn wasn't too far now. A minute later, the unforgettable odor of pigs hit him like a punch in the nose. He moved quickly past a pen holding an immense black sow and a small herd of squealing piglets.

A few more steps, and he was at the side of the huge barn. He rounded a corner, stopped, and turned. He was facing the front of the structure. The wide doors were open, but the sun was in his eyes so he couldn't see inside. He hesitated. It was very quiet. Where were the people he had seen from the crest of the hill? Now he did feel uncertain.

He walked haltingly toward the doorway, blotches from the sun's glare polka-dotting his vision.

He stopped at the threshold, uncertainty turning to sudden fear of the unknown. Was there someone inside? Heart pounding, breathing shallow, he stepped into the soundless gloom as the hair rose on the back of his neck. His eyes hadn't yet adjusted to the sudden darkness. He was blind, completely vulnerable.

A sudden scratching sound to his left, and his over-ratcheted nerves came undone. Overreacting to the small noise, his every muscle exploded in a huge sideways leap. He hit something made of metal, tall but light, leaning against the wall. A ladder. It crashed down, lacerating the quiet with a harsh clanging that set off a symphony of hysterical squawking and frantic wing flapping.

Instead of running back out the doorway, he inexplicably ran to the far end of the barn.

He saw some stalls and ducked into the last one. He stood there, shaking uncontrollably, watching the feathers float down in the pallid light that slanted in through high windows.

The next sounds paralyzed him. Somewhere outside, a man was shouting. Swift, heavy steps seemed like thunder in his ears as they pounded nearer and nearer. Then, he heard a hard metal click from the doorway. He was cornered. With a groan he sank down onto the straw and hung his head, despair sketching every line of his body.

A deep voice called out, a voice of authority. The chickens ceased their disgusted squawking. In the sudden silence he heard the soft, slow crunch of footsteps. They came agonizingly close. Then they stopped. Now there was only one sound in the thick silence – his own breaths, broken into shards by his uncontrollable shaking.

Two more footsteps, and a pair of legs ending in dirty boots were directly in front of him. He dared not raise his head any higher. He closed his eyes, stopped breathing completely, and braced himself for a hard fist, a slap, a vicious kick.

Nothing happened. He waited. Still nothing. And then something did. As the pain and fear drilled its way into him, an impulse escaped from deep inside — one that went against every lesson he had learned and every beating he had taken throughout his years of confinement.

He rose to a sitting position from his crouch. Lifted his head. And offered the man his paw.

* * *

There was a collar with tags around the dog's neck. The farmer ignored them. If the dog had allowed the farmer to touch him, the man would have taken the collar, tags and all, and thrown it down the old well in his front yard. A history of brutality was written all over the big Belgian Shepherd's face and body. Ugly scars, pulled tight, corrugated the skin on his head. Two small round burn marks punctuated the black skin of his nose. On his left side, a series of parallel welts reared up, parting the fur. Later, after he had collapsed into exhausted sleep, blood-encrusted puncture marks revealed themselves on his paws. The farmer recognized the type of wound and its source — barbed wire.

In sleep, the dog whimpered. The farmer felt an unaccustomed rage flare up inside him that, even in unconsciousness, the dog could not escape his brutal past.

For the next week, the dog followed the farmer every waking hour. The animal allowed no physical contact, flinching away at the slightest advance, but he gazed at the farmer with a yearning in his dark eyes that rocked the man's weathered, sixty-year-old heart. To the farmer, the yearning spoke of courage — the daring to hope for kindness even after unspeakable cruelty. He marveled, too, at the complete absence of meanness in the dog. Miraculous was the word that came to his mind. There was no snapping, no growling. Only the deep, scarring fear of being touched.

On the eighth day, from his porch rocker, the farmer gazed at the sun as it sank onto the pillow of the horizon and watched the rich oils of the painted sky fade into watercolors. The dog sat about a foot and a half away as usual, still as a statue.

Now, the farmer held his breath once more and, slowly, slowly reached out. With infinite care, he lowered his calloused, big-knuckled hand until it rested, light as a moth, on the dog's head. This time, the dog didn't flinch, but sat rigidly, eyes unfocused, for a long, hushed minute.

Finally, as the sky was pulling up its soft violet blanket, he sighed, and lifting his head, met the hand firmly and fully.

They kept the firmness between them as they rose together and went into the house.

THE OTTAWANNA WAY

Richard Hawley

The summer after fifth grade my mother realized I didn't like Little League anymore, that it was actually making me sad, so she decided to send me to Camp Ottawanna as soon as the season ended. Camp Ottawanna was an overnight camp on a big lake in Wisconsin. Mother told me that when she was a girl she had wanted to go to Girl Scout Camp more than anything in the world, but Nana and Papa couldn't afford it. She told me Camp Ottawanna would be wonderful. I would sleep in a cabin, and there would be boating and swimming and camping out in tents. She said there would also be sports, including baseball, and that I could bring my glove. I really didn't want to go. I wanted to go on our regular vacation with everybody else up to our own cabin in the north woods. I could see that saying this was hurting mother's feelings, so I stopped, but I really did not want to go to that camp.

Mother found out another boy from my school, Patrick Dannehey, was also going to Camp Ottawanna. She told me about it to make me feel better about going. She said, "You'll have a friend." I knew Patrick Dannehey was not going to be my friend. He was a grade behind me, and he had white hair and pale skin, and he was really weak. Thinking about Patrick Dannehey trying to hang around me for three weeks made me feel terrible.

I was right about it, too. Camp Ottawanna was completely terrible. The bad feeling I had about it right away was just a tiny hint of how terrible it would get. Mother took me to the train station on a Saturday morning where a special train just for the camp was going to take all the kids to Wisconsin. Mother said she thought it sounded like so much fun, but I didn't think it would be fun. The train started out in Chicago, and it was about half filled with kids by the time it got to us in Palatine. Patrick Dannehey and his mother and father were waiting on the platform when we got there. Mother went right over to them and started talking and laughing with Mr. and Mrs. Dannehey. She was always cheerful and polite with other people. I said hi to Patrick Dannehey, who looked weak and sick, and he started talking to me. He asked me if I had been to camp before and what I thought the kids would be like. I knew mother and the Danneheys were watching us, wanting us to get along and be friends. This made me not want to talk to Patrick at all. I didn't want to be mean to him, but I couldn't help feeling mean. I said no, I never went to the camp before and that I didn't know how the kids would be. I felt bad about not being nice, but when I looked at Patrick Dannehey's weak face and his soft white arms, I got even madder about having to go off to a camp I never wanted to go to and that nobody even asked me about before signing me up.

Two big boys from the camp who might have been in college or even men came up to us and told us which car to get into, and I realized that Patrick Dannehey was going to get on the same car with me and sit next to me in the double seat all the way up to Wisconsin. Mother helped me lift my suitcase, which was a huge blue plastic one of Nana's, up the steps of my car, and then she gave me a long hug and said goodbye. She was crying a little and being really nice, so I tried not to show her how mean I was feeling. I dragged my suitcase to the seat where Patrick was already sitting by the window. I lifted it up onto the seat so there could it be a wall between us, and then I sat back and got as mad as I could.

The train seemed to stop every three minutes to pick up more kids, and our car got noisier and noisier. Some of the kids who must have gone to the camp before were singing songs about Camp Ottawanna, which got me to hate those songs right away, songs like

We welcome you to Ott-a-wan-na
On the sandy banks of Lake Hathaway,
Where hearty braves can swim and play
In the old Ott-a-wan-na way

The songs were supposed to sound like real Indian songs with a *boom*-ba-*boom*ba rhythm, but they mainly sounded corny, and most of the kids couldn't sing at all, so they just shouted. For as much of the trip as I could, I shut my eyes and tried to look like I was sleeping, so I wouldn't have to talk to Patrick Dannehey or do anything.

When the train finally got to the last stop, I opened my eyes and looked out the window, but there was no camp or lake, just a station platform and some stores of a little town. From the train we all had to get in old yellow buses, which smelled like gasoline and sour sweat and throw-up. The ride was bumpy and kind of sickening, which made people stop talking and singing. The bus turned off the paved road and went through the woods for a while down a rutted dirt lane that came to a big clearing with a line of log cabins and behind them a big, shimmering lake.

Seeing the lake got the other kids excited again, and they started talking about camp things they knew and remembered from last year and the names of the cabins and the counselors. We were about the third bus in, and when it came time for us to get out, one of the counselors who helped get us onto the train stood on the bus steps and blew a loud whistle. He said his name really fast, but told us to call him either Kip or Mr. K. He told us we were all going to have a lot of fun, provided we did one thing, and that was to do what he told us to do, right away with no lip. He told us to get off the bus and form a circle around a log bench he pointed to. When we were all off the bus, standing around the bench with our suitcases, he looked at us for a long time and didn't say anything. Then he got up on the bench and turned slowly around, still not saying anything. He blew his whistle again, which was unbelievably loud, and said, "I hope we're not off to a bad start here. I hope we're not off to a bad start. Because it would be a very bad thing to get off to a bad start, because a bad start is a very bad thing." Somebody laughed, and Kip jumped down from the bench and went over in that direction. He looked mad. He was standing right in front of Patrick Dannehey. "Was that *you*?" he shouted at Patrick. "Did I say something *funny?*" I could see Patrick Dannehey say "no" but it didn't make any sound. "Well, I hope not," Kip said, and he clapped his hands down really hard on Patrick Dannehey's shoulders. "Because that would get us off to a bad start, and that would be a bad thing." I felt terrible looking at Patrick Dannehey's scared white face. I knew he wasn't the one who laughed, and that made me start to like him.

"We're off to a bad start," Kip said, "because you guys didn't listen to the one important thing I told you." I couldn't stand this. I wished I could turn completely invisible and pick up a rock and throw it at his head. "I told you to make a *circle* around this bench, and would anyone call this a *circle?*" He blew his whistle and clapped his hands, and kids started moving around trying to form a circle. Pretty soon everybody got the idea, and we were all standing in a pretty good circle. "Well what do you know," Kip said, "so it's true, chimpanzees really can learn." Some kids laughed, and Kip didn't mind. He looked like he was in a good mood now and told us the first thing we were going to do before we went to our cabins was to learn the Camp Ottawanna song.

Kip said, "Here's what we're going to do. I'm going to sing this song for you, one line at a time, and you are going to listen to it and remember it. Then I'm going to ask some *volunteers*"—he looked around the circle. "I'm going to ask some *volunteers* from last year to demonstrate how it goes, and then we're all going to sing. *Because*, my little monkey friends, nobody is going anywhere until we can sing Ottawanna Way by heart. Got that? No suppy, no beddy-bye until we sing it loud and clear. Okay!"

Kip said a line of the song in his talking voice, and then he sang it. When he was done, he sang the whole song through.

On the banks of great Lake Hathaway
Where chief Black Wing once came to stay
We will pitch our tent and stake our camp
In the old Ott-a-wan-na way.

At Ott-a-wan-na where we work and play
The weak go home but the strong ones stay
To greet the sun at the break of day
In the old Ott-a-wan-na way.

Undabunda dee, undabunda ray
Kowakumpa ree, kowakumpa kay
This is what the young braves say
In the old Ott-a-wan-na way.

And now you know our sacred song
And evermore can sing along
In joyful voices clear and strong
In the old Ott-a-wan-na way.

Kip sang the song in a loud goofy voice that wasn't really like singing, more like making fun of singing, and while he was doing it, I realized who he kept reminding me of—Wayne Stegner, my little league coach. It seemed like there was a certain kind of person, like Wayne Stegner or Kip or Lodi the German janitor in my school, who were in charge of kids or who worked around kids and everyone was supposed to like them because they wanted to be with kids. They all had that exaggerated way of acting and talking that kids were supposed to like but I never liked at all. Something, though, about that kind of person seemed to hypnotize a lot of kids, and they talked about people like Kip as if they were really funny or really great guys, even though they were actually pretty mean and sometimes got way too personal.

Our Youth Outreach minister at church was like that too, Reverend Klug. He was still partly in college, and you could see practically his whole scalp under the long strands of his hair, which made me wish he was just bald. Reverend Klug told all the kids in Youth Outreach that he believed God called him to work with us. He told Youth Outreach that we could tell him anything at any time and he would keep it to himself. Sometimes he was kind of interesting, like when he would tell us things he did when he was a kid in Duluth, Minnesota, but he wasn't very good at organizing us to do things or getting us to be quiet. It seemed like the main thing he wanted to do was talk to us while we sat and listened to him. Everything took him forever to explain before we could get up and actually do anything. Also, I didn't like looking directly in his face because he had some kind of extra lip behind his upper lip, and it would show a little when he said certain words. He wasn't very good at keeping us quiet, either. We would be fooling around, talking to each other while he was explaining something, and he would just stop talking and stare out at us, looking sad. I remember wondering what it felt like for him to be called by God to work with us in Youth Outreach. It was hard for me to picture, but it seemed to go with a lot of other church things like Sunday picnics and pancake breakfasts, which we went to but were never any fun. Almost everything about Reverend Klug made me want to get out of Youth Outreach as soon as I could.

We stayed in the circle and practiced singing Ottawanna Way about fifty times. Even after we knew it, Kip said it wasn't loud enough. He made us count off in threes, and had the ones and twos and threes sing it separately to see who could do it the loudest. By the end, everybody was practically screaming the words, so there was hardly any tune to it. Finally we were loud enough, and Kip led us over to our cabins so we could unpack and wash up before supper in Black Wing Lodge. My cabin was Laughing Bear, and there were twelve kids in it and six bunk beds. A big kid named Warren Keener was in charge of our cabin and had his own bed. Warren Keener was thirteen, and he got to be junior counselor by going to Camp Ottawanna for three years in a row and winning a bunch of Achievement Awards at the final Pow-Wow. Kip was in charge of Warren and the other junior counselors, but you could tell they were extra friendly and that he wouldn't make Warren do the kinds of things he would make the regular kids do. Kip told us Warren was our "lord and master" when we were in the cabin, and that if any of us gave him trouble, we would be spending time, he said, "with Mr. K.," and that we wouldn't enjoy it very much. Then he went away to the next cabin and left us with Warren Keener, who told us to form pairs and choose a bunk and decide who was on top and who was on the bottom. He said we had to keep our suitcases under the bed and out of sight and to keep our bed made all day and to leave the bathroom neat and clean. He said it should be "spotless." He said there were cabin inspections every now and then, and he wanted Laughing Bear to get a lot of Achievement Points, so we could win the special banquet, which was steak, on the last day of camp.

Warren Keener was tall and bony. His chest was caved in a little, and he slouched forward while he talked to us. He had dark hair in a short crew cut with a funny dent in the front. He didn't seem like a nice kid at all, even though he got chosen to be a junior counselor. He liked using dirty words like "piss" for peeing and "crapper" for the toilet. He told us things like, "We'll get along great if you don't give me any shit."

He told us to let him know if kids from the other cabins gave us any shit. He said sometimes there were midnight raids on the cabin from kids in other cabins. The purpose was to mess up your cabin and get away before anybody got caught. The other thing he said kids from other cabins might do is pants you when you were walking back to the cabin after Camp Fire or some other time when they could get away with it. Somebody asked what pantsing was, and Warren Keener said it was a kid holding you from behind while another kid pulled your pants down or even off. He said sometimes when you got pantsed they might goose your balls, sometimes not. He said most of the pantsing was for fun, and it helped keep up the competition between the cabins. He said the best way not to get pantsed was to stick together.

A big blond kid named Wally Kanicky said he would share a bunk with me and that he wanted the bottom. I said fine. We were supposed to take the things we needed from our suitcases, like our toothbrushes and toothpaste, and put them under our pillows, then to stow our suitcases under the bottom bunk so they wouldn't show during inspection. Nana's big blue suitcase was too big to fit under the bunk, so I asked Warren Keener what to do. He said "Fuckin A," and gave me a mean look. I had to keep looking at him, because I didn't know what to do with the suitcase. Finally he said, "Why'd you bring such a big suitcase?" and told me he didn't care what I did with it, just to put it somewhere.

That turned out to be the way everything was at Camp Ottawanna. Everything was supposed to be all set up on a schedule, which was out to the flagpole in the morning when the bugle went off, breakfast at the lodge, getting into our bathing suits and going to the lake for swimming practice and races, changing back into our clothes for field sports, then lunch, then back to the lake for sailing or kayaking lessons, then cabin hour, then to the ball fields for volleyball or softball, then supper, then Campfire, then either back to the cabin to bed or go somewhere for an overnight in a tent. After a day or two, I realized that each thing we did was terrible, and it wasn't going to get any better. The system was to make everything a little too hard or too rushed. For instance, when the bugle blew out at the flagpole in the morning, each cabin had to have every kid there in formation in ten minutes. This never worked, because some kids were so sound asleep they couldn't get moving even when someone pulled them out of their bunk onto the floor. Also there were only two toilet seats and two sinks in the bathroom, and everybody had to go and most kids wanted to brush their teeth, and there was no room, so most kids, including me, would go out and pee behind the cabin. I hated having to run out to the flagpole in my wrinkly clothes when the grass was still so wet my sneakers would get soaked through. Some kids were always late, and Kip would make them and sometimes their whole cabins do push-ups in the wet grass while everybody watched. Kids who made their cabins get push-ups would usually get pantsed on the way to breakfast.

The counselors worked it so that nothing could be fun or relaxing. The meals were terrible, especially breakfast, which was always the same, sour juice, cold toast, and eggs which were between scrambled and fried with streaky brown marks on them from the grill. They turned cold in your mouth, and there was no salt or pepper because when they used to have it, kids would unscrew the tops of the shakers so that the whole thing would come out on your food. I hated swimming the most, because it was right after breakfast when it wasn't really warm yet, and when it wasn't sunny, I would get so cold in the water my jaw would start shaking on its own, so I couldn't even talk. We'd have to start out swimming laps doing the crawl, breaststroke and backstroke, and then we'd have races against the other cabins, keeping score. There was a lot of screaming during the races, and if you didn't win your laps or fell behind during your lap of a relay, Warren Keener, who always had on dry clothes and a sweatshirt, would stand over you on the dock and say something like, "Thanks a lot, now we're in fourth" or "great speed." Some kids, like Wally Kanicky, could barely swim at all and were in a special beginners group during laps, but when races started everybody was supposed to swim for the cabin. Warren Keener would cheat every now and then by skipping Wally Kanicky and having some good swimmer go twice, but sometimes Wally had to swim, and Warren Keener would say something like, "Great, now we're in last," before Wally even started.

One of the main counselors, Mort Emerson, was in charge of all the boats, and when Kip introduced him the first day, he said Mort Emerson had been on a boat racing team in the Olympics. Mort Emerson was pretty serious and quiet, and he didn't seem to like teaching kids about sailing and kayaking. He talked in a quiet voice and kept the same expression on his face. He didn't seem actually mad, but you could tell he didn't really want to be around a bunch of kids, especially on the camp's big sailboat, The Ottawanna. Mort Emerson was really strict, and he meant it. He wouldn't let any kid sail by himself, even in one of the dinghies, until he could pass a test of boating terms and then prove he could tack, jibe, and land a boat without smashing the bow into the dock. This was actually pretty hard, so only about four kids got Sailing Privileges the whole time we were there. There was also kayaking, which seemed to me like it should have been simple, but Mort Emerson told us it was really dangerous, and that we had to learn safety techniques like rolling completely over underwater before we could take out a kayak by ourselves. In order to roll the kayak, we had to be strapped inside in a very complicated way, which I couldn't keep track of, and most of the kayaks were missing some strap or buckle or something, so almost no one got certified to kayak by himself. That actually disappointed me, because I liked the feeling of paddling the kayak through the water and it would have been nice to be able to take off somewhere.

The big treat in the boating program was supposed to be the day you got to sail out on Lake Hathaway in The Ottawanna. Starting the last few days of camp, each cabin got a turn, and even though I should have known better, I was kind of excited when it was time for Laughing Bear to go out. For one thing, The Ottawanna had a downstairs cabin with beds and sinks and cabinets and instruments built into the walls, and kids got to go "below" to see it. What I always liked best about ships in the pirate movies was that down inside they had big rooms with heavy dark furniture, like a house. The cabin of the Ottawanna was a little like that. All the woodwork and brass was polished and shiny, and it would have been nice staying down there, but something about being down out of the air while the boat was moving up and down made you automatically feel a little sick. Even if it didn't, we weren't allowed to stay down there or to do anything, just to look around. We were all supposed to do certain jobs on deck, things we practiced during boating instruction, like trimming the main sheet or raising the jib or setting the spinnaker. The afternoon of our sail was pretty windy, and none of us was strong enough to pull in the ropes that adjusted the sails by ourselves, so Mort Emerson had to step in and do practically everything. I mainly just stood there, holding onto a rope, feeling the boat dip down into a pocket then rising up to meet the wall of a wave, spraying me with cold water. As I stood there holding on and squinting at the shore, I kept thinking that if you took a picture of me and the other kids out on the lake sailing The Ottawanna, it would look exactly the way my mother pictured it when she decided to send me to camp, but thinking about mother only made me feel sad.

I don't think mother even believed in people like Warren Keener, people that mean. He wasn't mean every now and then or mean just to some kids. He was the kind of kid who tried to make you feel as bad as possible, no matter what it was about. If a kid got homesick and started to cry during cabin hour when the mail came, Warren Keener would go over to the kid's bunk and tease him. He'd say, "What's the matter? You miss mommy and daddy?" He'd keep going until the kid was really crying, until maybe the kid would start yelling swear words and swinging at him, and then he would jerk the kid around by the front of his shirt and tell him he was in big trouble. If Warren Keener was making fun of a kid, he tried to get other kids in on it, and some kids would join in, to get in good with Warren Keener for a while. Most kids, though, tried to stay away from him as much as possible. You just didn't want him to notice you, which was hard when he was with our cabin for most of the day.

You were supposed to be really excited and try really hard to get a lot of Achievement Points in everything, including inspections, swimming, boating skills, and crafts. The junior counselors reported each cabin's total Achievement Points at morning flagpole, but because Warren Keener was our junior counselor and got to give Laughing Bear's report, we pretty much stopped trying to get a lot of Achievement Points, which made Warren Keener start calling us "losers" when he talked to us after Lights Out.

Lights Out was really unfair, because the campers weren't supposed to be allowed to talk, only the junior counselor. But Warren Keener would get kids to talk by teasing them or by asking questions, and then, whenever he felt like it, he'd get mad at them and tell them he was reporting them to Kip. Sometimes he did report them, and they'd have to do push-ups or laps at morning flagpole, and sometimes he didn't. You never knew. Sometimes everybody was talking and laughing and screwing around after Lights Out, and Warren Keener wouldn't care. He would use really dirty words and let other kids use them, and this would get kids laughing, and it would get louder and dirtier until I had to go into a certain kind of trance. I hated talking and screwing around during Lights Out more than I hated anything else at the camp. At night in my bunk was the one time I had to make my pictures and tell my stories, but I couldn't do it with everyone making farting noises and Warren Keener saying your mother's this and your mother's that and getting kids to laugh at him. Whenever he felt like it Warren Keener could tell everybody to shut up and if they didn't, he said he would make sure something would happen to them on our next tent overnight.

Tent overnights were supposed to be where we learned camping and wilderness survival, but there was an old tradition where kids from a certain cabin were allowed to go out after Lights Out with their junior counselor and ransack the tents and scare the kids from the cabin that was camping out. Kip and the main counselors were in on it, and it was supposed to be fun because it was a tradition, but on our cabin's tent nights, some kids got into real fights. Weak kids got pantsed and tied up to trees, and some kids got their sleeping bags peed on. I think something bad happened to Patrick Dannehey on his cabin's first tent night, because a kid told me his parents drove up and took him home.

The final two days of camp were supposed to be the most fun. In the morning, instead of races and relays, there was free swimming. Kids who got certified in boating were allowed to take the sailing dinghies and kayaks out by themselves. Before supper on the second-to-last night was the Radio Show, which was supposed to be an actual program that went out over the radio in Wisconsin. Some of the cabins worked up skits, and kids who could play instruments or sing or do imitations performed at a big microphone in front of the whole camp. Before the show started, the kids in the audience had to practice clapping and laughing when the counselors held up a sign saying APPLAUSE or LAUGH. Almost from the time we sat down, kids started leaning over to other kids and saying it wasn't real, because the big microphone looked fake, and the headphones Kip was wearing didn't have wires connected to anything, but the kids went along with it, laughing and clapping when the signs went up. I couldn't understand what anybody was saying during the skits, and most of the kids who sang or played their instruments weren't as good as the kids at school. One kid was really good, though. He played a boogie-woogie on the piano, which was as good as an actual record. Toward the end of it, Kip stood up in front and made a big face and started clapping in rhythm to the boogie-woogie beat. Everybody joined in, but in my opinion it spoiled the song.

That night they put paper tablecloths on the tables for supper, and we got fried chicken. For the next-to-last Campfire everybody got marshmallows to toast in the fire, but the final Campfire was supposed to be the biggest tradition in the camp and people said that it made some kids cry. As I walked over to the fire pit from Black Wing, I wondered if they could actually do anything that would make me cry in a good way, but nothing like that happened. There were mainly a bunch of awards. You got a certificate for everything you did, for swimming, for boating, for softball, even if you didn't advance to a higher level. Kids got special awards for being the best in each thing. I had a feeling I might get the softball award, because I was one of the best players and was one of the captains, but I didn't get it. It went on and on, and even though you got up about every two minutes to get another certificate with your group, it was hard to keep paying attention and to keep clapping for everybody. When it was almost over, Kip gave special certificates and hunting knives to the junior counselors. Warren Keener went up to get his knife just like everyone else, and when he shook hands with Kip, he smiled and looked glad, just like a regular nice kid. It was like another awful thing he knew how to do. I knew that in a little while he would be lying close by in the dark after Lights Out talking about people's private parts.

Usually after Camp Fire the kids lined up behind their junior counselor, and he would turn on his flashlight and lead them back to the cabin. But the tradition for Last Camp Fire was for each kid to get his own candle, and Kip would light the junior counselor's candle, and the junior counselor would light the candle of the first kid in his line, and that kid would light the next kid's until everybody's candle was lit. Then they would walk single file through the trees singing *Fair Ottawanna.*

Though in the years to come
Our paths will surely stray
The sons of noble Dark Wing
Will softly make their way
Yes softly make their way
To our fair Ott-a-wan-na.

I held my candle out in front of me so I could see the path, and I tried to hear if anybody was crying. I hoped they weren't. I hoped that when I got back to the cabin and everybody was finally quiet, I could start thinking up things I could tell mother about the camp that wouldn't make her feel bad.

CARPOOL

T.D. Johnston

Charley Tolliver stepped past the dog bowls and into the middle of the kitchen. He scraped the flat of his black wingtip sole against the Spanish tile, back and forth, breaking the silence with the sound of sandy gristle. It was seven o'clock now. Nobody was home.

He opened the pantry door. Right, he thought. They're all hiding in here amongst the Chef Boyardee and the Del Monte and the high-fiber oatmeal packets.

Charley closed the pantry door and stood still again. If he strained hard enough, he might hear something, he thought. After ten seconds it occurred to him that the ringing in his right ear must be there all the time.

Where the hell were the dogs? Two Labrador retrievers don't ignore the presence of their master, or of each other, long enough to let a ringing go off in a man's ear for long. Especially not Sheff and Buster. Hell, the ringing probably came from those two knuckleheads in the first place. Normally the mere creak of the pantry door would have brought them barking and sprinting from the nether regions of the house, because the dog chow resided in the pantry.

Nobody was home. For God's sake, he thought.

Charley walked through the house one more time, his wingtips clomping loud on each of the sixteen wooden stairs. He entered the children's bedroom. The top and bottom bunks were made, the Winnie the Pooh and Tigger bedspreads perfectly aligned with the white side paneling of the bunk structure. *Naturally,* he thought. Julia wouldn't want to leave the house a mess instead of taking the time to call her husband at any of his *three* contact numbers to tell him that she's packing up the kids and the dogs and the hamsters and the fish and the bunny and there's Chef Boyardee in the kitchen so have a nice life, Charley.

He picked up a Leapster that had a game cartridge sticking out of the top. This one was Ashley's. Ashley would rather dive head-first into hot volcanic lava than go anywhere without her Leapster, Charley knew. He was comforted by the presence of the Leapster, and then even more so by the discovery of Kelly's Leapster next to a stuffed Eeyore on the girls' shared desk. Either Julia had not thought of the Leapsters in her rush to get the kids and the dogs and the fish and the hamsters and the bunny out of the house after making the bunk beds and not calling her husband with the news, or they weren't *really* gone. Maybe the dogs had to go to the vet for an emergency visit, and they'd all be traipsing back into the house with hot fried chicken from the drive-thru any second now. Maybe the dogs had an emergency. Sure! She didn't have *time* to call, because the dogs had an emergency.

Sure. And so did the fish and the hamsters and the bunny. Of course. Sure. And the feeling returned that he had been left alone, like a child counting to a hundred in a hide-and-seek game while the other kids are running away to watch TV and laugh at the sucker they left at the big oak tree.

Even Julia wouldn't do that, he thought. But the minivan was gone. No note. Just two Leapsters in the girls' room to say Julia wasn't perfect.

Charley walked swiftly through the master bedroom. Odd that the bed wasn't made, but he didn't have time for that right now, and he hurried back downstairs. Who could spend time looking at their own bed when their family was missing? Charley knew that he was a much better man than that, and checked the pantry one more time, peeking behind the hot water heater, before slamming the pantry door in agitation and heading for the TV room to—

He stopped in the marble foyer. The sound had come from the front door, as if beckoning him to check outside. But it was dusk now, the late September sun running away from the night. He did not want to check outside. After all, he had *begun* outside, hadn't he? He had pulled the Land Rover into the driveway at six-fifteen and the minivan wasn't there. What else was there to check outside, for Christ's sake?

He took another step toward the TV room and the doorbell rang. Charley froze. God, they could *see* him from out there, those stupid little useless windows framing the front door at night just so they can see in when you can't see out and God, oh God, what if it's the police and something's happened to Julia and the kids? The dogs too? And the fish and the hamsters and the....

It would not be the police. *Open the door*, a voice told him.

"I can't," he whispered. "I can't."

He left the foyer and continued on to the TV room, ignoring the ringing doorbell as someone obnoxiously kept pushing the damned thing and *please won't you just stop it I'm looking for my goddamned family won't you just give me a break?? Sell it somewhere else.*

Julia had left the TV on. She's definitely losing her touch, Charley thought. The volume was up, too. Funny, he thought, but the ringing in his right ear hadn't picked this up when he was in the kitchen. He glanced at the television screen in time to see a bathrobed man who had guest-starred on a million TV shows open the front door of his house and welcome a visitor. Charley recognized the disheveled, trenchcoat-clad visitor as Columbo from the old detective series he watched when he was a kid. But that did not matter now, not when he was searching for his family.

There were no Leapsters in the TV room, so Charley went back out to the foyer. He was relieved that the obnoxious doorbell ringer had given up and left, because he really needed to find Julia and the kids. It was time to check with the neighbors, just to see if anything suspicious had happened, maybe while they had been mowing their lawns or tending to their gardens.

He turned on the front porch light and peered outside through the stupid windows. He mused that they weren't so stupid when the front porch light was on.

There was nobody outside, at least not for as far as the porch light would illuminate. He considered removing his suit coat before going next door to the Hinmans', because they were casual people who couldn't wait to get out of their work clothes every day. Charley had never understood why Mark and Sarah Hinman always walked around the neighborhood barefoot at their age, but they did. Weird stuff, the Hinmans, but Julia liked them and was always going to their house to have a glass of wine when Charley was still at work and the kids were at soccer practice on somebody else's carpool day.

He decided to leave the suit coat on. If he had learned one thing in his years at the bank, it was that there was no such thing as being overdressed. Mark and Sarah Hinman had every right to do as they wanted in a free country, but the sensible thing to do when you were market vice president was to err on the side of being overdressed. He straightened his paisley tie, the one Julia was always calling a relic of the eighties, and ventured out onto the porch and down the steps to the brick walk.

Two spotlights switched on as the motion detectors did their jobs and Charley could see to cross through an opening between the Leland cypresses dividing the Tolliver and Hinman properties.

He rang the doorbell, re-straightening his tie. Julia wouldn't go anywhere without the Hinmans knowing about it. Especially not with the kids, the dogs, the hamsters, the bunny and the fish. Maybe she was even here right now. Except for the minivan, of course. The damned minivan.

Charley heard what sounded like mild argument from inside. Muffled, like angry whispers. They know something, he thought. They *know* where they've gone. And not even the consideration of a phone call, knowing that I'm pulling my hair out with worry over there…Talk about taking sides. Neighbors should choose neutrality, for God's--

The door opened. Mark Hinman stood there with a Heineken in his right hand and gave Charley the same goofy grin he always did.

Charley wasn't buying it.

"Evening, Mark," Charley offered.

"Why, Charley! What a pleasant surprise. Sarah! It's Charley Tolliver! Come in, Charley. Please come in. Can I get you a beer? Glass of chardonnay? I know you go back and forth."

Charley marched past Hinman and into the dimly-lit living room. He looked left and right and turned back to face Hinman.

"*I* go back and forth, Hinman? *I* go back and forth? You and your wife have been keeping secrets with Julia for months. *Months!* And now she's missing. Julia and the kids and the dogs and--"

"My God, man!" exclaimed Hinman, setting his Heineken down on the living room coffee table. "Missing? How do you mean? Sarah! Come quick!"

A door opened down the hall, and Sarah Hinman entered the room in bare feet and an oversized white tee-shirt that made her look like she wasn't wearing anything on the bottom.

"Charley! What a pleasant surprise! How's--"

"I'm not here to play nice, Sarah. You can stop pretending that you didn't expect to hear from me tonight. Julia and the girls aren't home. I was just wondering....if you saw anything strange today."

"Well, Charley," Sarah said, her face registering what Charley thought was a creditable attempt at surprise. "Maybe they went to soccer practice?" Nice, the way she said it as a question. Charley was disgusted at such pretense. He had never cared for it, socially or otherwise.

"They *did* go to soccer practice, Sarah. She had the carpool today, so I guess she didn't manage to be here downing shots with you and Mark and God knows who else you conveniently invite to your little shindigs. But she should've been home by six. I came home to an empty house, and, and--"

"Charley, why don't you sit down," Sarah said. "Can we get you a beer? Or..."

There it was. She shot a look at Hinman there. The briefest of quick, just the dartiest of a flick, but she sure did, Charley knew. They *know*.

"Look," Charley said, hands in pockets, trying to look calm. "They're not home. The *dogs* aren't home. She even took the aquarium. The bunny. The bunny's cage. Seven *hamsters*, for Christ's sake. She's left me, and I think you know why. So yes, Sarah, I accept your gracious offer. Beer sounds good."

Sarah Hinman nodded and left the room. The ensuing silence was awkward, as Charley risked a glance at Hinman.

"Where are they, Mark?" Charley asked. "I know you know."

Hinman shifted uneasily, taking a long look in the direction of the kitchen.

"Charley, I don't know what you think I know. We only had the occasional drink with your wife. Only when the kids had soccer practice. That's all, Charley. I'm sorry they're not there. I really am. But I'm going to say one thing without Sarah in the room. I'm sorry about Julia and the kids not being home, but it *really* gets to my wife when you talk about us as if we're lushes. You've talked that way about us for months, to anyone who will listen. You think it doesn't get back to us?"

Silence hovered expectantly. Charley mulled a response, but decided to take the high road and say nothing. Hinman was in denial was all.

"We're *not* lushes, Charley. A couple of drinks a night. We're not the reason your family's not at home, Charley. I think you know that. You've known that for a long time. Maybe if you—oh, here's Sarah with that beer for you, Charley."

Hinman stepped back, as if Sarah really needed five feet of space to give her neighbor a cold beer. They were acting strangely indeed, Charley thought. He accepted the Heineken and found a seat on the tan leather sofa facing the Hinmans' stacked-stone fireplace.

"Mind if I sit down?"

"Not at all," said Hinman.

The Hinmans did not sit down. They were hiding something, and Charley was going to get to the bottom of it, no matter how rude they could get with a couple of rounds in them.

"Look. I'm only asking you to help me here. They've gone somewhere. Julia didn't even leave a note. No phone call. Not even an email, for God's sake. A text message. *Nothing*. And I think it has something to do with her little visits here. I can't tell you the times I've come home, and the minivan is right there in the driveway, the kids are at soccer practice, and is my wife home doing anything productive? No. Of course not. She's over here. You don't want me to call you lushes, Hinman. That's fine. But you turned my *wife* into a lush, and God knows what else. And now she's packed up the kids, the dogs, the bunny, the hamsters, even the goddamned *fish*, and not even the courtesy of a simple note. Even just 'Have a nice life, Charley. You can keep the dog bowls.' *Nothing*."

"Charley, if you'd just listen to reason, maybe we could help you figure this out," Hinman said, but Charley knew he didn't mean it. They had certainly been Julia's closest counsel, meddling in another family's business when *nothing* was their business on their side of those goddamned Leland cypresses.

"The way you helped Julia figure it out?" Charley spit the words out and took a long swig from the green bottle.

"That's uncalled for and you know it." Hinman took a step toward the front door. "I'm a patient man, but I have my limits. Get out of my house."

"Mark!" Sarah Hinman gasped. "Please!"

"No, Sarah, there will be no more pleases. No more 'Try to understand where Charley's coming from' and 'Try to understand how people cope' and all that crap. *Charley* needs to understand where he's coming from. Don't you, Charley. And then go in another direction. Here's some free advice for you, jackass. Be the--"

"Mark! Please!" Sarah turned and ran from the room. Her oversized tee shirt hunched upward as she went. Charley noticed that she was indeed wearing something on her bottom, and was relieved that she wore something on her bottom at this hour. What with Julia being here about now on so many evenings.

Hinman pursued his point, moving closer toward the front door.

"You see what you're doing to my wife? Do you, Charley? Before I hit you in the ass with this door, I'm going to give you that free advice. Won't even charge you interest. That's a term you understand in your profession, isn't it? Be the banker, Charley. Be the banker. Do the calculation. Check the repayment schedule, jackass."

Charley tried to swallow the lump in his throat. The man's staggering insensitivity was....was....He could not cry in front of Hinman. Hinman might even tell Julia, and then she'd really have the upper hand. If she wasn't gone forever, of course, and if she didn't take the children to forever with her.

Hinman pressed on. "Whatever the damned hell you people do all day. You say we turned your wife into a lush, Charley? Check your precious compound interest, man. It's being compounded daily. You're the one who's paying it, Charley. Not us. Now get out of my house. *Now.*"

Hinman opened the door and stood aside, waving his left hand toward the gaping darkness.

Charley stood, raising a shaking green bottle to his lips, sipping at the lip of the bottle but getting only loud oxygen, moving toward the rectangular hole, passing through it into the night, hearing the door close but not slam behind him as he stumbled in the direction of the Leland cypresses.

When he reached the front yard, he looked back at the driveway, illuminated by the motion-detection spotlights that dutifully went to work upon his return.

The minivan was not there. Julia had not had a change of heart. No epiphany. No sudden thought that the children loved their daddy, would miss him terribly, awfully, all day at school, pining for their father as their lives were ripped to shreds in a single momentary lapse of judgment by their mother.

Back in the house, he checked the TV room again. It wasn't tuned to Nickelodeon. Boomerang? No. Cartoon Network? Stop it! *Stop it!*

Charley went upstairs and brushed his teeth. He allowed himself one defiance of Julia's rules, and skipped the floss.

He removed his suit jacket and tossed it onto the chaise in the corner. That was two, he thought. If she wanted him to floss and to hang up his clothes and put his socks in the hamper, she would just have to come home and quit this nonsense of being gone. If not for him, then for the kids. Kids needed a daddy to protect them, didn't they? Didn't they?

He stood and looked at the bed. He wondered whether anybody else of his gender had ever been in it. Whether anybody else who had ever been in it might be in the minivan right this minute with Julia and the kids and Sheff and Buster and....

Maybe they arranged to hook up for the trip at pickup time at soccer practice. Leave Somebody Else's car there and just drive off in the minivan and go to California or Canada or the Carolinas or wherever until Julia wakes up one day and says there are flings and there are real things and Julia's real thing and my kids' real thing is a market vice president waiting for Mommy to have the epiphany and bring the minivan home. Please, Mommy. Bring the minivan home.

He climbed into bed and set the alarm for six like he always did. He was about to pull the chain on the light when he remembered that maybe she called while he was at the Hinmans'.

He got out of bed and went downstairs, half expecting the dogs to follow him in a cacophony of excitement about the prospect of a treat or some leftovers. In the kitchen, he grabbed a pen and the pad of Post-Its, though of course he realized that if Julia left a message he would remember it. But you never knew. You never knew.

The machine reported that there were no new messages and said 'First Saved Message' before Charley hurriedly pressed the Off button.

He re-checked the incoming mail box in the plastic mail sorter Julia bought and put next to the phone when she was feeling particularly anal one day. He had forgotten to bring today's mail in tonight, so all that was in the sorter next to the phone was the power bill and the cards from his dad and mom and his brother and Julia's sister and her God-forsaken mom and dad and all those people from the church, and that big manila envelope from State Farm.

He knew he needed to try to sleep, even though it was only 8:15 and he usually checked the Now Playing list on the DVR right about now. If he went to bed early, he'd get almost ten hours. Enough to go on to forever tomorrow, contact the authorities, drive around, everything, because after all, he had rights. He had rights. She would have to come home. He had rights. The minivan would have to come home because he had rights and children need their daddies.

"They need their Daddy," he whispered hoarsely, and returned upstairs. Back in bed, he pulled the chain and the night went dark.

* * *

The alarm woke him at six. He stretched his legs, pushing them straight ahead past the foot of the bed to wake up every muscle and sinew and tendon. He hated the arrival of this time of year. There was no light in the morning. No light and no stars and no moon. Just pre-dawn blackness.

Quietly, he got out of bed and tiptoed into the bathroom. He took a quick shower, and shaved before brushing and flossing his teeth to make sure the nighttime plaque couldn't build up. He tiptoed on into the walk-in closet, where he put on fresh boxers, a white tee-shirt and black socks, followed by the sky-blue dress shirt with the white collar. He chose a paisley tie because he secretly enjoyed the ribbing he always took from Julia, the one about the relic of the eighties.

He put on a charcoal suit, and his favorite black wingtips, and tiptoed back through the master bedroom, not risking a glance at the bed because then he might wake her to make up the fun way and he didn't have time.

He was behind on the big loan to First Merchants, so he grabbed a cereal bar from the pantry and headed directly out the front door. On the porch he stopped when the motion detectors did their jobs, bathing him in white light. He really should pay that damned power bill, he thought. Pay it online and just get it over with.

He went back inside and grabbed the power company envelope. He considered opening the big one from State Farm, but he didn't have time, and besides, the premiums had probably gone up and they were killing a million more freaking trees just to give customers the bad news. The bastards. What a freaking racket.

He was at work by seven, beating the outer-belt traffic before the rest of the suckers were even out of bed. He opened his email, and sent a quick message to Sheila to please put the call through if his wife called, but otherwise he needed to work on the First Merchants loan and should not be disturbed.

One quick trip to the coffee station and he would be in good shape for a productive day. He considered leaving a quick voicemail at home that he'd be happy to do the soccer carpool tonight. Especially if it meant she would shut up with that nonsense about doing it all herself. But the lesson of being realistic, the cornerstone of banking after all, was that one should not promise what one cannot deliver. Julia could do the carpool.

Sheila would put the call through if Julia needed his help. Hell, the Hinmans ought to be able to do it. Maybe just this *once*, just this once, they could be real neighbors.

"When hippos fly," he muttered, and opened the First Merchants file, certain that if he could close the loan by four he could call Julia and let her off the hook.

He had been meaning to video the kids at soccer anyway. Like the Kodak commercials used to ask with that old Paul Anka song....how did that damned thing go anyway? Do you remember....something like that....*do you remember, baby? Do you remember the times of your life?*

Something like that. Cool song, kind of sentimental, and he found Year Four on the amortization schedule, because problems were made for solutions, and solutions were made for problems, and round and round we go.

"Round and round we go," Charley Tolliver whispered, and stood up to go make the morning coffee.

BURGLAR BOY WE NEED YOU

Paul Michel

If you're going to get into the habit of telling stories on yourself, you want to be careful about what you're putting in and leaving out. Also you want to make sure they're true, or mostly so, and that you completely understand the difference when they're not. Otherwise you risk misrepresenting yourself. Or worse.

I'm thinking of Alma, a woman I was dating recently. She isn't what you'd call my type. Generally I date library wallflowers and shy outdoors gals; women that are genuinely surprised when you ask them out. They always wear glasses. Always. I've known three that I might have married, but all of them turned me down, one just this past Christmas. So my self-confidence is not at an all-time high when a new woman appears in my building this past June, riding the same elevator as I do many mornings. She gets off at the seventh floor, all of which is leased by a television advertising company, where it turns out she is a production assistant. I smile at her every day and continue on up to nine, where I am a bookkeeper for a fish importing company. I don't eat fish. I've been sitting at the same desk and counting them, more or less, eight hours a day for the past nineteen years, and the thought of eating one of the slimy bastards turns my esophagus inside out. Funny, huh?

I've risen as far in the company as a bookkeeper can rise. Unless something dramatic occurs I'm thinking that I'll probably work here until I retire. The pay is decent. The benefits are generous. The people are friendly enough. My cubicle has a window facing a parking lot and two buildings of a community college across the street, between which I see a narrow slice of a green campus thick with trees and flying Frisbees. My days are neither long nor short. It's a life.

But I was talking about Alma. She doesn't look like the sort of woman who speaks to guys like me, not unless she's a clerk at a fancy boutique store where I'm struggling to buy something nice for a female that I don't understand —I mean the "something" I am buying, but then I rarely understand the girls I'm shopping for, so I mean both I guess. She dresses the way I would expect an advertising production assistant would be had I ever thought about it, which I haven't. Her shiny hair is nearly black, and falls halfway down her back like a shawl of fine silk. Her make-up is perfect, her smile is bright, her figure is ample but not fat. Her skin is dusky and soft. She does not wear glasses. Her eyes are an iridescent green. Later I learn that she is fifteen years my junior, and that she was born abroad, in what was Yugoslavia then, but she moved when she was an infant. But I don't know that about her for several weeks. I am too shy to introduce myself. But whenever I see her at the elevator I smile. I blush when I do, because she is lovely to look at, and I am not. She always smiles back.

One day I speak to her. I don't plan to. I am at least as surprised as she is to hear my voice.

--Two more floors and it's a whole different world, I say.

She smiles more broadly than I've seen before.

--Where you are the lord and master over all?

I do not expect this. That is, I hardly expect any reply, let alone one that is, what? Witty? Spontaneous? Flirtatious, even? I am too stunned to answer. The doors open, she laughs and theyslide shut behind her. I think about her that night. The next morning we exchange a few words. The following Monday we meet for coffee. Next it's drinks after work on a Friday. Soon we are sleeping together. I see this all happen like I'm watching an old B movie in an empty theater. The acting is bad, the plot is implausible, the directing is clunky, yet I can't pull my gaze away. We have almost nothing to talk about. We have incredible sex, and we go to a lot of movies and decent restaurants, but when we sit across a table from each other it's as if we lack a common language. Sentences trail off midway. Jokes fall flat. References do not resonate. Simply sharing a drink can be excruciating.

Yet we persevere. Two, three, sometimes four nights a week. I don't know what she does with her remaining evenings. I tend to stay home and lose myself in a book. A fire is nice, if the weather is right. And in the summer after dark, an open screen window can be like a doorway to a mysterious universe we know only by scent and memory. I try to explain this to Alma. She smiles nervously, her green eyes blinking fast. It strikes me that I don't understand this woman at all; indeed that I barely know her, and vice versa. And yet for no reason I can explain I begin to feel protective of her, bordering on defensive. I find myself making up conversations with friends and relatives in which I am insisting that yes she is the right girl for me, that despite our differences we are connected at some deeper level. These manufactured debates leave me tired and ill-tempered. I can't convince myself, even. Still we continue to see each other.

Then one night I go to her place, and she is upset. I am concerned, yet relieved. Something to talk about! I press her—What happened? What's wrong? What can I do? Her story is remarkable: she left a lunchtime restaurant earlier that day without paying for her meal. It was not an oversight. She'd arranged to meet a friend, who, once Alma was settled and ordered a cup of tea, had called to cancel with a perfectly legitimate excuse. Alma decided to have lunch anyway, and to read a book she'd tucked providentiallyinto her oversized purse. That's when things began to go downhill. The tea water was tepid. The service was terrible. The waiter brought her a Monte Cristo instead of a Reuben and wouldn't exchange it because the cook had stepped out. Then he actually asked her to finish up and leave when she still had a cup of tea and some chips on her plate she intended to eat. He said they had to close up, and it wasn't even three. So when he went back to the kitchen, she simply left without paying. Now she is wracked with guilt and remorse.

"Wracked" is not a verb I use lightly. She weeps profusely. Her body convulses, her chest heaves, her skin is hot and red with shame. I try to comfort her. She shakes her head, holds her hands over her ears, buries her head in my lap, and then turns her back on me. She is not to be consoled. She has robbed someone, she says. She has no excuse, she had no right, she is no better than a common criminal. She will return tomorrow and pay for her meal, with interest. But no—she could never face the man again, after what she has done. She is miserable and afraid.

What is remarkable to me is the depth and sincerity of her remorse. It has a curious frisson to it, like an overwrought vignette from a nineteenth century play. In this day and age, to regret something as insignificant as ripping off an insolent greasy spoon! There is an almost sexy innocence to her posture. I am fascinated by her despondence. I try my best to cheer her up.

I say this, then that—the predictable things. Suggestions of perspective, of humor, of fatalism. Nothing works. At one point I utter a vapid banality I'd sworn never to employ, but like my initial attempt at elevator humor, it slips out on its own:

--It's just not that big a deal, I say.

Her swollen eyes flash. She flips her hair back over her shoulder. This is an easy thing to say, she fairly sneers, when one is innocent. How, she demands, can I understand a feeling that I've never had?

So I tell her about the time I robbed the drug dealer. It's a true story and a good one, with no need for embellishment, though as I spin it out I realize that I'm tilting things a way that never had occurred to me before. Not that it's a tale I tell often. It's not a memory I'm proud of.

I'd just arrived in Seattle with my girlfriend from back east. We had shitty jobs and little money, so we couldn't be too picky about who shared our rent. We fell in with Rod and Tina, a couple of Midwesterners like us. We all lived together in a moldy two-story rental near Greenlake. Tina was a drug dealer. Cocaine mostly, but any number of other products passed through her hands as well, with stops for weighing, sampling and packaging at our dining room table. Rod grew marijuana in a room he'd built behind a fake wall in the basement. It was creepy and scary, but we were young and naïve enough, at least for a few weeks, to confuse creepy with cool and scary with new and different. Then they threw a couple of parties of the sort we'd never have been invited to if we hadn't lived there. People carried guns. Fistfights went outside. Women wept hysterically. All-night card games changed fortunes and made drunk men mean.

That's when we decided to move.

Three nights before we left, another fight broke out. I have no idea what the issue was, as only a couple of punches were thrown and a few insults shouted, and I was upstairs out of sight. Cool heads prevailed quickly and the whole small, stoned group went off to a bar near the freeway to play pool. When I passed through the downstairs I saw that the dining room table bore witness to the drama. Tina's scales and business ledger sat amidst a dozen empty beer bottles, a calculator and a newspaper folded around a fat envelope full of bills. I didn't even pause. I took the newspaper and envelope together. I counted the money in a bathroom stall in a bar on Aurora Avenue. A little more than three thousand dollars. I was making four bucks an hour, part-time, at an offset printing shop near Lake Union. I didn't have the money for the deposit on our new place. Okay, enough sob story. I wanted the money to buy good beer and dope and live it up for a while. And I did.

I tried hard to feel bad. I just couldn't muster it up. No one ever accused me or even suspected me as far as I know. Tina and her friends were all dealers,all paranoid, and they all mistrusted each other. She and Rod split up within months of our moving out. I'd burned through the money long since by then, with nothing even close to a pang of guilt. Maybe an itch, once or twice. But never a pang.

That's the big thing I change in the story. I tell Alma straight about taking the money, but then I tell her how I've tortured myself with shame and regret,though I've learned to see my little lapse in context as a lesson rather than a lifelong reproach. Oh, I say all kinds of stuff. Anything I can think of to stop the tears and swing her mood. After a while it appears to work. Her sobbing slows to sniffling. She wipes her eyes. She studies me. *Three thousand dollars?* She shakes her head. *You just took it? Weren't you scared? What if they'd seen you?* I shrug. There was no chance of being caught red-handed, I say. I was in the house alone. She laughs.

You're amazing.

That night we have great sex. Really great. I don't like sharing details, but let's just say that we do things I've only read about, and then some. Three separate times, while we're resting, wasted and wrung out on her damp sheets, she makes some reference to my story. *Three thousand dollars,* she says once. *Still waters,* she mutters next, and I know she's talking about my—Heist? Theft? I've never put a noun on it before. No nice ones come to mind. I go to the bathroom, and when I come out we do it standing up against the wall by the door. *My burglar boy,* she whispers just before her climax, which she announces with a full-throated holler I expect the neighbors on both sides can hear, and probably upstairs and downstairs too. I spend the night, which I've done only once before. She makes me breakfast. I look up from my eggs and she's smiling at me over the top of her coffee cup. I blow her a kiss and try to lose myself in the Sunday crossword. I can feel her watching me.

We don't see each other for a week. I'm busy at work with mid-year reports. Alma drives out to Pasco to visit her great aunt in a retirement home. When we get back together, at a new Chinese place near my place on Friday, she is subdued. I ask her if anything is wrong, and her quick denial is unconvincing. For a while we slip back into one of our awkward routines, eyes not meeting, busy with our chopsticks, as quiet as an old married couple. Out of nowhere I get it into my head to tell another story. It's a true one, but like the drug money tale I dress it up a little.

It's about stealing again, shoplifting this time, a phase my high school crowd went through in sophomore year. I hardly was a ring leader, in fact the whole caper drove me nuts with my constant certainty that we'd be caught and sent to some distant rural prison where burly, tattooed guards would abuse our rectums and mold us into hardened killers. In fact no one was caught, and we stole and resold enough blue jeans, coats and purses to stuff our pockets with twenties and rescue us for a while from the stinging poverty of allowance and babysitting money. It was strictly a tenth grade phenomenon. When we returned in junior year we didn't even discuss (or admit to) such infantile shenanigans.

I wasn't one of the actual shoplifters. I was deemed too jumpy and obvious to work the floors. My role was merely as a lookout, stationed at the big glass doors of whatever department store we'd targeted, or sometimes at the top of the escalators, scanning the aisles for security guards, watching the clerks and managers, poised to give the signal to abort should anything seem amiss. Thank god I never had to give it. We'd decided that, should I need to alert the sticky fingers in the racks, I would scream, falling to the ground, faking a crippling cramp in my leg. We figured that no one would be suspicious. That's one of the parts I don't mention to Alma.

I become something of a ring-leader in this new version; the one with the connections—"fences," I actually say the word—to turn the stuff over. In fact I was unknown in the criminal underworld. Left to my own devices I probably would have stashed the stuff in the back of my closet and worried myself nauseous about it. Hell, I'd probably still have it. As I hop-scotch over the details Alma perks up like a flower in a water glass. She laughs and sips her Cosmo. *You never*, she says, her eyes shining, unaware of how close to the truth she veers. I shrug. *Teen age mischief*, I say. Her foot touches my leg under the table. *Let's get out of this place*. I wake in the morning with the tracks of her teeth in my flesh.

A pattern is in place now, and I follow it like a tailor. We part, we meet, she is listless and/or sad, I tell her a story that is nearly true, she goes into heat like a lioness, we part again. At what point, you reasonably may ask, does a right-minded man complain about such an arrangement? It's a difficult question, I admit.

Easter approaches. She wants me to have dinner with her family. It seems a reasonable request. Not that we're "serious," necessarily, but I am having sex with this woman, if little else, several times a week, and I'm flattered that she wants me to meet her kin. Of course, I tell her. What should I bring? She shakes her head, her long hair dancing, though her eyes are dull. We've just met for drinks after work, and I haven't told any tales yet. Her mother, she insists, would be offended if I brought anything, even wine. Flowers? Yes, flowers are fine. Sunday at three. She has ordered red wine. Her glass sits untouched. I am ransacking my memory closets for the skeleton of a story.

--I was thinking, I say, about the time I got fired working as a vendor at a football stadium.

She cocks her head and lifts one brow. Already I see a sparkle deep in her sea-green eyes. As for the story, I'm on my own now. I make it a good one, in which I end up with a case of stolen beer and a wad of extra cash I haven't exactly earned. We spend the night at a nearby motel, our passion too urgent to endure the short drive home.

I wear a suit to dinner. I'm glad I do, as everyone is dressed up as if for a wedding. Alma has five brothers, all older. Her father has passed away, but present also are her mom, two aunts and a deaf and blind grandmother who lives in an overstuffed chair in a small dark room down the hall, in front of a television turned up louder than an ambulance siren. The brothers are tall, dark and big-boned. They look like mercenary fullbacks. Mom is petite and high-strung, and like the sons she has a Slavic accent. Just hearing it makes me feel exotic and adventurous, like I have stepped out of my small world and into the large one I really belong in. One of the brothers greets me with a glass of some clear, strong alcohol I have never tasted. Everyone hugs me. I am relieved.

We sit on straight chairs in a small, cramped living room. Although the day is warm there is a holiday blaze in the fireplace, lending a sauna-like feel to the gathering. My drink goes immediately to my head. I barely can follow the small talk, which seems to be about cars, cars, cars, cars of all kinds, bought, sold, traded and desired. It seems that cars are the brothers' business. I smile and try to look interested. One of them freshens my drink. I hope that dinner is served soon.

There is a pause in the conversation. The oldest brother, Vic, also is the tallest. He has short, curly hair so black it nearly glows. One of his eyes is half-closed, the result of some injury and its scarring. He nods at me, as though to say it is now my turn.

--So, my friend, he says, we hear that you are a thief.

The other men roar with laughter. Everyone leans forward. The spotlight is on me.

Alma has told them everything. They know details, some of which I do not clearly recall myself, about each half-invented adventure of my supposedly misspent youth. I hardly can believe that the person they are talking about is me. They ask questions, seek elaborations. They laugh as I oblige them, tossing their big heads back like bison, causing glasses to rattle on the table in the next room. Alma beams. I believe I've handled the situation well.

Dinner is served. There is no talk of me at the table, and I find myself beginning to relax. I'm not entirely happy that my fanciful stories were shared, but then it's not as if I'm going to see much more of these people. I'm starting to get tipsy, which is not something I'd planned on, but now that the process is underway I privately resolve to enjoy it. I feel like I've passed a test.

After dessert their mother goes to bed, and immediately one of the brothers opens a bottle of cognac. Another produces a deck of cards, crisp and new, with a back pattern of a painting reproduction: three clumps of gaudy, golden lilies in front of a purple pond. We are to play poker, specifically hold'em, a game I've seen on TV but barely understand. There is no refusing them. Drinks are poured, cards are dealt. The stakes are low, dimes and dollars. I sense that this is a friendly game with a newcomer, but that in my absence real money would be at risk. After a couple of hands in which I fold nervously, studying the play to try to get some sense of how least to embarrass myself, I am dealt two aces, with another on the flop, along with two queens. I am able to keep the betting alive long enough that when I do win it's a moment of real triumph. The brothers laugh and cheer. More drinks are poured. I feel a rush of adrenaline as though I've just bench-pressed a Volkswagen. On the next deal I start with a ten/jack pair and on the flop I'm one king short of a straight. I get it on the turn and rake in the chips while the brothers hoot and groan.

It goes on like this. I could not hand-pick better hands than the ones I'm dealt. When my cards are bad—or even average—I fold and sit quietly, realizing that I'm a good deal drunker than I intended to be. When they are good I play with a swagger and smirk that even I find amusing as my winnings grow and the clock ticks past midnight. Finally I have wiped out the last brother, Michael, and I am sitting at one end of the table amidst a ridiculous heap of chips, coins, bills and goofy IOUs promising houses, yachts and first-borns. Vic went out early, and has spent the evening watching me. He smiles as I pocket my winnings. The brothers groan and curse congenially as they pay their actual debts. Alma is asleep on the sofa.

Then suddenly, without warning, they are telling stories. I don't know who starts it, but soon all five of them are fully on board. I gather that this is some sort of ritual; a thing to do in that quiet time after the drinks and the boy games; a safe space to talk about a time that Alma has not mentioned to me, and that I would not have guessed about the brothers on my own. They tell stories of their homeland, twenty years old and more, stories from another time and place. They are horrible stories. They speak easily—or so it seems to me—of men killed, buildings torched, women maimed, children slaughtered, villages razed. They spare no details. You fairly can smell the scorched flesh and forests as they speak. There is no joy in their telling. Indeed, they weep and wring their hands. They offer no explanations, no justifications, though limp, pale excuses are dropped like fruit peels along the way: We were soldiers. We were zealots. We were drunk. We were young.

They sit silently, shaking their heads, which are heavy with the weight of their remorse. Alma is awake now. She weeps too. From the dark room down the hall we hear the roar of the television, a crime drama in full throat, guns blazing, bombs bursting, Grandma's musty air alive with the screams of the wounded. I look beseechingly at Alma, then at the door. Mercifully, she catches my drift. It will be nearly an hour drive back to her place, and I am looking forward to the time to talk through what has happened. Within less than a minute we are parked on the side of a road in the puddle of shadows between the glare of two streetlights. She is astride me in the passenger seat. Her mad cries rend the deep suburban night.

--Burglar boy, she sighs when we are spent. Welcome to the family.

We drive home in silence like usual, with the radio turned low to a country station. I keep my questions to myself. I don't want to mingle the brothers' dark memories with the immediacy of our lovemaking. She drops me at my place, and I don't see or even hear from her for three days. I begin to put the brothers episode behind me. Then I get a call from Vic. He wants to go bowling, me and the boys, maybe some other friends they know. Alma might drop by, but she doesn't like bowling alleys—says they hurt her ears. Tomorrow night. I will come, yes? I say I will. The truth is I don't get a lot of invitations to go out to bowling sorts of things. Other than dates with Alma I tend to go to meetings, sessions, workshops, birthdays and funerals. If entertainment happens, so be it, but it's never the chief reason for leaving the house. I forget, or refuse to remember—isn't that the same thing?—the surreal and disturbing night just last weekend. Bowling? Hell, it sounds like fun.

So does surf fishing, a baseball game and an afternoon of sweaty volleyball at one of our few sandy beaches. Soon I am accompanying the one or more of the brothers, usually Vic, on these outings and more. And it is fun, all of it. Alma is there, or she isn't. There is no further mention of the war. No one mentions the old days, no one says anything political. Apart from that one weird night it seems they've put their pasts behind them, and it seems fair to me to do the same. It's pretty cool hanging out with them. I start wearing suits to places I'd never have even thought of. I find myself sitting in cocktail lounges, more often than taverns, in an unfamiliar but comfy slouch, my legs parted wide, nodding in time to whatever music is playing, holding a bottle or glass in one hand at my crotch and gesturing with it, back and forth, in a way that almost, but doesn't, make me laugh. That first evening recedes in my memory like a man walking away on a long, straight road. Spending time around these guys is like being twenty-five again. I begin to drink a lot. I start smoking again, a habit I kicked a decade ago. I shave less often. I miss work sometimes, after late nights with the family. I'm having a ball.

Though the brothers don't talk about their pasts, they still ask me about mine. They love my stories. They buy me drinks and pry them out of me. I'm coy and modest, particularly as I'm constructing full-on fabrications now, without a nod to any cornerstone of truth. I'm not just an ex-thief but a fighter as well, a gambler, a con man and perhaps other things, this last just a hint, but I learn to leave dark holes in my stories, places where a man might vanish or worse. Their faces glow as they listen. Vic slaps my back and buys me drinks that taste like liquorish and rubbing alcohol. They sing a song in their language, their harmonies deep and rich, pausing to toast me between verses, glasses held high in the air. I raise my own to meet them.

I know this is not real. I know that these are not my people, and that this life fits me as poorly as a shirt two sizes large. But Alma and I continue to light up the summer evenings, and the brothers continue to treat me as one of their own. I go to concerts, to parties, to boat shows and picnics. I pretty much lose track of myself for a while. That's the best way I can describe it. Even now.

No doubt you see what's coming.

Alma shows up at my apartment one night after midnight. As soon as I hear my spare key in the door I know what she will say, and how this strange summer has brought us to this point. I think I knew it the night I told her about the drug money. I think everything since then has been like reading from a script. She slips into bed next to me. *Burglar boy*, she whispers. *We need you.*

Vic is in trouble. He owes a man money. Twelve thousand dollars. Alma does not say why. Threats have been made. Cars have been driving slowly past the house. Another brother has taken Vic out the back door and to a motel up in Lynwood. He can't stay there forever. And yet he can't leave without the money, which he doesn't have. He asked Alma to see me. He trusts me. He loves me like one of his own. He knows I will not let him down.

She is undressing under the sheets as she talks. Her body is hot, as if with a fever. Within seconds we have rolled off the bed and onto the floor in a twist of blankets and cast-off underthings. Her nails rip into my back. She is shaking so violently I wonder if she is ill. Then she is up on her knees, crouched over the bed, and I am behind her, my hands grasping her lovely, ample hips, ostensibly taking my pleasure. In the dim, filtered streetlight through the curtained window I see our silhouettes in the mirror over my dresser. We look like porn movie actors, grunting and gasping, calling our names out like curses. Indeed for me the act is much like a movie, for I find that, despite my thrusts and gyrations, I feel no physical sensation at all. We collapse in a heap, but I have had no satisfaction. I know too well what will happen next.

She knows I can do it. It is not so much money, she says, to a big company like mine. I've told her about the sums that pass over my desk, through my spreadsheets and calculator, rivers of money flowing with the slippery shapes of salmon and halibut, the vanishing wealth of frigid, distant oceans. My bosses are rich men who live by the water and watch red sunsets as they grill their Chinook steaks on alder planks, drinking fine Scotch and thumbing fresh figures into their Blackberries. I see them through her eyes as she quizzes me: Have they ever invited me to their broad cedar decks? Ever introduced me to their families? Victor is my family, she says. You cannot refuse family. It is family that gives you your soul. These rich men I work for? All they give me is smoked fish for a Christmas bonus. Fish I don't even eat. She laughs. *For me,* she says. *Do it for me.*

It doesn't matter what she says. I know I will agree, and so does she.

The money part is easy. I have password access to all the company accounts. I know where absent sums will not be missed. I do the job with a deft elegance that surprises me a little. It is as if I have been embezzling all my life. I take sixteen thousand, not twelve. I put the surplus in my savings account. The transactions clear on Wednesday. On Thursday Vic leaves his hotel, meets a black Dodge Durango in a grocery store parking lot in Lake City, then joins Alma and me at a bar across the street. It is one of those featureless, strip-mall taverns you pass by a thousand times without a thought of going in. I used to wonder who in the world kept such places in business. Now I know.

Vic is humble and quiet in his gratitude. I assume he's embarrassed. After his first drink he tells us a terrifying story of his creditor, of what happened to the family of a man who tried to take advantage of him. He speaks with weary resignation, as if similar fates await us all as long as such men drive black Durangos in grocery store lots. As if a bullet has missed him, but the gun remains loaded. We drink quite a bit, considering that it is barely after noon. Eventually, he asks me about the money—how did I take it? Was it difficult? Why won't it be missed? He studies my face. He smiles without humor. He watches me closely.

It is these last questions, finally, that bring me face to face with the man I so effortlessly have become. Vic's curiosity is no mere small talk, of course. He knows that he will be asking for more contributions from my company fund—he, or a brother, or Alma. He knows that, if he asks, I will provide. When we part there is a sense of sadness, as though we are mourning a death, rather than a narrow escape from it.

I go home unaccompanied, excusing myself with a headache and an upset stomach. In fact I have both, but they're not why I want to be alone.

I need an exit strategy. I sit at my kitchen table and remember a movie I saw in college; a stoner thriller about a pot-head loser who wakes up after a party with a wicked hangover, the dead body of a young girl in his bed, and no memory of how she got there. He spends the movie trying to reconstruct what has happened to him. I don't need to reconstruct anything. But I do feel like there's a corpse in my bed.

Alma leaves late that evening on a work trip to Los Angeles. They are shooting a commercial for a car rental company. She may have a walk-on role, and she is very excited. I drive her to the airport. I have come to no conclusions except that we need to break up, but this hardly is the time to tell her. We are mostly silent in the car, which is not unusual. I assume that I will drop her at the passenger entrance, but on the road into the terminal she asks me to drive into short-term parking. She says she has a surprise for me. I take a ticket and maneuver up the ramp, hoping that she has not bought me any sort of trinket in thanks for my becoming a felon. The short-term floor is crowded. I find a spot along the wall, far from the elevators. When I turn off the ignition she reaches for my belt buckle. I clasp my hand over hers and shake my head. I tell her I'm still not feeling well. She pretends to pout. I do not look at her. There is a new thing with us in the car; a palpable tension, a sense of unease. It will be best to end this soon, I think. As soon as she returns.

I take off work on Friday. The weather is beautiful, and a number of my coworkers also are making it a long weekend. I drive out into the mountains, first on the Interstate, then north on a smaller road that snakes through an old mining valley, dotted still with the husks of little towns and roadside Ma and Pa stores where you can get a six-pack, a plastic-wrapped sandwich and a shallow plastic pan for gold-hunting in the little streams that spill down from the glaciers and splash under short wooden bridges as you twist through the shadows of the peaks. I find a motel tucked into the trees behind one such establishment, at a deeply forested crossroads on the edge of a national park. I have no plan other than solitude. I buy beer and snack food at the store. I turn off my cell, and leave it in the car so I won't be tempted. I unplug the TV and the room phone, even though no one knows where I am. The room is Spartan: a bed, a table, a chair. Not even a picture on the walls. It is perfect. I want to force me to confront myself without distractions. I want answers and I want them now. I'm determined to leave this place a different man than the one that entered it.

I fall asleep with my head on the table, half of my seventh beer at my elbow. I awake in the middle of the night, cramped and disoriented. I make it to the bathroom, then to the bed, where I stare into the darkness at the little red smoke detector light above the door. Every couple of minutes it blinks. I haven't solved anything, haven't made a plan, haven't seen any deeper into myself than—well, than Alma and her brothers, I think. I'm as clueless about me as they are.

In the morning the monkish simplicity of the room is suddenly oppressive. My back is sore from the spongy mattress, and there is a taste of blood in my mouth from chewing my lips in my sleep, something I haven't done since adolescence. My little escape has solved nothing. I pack my toiletries and toss my bag into the car. In the store I pour myself a cup of boiled, bad coffee, into which I empty three packets of sugar. I sip it while I make small talk with the proprietress, an elderly woman in a pink sweat suit, her hair wrapped tightly in a turquoise scarf. No I'm not fishing, no I'm not prospecting, no I'm not on my way anywhere. I needed a night away from the city, is all. She nods and tells me that she gets a lot of single gentlemen seeking the same thing. A wretched sound of coughing comes from the back. Her husband, she explains, is bedridden, sick with something the doctors can't get straight, a burning deep down that leaves him gasping and weak. Never a smoker, never a miner, never sick a day in his life until this past January. Her mouth is set in a tight line. It's all she can do, she says, to keep up the store and motel. He needs her more and more. Sometimes she's at his bedside for hours, hoping nobody drives into the lot. What kind of way is that to run a business? She laughs and shakes her head. You want to count your blessings, she says, while you have them.

A hoarse voice shouts something indistinct. The woman hurries away. I take a glazed doughnut from the case by the register and leave two dollars on the counter. A mile from the parking lot I reach for a cigarette—I'm fully hooked again now—and find that I have none. I make a U-turn in a scenic view pull-out and drive back to the store. I leave my motor running. The old woman isn't in. The cigarettes are behind the counter. I slip around to grab a pack. The cash register drawer is pulled all the way open. On it are stacked banded bunches of bills. She was counting up her receipts when her husband interrupted her, no doubt, with one of his fits. There is a lot more money than I would have expected from a crossroads gas station. I take it all, without hesitation. I stuff it into the pockets and waistband of my khaki shorts. I even take three rolls of quarters. I take the cigarettes too.

* * *

I haven't seen Alma since my trip to the mountains. I think she might have met someone in California. She hasn't called me, nor I her, but still I have a feeling. Nor have I seen or spoken to her brothers. I receive a gift, I assume from Vic, a few days after I return: A shoebox that someone has delivered in person, leaned against the door of my apartment. In it is a bottle of that plum brandy, *slivovitz* they call it, that the brothers can't get enough of. There also is a deck of cards. I recognize it as the deck we played with that first night. I fan it out on my kitchen table and study it while I drink a glass of the brandy. It doesn't take me long to see that the cards are marked. It's the lily design on the back—the number of petals differs from card to card, as does the subtle slant of the leaves. Clearly there is a pattern and logic to their code. It wouldn't take long to learn it.

There is no note. The box might have been left by anyone, really.

* * *

Ah yes, one last issue. I knew you'd ask. Well, then: I made two more withdrawals from my company. One was for twenty thousand, the next for sixty. It wasn't enough money to retire, but it certainly was enough to relocate, and even to relax for a while. I waited until year's end to give notice. I was careful and creative in the ledgers. It still will be ages before they know the money is missing, and it will seem to have happened months after I departed. I hope that whomever they blame can acquit himself with a confidence becoming his innocence.

You bet I do.

THE TROUSSEAU BOX

Myra King

When the gulls haunt the sea-cliffs, dipping and climbing the wind like rising kites, and all the children of the houses that cling like periwinkles to the ledges above are tucked into bed three-apiece because that is all the comfort poverty will buy, a mother may tell in quiet words of the sea. What it gives and what it takes and sometimes what it leaves behind.

'Hush now, my little ones and sleep will come to you. And Ellie, lie still too, while your father fights with the ocean to bring us back the fishy in the morning. We'll have work aplenty then with the salting and the pressing.'

Her voice is soft, like the waves which froth in muted tones, curling the edged bed of the sea before hissing back to tuck the hidden depths.

And then Ellie, her eldest, says in plaintive pitch, 'Tell us again, Maither, tell us the story of the trousseau box.'

'Yes, yes,' Tommy and Markey, her two boys, clamour. 'Tell us about the pretty lady.'

And the mother sighs away the truth gnawing at her like the wave-eroded cliffs and begins her tale.

'It was not unlike a night as this, your father had not long gone a-sea, two nights before. Chasing the haddock he were. He were to be gone for three days more. And me alone, except for Ellie. But she had only seen four winters. The same as you two boys be now.' The mother pauses briefly. 'And me heavy with babe.' There is another short silence before she continues. 'I got up to the privy and then I saw a light.'

Then Ellie asks, 'Was it like the one Uncle Caleb sets up to guide in the ships?'

The mother gasps back a breath and pulls her shawl tightly around, her arms almost crossing herself. She doesn't answer, and bites her lip until the pain takes away the thought stinging her conscience like a wasp. When she turns away her face, she finds her voice.

'The wind was so strong the grass was flattened like a mat and it blew me towards the cliffs. The shawl I had was not enough. I was in sore need of my coat. I hadn't got it on. The privy only being a little walk. So I came back for it.'

Suddenly the wind rattles the windows of shuttered wood then scurries up the cliff face to rustle the trees. The boys scrunch down in the bed until it seems that Ellie is its sole occupant but for the two little bumps merging to one.

The mother continues: 'The moon was high and washed like the rain had cleaned it. And I could see ahead without the use of a lamp. And the little light I had seen before was still a-twinkling. Then I heard a sound.'

'That were the pretty lady,' says Tommy, his voice blanket-muffled.

'Maither, tell Tommy to hush. Markey wants to hear it too.'

'Hush now,' says the mother. 'Or I won't be telling it to any of you tonight.'

And so they are quiet while the mother tells of the pretty lady dressed in her finery lying on the sand and she as wet as the sea, and how the mother gave her coat to keep her warm. And how the lady kept asking for her trousseau box, saying how it contained much value. But how the candle in its silver holder, with its matching flintbox, to light it, were the only things she took with her when the sailors came. And how she begged them to bring her trousseau box to the lifeboat, but they'd said it would mean they could save one soul less.

And when the mother draws a breath, Ellie slips from the bed, comes back holding a candle and lights it from the lamp. 'Look, Markey, this is not the candle but the holder is the very same, ain't it, Maither?' And the mother nods and stares into the flame and goes as silent as the children have been until Tommy tugs her sleeve. Then she finds her voice again.

'She was the most beautiful woman ever I'd seen. Hair she had like this flame.' The mother's breath makes the candle flicker until it almost goes out. 'And her skin was white and as fine as what they use at the courthouse to powder their wigs.'

'And the colour of her eyes, Maither, what about her eyes?' says Ellie, who does not let any of the story be forgotten.

'Ah, yes, the colour of her eyes.' The mother pauses again. 'They were green like the sea of a summer storm.'

Ellie jumps up again, the boys watch as she goes to the curtained cupboard below the stairs and comes back with a yellowing nightdress. There are threads hanging loose around its bodice and edges. 'This had real pearls on it, didn't it, Maither, until the sea took them?'

The mother takes the dress, lays it over her lap, strokes the silk. She doesn't raise her eyes to her children until many are the minutes that pass.

'Ellie, you be putting back that candle now, do you hear? We don't have enough of them candles to be wasting.' Her voice is sharp and the boys cover their heads once more with the old grey blanket, the one with the holes from the moths that let the cold in like tiny needles, and Ellie hurries the candle in its little silver holder back to the windowsill where it lives.

The mother keeps on stroking the nightdress, her fingers playing with the twisted knots, teasing up the threads and plucking at them like she would a chicken.

'I made to leave the lady then, because the cold was taking me. I was shivering so bad I said to her, I need to go now and can you walk a little way? Then we can shelter behind that crag over there. But the words she answered me tumbled about each other. Saying how she'd been married for but a year and her husband was waiting for her in their new home. Then she touched my arm and asked again about her trousseau box. Had I seen it and could I look for it. It were as if it were just a summer day and we'd mislaid a shoe on the way to the market. She said it in such a manner. Not panicked as she were but light and hopeful. I was scared then, as I'd seen others before her taken by a fever much less than hers.'

Markey stirs and gives a little cry, for the sleep that was teasing behind his lids with pictures of the pretty lady has vanished and all he has left is the hunger ache in his stomach and the cold tickling his toes like frost.

'She got to her feet and we walked towards shelter, where the wind was not as fierce. And she went to lie down before we were there so that I had to hold her up. But I got her there and put the coat over her. She could go no more. When I came back the next morning she were gone and we never did find that trousseau box,' says the mother.

The boys are sleeping but Ellie sits as still as a wall, until her mother nudges her and tells her to climb back a-bed. 'And no more talk now, it's late and there'll be work for us all in the morning.'

* * *

The sea is stirring and grumbling like a drunken lover. The mother stares at the nightdress, hears the wind whispering, turns the pictures of the story around in her mind until they sit up straight and beg for the truth. The pictures become words of the lies she told her husband when he returned. How she delivered herself of two babes, not one, twin boys, and all on her own. Then she tells him of the lady, shows him the nightdress. But she has already washed the death-blood from its neckline and the birth-blood from its hem.

The contents of the trousseau box had bought them food and clothes for a year.

* * *

Later, the mother drapes the nightdress over a chair and goes to her own bed but she is not long there before she feels the blankets lift and Ellie slips in beside her like a fish. She pulls the girl close and feels her arms encircle her.

'What is it, Ellie, can't you sleep, girl?'

'Maither,' says Ellie, her voice a notch above a whisper. 'I remember that night.'

'What do you remember?'

'You were not with babe when you went to the pretty lady, cause our Tommy had already come. Don't you remember, Maither? I got you the cloths and the knife to cut the cord. And Tommy had blood on him and he was screaming. But you said the screaming were good to made his lungs strong.'

'Why have you not told me all this before?'

Ellie shivers and turns over, stares at the ceiling. The stars are flickering light through the cracks in the roof.

'I seen other things that night that I don't understand, Maither. I need you to tell me.'

The mother sits up in bed. 'Tell me first what you saw.'

'When you came back for your coat I followed you. But I kept back. I was scared then of the ghosts Uncle Caleb told me of. But now I know the ghosts is just a lie to scare people from finding the truth.'

'And what truth may that be, Ellie?'

'Uncle Caleb is a Wrecker. Aint he, Maither? He murders people and takes what's theirs. I know that he puts out the lamps for the ships to come up on the reefs.' Ellie's voice is loud and the mother snatches a glance at her two boys but they do not stir and for this she is glad.

The mother finds a memory of her own childhood, an awakening not unlike this night, but there was no pretty lady and all that she knew then was what her father and brother told her. It's the law, they'd said; if no one is found alive then the owners of the shipwrecks will have no claim. They did not tell her of the part they played to make sure of no survivors, be they man or beast. They made a thin line between salvage and plunder, she thinks.

'Hush now, Ellie, or you'll be waking the boys. And don't tell your father any of this. He's a fisherman and proud of it. As most of the men in this village are. He knows of it all. And I do not visit with my family or my brother now.'

'You lie.' Ellie spits the words like a snake.

The mother raises her hand but then her arm falls limp to the bed.

'Oh Ellie, I cannot abide this, what did you see?'

'I seen you and Uncle Caleb. But that were later. Earlier you came back for the knife, the same knife I had brought to you only a few sleeps before that day. When our Tommy was born.'

The mother takes Ellie into her arms, and whispers. 'Oh, my poor lamb, you should not have seen it.'

She sits up in bed and pulls her shawl around her shoulders. 'The pretty lady was with babe and it was coming and would wait for no one. That is why she could not walk. She was brave and I helped as I could. She was torn between this world and the other.'

Ellie is snuggling into her mother's side. The mother brushes away a strand of Ellie's hair.

'I kept thinking this is what my Ellie saw when Tommy came. Oh, and it is so beautiful, such a wonder. I took the babe to the pretty lady's breast. And how strong the babe were, Ellie. How it suckled. And its maither, her face were so soft it were like the silk of her nightdress. And her smile it were sunshine. I wrapped the babe in this shawl.' The mother touches her shawl with a fingertip caress. 'So I had only my dress. But I did not feel cold. The wind went away and the night went still. And that's no lie Ellie. I swear. Then the pretty lady were thanking me. Thanking me Ellie! Me, a lowly fisherman's wife and she so highborn. Oh, that moment I wished would never go.'

'But then Uncle Caleb came, didn't he Maither? Why was he angry? I got so scared, I ran home.'

The mother sighs a long breath. She hugs Ellie and lies back on the pillow.

She feels relieved that the child did not see what happened next.

Before she could stop him with word or action her brother had taken the knife and run the blade across the pretty lady's throat. A thin line. She had not made a sound and her eyes staring, green like the sea of a summer storm, were the last thing the mother remembers of her before snatching up the babe.

She told her brother that if he tried to take the babe from her she would tell her husband, when he returned from the sea. 'Not if you're dead, you won't,' her brother had said. But then laughter followed in her wake as she fled, and the words. 'You'll both stay safe enough if you keep quiet.'

Ellie says, 'Maither, Markey belongs to the pretty lady doesn't he?'

'No, Ellie child, not now, he doesn't. He is mine, and he is your brother and Tommy's twin. You must remember this truth and say no other.'

Ellie is silent and lays back to sleep.

The mother thinks of the trousseau box, carved oak, how she found it the next day, wedged in a cove, seaweed like sirens' tresses wrapping it hidden. She kept it secret from her husband. And what it held saved them all the following year when the fish did not come and when the winter was so harsh the boats could not go out even if they had.

The mother climbs from the bed, takes the nightdress from the chair and draws back the tattered curtain where an open wooden box, without its lid, stands on its side for a cupboard. She stares at the square oak plates, their backs ornately carved but their edges roughly cut, the knife pared by years of sharpening to a thin line.

A draught flutters the curtain and she thinks she needs to be putting more tallow between the cracks once again, come a pleasanter day.

WHY I'M HERE

Gary Lawrence

"On an experimental basis." That's how they worded it. And they scheduled it for seven in the frigging morning -- for graduating seniors only, honors students too, no less. When we heard Stokes had gotten permission from the school board to teach philosophy to us, we wondered what he had over them. How much it cost him. Rumor was that the school board thought that Plato was a planet, but they approved Stokes' request anyways. *Ideas of Man*, the class was called. Literature 352.

Stokes was a small man with a wiry build, five-foot-two, tops. If you saw him in the hall between classes, you might mistake him for a student, a freshman probably, a 98-pound wrestler, or a long-distance runner. Except for the goatee.

I met him that first day of the *Ideas of Man* class, in early January 1972. I was the fourth one of us to attend Rockford's West High. I'd already gone further in school than anyone else in my family. My sister got in trouble from (we think) Bobby Hedlund across the street and couldn't finish her senior year; she's never said who it was for sure because she was afraid me or my dad would beat his ass. My dad got kicked out of West in 1950 for riding his big Indian motorcycle through the halls. It's not real clear whether he was ever actually enrolled as a student or not --- they kicked him out anyways. My mom, in 10th grade at the time, quit school to marry my dad. Seventeen years later they'd had enough bickering and fighting. It was fun while it lasted, my mom always says, twisting her mouth tight in her way. It lasted while it was fun, my dad said, laughing and grinning broadly. Last time I saw him.

That first day of *Ideas of Man* Stokes sailed into class clutching a pile of books against his chest like a girl. He wore baggy khaki slacks, a loose tie, no suit coat, and rolled up the sleeves on his long-sleeve shirt. His clothes hung on his petite frame like rags on a scarecrow. His long black hair was combed straight back and hung over his shirt collar. Close up you could see specks of gray at his temples.

He heaved the books up on the teacher's desk, because he wasn't tall enough to just let go of them. When he set down the books he dropped his lunch bag on the floor. He fussed loudly about his yogurt spilling, and dove to get his dropped lunch bag. None of us even knew what yogurt was. I glanced at my practice partner, Kelly, the 175-pounder, and we just shook our heads sadly.

He ignored the large central desk and padded chair up by the blackboard, the traditional teacher's sanctuary, and came around to the first seat in the middle row (we'd all been warned ahead of time not to sit there). He flung the desk around and faced us: Still staring at us, he put his butt on the desktop, his feet in the seat, his elbow on his knee, and his chin on his fist. He let loose a big sigh.

We hushed each other and waited, hands clasped together on our desktops. But then he cocked his head back and forth like a chicken and squinted and scowled at us, shaking his long black hair. Finally someone snickered. Someone else laughed. Then we all laughed. Then Stokes smiled even more, too, his huge brown eyes dancing.

"This here's *Ideas of Man*," he said in an exaggerated drawl. "You all in the right place?"

We must have looked like a flock of little birds in the nest begging for worms, our heads were bobbing so much.

"What'd you say?" he yelled, raising his voice and widening his eyes. He put his hand up to his ear. "What'd you say? Speak!"

If he hadn't acted so funny we would have been scared. We looked at each other, raised our eyebrows, shrugged our shoulders, shook our heads, stared down at our desks. One of the girls up front, Janey Thompson, the cheerleader and class president, raised her hand.

"Yes, Miss Thompson?"

The air left the room suddenly. Magic had happened. We were shocked he knew her name. Without using a seating chart. Most of the teachers we had at West could barely remember your name even with the seating chart laid out in front of them.

Janey recovered quickly. "Sir?"

"I'm no 'sir.' I'm just Ernie Stokes," he said, getting up off the desk. He started pacing back and forth across the front of the room. "Why was it you raised your hand, Miss Thompson?"

"Well, sir… Mr. Stokes. Sir. You asked us if we were in the right place, I think, and… you know, I'm pretty sure I'm like, in the right place. Here. Actually. Today. This hour. I think. Sir." She clasped her hands in front of herself again, wiggled her ass into her seat, smiled and showed her dimples proudly.

Stokes stopped pacing. He put his hand back on his chin, his finger up to his cheek. "Hmmm. You 'think,' do you?" She nodded her head quickly. "Hasn't anyone ever told you that it's dangerous to *think*, Miss Thompson? Especially in a place like *this?*"

Janey nodded back, her golden curls bouncing, shining.

"But you do it anyways. Good for you, Miss Thompson. How about you, Mr. Miller?" he said, turning his head from Janey to me, trying to look mean. "You in the right place, Mr. Miller?"

I was sitting sideways in my seat with my feet stuck out across the aisle. The snow from my work boots had made a little puddle there where it had melted from the treads. "I'm where my schedule says I should be right now, anyways." I caught Kelly's eye. He smirked.

"So according to that dark and murky alternate reality that is your second semester schedule, you *are* in the right place, Mr. Miller. Good for you.

"But is this the right place for *you*, Mr. Miller?" He straightened up. "Why are you *here*, Mr. Miller?" He pointed down at the floor. "In *this* time and space, at *this* moment?"

I laughed and looked around. Took a few seconds to answer. "Sounded a lot better to me than a 7:00 a.m. gym class?"

We all laughed. And that's the way it started. Our little warm-up, our ritual. Every day he asked, "Why are you here?" to the class. Sometimes, most times, he called on someone, just to make sure everyone got a chance. Always people raised their hands. Kelly was here for comic relief --- his own and everyone else's. Janey Thompson was here to make the world a better place to live, she said. Dave Leske, the greaser quarterback with his styled hair, paisley shirts, creased slacks and Cuban-heeled boots, said he was here to please all the lonely, disappointed women in Rockford.

For the longest time, Walker, the only black kid in our class, couldn't think of an answer when Stokes called on him. "Mr. Walker, it's your turn," Stokes tried again one day. "Why are you here?"

We waited for a few seconds, then a minute. Some of the class started getting antsy. Kelly blew his nose loudly into an over-sized red-and-black farmer's hanky. He got the eye from Stokes. "Take your time, Jamal," Stokes said, quieting us and sitting on the desk. "We care about what you have to say. We want to know what you think."

Another couple minutes passed. Jamal muttered something. "What was that, Mr. Walker? I couldn't hear you," Stokes said.

"I'm here to learn how to tell the truth to people that don't want to hear it."

Stokes blinked, swallowed. "Very good, Mr. Walker. Very good, indeed."

* * *

First thing each class, Stokes asked "Why are you here?", until everyone in the class had had a turn. Then we started over. The unwritten rule was that nobody gave the same answer twice. "Why are *you* here?" started every class, every day that spring with Stokes.

Our *Ideas of Man* class quickly settled into a comfortable but lively routine. First we'd read a few pages in the book about the great philosophers and what they'd thought: Plato. Epictetus. Immanuel Kant. Nietsche. The Uphanishads. St. Thomas Aquinas. Then we'd talk it over until we could make some sense out of what they said. Then we'd write a few words about what it meant to us, today --- if anything, and hand it in for Stokes to grade. We'd get comments in the margins like "Yeah!" "Yippee!" "You got it, man!" One time we all got ink stamps on our papers from one of those cereal box toys --- one for "good," two for "great." Another time we got shiny gold stars from the Paralyzed Veterans of America foundation. Once we got Sierra Club stickers with the endangered species on them --- Kelly had to ask what "endangered species" were.

* * *

That year I wrestled 167 varsity. It was a lot better than the year before, when I had to make 155 every week in case Van Kessel, the senior, didn't, so the team wouldn't forfeit a weight class. If he made weight, he wrestled 155 and I wrestled 167, twelve pounds lighter than my opponent. I was strong from working so much --- I'd worked for a landscaping company since I was thirteen. My boss got a winter contract shoveling clinkers out of the coal-burning schools' chimneys and boiler rooms, dirty nasty work that nobody else wanted. He welded iron strips to the bottoms of our scoop shovels so they wouldn't wear out as fast -- but then they also weighed about twenty pounds empty. Toughen you up quick, he'd said. I could mop the mat with Kelly and probably anyone else at practice, except maybe Dempster, our heavyweight; but I got too nervous at the meets. I won about half my matches that year, good but not great. I was a hip-lock and arm-drag specialist, Coach Vitalli said --- "my 'take 'em down and squeeze 'em' man."

One match I remember all too well was against a tall, skinny, long-legged guy from Jefferson. He had to be six-foot-five or more; I'm six foot and I had to reach up to lock up with him. I was surprised he weighed enough to be a 167-pounder. The first round I took him down and threw him around the mat for the whole two minutes. The second round I took top position, then tight-waisted him hard but couldn't stick him. Last round, I thought I'd stand up and escape from him then throw him around some more, but he stuck his legs into me when I stood up, and I couldn't shake him off. He reached across my back and grabbed my arm while our legs were twisted together, then threw my arm behind his neck and arched his back -- a guillotine hold. Coach and Kelly were screaming at me from the side of the mat -- "Bridge, Miller! Bridge!" --- as I rolled over and got stretched out across his long frame. It was all I could do to arch my neck and pivot on my forehead or one shoulder to keep from getting pinned. The guy let me up enough to roll over after that, but then he just threw his legs into me again and rang up more points. In the end I didn't get pinned, but I lost 12-10 on a decision.

It was a long walk home that night, having to listen to Kelly go over both my early dominance and late mistakes again and again. "What'd you learn tonight, Muscle Boy? Huh?" He laughed. "Why were you *there,* Mr. Miller?" he mimicked. "Why were you *there*?"

The next day I got to *Ideas of Man* class early. I couldn't sleep anyways --- my neck was sore and I had a wicked mat burn on my right cheek and shoulder from having my face dragged under that guy. Stokes was already in the room. He came over to where I sat and eased into the desk in front of me, facing me.

"Tough night?" he said.

"You could say that."

I was afraid he was going to make me explain it all to him, but then he said, "I saw Coach Vitalli in the teacher's lounge this morning. He said you got out-smarted last night, but put up a hell of a fight."

My head shot up when he said this, but then Janey and a few of the other girls came in. "Live and learn," he said, standing up, and started to walk away.

"That's what Kelly said." I laughed.

Stokes grinned back at me. "Ah yes, more deep insight from our dear Mr. Kelly."

It hurt when I laughed. "Ouch," I said, touching the edge of my mat burn. And we laughed some more.

"What?" said Janey, looking down at her sweater, her skirt, her shoes, then at her arms. "What?"

* * *

The first time our comfortable class routine was interrupted in *Ideas of Man*, we were studying Thomas Hobbes. Stokes was trying hard, but he couldn't get anyone to disagree with Hobbes' basic premise.

"Really, people," he said, frustrated. "You all believe that the natural state of man is chaos --- *war?*"

Yeah, sure, we mumbled.

"You believe that? In your heart of hearts you believe that?" His eyes were wide. "*Why* do you believe that?"

We all assumed the position then and stared down at our desks. Finally Dave Leske raised his hand.

"Yes, Mr. Leske?"

"Take a gander," Leske said, sweeping his arm across his desk. "Right here in little ole Rockford, right here in little ole West High. Right here in this classroom." He stopped and flashed his best smile. "We all know what's what, what works around here. If you're strong enough to take it, you take it. If you're strong enough to keep it, you keep it. If you're not, you get it taken away from you." Our heads bobbed. "That's the way it is, that's the way it's always been, that's the way it'll always be." He crossed his arms. "Just ask Jarrard," he said, and shrugged his shoulders, and we laughed. We all knew Jarrard. Dave Jarrard was the greaser fullback, Leske's best friend. Everyone here had had their lunch money stolen by big blond Jarrard at one time or other. Janey blushed. Jarrard was her current boyfriend.

Stokes tished. "Thank you, Mr. Leske, for sharing your thoughts,

thoughts that are obviously shared by everyone here. But people: There really is another way. Can't you see it?"

We all sat there in his gaze. The room was deathly still.

"What if I told you that living the way Hobbes describes is a life of fear, a life of scarcity, a life of little-ness?" He stepped away from the board. "What if I told you that man doesn't *need* material things, that our first mistake a long, long time ago was building our world around 'things' that we think we need, things to keep and to guard and to hoard, like Mr. Leske says?" Stokes pulled himself up as high as his five-foot frame would let him.

"I don't know, Ernie," I said, breaking the silence. "That sounds pretty good but it's kind of *Fantasy Island* from where I'm sitting." We all laughed nervous laughs, then the bell rang, and we students hustled out quickly. We left Stokes standing in front of the blackboard, shaking his head, looking sad.

The second time our classroom routine was interrupted, Stokes did it himself --- he brought a new book to class not long after our "Thomas Hobbes" lecture. This day he sat cross-legged on his desk and just looked out at us.

"Pay attention, people," he said after a few minutes, and it took us awhile to get quiet because we thought he was kidding; it was hard to tell with Stokes. "This book," he said, holding up a slim blue-and-white volume in one hand, "is written by a man named Richard Bach. It's called *Jonathan Livingston Seagull.*"

"Yeah --- so?" Kelly said.

Stokes stared him down in the midst of a few giggles. "We're going to take the next few days off and read it. Out loud."

The room burst into snickers: "What -- story time?" "Bedtime stories?" "I gotta go home and get my blankie." "I want my teddy bear --- can I have a Hall Pass, Mr. Stokes?"

"It'll be my gift to you this week," Stokes said, unshaken. "Because you need to hear it. Not just read it. *Hear it.*"

I looked over at Kelly. We rolled our eyes. But then we listened as Stokes' read in his smooth, calm voice. We heard the story of a seagull who got tired of fighting for food every day and decided instead to be the best flier ever. All week Stokes read to us through first hour, and we sat as entranced as kindergarteners. Jonathan went away and found a great teacher and got better and better at flying and then came back to teach all the other seagulls how to fly better and be free. And then Ernie was done and when he finished, when he turned that last page and shut the book softly, we just sat there, still and silent, until the bell rang.

* * *

One Tuesday in March not long after Stokes read to us, Dave Leske made a pass at Danny Brown's girlfriend. Wasn't much of a pass, Dave said later, when he could talk again.

Danny Brown was black. Dave Leske was white. At West High in 1972, that meant war.

The chase started in the first-floor hallway. I was at lunch when the fight spilled through the cafeteria. First came Leske, flinging chairs behind him as he ran like a wild man. Then Danny Brown and his friends came running close behind like a pack of wolves, hurdling chairs, dodging food, and pushing people out of their way. I tucked two folding chairs under my arm for defense or offense, to fend off flying chairs or throw some myself, I didn't know yet.

Leske ran from the hallway through the lunchroom through the lunch line over a counter and then outside. Danny and his buddies chased after him. One of the lunch ladies yelled at them to slow the hell down. The whole thing happened in seconds. I wanted to help Leske, but I froze like everyone else.

When I finally did jump up to help Leske, "Wild Bill" Stoglitis, the boys' P.E. teacher, stopped me at the door. "Back off, dumbass," he said, stiff-arming my chest, staring me down. "Sit the hell down right now."

They caught up with Leske a minute later in the teachers' parking lot. In the end he was wheeled off on a gurney with a concussion, bruised ribs, and a broken jaw.

I should have been there.

The next day, Wednesday, Dave Jarrard got all us white guys together for a march through the halls. We gathered at the parking lot entrance wearing our winter school jackets and watch-hats and gloves and looking tough, and strutted through the first-floor hallways and cafeteria and out again. Thursday, policemen with side-arms and shotguns and dogs were in the school doing weapons checks on the lockers and on all of us. On Friday, by school board policy, the suspended boys came back to school. Not Leske, of course -- he was still in the hospital, jaw wired shut.

Over the loudspeaker that morning the basketball coach announced a prayer meeting "open to everyone," immediately after school. Teachers stood close to their doors, arms crossed, hurrying people on their way. Most of the women teachers looked scared. Coach Vitalli was assigned a spot in the first-floor hallway where the two corridors met; even he looked a little nervous.

Ten minutes into first hour someone yelled "Fight!" His voice echoed through the hallway. Every classroom emptied into the hall like they were spring-loaded.

The fight was in the stairwell nearest my *Ideas of Man* room, so I was one of the first ones there. The fighters were struggling under the Vietnam War display, the one that had started in the small shadowbox by the office but was moved last year and by now had wood-and-brass plaques bearing the names of graduates who'd died spilling over onto three walls.

Dave Jarrard gritted his teeth and grunted through his nose like a pig as he pounded on Danny Brown's back again and again. Spit and snot flew everywhere. A bright red arch of blood was already splattered across the pale green stairwell wall, but it was hard to tell whose it was.

Black and white students alike jammed the stairs. Teachers couldn't get through. Kelly and I held back what people we could to give the fighters room.

Danny Brown was a good athlete, but he was losing this street fight to the white boy. Janey Thompson, Jarrard's girl, was in the opposite corner crying, begging for someone to stop the fight, please, someone stop it.

Unlike all the screaming people around them, neither fighter said a word. They just grunted like hogs and made short rasping sounds when they breathed.

I could smell the spit and the sweat and the blood -- rusty, coppery -- I could taste it on my tongue. A fast punch from Danny left a long red mark on Jarrard's nose. He barely flinched and landed a right upper cut to Danny's gut that doubled him over and lifted him off the floor.

Small as he was, Stokes was the only teacher able to squeeze through all the bodies to get to the fighters. He passed behind me and clipped my knee going by so that I almost fell. Jarrard had just driven Danny's head into the banister when Stokes grabbed his arm. Jarrard flung Stokes away without looking back. Stokes grabbed his arm again and caught his balance. Danny Brown turned and swung blindly. He missed Jarrard but hit Stokes squarely in the face.

The air left the stairwell. Jaws dropped. Eyes flared. Nobody spoke. Nobody moved. Stokes lay stunned. When he finally stood up, blood trickled from his nose into his black goatee. He didn't wipe it off. Instead he went to Danny Brown, where he lay crumpled on the floor.

"Mr. Brown, you're hurt," he said, down on one knee, offering his hand. "Let me help you."

Jarrard stood over the two of them like a wolf, panting, feet spread shoulder-width apart, hands clenched tight, still churning in small slow circles at his waist. His chest heaved with every breath. His shirt was hanging open. Stokes made eye contact with him. "Mr. Jarrard. Your friend is crying. Help her." He pointed to Janey.

Still Jarrard stood there, breathing heavily through his cut mouth.

"Get out of my way, punks!" Above us on the third floor landing we heard Stoglitis bullying his way through the mob.

"David. Go to her. Help her," Stokes said calmly but firmly to Jarrard.

Then Stoglitis burst through the wall of students surrounding the fighters, wielding his rolled-up attendance book like a club, swatting anyone that didn't move out of his way fast enough. "What the hell's going on here?" he screamed. "Stop that crap right now, I say!"

But by then of course it *had* stopped. Jarrard spun and grabbed Janey by the hand. The crowd parted to make a path for them. and they ducked down the stairs in the other direction. Stokes stood up to take Danny Brown to the nurse's office. He helped Danny to his feet and looked at me. "Move it, Miller." His hand was warm and gentle on my arm, soft and small.

I shifted to one side. "You could have ducked that punch," I said.

He just smiled, his hand still on my forearm. "Maybe. I'm not an athlete, like you."

I stood there in the corner with my hands in my pockets and my head hanging down long after everyone else had left. A lady teacher appeared. Home Ec, I think. "It's all over now," she said, grabbing my arm and tugging me toward the stairs.

"Ma'am," I muttered. "Is it *ever* over?"

* * *

We were in lock-down for the remainder of that year. The draft lottery came and went in March; I got a high number, Kelly didn't. Leske got a high number too but joined the Air Force anyways, I heard. Jarrard became a Ranger. Danny Brown ended up somewhere in Canada, they say, playing saxophone in a jazz band. Graduation, when it finally came in June, was a solemn affair, with fifty police lining the walls of the auditorium. I returned to West High School as a Rockford College senior four years later for my student teaching semester. "You can do better than me," Stokes said when I asked him to be my supervisor, smiling. "Besides, I've already taught you everything I know." Miss Nyman, the department chair whose spot I would eventually take, took me on and let me teach *Siddhartha* to her junior honors class. Years after that, at our school district's annual party for the Rockford retirees, I pulled an old *Ideas of Man* book out of a plastic Ziploc bag, the book from what turned out to be the first and last philosophy class ever offered at West. "Property of District 205" was still stamped in bold black ink on the inside cover. I took the book out of the bag and held it out to Stokes.

"Stole it," I told him.

He took it from me and turned it in his hands several times, slowly. "Good man."

His hair was all gray now, even his goatee. But his eyes were the same brilliant hazel brown, the same dancing eyes that I'd first seen back in 1972, almost fifteen years earlier. He wrote with a flourish on the inside cover and handed the book back to me, then smiled and I moved away as he greeted some others. I waited until I got home that night to read it.

Mr. Miller, he wrote, *a guy who knows why he's here*.

My wife found me the next morning crunched into the bottom bunk with our son and daughter, our arms and legs tangled together like three dancers frozen in mid-leap. She took a picture of us that still sits on the shelf above my writing desk --- next to my copy of *Ideas of Man*.

SIDEWALK SALE

Jim Valenti

On a calm and colorless midtown afternoon a curious scene unfolded on the plaza at the corner of 53rd and 3rd. By Manhattan standards, an escalator standing square in the middle of the open-air sidewalk did not necessarily seem out of place. What did draw attention nonetheless was a sandwich sign placed nearby that advertised in handwritten bold chalk,

Stairway to Heaven
Today Only
$1

A bulldozer - watching the spectacle unfurl, sat off to one side idling at the ready. A crowd clustered around the unmoving staircase, the peak of which stretched skyward and was just visible from street level below. Prodded by an obese man in a sweat-singed red coat and matching beard, hundreds of people were offering their money and climbing up the silent stairs, each one following the previous and claiming a vacant step of their own.

"Deal of a lifetime, my friends!" he bellowed, winking at anyone curious enough to make eye contact. No one spoke back, their attention instead focused only on keeping strays from cutting into the line up ahead. Upon completely filling all the available spaces the stinking fat man slung a velvet theatre rope across the entrance at the bottommost tread, separating the riders from the waiters. After checking here and there to make sure his customers were comfortable and in good sorts, he released a lever which dually set the escalator in motion and roused the milling horde to silence.

Up into the thinning air the people went in a steady stream, grinning with delight at their fortune and at one another as the sounds of the city muted and time slowed in a collectively perfect moment. Then after about two seconds the first one fell onto the concrete at the center of the plaza from above with a searing scream and a resounding thud. And then fell the next - landing squarely and noisily on the back of the first.

As the escalator continued to rise upward they continued to fall in rhythm earthward, each one arriving no less loudly or promptly on the growing heap below than the one before. The torrent of bodies rained down unrelenting, until the last one came to a final painful stop following several unnatural cart wheels down the side of the oozing pile, and then the escalator was empty once again.

The crowd stood transfixed. The restored silence was soon broken by the rhythmic clapping of the fat man's balloonish fingers, which yielded shortly thereafter to a thrum of raucous applause, cheers and high-fives permeating the gathered throng as the bulldozer roared to life from the shadows. In slow sweeps it began pushing the accumulated mass of human carnage into one of several hulking dumpsters brought in just for the occasion.

The fat man unchained the velvet rope once more, clutching a fistful of sweaty bills and smiling devilishly.

"Step right up!" he crooned, "Before it's too late!" The waiting procession already reached Oprah-like around the corner and partway down to 52nd Street as the next customers in line started to fill the stairs.

LEX'S CASTLE

Lindsey Simmons

Lex's castle didn't have a door. It had four brown walls, and it moved, like a wizard's castle that Lex had once read about (Lex believed that mobility was an important quality in a castle); and its walls were strong enough to keep monsters out, because Lex's castle was her true home, and it protected her like a friend. And alone inside it—she was always alone inside the castle—she whispered secrets to its four brown walls, and it whispered back to her about deeper mysteries, and the difference between solitude and loneliness. Lex never felt lonely—her castle's brown walls held her like a hug. But her castle had no door.

Her mother asked her why, one day, as Lex clambered on top of the coffee table to lower herself down into it. Narrow pale hands settling on narrow hips, Lex's mother watched as grubby sneakers left crumbs of dried mud on her clean table, and she pursed her red lips.

"Alexandria, why don't you ask your father to cut a door in that old box?"

Lex looked over the top of her castle's walls in alarm.

"No! It can't have a door!"

"Why on earth not? It would stop you having to climb all over my furniture to get in," her mother said, eyeing the dirt on her coffee table with distaste. "Why can't your box have a door?"

"A door will let the monsters in," Lex said, eyes darting around as if expecting to see a monster hiding under the couch. She knew better than that, of course. No monster would hide itself so poorly.

"Alexandria, there are no monsters," Lex's mother said. She herself had believed in monsters, once; but that had been a lifetime ago. She knew better now.

But she saw in Lex's eyes that this battle would not be won yet, and Lex's castle would not have a door. Her mother sighed, smoothing her apron down across her flat stomach.

"Clean up that dirt when you're done," she said, and she went back into the kitchen to start dinner, leaving Lex alone again with her castle.

So Lex whispered to her castle, and it took her to forests full of creatures both bright and dangerous, and to mountains where the air was so clear she could see the filaments of magic sparkling in it, and to underwater lands where walls of seaweed sang lullabies to the fish curled up in their leaves. And no monsters got inside the castle, and the castle held her tenderly, and promised that the monsters would never touch her as long as its walls remained to keep them out.

One day, though, a knock at the front door interrupted Lex and her castle.

"Alexandria, answer the door please," her mother called from the kitchen.

So Lex tipped her castle forward, because it had no door, and crawled out, and went to the door.

There stood a boy and a girl.

The boy was taller than Lex, and had brown eyes and brown hair, and he smiled at her. The girl was a few inches shorter, and her hair was white-gold and her eyes were a quiet, solemn blue, almost grey.

"I'm Toby. This is my sister, Katie. We moved in down the street today," the boy said. He smiled at Lex again.

"I'm Lex," Lex said, offering a tiny smile of her own. The girl who had been introduced as Katie just watched them.

"Like Lex Luthor?" the boy asked.

"No," Lex said. "Like me. Want to see my castle?" She turned without waiting for an answer, and walked away from the door.

Toby and his sister followed. Toby closed the front door carefully behind them.

"This is my castle," Lex said when they caught up to her.

"Cool!" said Toby. Lex smiled; her castle was impressive, after all. "Where's the door?"

"There is no door," Lex said.

"Oh. It's a princess castle?" Toby's tone shifted subtly away from admiration to something Lex had never associated with her castle before—condescension.

"What's a princess castle?" she asked.

"Well, it's like in stories, how the princess gets trapped in a castle with no way in, and the hero has to climb up the walls or something to rescue her," Toby said. "That's what your castle must be. If it was a knight castle, it would need a door for all the knights and their horses to get in and out."

That's silly, thought Lex. My castle isn't trapping me, and I don't need to be rescued from it. She heard the castle hum in agreement. *Safe,* it whispered, so only she could hear. *I keep you safe from the monsters.*

But Lex didn't say anything, because Toby seemed so certain, and she didn't want to disagree. She hadn't played with many other children.

"Can I get inside?" Toby asked, but before Lex's hesitation became obvious, his sister spoke for the first time.

"Don't be silly, Toby." Her voice was light and clear as water. She shook her long blonde hair back over her shoulders. "You said yourself—it's a princess castle. Girls only. You should go home and help Mom unpack, anyway."

Toby looked like he would protest, but then he sighed. "Yeah. Okay. I'll see you later, Lex. Have fun, Katie." He let himself out the front door.

The girl watched him go, and then turned back to Lex. "I'm Katelyn." She held out her hand.

Lex shook it hesitantly. She had never shaken hands with anyone who wasn't an adult. "I'm—"

"Alexandria? Was there—oh! Hello! Who's this?" Lex's mother asked, coming into the living room, wiping her hands on her apron.

"I'm Katelyn. My brother Toby and I moved in down the street, and Lex and I were going to play for a while, if you don't mind," Katelyn said with a sweet smile.

Lex's mother seemed taken aback, but she smiled back at the petite girl. "Of course. Have fun, girls." She left Lex alone in the living room with Katelyn.

"You want to play in my castle?" Lex asked.

"Sure," Katelyn said, walking over to it. "How do we get inside?"

Lex climbed onto the coffee table and dropped down inside. Katelyn watched her, and then followed. She stepped delicately up and lowered herself down into the castle, gracefully, landing on her toes like a ballet dancer. Lex watched her, and felt a pang of envy. She moved like the princess Toby had claimed should live in Lex's castle. Lex felt clumsy for the first time.

The girls settled themselves onto the floor of the castle, knees hugged to their chests, backs pressed against the brown walls. They fit comfortably, with just a little room to move.

"Why isn't your castle in your room?" Katelyn asked.

"Should it be?"

"Of course. You don't have any privacy out here," Katelyn said. "How can you tell secrets with your friends?"

"I only tell secrets to my castle," Lex said.

Katelyn looked at her for a moment. "Don't you have friends?" she asked.

"Yes," Lex said. "At school."

"Oh," Katelyn said. "Well, now you have me, and we can tell secrets to each other. I'll help you move the castle into your room." She climbed out of the castle almost as gracefully as she had gotten into it, taking a long, reaching step up onto the coffee table. Lex followed, trying to move the way Katelyn had.

* * *

Lex was secretly delighted on the days when Katelyn brought Toby with her to play. They didn't play in the castle then—it was now kept in Lex's room, to Lex's mother's relief, and Toby never went into Lex's room.

The three of them played outside, when it was warm; and when it was cold or raining they played games of hide-and-seek inside, or watched movies, or played board games. Katelyn was always short with Toby, and Lex wondered sometimes if Katelyn wished he didn't come along with her to visit Lex. But Lex was glad when he came. He made her laugh, and he liked all the games Katelyn never wanted to play with Lex because they meant lots of running and yelling. And when Toby smiled at Lex, it stretched across his whole face and lit up his brown eyes.

When Katelyn visited by herself, she and Lex would sit in Lex's castle and Katelyn would talk about boys she knew at her old school, and about the friends she had moved away from. She told Lex how she loved to sit in the morning and watch her mother putting on makeup, slowly and subtly changing her face into what she wanted it to be. Lex had never noticed her own mother putting on makeup, but she looked, and sure enough there was a black bag of different colored powders and tubes in her mother's bathroom.

Katelyn snuck some from her own mother's room one day, and she and Lex smeared it above their eyes and across their cheekbones and over their lips. Lex wore hers like warpaint, in bold lines, but Katelyn sat on the floor in front of Lex's closet-door mirror and leaned in close, unblinking, to apply hers. Lex was busy drawing on bright red lips when she noticed how intently Katelyn was focusing on her reflection, entirely absorbed in what she was doing. Lex stopped to watch her, fascinated.

"You look like a grown-up," Lex whispered in awe when Katelyn finished. Katelyn started, her long white-blonde hair swinging out in a curtain as she turned her head to look at Lex—she hadn't realized the other girl was watching. Then Katelyn blushed a little, and smiled.

"I watch my mother do it every morning. I just wanted to see if I could do it, too . . . you know. For when I'm older. I'm not allowed to wear any now." She sighed. "Mother says maybe, when I'm thirteen, we can talk about it. I'll be thirteen in three more years. That's not very long, right?"

Lex nodded, but she hoped secretly that three years was longer than it sounded. Thirteen sounded so old, and she didn't like the wistful tone of Katelyn's voice when she said the word, like it was a faraway world, one she never wanted to come back from.

* * *

"You like Toby," Katelyn said one day.

"He's nice, I guess," Lex said. "For a boy." She turned her face to the corner of her castle, hoping that Katelyn wouldn't see her cheeks turn red. "He's good at hide-and-seek, and tag."

Katelyn smiled in a way that Lex wasn't sure she liked. "I'll bring him along tomorrow," Katelyn said, and Lex didn't tell her not to, and the blush spread down to her neck.

"Let's play knights and dragons," Toby said the next day. "Lex, we can use your castle. It'll be perfect."

Katelyn smiled in the way that Lex had decided she didn't like, and said, "Yes. Lex, you can be the princess first—I'll be the dragon." Toby would be the knight, of course.

Lex smiled, but it didn't reach her eyes, and she went to pull her castle back into the living room, where it hadn't been since the first day she met Katelyn and Toby. She didn't say that she'd rather be the dragon—or maybe the knight.

Katelyn wasn't a very good dragon, but she kept Toby from saving Lex effectively enough, until Toby ran her through with a broom handle-lance.

Lex watched, and didn't like that a battle was being fought while she stood, motionless, in the castle. For the first time she felt truly trapped by its four brown walls.

"Lex, you get rescued by the knight now. Toby, help her out of the castle," Katelyn said from the floor where she lay, dead.

"I know how to rescue a princess," Toby said, sounding annoyed. He walked to Lex's castle and offered Lex his hand. She took it and let him support her weight as she climbed back up onto the coffee table and then jumped down to the floor. Lex remembered how gracefully Katelyn always got in and out of the castle, and she remembered how she used to tip the castle forward and crawl out of it. This way, with her hand in Toby's, felt strange. She stood there, letting the strangeness settle over her like a wool coat, heavy and a little prickly. She shivered.

"What's wrong, Lex?" Toby asked, and his brown eyes were curious and bright. Lex blinked at him and didn't answer. He was still holding her hand. She started to pull away, but stopped.

Then Katelyn said, sending a secret half-smile to Lex, "Now, Toby, you have to kiss the princess. The knight always kisses the princess."

Lex stared at her, and then at the carpet, and then at her castle, refusing to look at Toby. Heat splashed across her face, and her palm felt slick in Toby's. She felt betrayed, humiliated—hopeful.

But—"No." The word was out of Lex's mouth, bubbling up and over her lips before she knew it. Her whole body was burning with embarrassment. "I don't want to play anymore." She pulled her hand from Toby's and took a stumbling step away from him. He didn't follow her, and Lex wouldn't look at him to see his expression. There was silence, stretched taut across the changing architecture of Lex's world.

Katelyn broke the tense, motionless silence. "Lex, don't you want to be the princess?" she asked, standing up and brushing her white shirt off. "I thought you'd like going first, since it's your castle. I'll be princess next, and you can be the dragon." She didn't say anything about kisses as she climbed inside Lex's castle, and Toby didn't say anything at all as he picked up his broom handle-lance.

Lex was much better at being the dragon than she was at being princess, and she roared and clawed at Toby, and flew down at him from the couch, and he almost didn't win, even with Katelyn calling encouragement from the castle. But when he did, Lex watched him help his sister out of Lex's castle, and she saw how Katelyn stepped down from the table, landing so lightly she could have been made of air, of glass—of nothing at all. Lex thought of Cinderella, pointing her toes to admire the tiny glass slipper, to show Prince Charming its perfect fit.

"I guess you're just better at being the dragon, Lex," Katelyn said, and all three of them laughed, but Lex stopped laughing first, and Toby stopped right after her.

"Maybe Lex isn't the kind of princess who needs to be rescued," Toby said, and Katelyn laughed at that, too, but she stopped when no one joined her.

* * *

That night, after Toby and Katelyn had left, Lex pulled her castle back into her room, and sat inside it, and—didn't cry, because Toby was right—she didn't need to be rescued. Her castle kept her safe, and there didn't need to be a door, because that way nothing bad could get in. *Safe,* it told her. *Here nothing can hurt you.*

She slept in the castle that night, and the monsters that she knew lived in the shadows didn't touch her. But Lex was bigger now, and she barely fit—even lying curled tight under her blanket on the castle's floor, her back and legs were pressed against the sides of the castle. Lex wondered how much longer the castle would hold her.

The next day, Katelyn didn't come over. Toby came by himself, saying that Katelyn had to go to the doctor's. Lex's mother gave him a long look when she answered the door, but then she smiled and didn't say anything. They played hide-and-seek, and Toby hid first.

Lex found him easily, hidden in the laundry room cupboard, and then it was her turn to hide. She smiled, as Toby began to count in the living room. She had the perfect hiding place. Lex ran into her room, and carefully closed the door behind her. Toby would never look in there—he never came into her room. She laughed a little, barely making a sound, and walked around her castle to the closet door.

Nimbly, Lex scrambled up to the top shelf, curling herself into a ball. From there, she could barely reach the door to pull it shut, but there was no sense taking chances, so she stretched until the tips of her fingers caught the door and she was left in the darkness. Lex was very quiet, so Toby wouldn't hear her. Her heart beat faster—it was so dark. But she remembered her castle sitting outside, in her room, and knew it was still protecting her. Nothing could hurt her here.

Listening for Toby, Lex could hear the faint sound of his voice as he finished counting. "Eighty-four, eighty-five, eighty-six," Toby counted, until he ended at "One hundred! I'm coming to find you, Lex!" She smiled, secret in her dark, safe corner of the world.

His footsteps started, going towards the laundry room where she had found him. Lex rolled her eyes. Would she really hide where he had just hidden? She heard him re-emerge a few seconds later. He went into the bathroom and opened all the cupboards, and pushed back the shower curtain. He peeked into her father's study, the door creaking a little, the way it always did. He checked the downstairs closet, and the kitchen, and then Toby's footsteps disappeared upstairs and Lex could only hear the creak of floorboards, so she couldn't guess where he was looking anymore.

Then Lex heard Toby coming back down the stairs, slowly, and she imagined the puzzled look on his face and giggled silently, alone in her closet. She shifted her weight a little, trying not to make any noise, because her leg was starting to fall asleep.

Her doorknob turned a little, and Lex was still again. Then her door opened all the way. Toby stepped inside of Lex's room for the first time. He stood still for a moment, looking around—to find any possible hiding places, Lex knew. He looked under her bed first. Then he looked in the big chest where her old toys were kept, because she was too grown up for toys anymore—mostly. He looked under the blankets piled on her beanbag chair. Then Toby walked over to the closet.

Lex's heart started to race. He would find her, now. But she had won the game—he had taken so long to find her! She must have won. The closet handle turned, and the door opened. Lex flinched from the sudden light.

"Lex? Lex, are you in here?" Toby asked, peeking around the door. He scanned the shelves, but the one Lex was perched on, heart pounding, was high enough and deep enough that he couldn't see her. Could he?

"I looked *everywhere*," Toby said, quieter this time. Lex smiled. She was safe! The closet door closed again. Lex waited for Toby to leave, so she could climb down. But he didn't leave. There was silence, and then he went back to her chest of toys, and Lex could hear him moving things in it.

Her mind raced. What was he doing? What was *in* the chest? Lex hadn't looked inside it in months. Her stuffed animals. Her toy horses. Her blue ball with the green stars on it. Her dinosaurs.

Her dress-up clothes, with the princess dress and crown, from when she was little. Toby would find them!

Lex edged her way down from the top shelf. There was just enough room between the shelves' edges and the closet door for her to slide to the floor, but she banged her knee on the way down. Toby must have heard the thud, because he ran over and opened the door just as Lex touched the ground, and she spilled over onto her back at his feet.

"Lex?" Toby asked in amazement. "Where did you come from? I looked in there..."

"I was on the top shelf," Lex explained, looking up at him and trying to catch her breath, rubbing her sore knee. "You couldn't see me."

"Are you okay?"

"I just hit my knee, a little. It doesn't hurt." Lex sat up. "What were you doing?"

"Oh . . . I saw your . . . dinosaurs. Before, when I was looking for you. I just wanted to see if you had any others." He looked down, not looking at Lex or at the chest of toys. "Sorry."

"It's okay, I guess," Lex said, standing. She walked over to the chest. The princess crown was just peeking out, next to her plastic brontosaurus. Lex slammed the chest closed and walked back over to Toby, her cheeks hot, wondering if he'd seen the crown.

He was looking around at her pale green walls. "I've never seen your room before, Lex." She watched him take in the drawings of herself in the castle, the tall white bookcase, her butterfly collection pinned down in black window boxes on the walls, the green-and-white flower pattern on her bedspread. "It's nice. Pretty."

"Thanks." Lex looked away when he tried to meet her eyes. Her heart was starting to beat faster again, like it had when she was sure that Toby would find her in the closet. Then he saw her castle, empty in the center of her room.

"You know, I've never been in your castle, either." He was already walking towards it, and Lex's throat was too dry to tell him to stop. "Can I?" Without meaning to, Lex nodded.

"Ladies first," he said, standing next to it, holding out his hand. Lex looked at him for a minute, trying to figure out what he meant. Then she realized he wanted her to get in with him. Oh. She walked to where he was standing. They wouldn't both fit, would they? He was bigger than Katelyn.

Lex was startled to realize that she was now tall enough to step over the side of her castle, instead of having to climb down into it from something else. Her mother would be happy—it would stop her having to stand on the furniture. She took Toby's hand and stepped over the side. Toby smiled when she let go of his hand too fast, plopping down gracelessly inside the castle. He threw one long leg over the side, and then the other, and sat down in the corner diagonal from her, facing her. They both drew their knees up to their chests, but even then there were places where their legs touched.

"So what do you and Katie talk about, in your castle? Sieges? Dragons? Knights?" Toby asked, looking across the castle at Lex.

"Um. We talk about lots of things. Her old friends. She tells me about them, and sometimes now we talk about the girls she knows here, but not much, because I'm not really friends with them. Or boys. Sometimes she talks about boys she knows," Lex said, staring down at her knees. Her jeans had a hole in the left knee, and she started to play with the frayed edge, twisting it in her fingers.

"But what do *you* talk about, Lex? That's just Katie talking. Don't you ever get to say anything? What boys do you talk about?" Toby teased, smiling, and then his smile faded as Lex took too long to answer. "Lex?"

"I dunno. We just talk. Does it matter?" Lex asked, for the first time embarrassed that she had so little to say to Katelyn when they talked. Except about Toby. She flushed, remembering Katelyn saying, 'You like Toby.' Katelyn had been sitting just where Toby was now. When Lex sat in the castle with Katelyn, their legs didn't touch.

"No, I guess not. I just wondered." They sat in silence for a while, and Toby went back to studying Lex's room, avoiding her eyes as adamantly as she was avoiding his.

He stood abruptly. "I think I'm going to go home."

Lex stood up too, and they were so close to each other, standing inside the castle's four brown walls, that she felt like she would fall over—like her center of balance had shifted somehow.

"You don't have to. We could play something else," Lex said, not knowing if she wanted him to stay or leave. "We can play knights and dragons, and I'll be the dragon *and* the princess, or we can play tag, or anything."

"No, I should go home and see if Katie and Mom are back yet." He stepped over the castle wall, and Lex followed, still unsettled by the fact that she was tall enough to do so.

"But..."

"It's okay, Lex. I'll come back tomorrow, with Katie. It was nice to see your room, and to get to talk in your castle." Toby smiled down at her—not so far down, anymore. Lex's heart pounded again, but this was different than it had been when she lay curled up in the closet, waiting to be found. And then he hesitated, and then he kissed her, and smiled at her again, softly, and stepped back. "I'll see you tomorrow."

Lex heard him close her bedroom door as he left, but she didn't watch him go. She stared at the floor as she listened to Toby's voice, faint through the door, saying goodbye to her mother. And then the front door closed. Her mother came into Lex's room a few minutes later, a dishtowel in her hand.

"Did you and Toby have a fight?"

"No," Lex whispered. She was still standing next to her castle. Then, louder: "No, we didn't have a fight. He wanted to see if Katelyn was home yet from the doctor's." Lex didn't look up. She walked over to her bed and sat on it, looking at her castle.

Lex's mother stood with her pale narrow hand on the door frame for a few more seconds, as if she wanted to say something, and then she left, closing Lex's bedroom door behind her.

Lex lay on her bed for hours, watching the shadows slowly move to take over her floor as the light faded, and she felt the minutes changing her body as she did so. She lay there until it was dark, and Katelyn's voice seemed to come from the shadows all around, saying that three years wasn't a very long time, was it? But now, having watched the shadows transform the familiar shapes of her room into a strange new topography in just a few hours, Lex knew the truth: three years was the longest time in the world, and in three years she would have changed so much that she would be unrecognizable. It was already happening—soon she wouldn't fit in her castle at all. She already had to fold herself into sharp angles to sleep in it. And maybe the monsters were changing, too, and maybe soon they wouldn't be monsters anymore. Would the castle still keep them out?

* * *

That night, Lex slept in her castle again, and this time she cried, and the castle took her to forests where the shadows held deep secrets and the sunlight held deeper ones; and to mountains where the magic in the air fell in flakes onto her pale skin and gilded the tear tracks on her face; and to oceans where her eyes and lungs burned with the salt water, and seaweed slid along her arms and made her shiver.

Lex woke before it was light out. She turned her bedside light on and stared up at the ceiling. Eventually she slid out of bed and brought back her mother's kitchen scissors. In the dim, yellow light of her room, with predawn just edging through her curtains, there was no sound except for the rasping as Lex sawed harshly through her castle's cardboard walls.

MY FATHER MOVES THROUGH TIME LIKE A DIRIGIBLE

Gregg Cusick

Lakehurst, NJ. September 2, 1925. 2:52 PM. Despite objections of Commander Zachary Lansdowne, an Ohio native, fearing line squalls and late-summer storms, the navy orders the 682-foot blimp Shenandoah *to set off for its tour of Midwest state fairs. As Lansdowne and his crew of forty in the rigid airship sail out over the pine woods of New Jersey, his wife watching from the ground turns her head away. So do wives and families of the other crewmen who have come to the field. It is considered bad luck to watch your husband's ship fade out of sight.*

I always sit down gingerly in the principal's office, into a chair surely more often reserved for the rumps of 13-year-olds. We smile, the principal and I, perhaps appreciating the same irony at the same moment. See, I'm 83 years old, while the principal of the Sam Houston Middle School is about my son's age, about 43. We've met before, and he knows what I want to discuss, again. My proposal for a school play. It's historical, I tell him again, and really about how time and memory work. As if anyone knows *that*, he's thinking.

But I can see it all, I tell him. At least the scene, the set and props, so clearly, the illustration of the smooth movement of time. I don't, at first at least, mention my responsibility for the crash of the dirigible *Shenandoah* in 1925, nor my responsibility for my father leaving just a few months later, although this is not because they have nothing to do with the story. It's more that if you go before a producer, say, to pitch an idea for a movie, if you start off with ramblings about guilt and responsibility and not fiery crashes and drama, you've pretty much shot yourself out of the air before you get a chance to fly, don't you think?

"So it's to be the Commander's, Lansdowne's, it's *his* story?" Principal Constantine asks. "Or is it *your* view of it now? Or is it the boy's, the four-year-old's—is it *his* story?"

"No," I say. "History," I say.

The principal is a smart man, and we've known each other for years. We live in the same Austin neighborhood and sometimes wave to one another as we put our recycling by the curb. He knows my son, I believe, though we've never discussed this. My son and I have been, I guess you'd call it estranged, since the divorce back now almost twenty years, but we still talk at the holidays and I call on his birthday. Maybe estranged is the wrong word, since we communicate, but it's like some form of distance or at least things unsaid, maybe *emotional estrangement*, you could call it. For my part, I wish we were closer but I'm not sure how to get there. I wonder if I may be like my own father in this way.

Speaking of whom, my father, did I tell you of my earliest lasting image of him? It was that afternoon, September 2, 1925. We're an Austin family, but my father was teaching then in Gettysburg, Pennsylvania, and we rented a little house outside of town, on what seemed to me then to be a huge tract of land but was actually less than an acre. I didn't know all this at four, of course, but I didn't recognize my father until then either.

I can hear his whistle this moment, cutting through the air on a bright, early fall day of much sun and scattered clouds, visibility probably fifteen miles or more. I've always been preoccupied with weather—I flew bombers in both WWII and Korea, was a commercial pilot after that. I've been forever fascinated by flight. But I was inside the house that afternoon when I heard my father calling my name and the name of my brother. My mother came running, too. I skidded to a stop at the huge unmoving feet that held up the statue that was my father, and I ran my eyes slowly up the legs, time-creased khakis, worn at the knees and white paint spattered, up to his plaid wool shirt, to shoulders and across the outstretched arm that pointed toward the distant sky like one of those memorable statue-stances of Stalin or, more recently now, Saddam Hussein. Pointing off into the glowing future. The sun behind my father haloed his head so that I could not see the features of his face, only shapes in bronze light. My eyes followed the line of his arm to see what my father, like a circus barker, was presenting to us.

It was of course the blimp, one of the great "rigids," an airship named *Shenandoah*, an Indian word meaning "daughter of the stars." My father always knew these facts, the details that make a story. And the dirigible, she was beautiful and massive but somehow seemed also light, moving smoothly, so distant across our view as if attached to my father's hand by some invisible, mile-long cable. I might've even imagined then my father being carried away by the blimp, like a clown by a handful of balloons. This was late afternoon, still hours before the *Shenandoah* would encounter the storms that would bring her down.

In the play, I tell the principal (Mr. Constantine his name is; mine's Joe, by the way), in the play it can be just as vivid.

Or if I were seated in an adult-sized chair before the massive glass-topped desk of the film producer, pitching the idea—I'd mention of course the natural forces, the storm and winds, and the looting after the crash. The looting could be a major sub-plot, sad and fascinating to a generation gobbling reality TV shows. Later, the surviving officers of the *Shenandoah* tried to keep watch, but souvenir seekers and worse materialized from the nowhere of rural Ohio and carted off the remains of the dirigible, leaving not even the skeleton as a fish picked by sharks, since there was really no flesh to the craft and the structure itself was all that was exploitable.

But I hesitate, and then I realize I'm asking the producer, the principal, for another chance, a new start to my spiel. I take a deep breath, and I hear my voice again, like an NPR reporter smart, confident, serious:

It begins and ends, and begins and ends again in my mind—I tell the principal. Curtain up, and it's the Jersey launch scene, wives and families crowding the stage while suspended upper right is a plywood cut-out blimp. Which is pulled, from the audience's right to left, smoothly across a clothesline, in front of a backdrop of clouds and blue-sky interspersed. Some plywood "clouds" are suspended in front of the backdrop, to give the scene depth and allow the "blimp" to pass through, at times "disappearing" behind "clouds." If your head conjures the tune, the words 'it's only a pa-per moon, floating over a card-board sea,' then you're getting it.

I tell all this to the principal, for the third time, I think, it's got to be three times at least. He could be my son, I guess, him forties and me eighties, his grown kids my grandkids if I had them. I tell Constantine for the third time that the school kids could really learn something from my play and, no, not just about the great "rigids," the airships, but about time and memory, about relativity, about personal responsibility. I can see what Constantine is thinking. At my age, maybe this is one of the few perks—I know he thinks I've got a whale of a story or, well, a decent tale, and a story that works on several levels. And I know he thinks I don't see it all.

"Your story works on several levels," he says then.

Three-quarters of a mile above Philadelphia, PA. September 2, 1925. 4:18 PM. The Shenandoah *passes over the city through scattered clouds, heading west toward the Alleghenies. She passes over central Pennsylvania in the late afternoon, cruising at 4,000 feet, the critical "pressure height" at which the ship's helium gas bags are 100% full. Lansdowne tries to rest but a brewing storm in the northwest has him back in the control room shortly after 3 AM.*

He's probably forty-three, Principal Constantine, as I said, though I'm a lousy judge of such things. As I was even before I got to the stage where everyone was decades younger than I, though I'm not looking for sympathy. He's got a peppery beard and big gray-blue eyes. He looks more like an actor who would play a middle school principal in the movie version. Divorced just a couple years, Mr. Constantine sports a once-white, wrinkled button down shirt, pleated slacks the same age and creases. He smiles, again, at my pitch for the Sam Houston Middle School's spring play. I know the two kids with the beeping cell phones in his outer office await his discipline. I can see in his face, his eyes that he thinks he knows me, and maybe I am the old man he sees. Still, I don't think he understands the *Shenandoah* story, what it means to the boy or what it meant when it crashed in 1925.

"Again," he says to me. "Fascinating." And there's both patronizing and admiration in the word voiced. "Think," he says to me as if I wasn't there. "Hundreds, maybe thousands saw it flying over that day, but how many are still alive? It's kind of a 'last Confederate widow' sort of thing, isn't it? I can't tell if he sees me as this widow, or if I'm the young writer, to his savvy producer. "I can see the cardboard (*plywood*, I say) blimp on the clothesline. And the first scene—Jersey, right? With the wives and families watching the dads fly away. Next the blimp is pulled slowly across, about center stage, where the father, *your* father, points upward and the boy and his family watch it pass. Interesting," Constantine says, "I like the symbolic images of the 'blimp-father' leaving the families. Your own father was about to leave his family then, right?" He pauses, picturing it, and I can't deny the images, yet of course I feel he's distorting my intentions for the play, reading too much in.

I think Constantine will ask then if I somehow caused the crash, caused my father to leave, but he does not. Instead he asks me about my health, what the doctors I've surely seen must've said about my declining health. And I tell him—I don't know from where inside me these outbursts come—that he can go screw himself. He laughs at this, tells me to come back and talk again soon, that he always loves my company. My mind is recounting the events in the life of the boy, but Mr. Constantine is on his feet then, extending his hand. Again, he's the producer behind the desk.

"About the play," I say.

"I'll pitch it to the drama teacher," the principal says, though I think this assurance is a falsehood. But as I'm leaving, my back to him, he calls out:

"About *flight*," he says, "have you thought about your own passion for flight? And your father's running away from your mother and his kids, or yours from your wife and son?"

Divorce, irreconcilables, I could scream. She cheated, the rumors were rampant, all over town, I could inform him. Instead I ask him if he's a certified psychoanalyst. And again, I remind him that he can screw himself, knowing still that he's a smart man and that he thinks he's seeing some levels I haven't considered.

A mile above Caldwell, Ohio. September 3, 1925. 5:05 AM. Battling headwinds, the Shenandoah *slows. Rising two meters per second, her ascent can't be checked. She is forced into a squall, the clash of opposing winds—one moist and warm, the other dry and cold. At 5,000 feet, the blimp is pointed up 15 degrees and still rises. Lansdowne orders helium valved off to check the ascent. Then, at 6300 feet, the cold force of the squall pushes the ship into a steep descent, 25 feet per second. Lansdowne orders tons of water ballast dumped to halt the plunge.*

And what I didn't get to describe to Principal Constantine (because while we met for an hour it seemed like seven minutes—is that the ratio of actual to perceived time, the formula I'm looking for?):

In this vision, *if you would*, I tell Constantine, substitute *time* for *sky*, sub it just as you sometimes will mashed potatoes for salad; it's that easy. And simply allow the plywood blimp to move ever smoothly but *between* a cloud or two, so that it's not always visible to the viewer on the ground or, I mean, to the audience.

* * *

September, 1925. I know, I know, it's an unbelievable amount of time to go back. But we must remain flexible, my yoga teacher tells me repeatedly. 1925, can you imagine what *hasn't happened yet*, not new VW Beetles or even the original ones, not Desert Storm or Vietnam or Korea even or WWII. Not yet even a Depression, though we're sitting flat in the middle of Prohibition, not that it stopped us. But I'm four, okay, four years old, and I don't have any idea who my father is. Until I hear that whistle. Thumb and index finger moist and pressed together, you know the sound.

I'm eighty-three, but I hardly feel it, isn't that crazy? And I know I sometimes fail to connect my thoughts, but that's only because I hope my listener knows the connectors that are, thus, unnecessary. You follow?

Yet in this college town sometimes girls of eighteen or forty-three look at me and I'm still at least mentally giving it a chance and they're casting aside glances, rolling eyes or snorting like I'm a doddering fool. They probably talk about me, pass rumors about my war stories and my eccentricities. But, point is, I feel pretty fit, intellectually in step, yet from their view, their perspective, I'm a crazed old man, a wild card. Like right now, I'm sitting, scribbling in my notebook, in a restaurant I lately favor. I've ordered the salmon entrée and what I'd have thought was a pretty smart glass of pinot noir. But my pretty young server seems hesitant, stays back a foot more than she has to her other tables, I can tell, don't tell me I can't. The air begins to smell of grilled pork, the special. And fall leaves, and late season grass clippings, when the door opens again and again then as the place gets louder and very busy.

Now at this late age I believe my father to have been, like all of us I guess, many people. He was gifted and angry, a reluctant father, a frustrated philosopher, a romantic maybe of the second kind—the first being those who pass away or are dramatically taken before the vision gets crushed; the second those who live the whole time believing or at least wanting to, that something or other could happen in this way or another, both rightly and beautifully, like an editor clips a movie. Me,

I see them both. I wonder does my own boy know me in these vague ways, or something more specific? And I think my father's violence and self-hatred were nothing of romance. And listen: when he moistened fingers to blow, and near-connected right thumb and index finger to whistle, that brought you running lemme tell you.

Get out here this is something to see get out here come on!

And so we ran to the yard and looked up to where he was pointing, my brother and mother and me not knowing what we were looking for, be it geese (we'd seen, but still beautiful), a funnel cloud (also seen, and we lost a garage this way), or something our father may never have seen with objective eyes (we'd been called to plenty of these false alarms, four-alarmers of his mind, and we so wanted to see them we nodded always as if we did but he knew, he knew). But we looked at his finger pointing, like hunting dogs, then beyond it into the sky and saw it. All of us saw it, we decided for ourselves and confirmed to each other later.

One couldn't forget such a sight, against such a painter's background blue sky, this buoyant blimp, some five decades before the Goodyear version showed up at sporting events, can you imagine what a sight the thing was? And I was four, did I tell you? What does one recall about being four? Nothing, I'd have wagered, yet I had this startling all-sense image: feel of warm wind, sound of father's whistle, touch of my brother's hand on my shoulder pulling me, smell of lye soap my mother was making, taste of the grit of blowing dust that was always in my mouth I think now at least, and the sight of the dirigible (I know now that's what it was), floating overhead, beyond my father's outstretched index finger (strangely his right, though he was left-handed). An observer of the scene could have drawn a straight line from my upturned head through my father's that was turned toward me, along his right arm that he wasn't looking at, through into the air and to the blimp that from that distance, in the vision of an observer standing perhaps ten feet from me, might appear to be not distant and huge but close and just a scale model or even a well-painted plywood cut-out maybe three feet long.

Mrs. Lansdowne—she was at the time just 27—spoke unrevealed words to her husband, in Lakehurst, NJ, and then she looked away as the ship sailed from sight. I had no reason, I think now, to believe that somehow I had caused the crash. Or that either of the above—words not spoken or the accident—had anything to do with my father's disappearance some months later. As much my fault as the damned Depression that was already part of our lives then but that they'd have you believe didn't really hit until '29, several years later. But I was just four then, when the blimp went over. And of course I digress. We were talking about my father.

Near ground, near Dayton, Ohio. September 3, 1925. 6:27 AM. Opposing wind forces wrench the Shenandoah. Amidships, steel girders tear and two crewmen are pitched out into space. The blimp falls, levels off, then again rises precipitously. Struts supporting the control car snap, the ship spins rapidly in a circle, Lansdowne and seven others in the gondola plunge to their deaths. Weighed down by three engines, the separated stern section falls like an arrow, glances against a hillside. Remarkably, the engines are scraped off by the earth, and the loose stern section floats up again. Men tumble from the wreckage, leap to the ground trying to avoid the crashing, disintegrating ship. Crewmen release helium and actually crash-land a section and survive. Debris is strewn over an area of twelve square miles.

So remember that I said that it begins and ends and begins and ends, and begins again. I realize for a moment now that I may be repeating myself. But each version's different, yes? And I only humbly wish to make the point that we're all, every one of us full of fact and fiction. The waitress before me now may not even believe I was shot down over Germany in '43 and, hell, maybe I wasn't. And just as much, I mean it depends as I may have said on one's point of view, where one places one's tripod and starts (and stops) the camera rolling. And see how perspective-talk leads us around and back right back to *TIME*? And of course its buddy, the great manipulator of time, memory. Memory that can leap forward and backward minutes, months, decades in single bounds that only take seconds.

* * *

On the next visit, or perhaps the previous one, I say to Constantine (like a kid, one whose tiny frame would fit this chair I'm in, would): "Did I tell you it was really all about time, that is, time and memory?"

His look is both pensive and somehow patronizing. Does he want me out of here? Is he comprehending my pitch, my theme? That is, either he's thinking of time, or of how to ask me to leave without offending me? His comments can be taken at various levels of seriousness.

"Right," he says to me, in a tone impossible to read, "about *time*," he finishes. I'm thinking he definitely italicized that *time* there. "Interesting," he says.

A plywood blimp, I say. Smoothing across a sharp cloudy late summer blue sky. The sky subs for time, the dirigible then being any of us, my father for instance, moving through it. Yet my father doesn't seem to move at all—he's there with his arm outstretched, whenever I look up. But he's actually moving daringly fast—rotating with the earth at 1037 mph, and revolving with the earth around the sun at a speed that is relative to the center of our galaxy, just as our galaxy is moving relative to the nearby galaxies.

But I too, just a boy of four, I'm moving at the same speed. So we're like the two motorcyclists speeding down the road side by side: we can toss a tennis ball back and forth, and to either of us the other seems to be motionless, relatively speaking. Which is simply to try to explain perhaps why my father seems to be motionless, and time seems the thing moving smoothly behind him. So we're back to point of view, as the dependent factor in measuring motion and, can we say, measuring time as well?

On the ground near Dayton, Ohio. September 3, 1925. 6:45 AM. All of the Shenandoah *is now down. Fourteen men are dead. The fragments of the ship and its 29 survivors are scattered over the flat Ohio landscape. First come the rescuers, followed closely by the curious, and the looters. By noon thousands of scavengers, armed with knives, hatchets, pliers, wrenches, make off with logbooks, steel girders, yards of fabric, and the ship's instruments. The still-dazed officers and enlisted men try unsuccessfully to keep guard. The gondola, miles from the other sections of the ship, is picked clean by nightfall. Even Lansdowne's Annapolis class ring is missing from his lifeless hand.*

I leave principal Constantine's office, sit down in a regulation-sized adult chair in this restaurant in town, where I watch my hand scribble these words that you might read in what might be described as real time, the description of our meeting. I know, again because I've known it before, that he won't be recommending to the drama department that they put on the *Shenandoah* play I proposed. And I'm not really agitated. Knowing, as I do, that I have my image. I have my father, moving in and out of the clouds, smoothly through the years, the sun behind him haloing his head.

HOLLARS

Susan Grothouse

The last meal to pass my lips in Ford County was a pizza in the shape of a heart, piled high with searing cheese that dripped down to my wrist and burned it white. I feel like that's a metaphor for something but I don't really know what. Before I got burnt, I was just an innocent tourist, visiting my aunt and uncle in Ford County, Kentucky – home of ancient Indian burial grounds and canned sardines. The son, the curiously named Clementine, was a lad interested in things like rap groups and fishing. The last time I saw him wear a shirt was at our grandmother's funeral seven years ago, but most of the time he wore his skin proudly, his broad shoulders back, his skin taut and tan. His best friend, Frank Hall, was the opposite; he was wiry and thin and scared. We all successfully co-existed until one day, something came up, you know, one of those times when the adults have to go away, and Clementine, Frank and I were all left alone.

We were sitting on the couch, staring at the TV, when a commercial came on that said Pizza Hut was having a special on heart-shaped pizza, due to the upcoming Valentine's Day. Clementine laughed loudly, grabbed the white phone by its cord, reeled it in and made an order – because there is nothing more hilarious than eating romantic pizza with two other guys.

When the doorbell finally rang, Clementine heaved himself off of the heap-like couch, straightened his backwards baseball cap, pulled his jeans down slightly so just the right amount of boxer showed and answered the door with his usual jocularity. After he obtained the goods from the glazed-eyed girl, he closed the door, hoisted the four boxes onto his bare shoulder with ease and began the procession to the dingy kitchen table. I followed him, pulled by allegiance to my older cousin, the allure of pizza and the desire to not be alone in the same room with Frank. I surveyed the kitchen as I stepped into it and was immediately steeped in the smell of cigarettes burning in a not so distant past. The room was bathed in yellow light and two salt and pepper shakers shaped like a fat man and wife in bath towels sat upon the waxy tablecloth. My imagination gave them life easily. Scenes ran through my mind of eating cereal while two fat barely clothed people argued about something pointless, their arm flab becoming progressively more active as they became angry – it flipped and floundered as if it wanted to slide off the bone entirely. This dysfunctional, awkward touch fit the room perfectly.

Clementine set the two boxes down on the table and went in search of the elusive plastic cups. Without having to be told, I went after the root beer, while keeping an eye on Frank, who just stood by the pizza, eyes bugging out and knuckles whitening, like a new father unwilling to leave his child alone in the nursery. Then he began to pry open the cardboard lid slowly, as to be imperceptible to Clementine, consumed in his search. Clementine glanced over and quickly established his dominance in the situation – "Get yourself a plate, Frank! You ain't a heathen" – and sent a paper plate flying in Frank's general direction.

Frank caught the plate with ease, scooped up an angular piece of pizza with his bony hands and began devouring the pie as if it was the last meal he would ever eat. I walked over to the flimsy table and placed the two liter of root beer next to the salt and pepper couple. Then I gingerly lifted a piece of pizza up to my mouth and took a small bite. It singed my mouth and my only option was to spit it out and look like a wuss or swallow it and take the pain like a man. I chose the latter.

"Sure is hot," remarked Clementine about a minute too late.

A couple of minutes passed purely devoted to the sounds of teeth gnashing, breathing and the squeaks of the table. Then Frank said mid-bite, "I, for one, thank the good Lord that I have any pizza at all. And you would do well to follow me." He pointed at me with his unnaturally large eyes, overlooking Clementine, for he was surely thankful enough.

"Why, praytell?" I said.

"Because in them Hollars – in the mountains – they don't got pizza, heart-shaped or otherwise." He inhaled another slice of pizza and Clementine spilled molten cheese on his bare chest.

"What's a Hollar?" Frank, who until this point had been wholly focused on the consumption of pizza, stopped abruptly to look at me like I was an idiot.

"Well," he stretched the word as far as it would go, "every educated person knows what a Hollar is. A Hollar is up in the mountains, where all the poor people live, because we don't like having them around. And all they do is grow their own food and get married so they can have more kids. And the houses are literally made out of dust and paint."

"Oh." I imagined a house completely constructed of dust, filled with dust people shuffling around. "And are the people made of dust?" I asked absentmindedly.

"No, you retard. They're…like normal people, except nobody likes them."

"Why not?"

"Because they're poor. And they're dirty. And they let old men marry little girls."

"Oh." I imagined an old dust figure in the house with a young dust figure. Age doesn't really matter, when you're made of dust and ready to crumble anyway.

"You don't think that's bad?" Frank menaced, between bites of love pizza. "You actually think that's acceptable?" I looked at him appraisingly; his small chest was puffed out like a dying bird and his eyes were popping and veiny. No doubt he would try to fight me over this timely women's issue, but it was unsure if he would be able to conquer me. Probably not. He was notably smaller than I was and I was infinitely smarter and faster.

"I didn't know you were such a fervent supporter of women's rights," I noted quietly, avoiding his gaze. Then Frank exploded, letting out a great roar that I didn't think he was capable of and shaking the table jerkily with his stick-like hands with an almost religious fervor. I didn't do anything. I just looked down at my hands in my lap. And I thought to myself, what could make a normally self-centered kid care so much about the less fortunate? Perhaps he had visited a Hollar before and witnessed the disparity. More likely he himself had been the product of an old man-young girl union. Only a person with something emotionally invested in the situation could get so upset about it. As Frank jiggled the table, I noticed something boxy jumping around in his front pocket – a box of matches or maybe a pocket knife. I wasn't sure what would happen next, but I knew that Clementine, the alpha male, would keep Frank under control. As I looked at him, Clementine looked down and raised his eyebrows. Not yet.

Then Frank started grabbing things on the table and throwing them to the ground. He seized the two-liter, which was uncapped and about three-fourths full and tossed it to the ground where it seeped generously into the rug. Frank picked up the pepper shaker man and threw him over his shoulder where he hit a wall and shattered in a puff of ceramic and pepper. His wife was not a widow for long, following him only seconds later. And then, with the desperateness of a man committing suicide, Frank picked up the second pizza box, which was about half full, and held it over his head, ready to destroy the pie.

He had gone too far. He had threatened the pizza. Clementine raised his hand, like an old Indian chief, and said, "No." Slowly, Frank lowered the box and placed it in safe territory. For a second we surveyed the damage sheepishly. Then Clementine broke in,

"Hey, hey! Um, let's talk about something more in the spirit of Valentine's Day! Like spreading peace and joy and good will towards women! Now eat your 'za, and speak no more of this!" Frank gave a heavy sigh and angrily bit into a piece of pizza. And in my mind, we were suddenly in the Hollars, eating dust over a table of dust, waiting for dust to fall through an hourglass made of dust. And then I put my dust hands into the pocket of my dust jeans and there was nothing at all in them. Not even lint.

MR. PENNY'S EXPERIENCE

Rolli

When Mr. Penny died that night on the surgeon's table, it seemed to him as if the ceiling became wax, then papery, fog, then melted altogether. Loose strands of it remained, like arms of jellyfish, and brushed against him as he rose - or should have brushed him, only he felt nothing, despite being a notoriously ticklish man. He tried looking at his arms, but couldn't find them, and had the same trouble locating the rest of himself. *But there I am*, catching sight of a familiar-looking fellow on the table below, being thumped and prodded by a growing horde of white coats. He reached out, tried swimming downwards like a desperate frog, but with his limbs a good eight feet below, that hardly worked. Shouting proved equally ineffective. Nothing seemed to slow or stop his steady upward movement. This was a conundrum, and conundrums always gave Mr. Penny a migraine. So he turned his head (preferring to think he had one), and waited, as patiently as he could, to see what happened next. There were stars overhead, now, and beneath him the frantic shouts and alarms grew softer every moment. He was glad to leave them behind. Soon there was nothing but darkness and stars all around.

Well, this is different, he thought.

Mr. Penny had a sudden, strong impression of brightness behind him, not that he could see any actual trace of it. Still, to satisfy his curiosity, he turned around again, half-expecting a last far-off glimpse of the operating room. Instead, he saw the Earth itself, radiantly glowing, a marble.

A little flurry of panic. After all, he'd never been up this high before. But he adjusted quickly - a surprise even to himself. In no time moving bodilessly through space felt as natural as – (nothing had ever really felt natural to Mr. Penny. At least not in a very long time).

Before he really had time to admire the beauty of the planet, it had shrunk to a star-sized dot. This was, of course, a major disappointment. Mr. Penny didn't know when he'd have the opportunity to view it from such a height again, and worried it was one of those "once in a lifetime" things people were always talking about. *I should have brought my camera.* As he moved along, the dot vanishing altogether, the likelihood that it was a once in a lifetime thing seemed strong. *It was a nice place*, he thought, trying to console himself, *but I've seen enough of it.*

The loneliness, the strange newness of the circumstances would have troubled most people, but Mr. Penny didn't really mind. He was by nature a solitary man, a retiring one, and when he did venture out found the world pretty baffling in general. Besides, there were so many interesting things to look at. There were stars, millions of them, but he couldn't find any of the constellations he liked. For a while he wished he had his telescope; though after passing right through one star (he liked to think it prickled), Mr. Penny realized he was as close to the universe as anyone could care to be.

There seemed to be no end of wonders. Flying rocks. Bursts of light. Clouds of all hues and sizes. The first time Mr. Penny approached one of these clouds (it was purple), he grew unbearably excited, and couldn't wait to see what it would be like in the midst of all that colour. The closer he came, though, the further away the substance of the cloud seemed to be, until, to his disappointment, it thinned out and faded into nothing. *A lot like walking into fog*, he thought. *You never really get to it*. Still, Mr. Penny enjoyed traveling through these elusive mists; liked going through the pink ones best of all, and imagined the whole thing was more fun that it really was. More than once he encountered burning ice, which he wouldn't have believed unless he'd seen it, and had the good fortune to catch a glimpse an outrageously big planet suddenly go flat as a cat's whisker, then vanish altogether. Though he'd seen that with his own eyes, he *still* couldn't believe it.

There were, of course, long stretches where there was nothing in particular to look at. To pass the time during these periods, Mr. Penny tried counting stars. But they vanished and reappeared so quickly that the whole thing was just too frustrating. Adding to the frustration was the fact that the speed at which he traveled never stayed the same for long. At times he went so fast that the stars around him went from streaks to long dotted lines to nothing at all, just hurtling darkness, and he missed lots of good stuff. At other times, he barely seemed to go at all, which was fine if there was something to look at, but ...

Just when he was starting to get bored, Mr. Penny noticed something that, even under the circumstances, he found strange.

At first, it looked like any of the small specks of light he'd been zipping past, for how long he wasn't sure. As he came closer, though, slowing every moment, he couldn't help but notice that *this* speck had a unique quality. It appeared to be, hovering in the middle of space no less, a nicely furnished living room without a roof (*like at a play*, thought Mr. Penny). From the main room lolled a long red-carpeted hallway, curving downwards where it ended. In the middle of the room was a low table, complete with silver tea service and a basket of what appeared to be scones. Around the table were a dozen or so high-backed wooden chairs, painted black. All of them were unoccupied but one, which bore the weight of a plump, sweet-looking elderly woman.

Alighting on the carpet, very close to the sloping curve, Mr. Penny was glad to see that, first of all, he had his body back, and everything was where it ought to be. He was also relieved that the carpet bore his weight as well as any solid floor, and he didn't go falling down into space.

He wasn't sure what to do next, so he looked around, and got to noticing things. It was a very nice hallway; probably the nicest he'd ever been in. Lining the walls were gold-framed paintings of men and women, some in old-fashioned clothes, some in modern ones. But they were all painted in the same fancy way, *and probably by the same person*, thought Mr. Penny. The temperature of the hall was just right. Mr. Penny had always found that most people's houses are far too cold. And though he couldn't find any source of light - there was no ceiling, after all, and nothing on the walls - the whole place was well lit, and as cheerful as he could have wished it.

From his vantage at the end of the hallway, Mr. Penny could see only a small portion of the room to which it led - essentially, the back of one of the chairs, and above that the head of the woman seated at the opposite end of the table. She smiled in silence. Mr. Penny took a few nervous steps forward. It was nice, after such a long journey, to finally have some company, *and she looks pleasant enough*. Still, he was skeptical. From experience, he'd learned that an awful lot of women who look pleasant and have nice painted-on smiles will nonetheless whop you with a purse if you get an inch too close. *This one doesn't seem to have a purse, thankfully*. On her cup fingers - I mean, the ones she was holding her teacup with - were several large, glittering rings. The other fingers toyed with a string of - *not pearls, but white beads around her neck*. Her tightly curled hair was almost certainly dyed (red). She wore a bit too much make-up.

"Mr. Penny," she said, refilling her cup. "I've been expecting you."

"*Me?*" He could hardly believe it.

"Tea?"

"Free," said Mr. Penny, thinking it was a rhyming game.

"Oh, it won't cost you a dime," said the woman. "Take a seat." He did - the one furthest from her, but nearest to the scones - looking about nervously as she filled his cup.

He was a bit reluctant to drink it. She was a stranger, after all. Though she was old, and most old people, Mr. Penny had found, are kind, he knew it was never a good idea to trust just anyone. But she downed the stuff herself without any apparent discomfort, and looked harmless enough. Besides, he didn't want to upset her. So he took a small mouthful, and was pleased to find that it tasted like plain old black China tea. He might have wondered where on earth she got it from - but didn't.

"Scone?" she asked.

Being partial to scones, he didn't hesitate to take one.

"No butter, I'm afraid," noticing how he looked about the table forlornly. "A little hard to come by in these parts."

"That's alright," he said, trying not to sound disappointed.

"How was the journey down?"

It had seemed more like a journey *up* to him, though all he said was,

"Fine, thanks." It was his favourite expression, and usually all he had to say to anyone. The same people, he'd noticed, who would stop him in the street to say "And how are *you?*" talked to other people about all kinds of things - movies, weddings, politics. But with him, strangely, they never wanted to know anything more than how he *was*. It was a conundrum.

"If you have any questions," said the woman, after a long pause, "don't hesitate to ask."

"Umm ..." Mr. Penny thought for a while. It's not that there weren't a million things he wanted to ask or could have asked. It's just that he wasn't very good at conversations, especially when the other person was looking you right in the eye. The newness of the place didn't help, either. So he timidly picked at the scone, and looked around the room.

Like the hall, it had an elegant, expensive look. There were plenty of tall, potted plants, and each of the several shelves and stands which stood in the corners had a doily and at least one glass curio on it. Though the room was bright - even brighter that the hall - he looked in vain for a lamp or a candle or even a switch. There were three doors: one just behind the woman's chair, and one each on the walls to her left and right. Just over her shoulder was a painting of - *well, it has to be her*, thought Mr. Penny. *When she was younger*. The painted figure reclined against a piano, smiling. And there was another painting, too.

"Is that *me?*" asked Mr. Penny, astounded. He looked so young - about nineteen or twenty - that he barely recognized himself. His picture-self sported a trim moustache (*I can never get it even anymore*) and the same orange coat he'd worn to the hospital, only brand new-looking instead of ratty. There was a briefcase in his hand. Suddenly, he didn't want to look at the picture anymore.

"You've had a very long trip," said the woman. "You must be tired."

Mr. Penny nodded. He suddenly was.

"Perhaps you'd like to go to your room?"

He nodded again, and said, "Yes, thank you. But - I'm afraid it's a long way off by now."

She smiled. "I wasn't talking about your *old* room."

"Oh," said Mr. Penny, slouching a little.

"I was talking about the *new* one."

"New?" said Mr. Penny, sitting upright.

"Of course. I should think you had the old one long enough. Ten years, was it? Dismal little place, especially after your mother died. Lonesome, too, I'll bet?"

A comet passed overhead, leaving behind a dusty trail that settled over the room. The woman quickly put her hand over her teacup, and Mr. Penny followed suit.

"It was lonely, yeah," he said. "But Mrs. Mickleson was just next door. She made very good scones. These ones are good, too," he added quickly, not wanting to offend her.

"No doubt, no doubt," she said, taking another big gulp. And after a while, "There's a time for everything, Mr. Penny, and I'd say it's high time for a *change*." She refilled her cup. "What do you say?"

He was about to blurt out "Yes, please," when the thought struck him that the new room might be more cramped and cold than the last one, so it wouldn't be a good trade after all. A person has to be careful. The new room could even have a rodent in it. Mr. Penny couldn't tolerate rodents. It's true that they're *sort of* cute when you see them in pet shops, or pictures in books, but when they're skittering up your pant leg, well, it's quite another matter. Mr. Penny's old room had rodents in it when he first moved in. That was before he had a dog. It was just awful.

"What *kind* of room," he asked, cautiously.

"It's a lovely room, really," refilling her teacup. The woman went on in short bursts between sips, "Four-post bed. Toilet with shower. Sink and stove in perfect condition. A window on each wall. A few cracks on the linoleum - but nothing's perfect, eh, Mr. Penny? Excellent view of the stars, of course."

"But what's it per month?" he asked, suddenly skeptical, knowing he only got so much, and the room sounded too good to be true.

"No charge," said the woman, finishing off the cup. "And you can stay as long as you like."

Mr. Penny was in awe. "Are you God?" he asked, finally.

The woman flushed. "Bless you, dear. I'm just the old housekeeper."

"Oh." Mr. Penny looked admiringly at the silver tea service, the paintings, the furniture. "Am *I* God?" he ventured.

The woman only smiled.

"Some more tea, Mr. Penny?" she asked.

Mr. Penny thought carefully, then answered, "Yes."

ON THE CHOPSHAW ROAD

Jon Zech

Right out there on the road to Chopshaw, Alabama, straddling the center rut, was a wicker love seat. From a half mile away Wisson Berryboy thought it was a cow. It could have been a cow, although pigs and chickens were more common on the Chopshaw Road. Either way Wisson didn't give it much mind, and he kept on walking. The sun, even through the thin scrim of clouds, was a force against his face and he mostly looked down at the flat-packed, sand-dust shoulder. Such dust as he raised with his thick brown brogans settled quickly; no breeze.

From a quarter mile away Wisson determined that if it was a cow that he was seeing, it was a dead one, or at least a downer fixing to die. At a hundred yards he saw that it was furniture. When he drew parallel to it he stopped.

Some wicker is painted white and sits on a veranda and creaks when you first settle into it. Other wicker, older wicker, wicker that's been retired from the veranda, might spend its last years out of doors, under a tree, fading into a soft, bleached, straw color. But this wicker, the wicker that Wisson Berryboy was studying, had been stained and finished to a dark red-brown that shined as though varnished or shellacked. Wisson had never seen wicker in a proper living room in a white man's house, but he imagined that if ever that might happen, this was the piece that would fit.

With that thought Wisson began to consider what he should do. If he were to continue walking toward town and if something were to happen to this piece of wicker and if he had been seen near it, there might be blame. And at seventy-eight years, the last thing Wisson wanted was blame for something happening to a white man's property. It didn't look heavy and he decided to just move it to the side of the road and then walk on, but having taken only a single step he caught sight of a plume of dust rising from the road to the east. He stood by as the plume approached in the form of a brand new, black, DeSoto sedan. The car slowed and a man wearing a cream colored suit with a matching hat called from the window, "Why don't you move that damn thing? Is it yours?"

"No, Sir," said Wisson. "It's not mine at all. I'm just minding it."

"For who?"

"For Mister Dick." Randolph Dick was a white man who Wisson considered might just have a set of wicker like this. And if he had such a set and this one piece had fallen to the road, and if he had seen Wisson walking, why it would be just natural that he would ask him to mind it until he could send someone to retrieve it. And surely if it were not Mister Dick himself, then it was another white man from not too far away who would have made the very same request.

"Randolph Dick?" asked the man. He consulted briefly with a woman sitting next to him. Then he said to Wisson, "I could take that loveseat to Randolph Dick myself. You could put it in my trunk and I could carry it to him."

"Well, Sir, Mister Dick didn't say nothing about moving this here furniture." And that was the truth. Wisson Berryboy felt safer with the truth than with the merely plausible.

"So you're just going to stand here and wait?"

"I'm just supposed to mind it for a while."

"Fine," said the man, clearly disgusted. The DeSoto kicked dust and left.

And now Wisson had a problem; having been seen with the love seat he could hardly leave it, but also having refused to have it moved he had made a certain commitment. He resolved to mind the furniture for a while as he had said. He pulled the loveseat to the shoulder and sat down on the ground next to it. It never occurred to him to sit on the loveseat itself. The wicker cast a dappled shadow and that was enough.

He must have dozed because he didn't hear the clattering pre-war Ford until it was nearly upon him. In the Ford were three young men of varying shades of black, but all with the very same eyes. They were the sons of Pamela Bacon and they lived not too far from Chopshaw, down the Old Dam Road and a bit east. Wisson didn't know they had a car now.

"Hey," called the one who was driving.

"Hay is for horses," said Wisson.

The driver's door opened and the first lad slid out, all slow and loose in his limbs. The two others followed through the same door. "Well then, how do you do, Mister Berryboy? That better?"

Wisson nodded, "Better. When did you get a car? Is that your car?"

The second boy said, "Momma's friend. He's got two cars."

The driver, Maurice, said, "Mr. Berryboy, how come is it that you're sitting by the side of this road with a sofa?" The third son of Pamela Bacon snickered. His name was Charles.

"I'm to mind this here wicker loveseat for a little while for Mister Randolph Dick."

"Is he paying you?" asked Charles.

"Yes," said Wisson. "Mister Dick is paying me two dollars to mind it here until dark."

"What happens after dark? Is he sending a car? How did it get here?"

"You don't need to concern about any of that," said Wisson. "That's all Mister Dick's business. And mine."

"We'll mind it with you," said Maurice. "Keep you company."

Wisson thought for a minute that he wouldn't care for any company, but then decided that it might be more comfortable sitting in the old Ford than on the ground so he didn't object.

Wisson awoke an hour later in the front seat of the Ford and saw that two of the Bacon boys, Charles and Maurice, were sitting on the loveseat and their brother Pinchon was talking with a fourth person. This fourth person was known as Alan but nobody knew his last name. He lived in a shack out behind the deserted peach cannery and kept pretty much to himself unless he'd been drinking, which he appeared to be doing at this moment. Wisson got out of the car.

"No," he shouted. "That loveseat isn't for sitting on. We're just to mind it."

The boys stood up. Alan took a swig from a bottle in a paper bag and stared at Wisson.

The air was cooler now and the shadow from the loveseat longer. Wisson told Maurice Bacon that he was disappointed to see him sitting on the wicker and he was sure Mr. Dick would have been upset to have seen it, too. He heard a rustle and turned around to see the paper bag passing from Pinchon to Alan.

"Now what is this? What is this? Pinchon, what are you doing with that bag? Nothing you need in there." Pinchon grinned.

Alan passed the bag to Wisson. He hesitated, but it had been a long day so he took the bag and took a full swallow. The cheap whiskey burned, but it cleared his eyes and settled him down a bit.

An hour later the sun was down and only a thin band of indigo hovered in the west. The bottle was half empty and Wisson was sitting on the loveseat. He figured he was protecting it.

"Mister Dick isn't here yet," said Alan.

"No," said Wisson. "And it's near full dark, pretty near." He was preparing to ask the Bacon boys to give him a ride home. He lived with his daughter, only about five miles down.

But then there was a scuffle in the weeds and two people stepped out and onto the road. The boy led the girl by the hand. She whispered something to him and he hitched up his pants. He was Antonio Brown, tall, light skinned, broad shoulders and not yet sixteen. She was MayAnne Spencer and MayAnne Spencer was known to be good for only one thing and it appeared that Antonio Brown had just learned about that one thing in some detail. MayAnne had a homely face but her body had been full grown since she was eleven.

In the twenty minutes it took for the sky to become full dark, Alan's bottle was empty. MayAnne said, "That nasty old car got a radio?"

"Yeah," said Charles, "but there's something wrong with the speaker. It don't play good."

"Let me see," said Antonio, and he slithered on his back under the dashboard. "Just a loose wire," he called, and in seconds he had the latest song from Big Momma Thornton blaring through the tinny speaker. "And that's not all."

He snaked his way from under the dashboard and onto his feet. He held one hand behind his back. "Look what I found." It was a nearly full bottle of Lord Standish Sloe Gin.

The moon came up and the level of the Lord Standish Sloe Gin went down. Twice Maurice had to start the Ford to recharge the battery. There was a slight breeze and a slight chill and about ten o'clock Pinchon and Charles dragged some brush and dry tall grass to the side of the road and lit it with a kitchen match. Alan figured the fire was far too small and went off to find some real wood. He hauled back a twelve-foot elm branch which he proceeded to stomp into relatively small and burnable pieces.

MayAnne and Pinchon danced in the half-light a dozen feet from the fire. Maurice and Alan jitter-bugged and Wisson found himself wagging his foot to the beat. The gin left a sour candy taste in his mouth and only another swallow would clean it out for a few minutes. Between songs on the radio MayAnne and Pinchon left the light of the fire.

"He's too young for all that," said Wisson.

"Thirteen," said Charles. "Not too young. I was fifteen before I met a willing girl."

"How old are you now?"

"Sixteen. Mister Berryboy? How old were you your first time?"

"People ask the damnedest things nowadays. Whoever would have thought? A sixteen-year-old boy asking a grown man…an old grown man…about things like that. Truth is I don't rightly know. I didn't mark it on a calendar or anything."

Charles asked, "You don't remember your first time?"

"Oh, I remember just fine. Just fine." He collected his thoughts for a minute. "School teacher's daughter," he said finally. "Older than me. Skinny shy girl. But she knew what she was about. I think I might have been your age. It was while my momma was still alive and she passed when I was seventeen. Maybe the summer before that." Wisson Berryboy smiled. "Oh yes, I remember just fine. I remember a lot more than I'll tell."

Pinchon and MayAnne returned. Maurice had found more wood. Wisson was feeling tired.

There was a high sharp cry and Wisson saw that Alan had MayAnne by the arm and was leading her to the shadows, but she was having none of it. She tried to pull away but he held firm and she snapped back to him like an elastic band and cracked his face with her free closed fist. He stumbled backwards, still hanging tight to her arm and the pair lost their balance and fell, MayAnne on top of Alan and Alan slamming flat on his back into the fire.

Alan was screaming before he touched the embers and MayAnne, now free, was slapping him with both hands as the soot and ash and a massive shower of sparks sprayed around them. The hem of her dress caught fire and she just kept slapping. Charles and Maurice and Pinchon grasped and grappled at the pair to pull them from the fire and each other.

At last Maurice and Charles held Alan, one at each arm, as he bellowed that they were grabbing where he was burned. They didn't let go. Pinchon had MayAnne on her back and had swatted her burning skirt until all it did was smoke. Her eyes never left Alan.

Wisson saw it all and he turned to catch his breath just in time to see that stray sparks and bits of burning elm had found the wicker love seat. Small flames ran up the left arm and started across the back. Wisson snatched up the blanket and threw it over the flames. He pulled back the blanket and sent a rolling cloud of white smoke upwards. Charles and Maurice and Pinchon stood by him. MayAnne sat by the fire, still muttering curses at Alan. Alan was gone.

"Well now," said Wisson. "Well now. This is a kind of a problem."

Charles said, "Yeah. Mister Dick. What's he going to say?"

"Hmm," said Wisson Berryboy. "Hmm. If this here wicker was found to be damaged, I expect there would be trouble."

"But?" asked Charles.

Wisson smiled and reached for the scorched arm. "Here. You grab the other arm."

They dragged the love seat over to the remains of the fire and tipped it onto its back. It caught in seconds. It burned bright and fast and satisfying. Even MayAnne was grinning in the orange light.

A short while later they spread the ashes of the fire and of the loveseat and of the evening and scuffed it all into the dust, leaving only a slightly darker patch of road for the morning to find.

The sons of Pamela Bacon offered Wisson Berryboy a ride home. As he settled into the back seat he thought to himself, "And the hell with you, Mister Randolph Dick."

THE CURSE OF PENNY STATION

Brian Sanders

It was Christmas Eve, and all the sound-minded people in Hucksville were indoors keeping warm by hearth, radiator, or lover. But not so the young man, Chris Becker, who shuffled up the stairs and sprang onto the platform at Penny Station. He swiveled his head left and right, hoping to see the faint glow of the train that would deliver his beloved to him. In his eagerness to see her, he blinded himself to the one other person on the platform.

The man in the gray wool coat and fedora hat sat on a wooden bench. The newspaper from which he read obscured his face. He sat as still as the night, allowing snowflakes to collect on his hat and thighs. A cloth bag rested at his feet, keeping warm the whisky bottle therein.

Chris fetched his cell phone from his red jacket and was about to dial the train service to speak with an operator. Alas, at the remote station, which was frequented more by deer than men, his cell phone found no signal. "Dammit," he muttered. He checked his wristwatch. It was ten o'clock, the exact time she told him to be there.

"Excuse me, sir," Chris said to the stranger. "You wouldn't happen to have a phone I could borrow. I don't seem to be getting any reception."

The man neither stirred nor lowered the newspaper, but said: "Can't say that I do. Though if it's Train 32 you're waiting for, I'd recommend getting comfortable."

"Why's that?" asked Chris, folding his arms. He felt uncomfortable conversing with the classifieds.

With a snap of his arms, the man folded the paper, giving Chris a glimpse of his wild gray beard and pallid blue eyes. He looked to be in his late seventies, but was probably only sixty. No doubt, his face aged him. It was the face of a weathered stone – whipped by wind, cracked by ice, and loved by no one. "She's always late," he replied.

"Always?" asked Chris. Before the man could answer, an unseen train howled its approach like a banshee.

"Here she comes!" Chris cried, rubbing his hands together. The smirking old man knew better. Still, he let Chris approach the platform edge without issuing warning or reproach. The passenger train blew its horn once, now twice. The engineers crossed themselves, hoping the man on the edge would not jump. It had happened before, and always around this time of year.

The train barreled past Chris, nearly knocking him over. Chris cowered and shielded his sensitive ears. After five seconds the train, which was evidently not 32, was gone.

Chris picked himself up and, in his embarrassment, glanced at the old man in expectation of a grin or jest. But the man read his newspaper and paid him no mind. Chris paced the track for want of anything better to do. The wind flung ice at him, and for the first time that evening he felt a chill.

"What's her name?" asked the old man.

Chris spun around and answered, "Sarah." Then, it dawned on him. "How did you –?"

"It's Christmas Eve," said the old man, peremptorily. "A single man without luggage waits for Train 32. A train comes down the track. His eyes light up. Pupils widen. Could it be? Might it be? No! Icicle in his heart! Unless you're waiting for Jolly Ol'Saint Nick, I'd say there's a girl."

Chris smiled. The old man had unexpected charisma, the words rolling off his tongue as facilely as a used car salesman's. Chris offered his hand. "Chris Becker."

"Victor."

Chris sat beside him on the bench. "So, Victor, I take it you're also waiting for someone?"

Victor turned from Chris and rested his forlorn eyes on the rails. "Railroad stations… loneliest places on Earth."

"I'm sorry. I didn't mean to –"

"No, no. It's quite all right. When I was a young man, about your age actually, I was out here on Christmas Eve, waiting for Train 32 to Hucksville. It was unusually cold for December. Why, I believe it was the coldest day all that year. But I was kept warm by the very thought that on that train was the love of my life. Or so I thought…"

"What happened?"

"The train arrived at midnight, nearly three hours late. I waited out here the whole time, each minute my heart growing as numb as my hands. The passengers left the platform and the train started off. Fool that I was, I ran after it. She had

fallen asleep, forgotten the station stop, or could not circumvent a fat man blocking the aisle, I told myself."

"And?"

"A few days later, I received a letter from her. To summarize, she had fallen in love with another man. Old college buddy of mine, actually. He was taller, richer, and handsomer than me." Victor stooped for his bottle of whiskey. He unscrewed the cap and stared at the alcohol reflectively. "And, as they say, to the victor go the spoils." He took a hearty swig and wiped his mouth on his sleeve. "But not to this Victor."

He offered the bottle to Chris, who politely declined. "So," Chris said, "you come here to... nah, never mind."

"Go on. Say it."

"Reminisce? Grieve?"

Victor chuckled. "Not quite, my friend. I come to Penny Station for business reasons, though I must admit nostalgia chills my heart every time."

"And how often is that?"

"Every Christmas Eve."

"And what, if you don't mind me asking, is your business?"

"I'm a writer, Mr. Becker." Victor parted his coat and removed from the inside pocket a leather journal. "I specialize in stories of heartbreak and loss."

Chris looked at the old man strangely, wondering if he were telling the truth. It seemed ridiculous for an old man to trudge to a train station, braving ice and snow, just to write a story – especially on Christmas Eve. Did he not have family or loved ones to be with? Did he not have sanity?

Victor noticed Chris's bemused expression and explained: "You see, the year following my tragedy had not treated me particularly well. Come Christmas Eve, I felt more alone than ever. Restless and inebriated, I wandered the streets until I found myself at Penny Station. There, I met a young man who was waiting impatiently for Train 32. He was waiting for a girl. Once again, it arrived two hours late. And, well, I don't think I have to tell you the rest."

"She never showed?"

Victor helped himself to another swig of whiskey. "It's a curse. It's a cruel, cruel curse this station puts on young men's hearts every Christmas Eve."

Chris shook his head and laughed uneasily. "I don't know about all this curse stuff. I'm not the superstitious type."

Victor turned toward Chris with tiger quickness. "It happens every year! Once is a fluke. Twice, a coincidence. Ten times, tragic. But forty times? That, young man, is a curse!"

Chris sprung from the bench. He did not like the mad glint in the old man's eyes, nor his shrill tone. He walked to the edge of the platform and stared hopelessly down the track. For a moment, he thought he saw a light, a train. But it was only the sheen of moonlight on the snow-laden rails. Why worry? he asked himself. The old soothsayer was a loon. Only a crazy person would be out here on Christmas Eve, anyway. Yet, for some reason, some secret angst, he began to believe Sarah would not come after all. Tomorrow morning he would open presents alone, toast egg nog to the birds, and fa-la-la-la-la to the echo of his own voice.

"Come on," Chris said in vain invocation. "Come on, you stupid train." Hearing this, Victor laughed a high-pitched trill that rattled Chris's heart.

"She'll come!" cried Chris. "I know it!"

"I'm sorry," said Victor, stifling himself. "It just never fails, that's all.

It's so sad, beautiful, and funny all at the same time. That's why I come here, you know. Watching a young man's heart break every Christmas Eve is my inspiration as a writer. If this sounds selfish of me, remember I've been in your shoes before, my friend."

Chris sauntered to the bench and sat, shoulders slumped in dejection. "Yeah, well, you could try laying off the jokes."

Victor fetched a pack of cigarettes from his coat. "Would you like a smoke to take the edge off?"

"I'll take some of your whiskey."

"Sure, you will." Smiling, Victor handed Chris the bottle. He watched Chris gulp down the whiskey with the delight of a grandmother watching her grandchild eat her cookies.

Then, Victor set his journal on his lap, opened to a blank page, and uncapped his pen.

"Sarah," said Chris musingly, "I don't know what I'd do if she didn't come tonight." He tipped the bottle over his mouth and let the liquid warm his tongue and soul.

"Say," said Victor, "why not tell me a bit about her? We have more than an hour till midnight. It would be a shame to sit here in silence, don't you agree?"

Chris belched, his propriety fading under the growing doubt he would ever see his lover again. "What do you want to know?"

"Why not start at the beginning?"

"Well, I met Sarah a year ago. It was the second week in October. Back at the carnival…"

A half hour later, there were still only two men on the platform. The distance between them on the bench was much smaller now. Chris sat nearly on Victor's lap as he waved the hollow bottle and recounted the happy couple that was he and Sarah. Victor took no notice of the drunkard's foul breath or gratuitous touch, for he was writing in his journal with unalloyed concentration.

"And this one time in July, ol' Victor buddy, we were in bed and we had just seen the fireworks and been drinking a lot of vino – a whole damn bottle we downed – and she jumped on top of me and we…"

Had not a freight train rushed by just then, Victor would have had to endure the vulgar and explicit details of Chris's sex life. Instead, he merely watched Chris stagger to his feet, thrust his hips back and forth, stick his tongue in and out, and jump up and down like a monkey.

The train passed. Chris sat, turned to Victor, and, sparing a hiccup, asked, "You ever do that, huh? Ever try that one?" His head wobbled and his eyes were half shut.

Victor flipped back through the pages of his journal, reviewing what he had written.

"Hey, Vic, I'm talking to –"

Victor looked up at Chris sternly, his former friendliness all but gone. "Look, Chris, you've told me all the things you love about your 'sugarplum,' and it's all nice and well. But there has to be more."

"I just told you the best part!"

Victor grabbed Chris by the collar of his jacket and shook him like a snow globe. "There has to be something about her you don't like. Something you just can't stand! Quickly! We haven't much time!"

Chris batted Victor's hand away and lurched awkwardly onto his feet. He reached out his hand and, in his mind's eye, beheld Sarah – her curly brown hair, her lips as full as her hips, and the resplendent fur coat she wore. "Sarah!" he cried. "I love you!"

With these words, Chris collapsed. Victor set aside the journal and hurried to his side. He peeled the scrawny young man off the ground and laid him on the bench. Resting his hand on Chris's shoulder, Victor stared into his twilight eyes, whose lids had all but set.

"Tell me," said Victor. The urgency in the old man's voice was gone. His request mellowed into something hypnotic. "Tell me what you hate about her."

"She… she never…"

"Yes?"

"She never said, 'I love you.'" His eyelids set. Chris left to meet Sarah in his dreams. Victor hovered over him a while, motionless, contemplative. When he sat again, a terrible smile arose on the left side of his face. An asymmetric, ugly smile that undoubtedly would have frightened Chris had he not left so soon. Victor unsheathed his pen, wrote with incredible speed on a fresh page, tore it from his journal, and tucked it into his coat pocket.

In the distance came the bells and whistle of a train. Victor looked to Chris, still smiling diabolically, and shoved him. As Victor had hoped, Chris tipped over, whiskey comatose, but did not move or utter a sound. Victor rose and hoisted Chris over his broad shoulders. The train slowed into the station, its brakes squeaking like a flock of geese. Several passengers descended the train assisted by a ruddy-faced conductor in a navy uniform and cap.

When the last passenger, a sprightly grandmother with a suitcase bigger than she was, exited the train, Victor approached the conductor. "Excuse me, sir."

The conductor cast a wary eye on the pair – this gentleman who wore a younger man over his shoulder like a sash. Victor smiled warmly and, in his most humble tone, spoke: "I'm terribly sorry to trouble you, but my friend here has had too much to drink and desperately needs to get home to his family up north. He has a ticket." Sure enough, Victor pulled a ticket from his pocket and handed it to the conductor. The latter held the ticket up to his eyes and carefully inspected it.

Satisfied as to its authenticity, he leaned toward Chris and sniffed. "What's his poison?"

"It was the whiskey."

The conductor leaned back and scratched his chin. "Please," said Victor, "have mercy on this drunkard's soul and see that he reaches his family. It's Christmas!"

Well, who but the Grinch or Scrooge could ignore a plea for compassion on Christmas? "Ah, damn," said the conductor. "I'll look after him for a ways. Till he comes to his senses." With that, Victor set Chris onto his feet. The conductor tucked his arm under Chris's and led him up the steps into the train.

"And a merry Christmas to you!" called Victor and waved good-bye to Train 28.

* * *

At midnight Train 32 pulled into Penny Station, just as it had done for the last forty years. On most nights, it arrived in the quiet town of Hucksville at 10 pm. But every Christmas Eve, due to increased freight train traffic, it came approximately two hours late. Of course, this was not known by many, especially not young men who thought of little else besides their Kelly, Mary, or Sue.

A pretty girl in a fur coat rolled her suitcase across the platform. She peered this way and that, but her Chris was nowhere to be seen. So, she crept toward the man who was leaning against a pillar and smoking a cigarette. She could scarcely see his face, for it was masked in smoke and the shadow of the pillar.

"Excuse me, mister?"

The man might have been dead, so still and vacant was he. Sarah felt greatly intimidated, but she had already engaged him and could not retreat now.

"Have you seen a young man? Blond hair, about five foot six? He was supposed to pick me up at--"

"Chris," said the man. He stepped out of his veil of smoke and into the moonlight. "That's his name, right?"

"Yes! Yes it is! Where is he?"

At this, the man doffed his fedora and held it against his heart. With a weighty sigh, he looked into Sarah's eyes. "I hate to be the one to do this. But it was me he asked and I gave him my word I would."

"What? What is it?"

The man reached into his coat. Sarah held her breath, and her muscles tensed. But no weapon or dismembered body part did he produce, only a folded piece of paper. He held it out for her to take. She glanced warily at it and at the man, back and forth.

"Go on. Take it. He told me to give it to you."

She snatched the paper from his hands, lest he try to bite her.

"You see," said the man, "as I was exiting the train a moment ago a man stopped me. He seemed to be in such a hurry that I forgave his impetuous manner and listened to his plea. He confessed that he had been leading a double life – that is, with two women. He explained that after weeks of wavering, he decided to take a north-bound train to meet a woman who…"

"Who?"

"Well," said the man, gesturing to the paper, "I'm sure you'd rather read it in his words than hear it through a stranger's."

And so, she read:

> "My dearest Sarah,
>
> I'll make this short and sweet. I love you, and have loved you since we met at the carnival (P.S., you're still the best ring tosser in the whole wide world!). But even though we have been through so much (who could forget that night in July?), I have never heard you utter the words, 'I love you.'
>
> Then, a while back, I met another woman. She is taller, wealthier, and prettier than you. And at night she fills my ears with words of love.
>
> I hope you understand why I had to leave. Good-bye, my sugarplum.
>
> Yours truly,
> Chris"

Sarah crumpled the letter and wiped her tears. The part about the woman being taller, wealthier, and prettier hurt her most. She stood there rigidly for a moment, sniffling, wishing to deny it all, to deny the effect of her reticence. But the evidence was plain. While the neat block letters were rare for him beyond grocery lists, the corny accolade of "best ring tosser" bespoke of Chris. If only she had told him the truth.

* * *

Victor watched with feigned sorrow as she sauntered to the bench and dropped onto it lifelessly. Burying head in hands, she wept. Victor approached her, his boots soft on the snowy platform. He opened his mouth and was about to give consolation, but Sarah spoke first: "Please. Just leave me alone."

He did as she wished. His business was done, anyway. He put on his fedora and walked the platform to the far end. Beyond the tracks, miles past the shivering trees, the houses of Hucksville twinkled red, green, and yellow. Victor thought of the people in the houses, keeping warm by hearth, radiator, or lover. Yes, he thought of these fools and Chris and all the other young men who came to Penny Station. And he thought of himself.

He started down the track with a smile snaking up the side of his face. As he disappeared into the night, he whispered something. The Wind seized his words and sailed them across the forest, down the hill, and through the lamp-lit lanes. And, had you been there just then – stepped out for a smoke or to adjust the wreath – you'd have shivered and heard the echo of the cursed:

"Railroad stations… loneliest places on Earth."

A GOOD YEAR

Ray Busler

The coffee burned my mouth as I sat down, out of Emma's way, at the table. She fussed around the kitchen getting breakfast ready, hanging coats on pegs by the back door, and setting a bottle to warm in a pan of water on the stove. Claire sleeps through the night now, but she would be awake soon. Emma usually feeds her while the boys and I eat.

"What will you do today, Emory?" The creak of the oven door, the scrape of the biscuit pan almost drowned her words. I cut only hickory for the stove. Emma claims it bakes better.

"Mend the axle on the hay trailer, I guess. Then there's the shed roof I need to see about. Why, is there something you need done?"

"How long has it been since we got the corn in, a month now?" She was buttering the biscuits while they were still hot, the butter melting right into the flesh of the bread.

"A month. Yes, about a month since harvest. You know that."

"Emory, why hasn't Chandler burned his corn? Every day I expect to see his fields laid by, smell the smoke from his corn stalks burning. Not long 'till first snow and he hasn't touched his fields."

"Plenty of time for that," I said, looking out the window into the false dawn in the east. The bottoms of the panes were rimmed with frost that was beginning to melt and run in the heat of the kitchen.

"Why don't you go down and see him today? You haven't been down there since... Well, since right after the harvest. That axle can wait, it sure isn't going anywhere."

"Emma, if Walter Chandler needed my help he'd--"

"No. No, he wouldn't, Emory. He wouldn't ever say a word. If I was a man I'd go see him. I'd go today and let the shed roof and all the hay trailers in the county go to hell."

The boys came trooping in then. I helped their plates as Emma went upstairs with the bottle.

From my workshop I can see the road wind down the valley past my farm, then Chandler's, before it disappears over the hill. The county tarred and graveled the road last spring, so when the yellow and black school bus stopped in front of my house there was no plume of dry November dust rooster tailing behind it. My boys waved up the hill to me before boarding. Ted, the youngest, had already unbuttoned his coat. I was glad Emma didn't see him.

I could see Chandler's fields, row after row of dry, barren cornstalks reeling in drunken ranks. I knew Emma was right, the stalks should not still be standing. There was a winter smell in the air. The corn still in the field was an affront, like a roach on a wedding cake. I put my toolbox back on the work bench and got into the Ford.

I almost didn't see him. His clothes were as brown as the corn stalks; the blue chambray collar of his shirt caught my eye. I got out and waited to the fence line, my forearms resting on the top strand of wire. I liked it better this way, seeing him at the edge of the field. I didn't want to be in his house. He made a raspy sound, like pages being turned as he came through the corn.

"Emory," he said, simply as a matter of fact. We didn't shake, we seldom do, and his hands were occupied rolling a cigarette.

"Walter," I replied. An awkward silence hung between us until he lit his cigarette and fanned out the match. "See you got your corn in," I said.

"Yes, barns are all full - silo, cribs, and every vessel I own, even had to stack a few dozen bushels in the parlor."

"Yeah, it's been a good year." I regretted this as soon as I said it, but Walter didn't seem to notice. "You know I got that new John Deere? I can pull the center plows off and run the middlins. The outboard plows lay those stalks over just like they were hand stacked. I'm just about caught up. I thought if you wanted I could come down and give you a hand?"

"Been a little windy for burning," Walter said. He was resting on the top wire, the smoke from his cigarette rising straight up in a blue stream.

"Smelled like snow this morning. You know how it smells this time of year right before that first one? I smelled that, thought about that John Deere and just got it in my head I might come see you."

Walter Chandler pinched the hot ash from his cigarette and watched it fall. He looked me full in the face before he spoke again. ""I'm just as good a farmer as you ever were. I can smell what's in the air as good as you. I got a Case tractor sitting right over there as good as any Deere ever made."

"Walter, I didn't mean anything like that…"

"I'm as good a man as you are, you son of a bitch. I can take care of this place, I can take care of-"

"Walter, it was the diphtheria. There was nothing you could do. Nothing even a doctor could do. It was God's will."

"Get off my fence. Get back up the hill to your wife, and those children, and your God damned John Deere tractor. Don't you ever come back down here and tell me about God's will."

After supper Emma informed me we would be having ham for this year's Thanksgiving dinner. I had seen this decision coming since the day Ted named the turkey I was raising with the chickens. She stopped in mid-menu and a strange look came over her face. "Emory! Do you smell that?"

The instant she spoke I smelled smoke. I ran straight upstairs to

Claire, but she was sleeping quietly, then I saw the glow through the window, from down the valley.

I rushed out of the house toward the workshop and my truck. Over my shoulder I yelled one word back to Emma. "Chandler!"

I could see it all from the shop. A thin line of fire snaked across the fields; the barns were going, sending volcanoes of sparks up through incandescent clouds of smoke. I stepped on the starter as flame came up through the roof of Chandler's house. I rushed, that's what you do when there's a fire, you rush toward it or away from it, but I knew it was too late. I knew what I would find. Walter Chandler was burning his corn.

He was burning all of it.

THE HANGING MAN

Lawrence Buentello

At midnight Manny Royce was wakened by strange sounds.

Why these sounds, voices and an idling engine, should raise such fear in him he didn't understand. A rush of adrenaline burned through his chest, as when he was a child and heard the faint scratching of vermin in the walls. But the sounds reverberated beyond the house, beyond the windows and doors. He'd lived in the house for only a few months and still hadn't gotten used to the isolation. It must have been joy-riding teenagers searching for a place to perform their adolescent rituals. Yes, that was the most likely explanation.

Royce turned and saw that his wife was still sleeping. He was always the one to rise in the middle of the night in search of the source of unidentifiable sounds. He felt foolish for being so sensitive about such things, but he'd grown up poor, his nights infested with the presence of too many rats; to young Manny Royce, they were demons floating from room to room, waiting for him to fall into a defenseless sleep. His brother, sleeping next to him one winter night, had actually been bitten—

Royce cursed his own foolishness and rose from the bed.

He slipped on his robe as he walked through the dark hallway to the living room. The sounds intensified once he left the bedroom, and, as he walked to the large window at the front of the house, he realized that the voices were deep, rough and angry. The engine noise had ceased, but the voices were rising in tone, as if they were approaching the house.

The muscles in his back tensed as he moved the curtains away from the window carefully.

Beyond the window glass were the wavering shadows of the trees, and the silhouettes of several hills. The moon was above the house, the trees and grass lit by a faint light. When his eyes focused more clearly he saw the figures moving over one of the hills toward a grove of trees. His heartbeat increased as the headlights of an invisible truck flashed once and then died. The truck was parked about fifty yards from the house on the dirt road which wound through the hills and back to the highway.

What in the world is happening? he thought, and for a moment his breath fogged the glass before he turned his head slightly to avoid breathing on the window. When the condensation faded he saw a pair of flashlights bobbing in the crowd of figures moving over the hill, circles of light playing over the grass. He still heard the voices, low and angry, and an occasional cry, as if from a man in pain.

What's happening? he asked himself again. He was suddenly aware of the heavy fabric of the curtain sliding across his cheek. He gripped the edge of the cloth and tightened it into a small portal through which he couldn't easily be seen—how many times as a child had he rushed to the window, the curtain wrapped tightly in his small hand, to stare at the street after some terrible fight between the gangs, or as a drunken husband assaulted his wife, or after the sound of gunshots moved his curiosity? A life influenced by harsh memories, a terrible place to be a child—

These were no teenagers, he thought.

Royce watched as the parade of figures moved along the hill and threatened to vanish below his line of sight. But then the figures stopped and the flashlight beams played over the ground. He watched, transfixed by the beams of light, occasionally seeing a pair of shoes or boots hitching in the grass. And then a circle of light began playing over the broad trunk of an oak tree. Royce could barely hear the voices now, but there seemed to be a consensus sound that rose once, and then faded. He watched the events as if he were staring through the wrong end of a telescope, uncertain of what was happening—until he saw a thin line flung up through the flashlight beams into the dark boughs above the men.

A rope.

Dear God, he thought. This can't be happening.

Then he heard a voice, as if in sudden pain, rising through the hills. The flashlight beams moved violently in the air, as if the men holding the flashlights were suddenly confronted with the thrashing of a wild animal. Through the light he saw faces, but they weren't faces at all; the men wore kerchiefs over their mouths. Only their eyes flashed in the beams.

No, no, he thought, this can't be happening. But it *was* happening. The rope swung wildly in the light, and then one of the men looped it around the trunk of the tree. Royce heard laughter, a short staccato sound that made him afraid. He felt tears in his eyes, but couldn't move to wipe them away. The men moved diligently, and then he saw the flashlit face of the only man without a kerchief gazing in terror as the loop of rope passed over his head and tightened around his neck. A noise moved through the air, but he couldn't accept it as human—it was the cry of a spirit in the trees, a lifeless soul caught between worlds. As three of the men pulled the rope taut around the trunk the body moved slowly into the air above the grass, struggling horribly, hands tied behind, feet flailing, a dying fish struggling helplessly on a line—

Then the men secured the rope and stood away from the tree.

All this happened in the few minutes that Royce stood at the window, his ears filled with a pulse that made an ugly music. Oh God, he thought, oh my God—

"Manny?"

Royce turned suddenly, startled, but managed to keep from stumbling against the window. He said, "Don't turn on the light."

His wife, Gayle, stood in silhouette at the end of the hallway. "What's that noise?"

"*Don't* turn on the light," he said again, with an urgency she couldn't misinterpret.

"Why not?" She stepped forward, a spectral figure in her nightgown. "What's happening out there?"

Royce stared through the small opening in the curtain again, then let the fabric fall back into place as he moved toward his wife. His arms fell around her shoulders and he held her. She didn't fight against his embrace, but raised her head away from his chest.

"Manny?"

For a moment Royce could only hold his wife wordlessly; the event beyond their door made no sense to him. How could it be occurring in these times, so near his home?

"What don't you want me to see?" she said, trying to move away from him. But he held her firmly. "Was there an accident?"

"No," Royce managed to say. "We have to call the police."

"Why?" She stared into his eyes, and he could see her confusion even in the absence of good light.

"I think a man's being killed," he said.

She exhaled fully, then caught her breath.

Royce quietly described what he'd just seen through the window. He knew he had to remain calm, because his wife was a nervous woman and would certainly panic. When he finished speaking, he released her and moved toward the telephone.

"What are you doing?" she asked as she moved by his side.

"I'm calling the police," he said.

"No, Manny," she said in a whisper. "Wait."

She moved away from him, stepped to the window and peered from behind the curtain. She stood watching for a moment, saying nothing, then moved to the door to check the locks. When she was satisfied she returned to his side and placed her fingers on his arm.

"Are they still out there?" Royce asked.

"Yes."

"Then we have to call the police."

"No, Manny."

"Gayle, we *have* to call," he said, incredulous. "A man is being *killed.*"

"No!"

Her fingers closed around his arm, and he felt the pressure of her fear down to the bone.

"Let's leave it alone," she said. "It's none of our business."

"Do you know what you're saying?"

"Manny, they won't come after us if we leave it alone. They'd have no reason to. Let them go, it has nothing to do with us."

"I don't believe what you're saying." He moved to reach for the telephone, but she pulled his arm away.

"*Listen* to me," she said, desperately trying not to raise her voice. "Those men don't know who lives here, do they? How could they know? But if we call the police they'll know it was the people in this house. What if they come back and see the color of our skin? You tell me what people like that will do to us."

"Gayle, we can't just let this happen."

"No, we'll let it *go*. The police will ask us what we heard, but we'll tell them we were asleep and didn't hear anything. Then they'll know we didn't talk to anyone and they won't come back."

"We have to tell them what we know."

"Why? So those men can come back and hang us, too?"

Then his wife began to cry, and he held her. He knew her argument only came from fear, but for some reason he didn't reach for the telephone. In the city, there was never a telephone call—murders, drug dealers, gang shootings, terrible things for a child to witness, a teenager, a young man. His dream had been to get an education and buy a house in the country; far away from the life he'd known growing up. And he'd fulfilled his dream, through years of study and work. Commuting to the city now was the least of his worries, because he knew he had a peaceful home to return to every night. Accounts manager, CPA license, retirement package, an office of his own, the respect of his co-workers—these were the things that mattered to him now, and as much as he'd endured because of the color of his skin—

But was she right? *Would* they come back?

They sat together on the sofa, and he held her as she cried. When her crying ceased, they sat quietly, listening for the sounds of the men beyond their house. Royce forgot about the telephone, because he had too long to think about his life in the city, and what could happen to a black man alone in the country if those men decided to come to his door.

* * *

By one o'clock the sounds had vanished into silence.

Over the last hour Royce had listened with his eyes closed, wondering if the men would come to the door, or peer through the curtains. But no one came to the door. The engine turned over, the sound moving nearer to the house, but then dissipating. The house was quiet again. They sat together for another few minutes before the silence began to speak to him, reminding him of what he'd let transpire.

"They're gone," he finally said.

"How can you be sure?" his wife said, squeezing his hand.

Royce flexed his hand to let her know she was squeezing it too tightly. "Gayle, they're gone."

She began to cry, and he wanted to hold her, but he didn't hold her. Instead he stood up and pulled his hand away.

He moved to the window and stared beyond the curtain to the stand of trees, studying the shadows carefully for a moment before finding the silhouette. He stood transfixed by the image, and the thought came to him that he was staring at his past, the past of distant relatives; a depraved image of Christ on the Cross. His fear was an ugly thing, living in his heart, telling him that it could easily be him, or anyone in his family. That it *had* been someone in his family, and not so many years ago. But if it had been the savior hanging from that tree, what accounting would Royce give of his conduct in the face of his enemies?

He moved away from the window and hurried to find his shoes, and then to the kitchen to find a flashlight. When he returned to the living room his wife moved to block his way and grabbed his arm. He tried to walk past her, but she held him desperately.

"What in God's name do you think you're doing?" she said.

"I have to see," he said. "I have to know."

"Know what? You don't have to know anything, least of all anything that could get you killed."

"Those men are gone. They're not coming back."

"You don't know."

"I know," he said. He pushed her away from him gently. "I know that kind of men. They've done what they came to do."

She seemed to wither against his hand, and then sat on the sofa. She sat staring into the darkness. He moved to the front door.

"Stay inside," he said without turning. "I won't be long."

* * *

He walked without using the flashlight, and since he knew the way, it wasn't difficult. The sounds of hidden animals reminded him of the rats again. The bedroom he shared with his brother was always cold in the winter, never warm, but that didn't dissuade the rats. He always lay with the blanket pulled tightly over his head. He thought that if only he hid himself well enough he could keep the rats away. But they never went away.

He walked up the hill where the trees stood blackly against the stars, his shoes crushing invisible leaves; the sound intensified his fear, but he refused to surrender to it. His eyes were focused on the silhouette of the man hanging from the tree. As he climbed the rise the man grew in dimension, and the sound of the moving branches called out like a hoarse whisper. He topped the hill, transfixed by the human shape before him.

In the silence of the country he could hear his own breathing, and birds moving in the foliage. The man hung almost three feet off the ground. In the darkness Royce could only see the shape of the body, the arms and legs hanging, the irregular outline of clothing—the head bent at a sickening angle, and the odd elongation of the neck. His stomach tightened, and he felt a queer nausea. He raised the flashlight, his arm trembling.

The small circle of light fell on the man's shirt. Royce slowly pulled the beam over the pearl buttons, past the collar to the man's face. The rope creaked against the high bough as the body moved gently in the breeze. He felt removed; he felt as if he wasn't there at all, that he was seeing the dead man in a dream. The light shone palely on the acne-scarred cheeks; the tip of the man's tongue was wedged between his lips. The man's eyes were closed. Thinning brown hair lifted on the wind. Suddenly the middle-aged, Hispanic features seemed familiar to Royce, though he couldn't remember ever seeing the man, but the sense of knowing him was almost overwhelming. He traced the beam over the man's neck and saw the bruising from the rope. He stepped around the body and shone the light on the man's arms. They were tied behind him at the wrists, the cord stained with blood.

Are you really dead? Royce thought, and hated himself for doing so, because he knew he would have to verify it for himself. He stepped closer, the beam rising and falling, until he was near enough to reach out and touch the man's arm. His fingers pressed the flesh of the wrist, though the cord obstructed his attempts to find a pulse. The man was hanging too high for Royce to find the artery in his neck. God, he thought, I can't leave you hanging like this. I can't.

He stepped behind the tree and found the place where the rope was tied. He held the flashlight beneath his arm as he pulled futilely at the knots. The tension on the rope made the knots impenetrable. His fingers grew sore as he picked at the fibers. He leaned back against the trunk and cried out softly. What am I doing? This man is dead, he's dead and nothing I do will bring him back.

When he'd swallowed the tears in his throat he stepped from behind the tree and shone the beam on the body again.

He dropped the light from the man's face to his torso, along his abdomen to his pelvis and legs. The dungarees were stained with urine. You poor soul, he thought, this is no way for a man to die. Then, as the beam dipped to the grass, he noticed an object below the man's feet. A wallet. Had it fallen from his pocket? Or had the men left it there intentionally—

I shouldn't touch it, he thought, it's evidence in a murder. But he felt a sudden desire to know the man's name, so he pulled it from the grass and opened it in the light.

He found the driver's license and read the name. Garcia. Yes, now he remembered. He shone the light on the man's face again. Yes, he'd spoken to the man in town. A few weeks earlier Royce had stopped into the hardware store to buy some paving stones for his house and spent a few minutes speaking with the man. He was a gardener, and asked Royce if he needed any help with his land. Royce declined, but they spoke another few minutes about the town—Royce remembered remarking how much safer he felt in a smaller community. The man, Garcia, stood listening without responding; then Royce closed the trunk of his car on the paving stones and drove home.

Why would anyone want to kill you this way? he thought. What did you do to provoke such hatred?

Then another thought occurred to Royce—why had they decided to hang the man so near to his house? Had they seen Royce speaking to him in front of the store? Or was this just a coincidence?

The nausea returned to him, or perhaps it was something more—dread, a sensation he hadn't felt so intensely since childhood, a belief that at any moment his life might be taken from him by unseen men in the shadows of the trees. I thought I was in a good place, I thought I was safe—

Or perhaps it *was* only a coincidence; perhaps the men only came to this place because it was right off the main road.

But would he ever to know?

He'd certainly find out if he called the police. They'd know they were seen by a man with dark skin, and then what would they do? There was no more security for him in the country than in the city. He would have to leave, find some place where such things didn't happen—

Royce dropped the wallet and shone the light again on the hanging man.

Did he have a family? Were they wondering where he was right now? And how would they accept the news that he'd been murdered so obscenely—

"I'm sorry," he found himself saying. His words sounded strange to him, as if they were coming from someone else. "God forgive me, I'm sorry I did nothing to stop it. I don't know that I could have, but I should have tried."

The only sounds he heard in response were the birds in the trees and the groaning of the rope against the bough.

The first time Royce saw a man shot he was eight years old; a drug deal gone bad, an argument outside his window in the parking lot of the apartments. He'd just come home from school and heard shouting from outside. He'd parted the curtains in time to see a gunman taking aim at a man standing by the railing of a second floor apartment. The gun discharged, and the man by the railing clutched his shoulder and fell to his knees. Royce shrank from the window in terror and sat crying until his older brother came home later that day. The shooting was his introduction to violence on a mortal level.

But this was something he never thought he'd witness. All Royce had ever wanted in life was to live peacefully, to be free of the fear that haunted him since that moment so many years ago.

But here was a man he knew, if only incidentally, hanging from a rope less than a hundred yards from his beautiful country house.

I don't want to lose any more of my life, he thought. I don't want to see any more violence.

He shone the light on the man's face again, but all human expression had been stolen from it.

Then Royce became deeply aware that he was standing alone beside a man who had just been lynched.

He dropped the flashlight beam and began walking back toward the house.

His wife was standing by the door as he stepped inside.

Royce turned the deadbolt and set the chain. He turned on the living room lights and stepped toward the sofa.

"What did you see?" she asked, her hands twisted in her robe. "Was he dead?"

"Yes," he said, staring down at the telephone. He couldn't look into her eyes—he didn't know if it was shame he felt or an abiding fear. But he didn't want another human being to see his face.

"I'm going to call the police," he said.

She moved to him and held his arm.

"It's not our problem. It's not our business."

"Gayle, I *knew* the man. I met him in town."

"Oh, my God, Manny, that should convince you not to get involved. If they know you won't make trouble for them they'll leave us alone. You know that's how it works in this world. They'll leave *us* alone if we leave *them* alone."

Now he couldn't avoid looking in her eyes. The terror he saw in them nearly brought him to tears. Yes, it was frightening to think about the consequences of becoming involved in something so inhuman. But he was so tired of being afraid—

"I love you," he said, touching her cheek. "I love you more than anything in this world, but I can't let it go."

Her tears felt warm against his hand.

"What if they come back?" she said. "Manny, what will we do if they come back?"

"I don't know," he said, studying her face. "God knows I don't want to die like that. But I don't want to live like this, either."

She stared into his eyes for a long time, then closed her eyes and nodded. She sat on the sofa, her head bowed as if waiting for death to come to the door.

He sat next to her and reached for the telephone.

"Hello," he said, as the operator's voice came on the line.

For a moment he saw the man again in his memory, hanging lifelessly from the bough. He saw his own face hanging in the light—

Then he said, "Something terrible has happened. A man's life has been taken—"

A knocking silenced him. Three loud raps at the front door. He tried to speak, but couldn't. If they had seen him—

His wife gripped his forearm. "*Manny*—"

Four loud raps. Silence—

He refused to be afraid, and spoke again into the phone. "A good man's life has—"

—the sound of splintering wood.

JANGO JACKS

Laury A. Egan

He'd been called "Jango" for as long as dogs could bark. That's what he always said when anyone asked. Mostly, Jango kept on the move until he was out of money and his belly was echoing with hunger. Right now, he was in southwestern Pennsylvania. He'd walked up and down a lot of roly-poly hills and into the Laurel Highlands on route to Johnstown or maybe Pittsburgh. His itinerary was predicated on the whim of the wind or where the sun was or whether he was too cold or too hot. More or less, it didn't matter where he went. Kith and kin from Kentucky he'd kissed goodbye long ago.

Jango didn't own much. He owned even less when the liquor was gone from the pint bottle he'd buy when he could afford it. Everything else was stashed in an army duffle: jeans and shirts, a few paperback books, and some toiletries, though he only used the razor when he needed some sprucing up before knocking on a door for work. His prized possession was his mother's old guitar which he protected with a trash bag when it rained. His philosophy was to keep things simple. No good accumulating anything or anyone because the day would come when the possession would be too heavy to carry or the person would be too hard to live with, although Jango allowed as how he was the most impossible man alive and that no one would hitch up with him for long.

Over the last week, he'd had no luck outwalking the heat. As fast as Jango moved north, so did the wave of August misery. This particular morning was a beaut. Hot and steamy, with the air hanging heavy with unspilled rain. For several days, clouds had thrust against each other, promising wind and lightning, but each evening the weather forgot what it was threatening to do and slipped into night, carrying over the expectation of storms to the coming dawn. Today, all the compressed humidity made the sun look like it was hungry for more yellow. Pale as it was, the washed-out lemon disk hurt his eyes. Of course, mostly they hurt because of a visit with Old Grand Dad, a bosom-buddy acquaintance to whom Jango had been reintroduced last evening.

Despite the soreness in his bones and the desert he'd swallowed overnight, Jango had all his parts and even a few dollars in his pocket, which was a blessed event if there ever was one. Yesterday, he'd earned some money pulling weeds for a widow, Mrs. Audrey Dalton, a nice lady and pleasing to the eye. Graying hair with streaks of the original gold, large blue eyes, and a figure kept trim from running a small farm with only one old man to help, Shef, who had just left after years of working for the Daltons. He'd gone south to one of the Carolinas—Audrey couldn't remember which one. Because she was alone, Jango was surprised she'd been so friendly when he called on the telephone about her ad in the local paper and then later when they met. In his experience, it was unusual for a woman to hire a stranger, one without references, and especially a big man like himself. Audrey had paid him to neaten up her garden—a job that was half done—fed him a chicken dinner, and let him take a shower, though he'd refused to stay overnight in the house because he planned on a foray to a gin mill he'd spied in town and knew he might not be presentable upon his return. He'd left his guitar in her living room, however, figuring she could take care of his better half.

Jango tumbled out of the haystack. After flicking off bits of straw that clung to his clothes, he sniffed his shirt, which smelled of mildew, dirt, and moldy hay. Upon closer examination, Jango saw that the stack hadn't been freshened in weeks and wasn't as sweet as he thought when he'd selected it for his sleeping quarters. Overall, however, he felt pretty clean from yesterday's shower, though his breath was probably raunchy from the bourbon. He rooted around in his duffle bag and found his toothpaste, which he squeezed generously on a toothbrush and ran the combo around his teeth a few times before spitting it out on the grass. As he did this, he tried to remember his return trip from the bar last night and couldn't. He hoped he hadn't taken to singing one of those fool hound-dog songs and made a ruckus. He didn't want Audrey to regret her charitable behavior or think badly of him.

Jango zipped the duffle and walked toward the Dalton house past an acre of corn and a large plot of tomatoes. The farm appeared to be modest in size, but most of the land lay fallow, overgrown with blue chicory, goldenrod, and lacy cowslips. Cabbage white butterflies were flitting about, cheerfully investigating the bountiful wildflowers.

The residence was a two-story clapboard affair, needing a coat of white paint, though the black shutters were relatively new. A brick chimney and a small stove pipe sprouted through the dark gray roof. An ancient well and outhouse, which were providing happy meals for termites, were separate from the house as was a garage that butted next to a silo and a red barn. Inside the barn were tools, a green tractor, and other farm equipment. On the earthen floor, tall piles of *National Geographic* were stacked. According to Audrey, Mr. Dalton had been an avid reader and armchair traveler before he'd died from a heart attack last week. She said his heart had been weakened from heavy smoking, one vice Jango didn't have. His vice was even more wicked, Jango thought, as he approached the front door, straw hat in hand, feeling a might ashamed that he'd look like what he was—a hung-over drunk.

After spitting on his fingers, he applied them to his hair in the vain attempt to subdue his springy ash-colored hair. Some men were half bald by his age, but he took after his father in the hair department but thankfully not in other ways. Dad had been a mean bastard, a coal miner with a temper as combustible as the explosives they used deep within the mountains. He'd died on his sixtieth birthday. If his accounting was correct, Jango had five more birthdays to celebrate before he achieved that mark.

He tucked his blue denim shirt in his jeans, squared his shoulders, and gently rapped on the door so as not to startle Audrey. It was probably about eight o'clock. He hoped she wasn't a lady of leisure.

The door opened and there she stood, looking cool and cheerful even in the heat. She was dressed in a black cotton dress, a small gold cross at her neck, the same outfit as yesterday.

"Good morning!" Audrey smiled at him as if he were bearing an armload of yellow roses.

"Good morning, ma'am."

She opened the screen door. "Come in and have some breakfast."

"Thank you. That'd be mighty welcome." As he entered the house, Jango tipped his head slightly because he felt like a huge lug compared to Audrey, who he dwarfed by almost a foot. She smelled of clean soap and maybe a spritz of perfume. Had she put on scent for him?

Audrey ushered Jango into the kitchen, a big, well-lit room with white curtains gathered with red and white gingham sashes, and an oval table covered with a blue cloth trimmed with little red balls. The decor was patriotic right down to the eagles, crossed muskets, and Liberty Bells on the wallpaper.

This outburst of red, white, and blue sentiment wasn't to Jango's taste. He'd served in Korea during the war—not of his own volition—and been shot up twice, losing his love of country in the process, though at best he had only nursed a lukewarm affection prior to being drafted. Over the ensuing years, the scoundrels in Washington hadn't done much to win his loyalty, whether they sported a donkey or an elephant on their lapels. Though the room was too "Uncle Sam" for him, Jango decided if Audrey wanted to salute America every time she made a cup of coffee, that was her inalienable right.

He placed his hat on a chair. "What can I do to help?"

Audrey was a bustler, with the kind of hands that fluttered around, making even simple gestures appear complex. "Nothing at all," she said, rushing over to the stove and turning on the burner for the teakettle.

She didn't ask what he wanted to eat. That was okay because this morning he was famished and prepared to consume frog's legs if she served them. Audrey began frying bacon and eggs, popping bread in the toaster, and slicing tomatoes. It looked like he was going to have quite a repast, much like the chicken dinner she'd whipped up the night before.

"Now, why don't you sit down and coffee will be ready in a minute?" She gave him a quick smile because the kettle was already gurgling and she seemed to be the type that had to attend to things pronto.

As he surveyed the room once again, a black-and-white photograph snagged his attention. The portrait—presumably of Mr. Dalton—was placed to the right of the sink, hanging crooked. This struck him as peculiar since everything in the house was tidy and square except for this photograph which Audrey could reach up and straighten without any effort. Was she implying something wasn't straight about her dead husband? The portrait gave the impression of a self-righteous man whose starched collar was too tight. Narrow-set eyes were protected by high cheekbones so sharp they'd cut any hand that caressed them. The pointed chin jutted aggressively, and the mouth drooped with disdain. He'd make a perfect old-time hellfire preacher, Jango decided, and had probably been an impatient son of a bitch.

He felt sorry for Audrey having to tolerate this man who surely hadn't been a tender husband. In comparison, Jango imagined Audrey might find his easygoing personality a soothing contrast. By and large, he was a peaceful sort whose feathers weren't often ruffled. And when they were, he and his guitar found someplace else to go.

Audrey set a steaming plate of food in front of him. The bacon smelled delicious, trailing the welcome scent of warm fat to his nostrils. The eggs were scrambled just as he liked them, in a loose kind of way, not tight and dry, and spiced with freshly cracked pepper. There was also strawberry jam in a white dish with a tiny spoon the size of his little finger nail. He looked up at his hostess and gave her a big smile. "Why this is the finest spread I've had since…last night!"

She smiled back, wiping her hands on her apron and taking the chair across from him.Audrey wasn't much of a talker, perhaps because she was in mourning, so Jango ate in silence, making appreciative noises and frequently wiping his mustache and lips with the red-checked napkin. "I'll finish your flower garden today, I think," he said at last.

"Thank you."

He studied her, trying to decipher if she liked his company or wanted to be rid of him. She'd cooked him two meals and treated him nicer than anyone had in a long while so perhaps things were okay.

As if reading his mind, she said, "Maybe we'll have dinner on the porch this evening. Pork chops." She observed him intently, her eyes fixed on his. "I'd like that, wouldn't you?"

Was she suggesting more than dinner? It certainly appeared that way, which was surprising behavior for a recent widow. "That would be a real pleasure."

"Good." She sipped her coffee. "You know, Jango, after you take care of the garden, I might need your help with some other things."

"Oh?"

She nodded. "Shef's gone and there's work to be done." She set down her mug. "You know how to run a tractor?"

"Yes, ma'am."

"Well, if you're willing, I'd be happy to offer a few weeks of employment. The corn needs to be harvested, and the ripe tomatoes need to be picked. Might be a good idea to turn over one of the fields and add fertilizer, maybe some lime. We can plant a small fall crop, too." Audrey paused, to see if he was interested. "Same rate as we agreed: meals and use of the guest room downstairs."

Jango leaned back and kept his face serious. This was, after all, a business transaction and should be considered in that light. "Sounds fine to me."

"It's been difficult working the place this year. We don't have much growing, as I'm sure you've noticed. We sell vegetables to a neighbor who supplies local markets and has a farm stand. And hay to several dairy farms. That's about it."

Jango couldn't see how she could manage on this income, especially if she had to pay for help. Had Mr. Dalton left her money? He hoped so or that he'd taken out a big life insurance policy so she'd be provided for. In either case, it was none of his concern, though it did make him reluctant to accept the rate she'd offered yesterday—three dollars over minimum wage.

The thoughts about money skipped into his usual worry. Although he was grateful for the work, Jango was concerned about how to tailor his drinking to the obligations inherent in her proposal—those attached to employment and those that might be more social in nature. Although he didn't consider himself addicted to liquor, he had an outsized fondness for it. When he was short on cash, he didn't partake, which was more or less okay. No shakes, just a kind of sad melancholy would steal up on him. Sometimes it happened when he was drinking, too. Jango assumed he was born with a blue personality whether he imbibed or abstained, but all in all, things went better when he was properly oiled, especially if socializing was on the agenda, which apparently it was. He remembered that nine dollars were in his pocket, so he decided to walk into town later and buy a bottle of wine for tonight's dinner. Audrey might construe this gift as courtly behavior, though to him it was something a fellow should do if a lady cooked supper.

After breakfast, Jango helped her dry the dishes while she explained what needed attention outside. Later, as they walked to the barn, it occurred to him she was a trusting soul, allowing him keys to the John Deere tractor, freedom to come into the house when he needed to use the facilities, and guest room privileges. Yesterday, he'd refused to sleep indoors, but today he decided that sleeping within four walls would be acceptable; indeed it would be rude and ungrateful to do otherwise, especially after an evening with Audrey sipping wine on the porch and perhaps strumming a tune or two.

The day was one of the hottest he could remember. First, he removed eight 40-pound bags of lime from the trolley, then hitched the trolley to the tractor, which he drove out to the corn field. All morning, he picked corn until Audrey called him for lunch. He asked to sit on the porch to eat his two ham sandwiches because he didn't feel fit to be inside the house. Sweat was pouring down his face and large dark stains of perspiration ringed his pale blue shirt. He drank three tall glasses of sweet iced tea, wishing for cold beer instead.

In the afternoon, he turned his attention to the tomatoes, stacking them in bushel baskets. As instructed by Audrey, he also cut some sunflowers from her garden and then drove the trolley to the neighbor's house and delivered the goods to John Willis, who was manning a farm stand at the foot of his long driveway. In addition to tomatoes, corn, green beans, zucchini, and squash, big glass jugs full of tall pink and purple gladioli sat on the bottom gray plank of the stand. On the top shelf, jars of honey gleamed gold in the late-afternoon sun.

After introducing himself, Jango helped John Willis unload the corn and baskets.

"Thank you," John said after they'd finished. "Shef usually dumps everything on the grass and takes off."

"Well, I understand he was getting on in years," Jango replied, thinking that John was an affable fellow with his quick grin and dusting of tan freckles across his face.

John raised an eyebrow. "Not really. Younger than you, I'd guess. I don't mean to be critical of him or anything. He's nice enough and he's a big help to Audrey."

This surprised Jango because Audrey had described Shef as well past retirement age. It also sounded like John Willis didn't know Shef had left.

"Yeah," John continued, "without Shef, Audrey wouldn't have managed these last few years, seeing as how her husband, George, is pretty much worthless." He wiped his forehead with a handkerchief and laughed. "There I go again, talking too much. Fact is I don't know George well. He doesn't attend church or even come into town often. Audrey runs the farm so far as I can tell, but she keeps to herself, too."

From this, Jango assumed that John hadn't heard about George Dalton's death, which was curious since most neighbors in small towns know each other's business. He supposed Audrey was a private woman who didn't broadcast her troubles. He could sympathize with that.

"I see." He turned his attention to straightening the sunflowers in their jar while John arranged the vegetables. After they finished, Jango started to leave but couldn't resist asking how the Daltons lived on the income from such a small crop.

John shook his head. "Don't know for sure. Rumor has it that Audrey inherited some money when her father died. Quite a bit, though I don't have any idea how much. George must've decided working the land was too much trouble." John glanced at Jango. "And of course, George liked to drink."

Jango took this in, then thanked John Willis for the chat.

* * *

By four o'clock, Jango was enjoying a long, cold shower, feeling the sizzle of water against his hot skin, knowing he'd be stiff and achy later, especially without sufficient alcoholic lubrication. When he finished toweling dry, he went into the adjoining guest bedroom and was surprised to find a folded pair of khaki pants and a white shirt neatly placed on the chair. A rolled-up brown belt was there, too—a real improvement over his—with its gold buckle pocked with tarnish. He presumed these duds were Mr. Dalton's, though from the photograph, he had appeared to be a man with a slimmer build. Jango held up the shirt and decided it would fit fairly well. On the bed, Audrey had also left a pile of socks, tee shirts, boxers, and pressed shirts and trousers—everything in his duffle bag that had been dirty was now clean except for the clothes on his back earlier today.

"Damn!" he said, feeling embarrassed that she had witnessed the sorry state of his laundry and had touched items that had been worn for days. Jango slumped on the white chenille bedspread and shook his head, then chuckled. "Guess I've been adopted!"

* * *

After he'd thanked Audrey for the clothes, Jango set off toward town, whistling and wondering what kind of wine to buy to accompany the pork chops she was preparing for dinner. Not that he personally cared about matching things up, but he wanted to appear knowledgeable. After all, it seemed tonight was more of an occasion compared to last night. Supper on the porch rather than in the kitchen.

At the store, the clerk handed him a bottle of chilled white wine. Its label had a lot of curlicues around the letters that looked sophisticated. Jango also bought a pint of bourbon, which he could afford because Audrey had paid cash for the day's labor. On the way home—and he now thought of her house that way—he was sorely tempted to start in on the bourbon but controlled the urge. This skirmish with temptation lasted the return two miles as pleasant little sitting spots afforded opportunities to stop and partake. By the time he was at the house, Jango felt pleased that he hadn't heeded the siren call of the alcohol—at least for now.

What he hadn't banished was the conversation with John Willis regarding George Dalton and the man called Shef. Jango couldn't explain why he felt unsettled when he turned John's comments over in his mind, but he did. It was not his nature to be concerned with other people's affairs, he reminded himself. Soon enough he'd be heading elsewhere, though he admitted to being partial to Audrey. Jango recalled that it'd been awhile since he'd entertained an attraction for a woman. The last time had been before Christmas, in Florida, when he'd been hired to fix two broken harvesters at a large orange grove. The next day, the owner departed for weekend National Guard duty, leaving the lady of the house to run things. She'd run things, all right. Two days of running him ragged on a wild whirlwind of passion.

He hadn't been proud of bedding another man's wife, especially a Guardsman's, but life on the road created odd unions. People who normally wouldn't step out of line seemed to discount dalliances with someone who was just passing through. Sometimes Jango obliged; sometimes he had enough sense to leave. It occurred to him that leaving might be the sensible course of action now. But it was hard to refuse a dinner with wine and female conversation. Besides, he'd agreed to stick around for a week or two.

He knocked on the farmhouse door. It was probably okay to walk inside but best to err on the side of politeness. After a few minutes, Audrey opened it, smiled, and accepted the bottle of wine with thanks, saying it was thoughtful of him to buy it. Feeling pleased, he went to his room and washed his hands and face. The pull of the bourbon grew strong after that, so he lay down on the bed and forced himself to read a newspaper until the urgency quieted. He composed himself and then made an entrance into the kitchen, where he noticed that Audrey had changed from her black clothes into a pretty pink blouse with the top button undone and a cream-colored skirt that showed off her legs. She looked like a different woman. A very attractive woman.

Audrey put him to work shucking corn and slicing tomatoes. After that, he helped her set the wicker table on the porch, carrying out silverware, napkins, two candles in hurricane lanterns, and a bouquet of plump blue hydrangeas.

"Well, I think we should photograph this spread," he said. "Looks like something out of *House Beautiful.*"

She handed him a box of matches so he could light the candles. "It's nice to have your company, Jango."

"My pleasure." He gave her a warm smile, one that was just shy of flirtatious.

* * *

During the meal, Jango told stories and Audrey laughed. A good, easy laugh that heartened him and filled him with delight. In turn, she recalled her college days at Chatham, studying English, displaying a wry skill with words that fascinated him. As he watched her, Jango thought of the white butterflies he'd seen that morning. Perhaps it was the wine, but Audrey suddenly seemed to possess a bright exuberance that lit him up, made him feel happy and good in her presence.

Dinner was fine and so was the wine. As it happened, Audrey had chilled a second bottle, which was a gratifying sight. He opened it after they finished the first, equally pleased that Audrey wasn't a teetotaler. She was almost matching him glass for glass, though Jango tried to restrain his intake.

After the plates were scraped and they had returned to the porch, he realized she was a trifle buzzed. They sat together on the wicker sofa, listening to the crickets and watching the fireflies pulse yellow against a dark cobalt blue sky. The air was dense and warm, almost still except for the occasional breeze that shivered through the oak leaves. Audrey's perfume—a rose scent—seemed to intensify as the evening progressed, or perhaps this was only because she was closer to him. Jango had been delighted when she'd chosen to share the couch rather than sit in an armchair.

"So, my bet is that your mama never named you Jango," Audrey said, after a sip of wine.

"And you'd win that bet." He waited and then added, "Janson. Don't know how that name got twisted around, but I suspect it's because I was always on the go even as a toddler."

Audrey laughed. "Like you still are."

"Yes, I suppose so."

"Must be strange. Arriving someplace and not knowing anyone."

He'd mentioned this when she'd asked for references. "I have a few acquaintances in Johnstown and Pittsburgh, but not what I'd call friends. That's kind of true in general. I've lost touch with anyone I knew growing up." Jango had said this many times before, but this time he felt a little sad admitting he was a totally rootless, unattached human being.

Audrey took this in and was quiet a few minutes before asking how long he'd been on the road.

"I did a stint of walking when I was discharged from the army in 1953. Went home when my mother passed in 1969, but I shouldn't have bothered." He paused and then added, "I took off after that."

She raised her eyebrows at this but didn't question him. "Did you serve in Korea?"

"I did." Jango didn't like to talk about the war or his mother, so he reached over and topped up Audrey's glass and his own, before going inside to get his guitar.

When he returned, he busied himself with tuning the strings. He glanced at Audrey several times, making a few jokes about how awful his guitar-playing was. Actually, Jango thought he wasn't half bad.

"Did you ever study music?" Audrey asked.

"Me?" He chuckled, then strummed the guitar to hear how it sounded. "Hell, no. My mother taught me how to play when I was a boy. Never tried other instruments. Never studied anything except for learning to be a mechanic in the army. School and I weren't much of a match."

Audrey frowned. "I married George right after I finished college. He didn't want me to have a career or kids, so mostly I've kept house and helped on the farm."

"That's a shame," he replied, thinking she was too smart to waste her life on a no-account farm and with a man Jango knew he wouldn't have liked. This wasn't any of his business, though the sadness in her voice when she mentioned kids and her homebound fate was unmistakable. "Must have been tough losing your husband," he said, wondering which was the biggest loss of her life. He suspected it wasn't George Dalton's passing.

Audrey's mouth tightened a little. "Yes, it was."

The silence became awkward, so after they drank their wine, Jango played "Amazing Grace" and "Blowin' in the Wind." He sang along as he strummed the chords, doing a few riffs and some fancy picking as embellishment. Audrey regained her good humor and was an attentive audience. Jango thought she looked beautiful, nodding to the music, her blue eyes shining in the candlelight. There was a trace of sorrow in her expression, but perhaps it was often present and he simply hadn't noticed it before.

Jango mused on this. Was her sadness what attracted him to Audrey? Or perhaps it was that they'd both been searching for something they hadn't found. Whatever it was, he was having feelings for her, which made him anxious. He looked down at the empty wine bottle and thought about the bourbon stashed in his room. An unwelcome yet familiar yearning flared through his body and permeated his mind. He told himself he'd had enough, but part of him insisted it was only a start. To distract from this temptation, Jango played a rendition of "Leaving on a Jet Plane," one of his favorites, which Audrey said was a song she loved. After he finished, he leaned the guitar against the porch railing.

"That was beautiful! You have a wonderful deep voice, Jango." Audrey observed him for a moment before offering coffee and some brandy.

Jango couldn't hide a smile. "Damn! That's a fine idea!"

She laughed at his eagerness. "Would you mind—"

"Sure. My pleasure."

"The coffee tin is in the refrigerator and the brandy is in the cupboard."

He rubbed his hands together, making light of his eagerness for more liquor. "Well, aren't we going to have a great old time this evening!"

As he walked into the kitchen, Jango wondered if Audrey was a drinker like himself. He hadn't seen any of the usual signs during the two days of their acquaintanceship, but she certainly was enthusiastic about the brandy. He reasoned that his perspective was probably coloring his interpretation of her behavior. Most likely Audrey was just worried about where the evening was taking them, perhaps anticipating romance and being afraid of it, imbibing more than usual in order to muster courage. She had a lot more on the line than he did, Jango reminded himself. She'd recently lost her husband and was vulnerable and alone. Jango weighed this and realized he needed to act in a considerate and unselfish manner. It wouldn't be right for him to woo her and wander off, compounding her misery. This left him with the decision as to whether he should derail the present course and keep things friendly, strictly employee to employer, probably disappointing Audrey, or allow matters to progress, in which case he would hurt her when he left. The third possibility—that he would stay—was one he hadn't entertained in years.

"You'll turn out to be a cold-hearted bastard," he muttered. "Again."

Jango sighed, filled the cast iron kettle with water, and dismissed the idea of a fast getaway. Instead, he busied himself with finding mugs and two brandy glasses. When the water boiled, he made coffee, and placed everything on a tray which he carried outside, unsettled despite the delightful promise of more to drink. He poured two generous tots of brandy and hesitated before taking his place on the sofa. Audrey gave him such a warm smile, however, that sitting elsewhere was unthinkable.

"Thank you, Jango." She squeezed his arm in appreciation.

"You're welcome," he said. "My, you have strong hands for such a little lady." He accompanied this with a teasing smile. "Good to have for farm work, I suppose." As he said this, Jango imagined her fingers touching his face.

They drank some coffee, then took up the brandy glasses and clinked them together. The liquor was dark and smoky, not the most expensive, but ambrosia compared to the rotgut he usually drank. Having a full glass and nearly full bottle in front of him usually was the high point of any day, but tonight he couldn't erase the confusion he felt; confusion mixed with foreboding, like an internal gauge was warning of danger ahead.

Jango took a second swallow of brandy. He wanted to make love to Audrey, but not just for sexual gratification. That's what worried him, that and something else he couldn't identify. He draped his arm across the back of the sofa, giving her room but also the opportunity to move closer. As he did this, he accused himself of being a coward, of leaving Audrey to decide whether they should transgress into physical territory, a place they should probably avoid.

"I haven't had brandy in a very long time," she remarked.

He laughed. "I can't say the same." While he meant to sound humorous, he wasn't proud of this admission and disliked that he was making light of a serious problem. For some reason, Jango felt he owed her an honest assessment. "I tend to drink too much, Audrey." He wanted to look away, but he forced himself to hold her gaze. "I wish that weren't the case."

She observed him candidly, without disapproval. "I know that. We all have things we're ashamed of. Either something we are or something we've done."

Jango tried to read her meaning, sensing that she was telling him something about herself. "I can't imagine someone as lovely as you could do anything wrong."

She stared at the brandy in her glass. "Thank you, but you'd be surprised."

Although this aroused his curiosity, he also felt protective. Without thinking, he set down his brandy and folded her in an embrace. She felt small and fragile in his arms. Her hair smelled sweet and clean.

"Audrey, I wouldn't be surprised by anything that happened in this world. I've seen it all at one time or another. Memories that chase me over the hills, day after day, night after night. There's nothing you could say that would shock me." As he said this, he wasn't positive it was true. Jango knew some defenseless places still lurked in his heart.

She pulled away a few inches, perhaps to see his expression, then placed her mouth against his. The gentleness of the kiss was different than the alcohol-fueled crush that Jango usually encountered. He responded in kind, tentatively, which led to a longer, more intense kiss. "Are you sure this is a good idea?" He half hoped she'd be wise and sensible, half hoped she wouldn't.

"It probably isn't." Audrey nestled against his shoulder, making no move to separate.

Jango stroked her neck and hair and remained silent, wrestling with desire and apprehension. As always when matters of the heart were weighing on him, he remembered his mother, whom he'd loved, and whose death at his father's hand pained him acutely even all these decades later. After her funeral, he'd tried to walk off his anger, but the hatred for his father was still with him, even though the man was now dead. He disliked recalling any of his past—his childhood, his parents, or his army service—a lot of bad stuff to lug around the countryside. Usually, he managed to shove all these memories out of his consciousness. However, something about sitting here with Audrey knitted all of the fragmentary experiences together and made him feel more like a whole person, with a history and perhaps a future. Although he hesitated to wonder what lay ahead, he was surprised Audrey had elicited this reaction. No one else ever had.

They stayed together for several minutes, the silence feeling right;

communication occurring without words. A strange contentment floated over him, one that was akin to intoxication but different. In fact, as he held Audrey, Jango realized he hadn't broken their embrace to reach for his brandy. That he didn't mind was impressive, gave him hope and a tiny flicker of expectation. He leaned down and kissed her again, trying to express the powerful emotion he felt. Her response seemed to convey the same feelings.

"You know I'm not the kind of guy to fall for," he told her.

Audrey didn't answer for a few seconds. When she drew away, Jango feared she had reconsidered, had recalled that he was only a lowlife drifter not worthy of her affection. Then he saw how serious she looked. Almost solemn, like she'd made a decision.

"Promise me something," she said.

Immediately, he wanted to refuse, worried she'd ask for a promise he couldn't honestly give. But before he could say this, she continued.

"Promise me that if we make love now…that later tonight or in the morning you won't despise me for anything I might tell you."

Jango was surprised by this request. Audrey seemed incapable of any wrongdoing and yet clearly was suffering because of something she'd done.

He kissed her. "I promise."

Audrey led him upstairs to her bedroom. A four-poster maple bed dominated one wall; a black Franklin stove was opposite, its doors folded half open. An oval hook rug lay between. They placed their brandy glasses and candles on the end tables flanking the bed. Rainbow refractions from the crystal facets of the glasses danced on the white ceiling along with reflected amber from the brandy. Their bodies cast black shadows that stilled when they came together in an embrace.

As he kissed Audrey, he smelled her rose perfume and the faint remnants of wood smoke from the stove, which evoked a picture of the two of them lying together in bed during a snowy night, the fire hot and flickering. As he imagined this, Jango realized he wanted more than one special evening with Audrey. He thought of all the winter nights he'd huddled in barns or lay drunk in an alley, nearly frozen, and knew he was growing too old for the itinerant life. Mostly, however, he was growing too old to be alone, to want nothing and no one.

Instead of drinking his brandy, Jango helped Audrey unbutton her blouse. He'd noticed how ill at ease she was, how her fingers shook as they tried to grasp the buttons. Seeing this, he removed her clothes slowly, item by item, leaving time for her to adjust to each stage of nakedness. Their lovemaking was equally slow. For Jango, this was deliberate. He wanted to savor each moment, to remember this first time because it might be the only time.

* * *

He didn't know when they'd fallen asleep, but when he opened his eyes, the sun had risen high above the hills of green trees. Through the open windows came bird song and a warm breeze. Jango felt happy as he slipped out of bed, trying not to disturb Audrey, who faced him, her hands tucked beneath her chin. In the morning light, Jango saw that she was growing old, as he was, but unlike his face that had been ravaged by weather and hard drinking, Audrey's retained a delicate beauty, her face serene with sleep.

Quietly, he walked into the adjoining bathroom, though he felt a little presumptuous using it rather than the one downstairs by the guest room. Jango imagined that the counter had once held razors and shaving cream and maybe a bristle brush and black-toothed comb, possessions of Mr. George Dalton, but now only Audrey's bottles of make-up were lined along the backsplash. After squeezing out some toothpaste on his finger and working it around in his mouth, he scooped water in his hand, rinsed, and dried his mouth on one of Audrey's hand towels. Then he returned to the bedroom and hesitated, unsure whether to put on his trousers.

His entrance woke Audrey. "Where are you going?" She smiled and patted the bed.

"Well, nowhere that I know of." He returned her smile and sat beside her. "And how are you this fine day?"

In response, she drew him to her. They kissed. He removed the sheet that separated them, slipping his arm under her head.

"This is nice," he whispered.

They began to touch each other with more assurance than the night before.

* * *

Afterward, Jango lay back against the pillows, holding Audrey and luxuriating in the peaceful joy he felt. She sighed and seemed equally content to treasure the silence. Finally, she rose and examined him with tender regard. "You know you'd be a handsome fellow if you had a haircut."

"Now you're just flattering me, ma'am. You and I both know I'm an ugly old dog who's been out in the rain too long."

She laughed, then a look of concern shadowed her face. He saw the change instantly and raised to a sitting position. "What's the matter?" He could think of a slew of things that she should be worried about, but he recalled the promise from the night before and sensed she was about to confide some uncomfortable truth.

Audrey pulled the sheet to cover herself and stared out the window.

He placed an arm over her shoulder. "You can tell me. I think you know that."

She glanced at him, her lips compressed, as if she didn't wish to speak. "That's where it happened." She pointed to the Franklin stove.

Jango stared at the stove, bewildered, and waited for her to continue.

"George deserved it, of course," she said. "Though I didn't mean to do it."

Instantly, he understood. "Self defense?"

Audrey nodded. "He kept the cast iron teapot on the top burner. Kind of silly, since it was just about as easy to go to the kitchen and heat water. However, George liked the idea of having tea at night while he was reading." She sighed. "And whatever George wanted…"

"Go on."

"Well, he got mad at me. He was always furious about something. This time it was about spending too much at the store. Which was ridiculous because I paid for the food to avoid trouble with him—I inherited money from my family, which George resented, too. At any rate, he found the receipt in the kitchen and charged up the stairs, yelling and screaming. He dragged me out of bed and knocked me to the floor." Audrey turned toward him again, tears welling. "When I got to my feet, I grabbed the kettle and hit him on the head. He fell. Then he tried to get to his knees. I hit him again. Harder."

Jango exhaled slowly, imagining how horrible Audrey's life with George Dalton must have been. He grieved for her, as he had for his mother, who'd been battered by his father over and over until the bastard had finally killed her. He understood Audrey, the frenzy of rage that had exploded within her. He had wanted to murder his own father. His hands had itched to do it, but he'd packed his bag instead.

"I'm so sorry, Audrey," he said, pulling her close.

She began to sob. "I didn't mean to do it. I…I—"

"I understand. It was an accident."

She pressed against his chest. Jango felt the wetness of her tears on his skin, her body shake with emotion. As best he could, he comforted her, imagining that she felt glad the abuse had ended; guilty for ending it.

When she stopped crying, Jango handed her tissues from a box on the end table. She wiped her face and nestled against him.

"Don't be ashamed of what you did," he said. "You did the right thing."

Audrey looked up. "I know, but every day I have to live with what happened. With the fear of being found out."

He nodded and thought about this for a moment. "What did you do with—"

"The body?" She shook her head. "Thank God for Shef. He knew what was going on. About how brutal George was. He carried George out to the barn and buried him there. Dumped some bags of lime on top." She gave him a rueful smile. "He's under the piles of *National Geographic*.

George always wanted to travel but was too cheap to pay for a trip."

Jango laid back against the headboard. He was disturbed by Audrey's smile and expression. There was something wrong, something very wrong. "So, Audrey, what was your plan after that?"

A flash of wariness passed over her face, concealed almost instantly. "I don't understand."

"You don't understand? I know what you did with the body." He rubbed his chin, and sighed. "But how were you going to explain that George was no longer around?"

She shrugged. "That he just took off, and I have no idea where."

Jango didn't believe her. He wished he did. Suddenly, he was more disappointed than he'd ever been in his life, which was saying a lot. "I think you figured a way to blame someone else. Didn't you?"

As his swarm of suspicions settled into place, Jango swung his legs over the side of the bed and stood up. He leaned against the windowsill, looking out at the tranquil landscape, and felt winded and sick.

"Maybe find some no-account drifter who'd answer an ad in the paper," he said. "Someone who didn't know anyone. A stranger who took a fancy to the lady of the house. Got jealous of her husband." He paused, thinking through the possibilities and of all the things in the house he'd touched, including the tea kettle. The shovel, bags of lime, gloves, the bed post. His fingerprints were everywhere.

She removed the sheet and came to her feet. "No, Jango. Please."

"Please what?" he said softly, almost to himself. He turned toward Audrey, appreciating how the sunlight illuminated her body. He still desired her, wanted nothing more than to erase the last few minutes and to make love again. Instead, he reached for his clothes.

"Please! Believe me! None of that will happen now."

Jango stepped into his boxers and slipped on his shirt. She stood before him, naked. His instincts told him to run and yet the urge to stay was powerful. "Last night you made me promise not to despise you, no matter what you told me."

For a second, she seemed relieved, though she clutched at her hands. A nervous gesture that Jango noticed.

He hesitated. "Well, I don't despise you for what you did to your husband."

She took two steps toward him. "I didn't know you then. When Shef and I—"

"No, you didn't," he muttered, pulling up the zipper of the khaki trousers. As he placed his feet into his work boots, he noticed a small dark stain on the pants' cuff. He bit his lip. Shef's pants. George's blood.

Audrey saw his expression and grabbed his arms. "Shef won't go to the police!"

"Oh, so old man Shef is still hobbling around these parts?" His voice sounded brittle, rusty, with a derisive tone he seldom used.

"I'll stop him! He's not supposed to go to the police yet." She walked to the dresser, grabbed her wristwatch, and placed a hand over her mouth. "Oh, my god!" she gasped.

Jango snatched the watch and checked the time. Nearly nine. He stepped away from her. "You and Shef. He's been in this bed, hasn't he?"

She shook her head, but her eyes betrayed her. "Don't go."

"Don't *go*? Hell, that's what all the ladies say. Love 'em and leave 'em, that's my motto." He chuckled at this, but only to hide the hurt and anger he felt. It was all he could do to leave the room without admitting how hopeful he'd been, how much he cared for her. He took the stairs quickly, rushed to the guest room, and threw his possessions into the duffle bag. Then he carried the bag and his guitar to the kitchen and used a tea towel to wipe his fingerprints from the kettle. Not that this would do much good, with all the other evidence he'd left around the house.

Audrey hurried into the room, belting her bathrobe. "Jango, don't leave! I'll explain to the police!" Tears coursed down her face.

Jango ignored her. He wrapped a loaf of bread and some tomatoes in the towel and shoved it in the duffle bag. "And tell them what, Audrey? Sounds like you and Shef have it all worked out."

She swiped at her wet cheeks. "Don't you understand? I might be falling for you."

"Might is a lousy word," he said. "Maybe I might have loved you, Audrey. Eventually." He walked into the hall and grabbed his straw hat from the hook, opened the screen door, letting it slap loudly behind him, and marched around the side of the house.

A north wind was blowing hard, driving massive thunderheads across a tormented gray sky. A big gust decided him to head south, to West Virginia. Maybe Tennessee. As the first raindrops began to fall, Jango heard Audrey calling his name. He reached inside his duffle bag for the bourbon, took a long swallow to help forget her voice. The alcohol tasted bitter, poisonous. When it hit his stomach, it burned as if it were battery acid. He stared at the label for a moment, studied it like a lover's face, and tossed the bottle into the bushes.

Jango hurried past the haystacks and through the meadow, then paused to glance at the farmhouse. Audrey had turned away from him. She was waving at something in the distance. He blinked the rain from his eyes. A black truck and a white police cruiser shot down the far hill, vanished behind a rill of trees, and came into sight several miles down the road, aiming for the Daltons' driveway. It was tempting to hide, to see if Audrey would point out where he was headed or send the police north, in the opposite direction. He could climb a tree in the woods up ahead and watch. That way he would know the truth.

He sighed. Searching for the truth had never been a part of his life.

In fact, he'd tried to outrun the truth for as long as he could remember. This time, however, the not knowing hurt. Not staying with this one, this woman, cut deep.

Jango slung the strap of the duffle bag across his back. Instinct told him to drop the guitar so he could run faster, but he had already lost more than he could afford to lose. He squeezed through the clacking stalks in the cornfield, the tawny sheathes slapping at his shoulders, and sprinted toward the forest, thankful that it was crisscrossed with streams and rivers where he and his footprints could disappear.

THE TAKING

Katherine Tandy Brown

A bead of perspiration slides from my temple along my cheek and wakes me as it drops on the back of my hand. Tortola's near equatorial sun sears my back. I can't have napped for more than fifteen or twenty minutes, but my head feels filled with cotton. My mouth is dry, my body sticky with sweat.

Groggy, I sit up and slide into orange rubber thongs, protecting my feet from the sweltering cement surrounding the swimming pool. My forehead throbs till I'm used to the elevation. I touch the scar on my head, gingerly fingering the stitch lumps, still prominent as railroad tracks.

Squinting into the early afternoon brightness, I regard the Caribbean Sea, a placid quilt of turquoise and azure speckled with dozens of sailboats at rest, waiting for wind. From my vantage point on the bluff I can see blue-tinged reefs a hundred feet or more below the surface. Calm ocean waters beckon but I'm not yet strong enough for clandestine currents. Laps in the clinic pool are challenge enough.

Only a month ago the headaches began. I was on assignment, writing a story on Jost Van Dyke for *Islands*. My first piece for a national magazine. Finally. The weather was January-perfect — hot, dry and sunny. I'd hiked the island's four square miles for three days interviewing local guest cottage, campground and restaurant owners. Just as I was taking the last bite of fresh-caught lobster at Johnny's Beach Eats, a hatchet split my brain. At least that's what it felt like. God, it hurt. I remember hearing my fork clatter to the floor as I grabbed my head and shrieked. Then "everything went black," as they say. It really did. When I came to, I was on the cement floor. Virgie cradled my head and I looked at her through a dream. The late afternoon sun glistened off her sweaty sienna skin and the whites of her eyes were a sort of yellowish pink. I had no feeling in my legs. And they didn't work. That's how I ended up here at the purple stucco clinic — under the knife with a prognosis of "probably" — instead of at home in Ocean Springs on my twenty-eighth birthday.

"Ya doin' okay, darlin'?" The nurse's Jamaican singsong finds me from her window on the office deck. I give her a thumbs up. She grins, her teeth a dazzling white, before she disappears.

Crimson tamarind blossoms stir lazily overhead, caressed by puffs of a gentle tropical breeze. Unsticking my thighs from the plastic chaise longue, I stand, allowing my head to settle before I walk the six steps to the pool. These Virgin Island swims have turned my skin golden, making my yellow bathing suit glow neon in contrast. I kick off my thongs and slide goggles over my head.

Sitting on the edge of the pool, I slip my toes into the water, then my ankles, then calves, next thighs, and finally, I slide off the green tiled edge into the liquid depths of the pool. The water feels cool on skin still warm from the sun. I gasp when its chill reaches the small of my back. A scent of chlorine tinges the salty ocean air.

Adjusting my goggles one last time, I steel myself for the plunge, bend my knees, take a deep breath and push off toward the nine-foot bottom. First I angle downward with a long, gliding breast stroke — a hard pull of my arms down to my sides, then glide, then a whip kick followed by another glide. A bubble or two at a time I release tiny bits of air, gliding, stroking through the coolness of the pool. My body welcomes its daily return to the womblike comfort of the water, a ginger ale effervescence around my face and limbs.

I break the surface, inhaling the moist, chlorined air. My first laps are always the crawl, so I reach and pull with the right arm, then the left, kicking one, two, three for each arm stroke. The water caresses me like fresh mountain air.

My mind eases into its swimming mantras. I'm always most comfortable in the water. On land my long, lithe limbs feel awkward. Water is home, a place to play, to swim, uninhibited and joyous. The first lap completed, I smile, turn quickly, and with a strong thrust, push off, returning to long, smooth strokes and glides.

When I first notice him, he is floating in the far corner while paddling slowly, childlike, with slightly pudgy arms. His skin is the translucent white of a corpse. His neck-length hair floats on the water's surface like seaweed circling his head. Soft and thick, his trunk descends into whitish swimming shorts and then down to flabby, stumpy legs with short, wide feet. He doesn't look the least bit athletic, and for a moment I wonder why he is here. A short stab of pain behind my left temple reminds me this is a surgery clinic.

My prayer to the water has just begun, with nineteen laps left to go, and I continue to stroke and kick, stroke and kick. Absorbed, I am oblivious to anything but the sensual touch of aquarian fingers on my skin.

A transient sense of dark, of chill, passes through me. But I swim on, choosing to ignore the shudder which, for an instant, sets my instincts on alert. Though the surgeon believes he removed all the tumor, twinges of head pain under the scar still make me wince for seconds at a time and strange neurological impulses sometimes skitter at random throughout my body. I dismiss this as such, continuing to stroke and glide.

He must have watched me enter the pool, observed my lap cadence, noticed my total absorption.

So completely am I immersed in blue-green meditation that I don't notice he's moved closer. Suddenly he grasps my hair, pushing my head underwater. Because he's behind me, I can't see him. I have no idea who he is, but he's surprisingly strong and very white. Maybe a tourist. His hold on my hair hurts my head. I reach up with both hands to loosen his grip and free myself from his rough play. His fat fingers hold firm. I struggle to grab some part of him, my arms flailing like tentacles, but he's soft and slippery with no edges. I seize a handful of his swimming trunks. They're slimy like pond scum. My throat slams shut with terror. My head throbs. I can't think, can't fight back. I *must* get free but I can't I can't I *can't.*

He reaches with his other hand and clasps my arm, pulling me down deeper. His fingernails dig into my wrist, paralyzing my hand. Heeding instinct, I scream long and loud. "*Nooooo!*" reverberates through every brain cell, all now on fire. The sound leaves my lips in an immense opalescent bubble, pink and pearly. Mesmerized, I watch it float round, shining and full to the surface, where it quietly bursts, my last hope.

My lungs are empty and aching. No longer able to hold back the reflex, I squeeze my eyes shut and gasp a breath of water. It surges into my nostrils and mouth. I choke, coughing violently. Searing pain shoots down my throat. My eyes pop open. *Oh God. Where's the sunlight? Where's the surface?* Hues attack me, dimming and clouding, tiny interspersed flashes of light, intense violet, fluorescent green, like nerves sparking in my brain, synapses firing like laser beams. My head throbs, my limbs tingle, I taste bile in my throat. The colors strobe against a field of dark. Utter black. *Like death? My God, no.*

I scream again. This time there's no sound. No bubbles. No hope. No strength. I can't fight anymore.

A great sob wracks my body. *God, not now. Not after the tumor, the surgery. And the pain. Constant, all-consuming pain! It's not fair. I just want to swim and get strong and live. I haven't done anything wrong. God, where are you? How could you do this to me now? Now? What kind of god are you? I don't want to die. Not like this. I need air. Help me, God. Please. Please. Help me.*

I inhale long and deep. Liquid fills my chest, easing the pain in my throat. I exhale, then draw a tentative breath. Water floods my lungs again. I wait for them to collapse, like pin-pricked balloons, but instead… they *expand.* It *works.* Amazed, I try again. As I breathe water, my head clears and the ache subsides. I open my eyes wide to see crystalline turquoise cut with shafts of sunlight all around. The vivid flashes subside. My brain quiets. He releases my hair. Strength returns to my limbs, and I pivot to face my antagonist.

Now for the first time I see him, really see him. His watery features are blurred. His smile is angelic, alluring. His eyes are a soft green with tiny bubbles clinging to the lids. There's no trace of malice. A feeling of trust for this — somehow I can't call him a man — creature overwhelms me. I relax.

His grip on my arm is still firm but no longer hurts, as he pulls me down the tiled slope of the pool towards the drain. Deftly, with a flick of his index finger, he removes the rusted metal grate and, sliding through feet first, he pulls me after him into a chilly, murky tunnel. Still breathing water, I strain to see ahead. But the passageway is dark, barely wide enough to fit our two bodies. I trail my finger along its wall. The surface is soft and spongy, like moss or algae. His feet kick rhythmically, gentle by my thigh.

Soon the black, wet atmosphere lightens and brightens. Warm, shimmering water teeming with aquatic life surrounds us. Giant coral reefs tower overhead, pulsating with the ebb and flow of the sea. A tiny octopus camouflages from vivid scarlet to drab gray, its pliant tentacle briefly brushing my leg. Vibrant blue, yellow, green and red Caribbean fish frolic around a kite-like Manta ray that glides serenely, harmlessly between us.

Strange as it seems, I feel that I know these creatures. I feel safe and comfortable. Like I've come home, whatever that means. For the first time in a month my head is free of pain. The gentle brine is warm and soothing as it enters my lungs.

His smile radiant, he releases my arm and beckons to me.

An invisible force – the hand of God? – rocks clumps of pencil-thin, olive-green seaweed on the soft sand beneath my feet. Back and forth. Back and forth. Its lullaby mesmerizes, and a peace born of the tides fills my soul.

Joyously, I follow.

A SONG FOR ONE-EYED LOU

Martin McCaw

I was glad when the music started. I'd gotten bored making Luke guess which fist held my collection-plate nickel. He hadn't guessed right yet because I was sitting on the nickel. The congregation was crowded into the back two pews on both sides of the aisle, meaning late arrivals would have to sit in front where they couldn't pick their noses. By standing tiptoe I could see over Bertha Welch's shoulder to where Mama was playing the piano up front. All these people, fifteen at least, and Mama was leading them all. Without her piano they wouldn't be able to find the right notes. The only grownup who wasn't singing was Daddy, though he held one side of the hymn book while I held the other, Luke and Nadine being too small yet to read the big words.

After the benediction the congregation shuffled into the aisle, the men shaking hands and chewing out President Roosevelt. Outside on the sidewalk, I told Mama, "Daddy was so proud listening to you play that he forgot to sing."

She laughed and tousled my hair. "He can't carry a tune," she said.

But Daddy whistled as he started the car. That's how we always knew he was happy. In the back seat we kids held our usual contest, trying to be first to smell the rotting pea vines Daddy got last summer from the cannery. The smell had worsened lately as the weather turned hot. The hogs seemed in no hurry to finish off the pea vines, for which I was grateful. Once the pea vines were gone, we'd be able to smell the hog pen again.

"I smell the pea vines!" Nadine yelled.

"No, you don't," I said. "We're only two blocks from the church."

"Roll up your windows," Mama said, giving Daddy a dirty look.

Back at the ranch, a column of blue smoke rose from the burn barrel behind our house. Mama took a deep breath on the porch, savoring the smell of singed chicken feathers.

While she rolled the chicken pieces in flour and poured bacon grease in the skillet, Luke practiced the piano. Mama had started giving both of us piano lessons last fall, gambling that we had inherited her musical talent instead of Daddy's. She broke even. After eight months of lessons, I would entertain Nadine with my best piece, "Chopsticks," then wander into the orchard so I couldn't hear Luke play Haydn's "Surprise Symphony."

But Luke had to think about what he was doing, mashing the keys so hard the tips of his fingers would whiten. Mama just looked at the music and played, her fingers skipping over the keyboard like water bugs. To

Luke the piano was a mule that had to be spurred, to me it was a bucking bronco, but to Mama the piano was a winged horse that carried her across continents and time, away from our treeless hills.

When she played "Home to our Mountains," she again would feel the Rogue River's spray as she picked blackberries with her sisters. When she played "Little Mother of Mine," she would brush egg whites over a pan of steaming scones and watch her mother slide it into the oven. She would sit once more on the piano bench alongside her father as he tapped the keys with one finger and sang "The Ninety and Nine" in a trembling tenor. "Loch Lomond" would whisk her to a Scotland she had never seen, where she and her grandma would climb a hill of purple heather at dawn to watch the loch light up in gold. "Let Me Call You Sweetheart" would find her sitting in Daddy's car at the Whetstone depot, waiting for the train that was supposed to take her home to Oregon, a train she would never take because Daddy, watching the engine approach far down the track, would clear his throat and say, "Think you'd like it up here?"

Mama lost track of time when she sat at the piano, and like all children of addicts, we suffered. We often waited patiently at the table twenty minutes past the six o'clock supper hour, listening to our stomachs rumble, reporting each minute as it ticked off the clock, while Mama scurried around the kitchen. None of us kids offered to help because we didn't want to encourage any more six-thirty suppers. Also, we knew Mama would have supper ready by the time we figured out whose turn it was.

The way Mama put it was, "I'd rather do it myself than listen to you kids quarrel." But of course she didn't understand we were helping her most by not helping. Daddy would spoil our therapy by asking if there was anything he could do to help. He fueled her addiction in other ways, too. When he came in for supper after feeding the pigs, he would stand on the back porch with one boot off, listening to Mama. Somehow she always knew he was there, because her next song would be "Let Me Call You Sweetheart." Then she would jump up from the piano and exclaim, "Where did the time go?" Daddy would put his arm around her shoulders and give her a squeeze and say, "I'd rather listen to you play than eat." It seemed strange that a man could farm all his life and not appreciate the importance of food.

After we finished our chicken dinner, Daddy and Charley Flathers, our neighbor, climbed the big hill behind the barn to check the wheat. I tagged along a few feet behind. It hadn't rained since Easter, and the yellowing wheat stalks rubbed against my legs, hoping to filch a drop of sweat. By the time we reached the hilltop, a wet half-moon had formed on the back of Charlie's shirt.

Daddy broke off a head of wheat and pinched its kernels. "Another week without rain and we might be hurting a little."

"Another week and we can forget about harvesting." Charlie clapped

Daddy on the back. "Look at the bright side, Eddie. We won't have to bother getting our combines in shape."

After Charlie cranked up his Model T and putted off, backfiring instead of waving goodbye, I kicked a clod and watched the dust float away. "What are we going to do, Daddy?"

"Don't pay attention to Charlie. He loses his crop every year and then harvests forty bushels."

I went inside, but Daddy stayed on the porch awhile, looking at a wisp of gray cloud in the west.

At dusk our family huddled around the radio, listening to *Ted Mack's Amateur Hour*. Ralph Sigwald seemed determined to shut out the other contestants by taking the whole hour to sing "The Lord's Prayer."

"Lead us not into temptation," he sang, holding each note so long I was afraid his lungs would give out, "and deliver us from evil." No worry there, Ralph. I could spot the bad guy in a movie by the shape of his mustache.

When the "Amen" trailed off into silence, Daddy said, "What's that sound?"

He opened the door, and we could see the shimmer of raindrops against the darkening sky. Daddy started whistling. It was a tune we never heard from anyone else, the same few bars over and over, slightly off key like a meadowlark's song.

Next morning Daddy stuck a ruler in the tomato can he kept in the back yard to measure rainfall. "Sixteenth of an inch. Hardly enough to wet the dust."

By June fourteenth it hadn't rained again. We all stood in the back yard, surveying the blackberry bushes Mama had planted to remind her of the Rogue River. "Everything's turning brown and it's only June," she said.

Nadine squealed, "Look!" and pointed at the south hills across the river. Huge clouds rolled toward us, the shape of black widow spiders.

"What is it?" I asked Daddy.

"I don't know," he said. "I've never seen anything like it."

"Rain's coming!" Nadine yelled, clapping her hands.

"If those are rain clouds we'd better build an ark," Daddy said.

We watched the clouds boil toward us, blotting out the sun. Birds stopped singing. Our collie whimpered. I got impatient and took a forked stick out by the gas pump to play Uncle Wiggily. The sky got dark.

The first blast of wind almost knocked me over. I opened my mouth and gagged on dust. I could see only a whirling gray haze. My eyes stung, and I shut them tight. They felt gritty, but I didn't dare open them. There was a steady roar, like barley whooshing down an elevator chute.

I stumbled into the wind. Something whacked my face, and I sprawled in the dirt. I touched my forehead – wet and grainy. My nose plugged up. I turned my head away from the wind and sucked in a big breath. Dust filled my mouth, my throat, my lungs. I began to cough and couldn't stop. Gasping, I curled into a ball. The roar inside my head got louder. Something brushed my shoulder. With my eyes shut, I pictured a white-bearded figure bending over me.

"No!" I flailed my arms, grabbed a bony thing that raked my palm and thrashed free. Something was clenched in my fist – leaves, big leaves. I'd walked into a branch of the maple tree. That meant the house was east, but which way was east? The clouds had come from the south, so if I kept the wind to my right … Coughing and wheezing, I began to crawl, fingering each weed for clues, the wind pounding my right side. Stickers jabbed my face and hands. Russian thistle. Too far south, veer left. My hand flattened against smooth wood. The porch. I crawled up the steps.

"Stay inside!" I heard Daddy shout. "I'll go out again and look for him."

I touched his shoe. He scooped me up and carried me into the house. Other arms circled me. I opened my eyes. Inside, the haze was yellow. Mama and Daddy were both hugging me. Luke and Nadine crowded close, trying to pat my head.

"Give me room to breathe," I whispered.

I shut my eyes and flinched while Mama dabbed iodine on my forehead with a cotton swath. My hacking had dwindled to a cough every few seconds, like hiccups. I opened my eyes and saw Mama's father looking at me from the photo on top of the piano. His mouth curved down into his long white beard, but his eyes crinkled. This piano had been one of the few possessions saved when the bank foreclosed his mortgage after he died, scattering his family.

"There's dust all over your piano," I said.

"Might make it play better," Daddy said, winking at Mama.

"Let's find out," Mama said. She swiped her hand over the piano bench, raising a puff of dust. Then she sat down, thrummed the keys, and began singing "Wait 'Till the Sun Shines, Nellie."

In the morning we waded through foot-high dust dunes into a wheat field. Daddy rubbed a shrunken head of wheat between his thumb and forefinger. The husks at the top were missing their kernels. "Wind shattered it," he said.

We all watched Daddy. There was no expression on his face. Mama laid her hand on his arm. He looked at her, and his eyes twinkled.

"You've got to look at the bright side, Lola," he said, jostling her shoulder like the calves did to each other when they felt playful.

"Stop it," Mama said, trying to look cross. "What on earth could the bright side be?"

"You won't have to get up at three to feed a harvest crew," Daddy said.

* * *

Mama got to sleep in till five all summer. One day in late August dozens of trucks with rickety sideboards clattered into the field south of the house, crunching tumbleweeds and raising dust so thick I couldn't see the highway. In other years gunny sacks full of wheat would have dotted the field, but this year the wheat stalks, their shriveled heads still attached, lay twisted in every direction, like my hair when Mama forgot to comb it.

By noon the trucks' owners were bunched in front of me, squinting south into the sun. Their necks were burned leather-brown, even though their hat brims slanted low all the way around instead of curling up over their ears like real cowboys' hats in the movies. It was so hot the flies on the hats had quit crawling to save their energy. I stood on top of an upside-down apple box and listened to an auctioneer I couldn't see.

"Lot number thirty-seven, blue mare name of Susie." The auctioneer's voice changed to a sing-song. "Got forty, forty now five now five now two fifty, going at forty ... sold for forty to Sam Woods of Waitsburg."

Daddy emerged from the crowd, leading Susie, the last of the team of thirty-two horses and mules that pulled our combine. A gaunt-faced man threw a rope around her neck and knotted it. Daddy untied his own rope, patted Susie's neck, and watched the man lead her into the loading chute. Daddy climbed the porch steps. A rancher came through the front door, walking gingerly, as if his glass were brimful of nitroglycerin instead of lemonade. Daddy stepped aside to let him pass. Through the kitchen window I could see Mama pouring lemonade from a pitcher into a row of glasses on the table.

"Lot number thirty-eight," said the auctioneer. "Clarendon piano."

From the porch Daddy looked toward the voice. He rocked on the balls of his feet, his thumbs hooked under the straps of his bib overalls.

"Got eighty now five now five, got eighty-five now seven fifty now eighty-seven fifty now seven fifty, going at eighty-five ..."

The auctioneer waited. I stood on tiptoes, and the apple box under me creaked. Between two men's hats I could see the top of Mama's piano. Beyond the piano, along the river half a mile away, cottonwood trees shimmied in the heat. I looked back at the house. Daddy stood on the porch, overall straps balled in his fists. Inside the kitchen, Mama reached up and pulled down the blind.

"Sold to Harvey Drumheller for eighty-five," said the auctioneer.

I heard a wail from the front of the crowd, and a moment later Nadine ran past me toward the house. Daddy came down the steps, squatted, and took her in his arms. She tried to tell him something between sobs. Then she pulled away and ran into the house. The door slammed. Daddy looked at the door, then at the kitchen window with its closed blind.

He walked toward the loading area, where a truck was backing up to the chute. The chute trembled, and the truck stopped. I caught up to Daddy as a man with a handlebar mustache climbed down from the cab.

Nadine ran toward us from the house.

"What would you take in place of that piano?" Daddy said.

The other man was up in his truck bed, pulling the end gate out of its slots. "Well, I don't know, Eddie. MaeBelle's been wanting a piano a long time."

"You know my saddle horse?"

"Blackie?" Mr. Drumheller set the tailgate against the truck's side panel and pulled a tin of Beechnut tobacco out of his hip pocket. "Well now, Blackie's a real good horse."

"Would you take Blackie instead of that piano?"

Mr. Drumheller tucked a pinch of tobacco between his gums and cheek, then worked his jaws until the tobacco settled where he wanted it.

"Reckon I would," he said.

"But Daddy," I said, "how will you find the cows – hey!" I bent to rub my ankle where Nadine had kicked it.

I expected Mama to act happy when Daddy and two other men rolled her piano into the living room, but instead she scolded him for giving away Blackie. Daddy and I went out on the porch to watch the auction. I couldn't decipher the auctioneer's drone because Mama started playing the piano.

"Let's move closer," I said.

"Soon as this song is over," Daddy said, although he must have heard "You Are My Sunshine" a thousand times before.

* * *

After I graduated from grade school, the other freshman boys proved their manhood by smoking Camels, while I proved mine by singing bass in the church choir. One Sunday as we began "Love Lifted Me," Mama hit a wrong note and quickly shifted upward to the right key. I wondered if she'd been making mistakes for years that I hadn't noticed, and now that I was an adult I'd become more perceptive. Each time she played a wrong note, I slid backward a few inches so the sopranos blocked me off more from the congregation. After the sermon, instead of edging down the aisle chatting and shaking hands, I slunk out the back door, hurried to our car, and crouched low in the back seat.

On the way home Mama said, "It's my arthritis. I can't move my fingers fast enough any more."

"I've never heard you play better," Daddy said.

"How would you know?" Mama said. "You're tone-deaf."

Nadine said, "The piano sounded great," and Luke agreed. I snorted and looked out the window.

"Maybe we could move Aunt Mary's old organ up from the church basement," Mama said.

"Maybe it's time Jeannie Bowe took over the piano playing," I said.

Daddy turned around in the driver's seat and gave me a look. Then he patted Mama's shoulder and said, "We'll move the organ up tomorrow."

* * *

Switching to the organ didn't faze Mama. She'd been playing it all along for the Beginners' Sunday school class. The week before, our Juniors' class discussion had been drowned out by "Amazing Grace" surging up from the basement as I was explaining why a murderer could never achieve redemption.

"Amazing Grace" isn't a kids' song," I'd complained to Mama after the church service.

"I liked it when I was a little girl," she'd said, as if that made it okay for every kid.

Although the organ blurred Mama's mistakes, it magnified mine. Singing along with the piano had been like sitting down in a wooden chair, straight-edged and hard, but trying to follow the organ was like sinking into the sofa Aunt Agnes broke after she went off her diet. Singing in the choir, I had no choice but to ignore the organ and follow the rumbling bass of Mr. Langley, our high school math teacher. He was pleasant enough at school, but in church he wore a fierce scowl, which I attributed to his belief that only a hundred forty-four thousand preordained souls would be allowed into heaven. He understood the laws of probability, so he knew what odds we were bucking.

Because his scowl lowered the corners of his mouth, he would sing half a note flat and drag me down with him. Once I tried to strike out on my own, but our minister looked up from behind the pulpit where he'd been studying his sermon notes, so I went back to Mr. Langley's key, whatever that was.

One day Bertha Welch came up to Mr. Langley and me after church and said, "It took some getting used to, but I've kind of grown to like hearing you basses sing in a minor key."

* * *

A few weeks before Mr. Langley died, after we both had quit the choir, I confessed to him, "I never could hear the organ's bass notes. I had to follow you."

He did a double-take. "Are you kidding? I was following you." He shook his head, and the scowl came back. "Boy, did I get mad when you'd stray off key and pull me along with you."

* * *

At age nineteen, with time to kill before harvest, I got a job at the Walla Walla Cannery. I pushed steaming tubs of peas past conveyor belts where women picked black balls of deadly nightshade from the peas. A dark-haired woman at the end of a belt picked frantically, like an angel charged with saving a fleet of rafters before they plunged over a waterfall. She had a purple bruise on her swollen left cheek. Sweat glistened on her throat, and her belly stuck out like a pumpkin. She shouldn't be here, I thought. I remembered Mama rubbing shirts up and down the washboard, her stomach bulging with Nadine.

"What if they miss some nightshade?" I asked my boss.

"Symptoms resemble a heart attack. The coroner won't suspect a thing." A machine shrieked behind us, and he raised his voice. "Don't you have two tubs of peas backed up over there?"

That night he told me to wash out the tubs, pointing to what looked like a fire hose. When I turned the faucet's handle, the nozzle twisted in my hand and water blasted my face, snapping my head back as if I'd been punched. The hose leaped out of my hand and writhed on the floor like a python. With blurred eyes and stinging nostrils, I dropped to my knees and groped for the hose. My knees skidded on wet cement, and I splashed onto my stomach as the hose whipped away. By the time I got the nozzle aimed at a pea tub, the women at the conveyor belt had forgotten about the nightshade. It was the first time all day I'd heard anyone laugh.

Behind me, my boss said, "Why didn't you just turn off the faucet?"

My shirt and pants were still wet when I parked outside Shep's Smoke Shop and squished into the poker room, past the "No one under 21" sign. I handed the house man a five-dollar bill and held my breath. He glanced at my wallet as if about to ask for ID, saw more bills, and counted out chips.

"Fresh blood," said a man with matted gray hair and a bulge in his cheek. Spittin' Joe, someone had called him a week before when I'd watched all afternoon from the doorway. "One seat open," he'd said to me then. Now he licked his lips. What he didn't know was that I'd figured out which hands usually won pots, and they weren't the cards he most often turned over at the showdown.

Another man I'd pegged last week as a poor player was also in the game tonight, a burly man with tight neck muscles and angry eyes. Last week I'd given him plenty of room when he'd passed through the doorway on his roundtrips to the bar. As I sat down alongside him, he cursed and threw his cards into the muck. He reached for his hip pocket. I could see into his wallet as he drew out his last bill and handed it to the house man.

I threw away eight hands in a row without playing a pot. So did a player who had three stacks of yellow chips. He was watching me out of one eye. The other eye had a patch over it. His face looked as if sore losers had gone after him with beer bottles they'd broken off at the necks. The fingers of his right hand moved constantly, shuffling two short stacks of chips into one stack, separating them, clicking them together again, like a hawk flexing its talons as it waited for a field mouse to scamper into the open.

"Professional gambler," the busboy had whispered the week before when we'd stood in the doorway and watched the one-eyed man turn his hole cards face up, then drag in a huge pile of blue and yellow chips. "Professional gambler," I'd echoed, feeling my cheeks puff and hollow.

I looked at my hole cards. A six and a deuce, trash. I pitched my cards toward the discard pile, but Spittin' Joe picked them up and ran a forefinger over the backs of both cards. He shook his fingers as if he'd dipped them into a toilet.

"Get a new deck," he said. "Somebody here must be awful nervous."

While the house man broke the cellophane on a new deck, I wiped my palms on the underside of the table. I took out my Camels and jiggled the pack – I'd practiced this move for weeks – until one cigarette shook out far enough for my lips to clamp onto it. I let it droop while I fished in my pocket for a matchbook. The match didn't light. I struck it harder, and the tip broke off. The one-eyed man threw me his matchbook. I held a burning match under my cigarette and inhaled. All I could taste were flakes of tobacco. I took the cigarette out of my mouth. Damp. My face got warm.

"Try my brand," said the one-eyed man, tossing me the pack of Lucky Strikes that had been lying by his chips.

As I lit up, I said out of the side of my mouth, "Been thinking of switching to Luckies anyway."

"Jack?" said a soft voice. A woman stood in the doorway, her stomach protruding into the card room. Except for the purple splotch under one eye, her face looked even paler in the card room's light than it had above the conveyor belt.

"Jack?" she said again.

The burly man shifted his chair so his back was to the woman, sending a whiff of second-hand beer my way. When I looked up again, the doorway was empty.

I squeezed my cards, and my scalp prickled. Two queens in the hole with another queen face-up. I bet a blue chip. Across the table the one-eyed man had a chip in his hand, ready to call, but now he looked at me and threw away his cards.

Spittin' Joe said, "Up it a buck," and raised me a yellow chip. The burly man hesitated, looked down at his small stack, and pitched two chips into the pot.

"Raise it again," I said, hoping the two men couldn't hear my heart thudding. The dealer turned more cards face-up, and the pile of chips in the center grew. The burly man tossed in his last chip. I turned over my queens.

"Beginners' luck," grumbled Spittin' Joe. He flipped his cards into the muck and shot tobacco juice toward the spittoon and my shoes.

The burly man tore up his cards and flung them into the air. I sat still, looking straight ahead, as bits of pasteboard fluttered onto the table. He stood up, kicked his chair backward into the wall, and stalked out of the room. I heard a whang and guessed he'd kicked a counter stool on his way through the bar.

"Well, his wife wanted him to come home," the one-eyed man said.

I rose from my chair, banged my head on the brass lampshade that hung over the table, and raked in the pot.

The one-eyed man pushed out his ante for the next deal and said, "You may look like you shouldn't be shaving yet, but you play poker like a man."

I'd arrived in heaven sixty years ahead of schedule.

In two hours I won seventeen dollars, more than I'd earned all day at the cannery. After my shift was over the next night, I won twenty-six. The third morning I didn't show up for work; my cannery career had ended. Two weeks later I came home at dawn. As I sat in the car counting grainy five-dollar bills – I'd won exactly thirty dollars – the smell of frying bacon seeped through the car's open windows.

I sat down at the table and pried a waffle loose from the waffle iron. "Night shift pays twenty cents an hour more," I said.

"You'll have Sunday mornings free again," Mama said. She forked bacon from the frying pan onto my plate. "Everybody misses you at church."

"Can't make it to church anymore. I'll need to sleep."

"Pea season's about over, anyway," Mama said.

"They want to keep me on at the cannery year around." I turned to Daddy. "You'd better get another truck driver for harvest. My hay fever's got so bad I'll have to quit farming."

Daddy looked out the window toward the orchard. Twenty years before, his father had gone out there in a drizzling rain to pick pears, wanting to help the family some way even though he was just getting over the flu. There had been no antibiotics to fight pneumonia in those days.

"Well," Daddy said finally, "you've got to do what's best for your health." He picked up his plate and carried it to the sink. The creases of his fingers were black with grease. Last summer I'd helped him change the cylinder teeth, curled on my back inside the combine's womb in hundred-degree heat, sweat dribbling into my eyes, wheat chaff falling on my face. Even though I'd scrubbed my hands with Lava soap, I couldn't get them clean.

I admired my white fingernail tips. One-eyed Lou and I wouldn't get our hands dirty the rest of our lives.

Daddy took his hat off its nail by the pantry door. "When Luke gets up, tell him I'll need some help on the combine," he said to Mama. From the kitchen window I watched dust rise behind his pickup as he headed out the lane.

Mama sloshed dishes in the sink. I picked up a dish towel and dried a plate. She looked at me in surprise.

"My, those people at the cannery smoke like fiends," she said. "I hope I can get the smell out of your clothes."

I dropped the last knife into the silverware drawer and followed Mama into the living room. She sat at the piano and began to play her father's favorite song. She sang, "There were ninety and nine who safely lay in the shelter of the fold –"

"I better get some sleep," I said.

"But one was out on the hills away, far off from the gates of gold."

"Could you have my dinner ready a little before noon?"

Mama sang louder, "Away on the mountains wild and bare, away from the tender shepherd's care."

"I've got to be at the cannery by one," I shouted.

She stopped playing. "That new job sure has you working long hours."

"Pays better, though."

"What is it you do?"

"Oh, different stuff."

"Well, I'll tell Aunt Agnes she ought to scold whoever told her that nasty rumor."

* * *

Ten years later, after Daddy's heart attack, I had to leave a poker game loaded with amateurs to join the family at the hospital. I walked down the corridor toward Daddy's room, wishing I was still at Shep's where the chips would be wandering back and forth among the amateurs like homeless children. I passed a "Keep door closed" sign on room 326. I stopped, remembering. Four years earlier I'd stood inside that room looking at the oxygen tubes curled into One-eyed Lou's nose, listening to the rattles as he breathed.

"You're his only visitor so far," a nurse told me. "He won't last the night." She fastened an empty plastic bag to the catheter hose under his bed. "He brought all his money in a paper bag, wads of twenty-dollar bills. Wouldn't let us put it in the safe. Said he didn't trust anyone." She checked the IV needle taped to his wrist. "We had to wait till he was sedated to sneak it out from under his pillow."

After the nurse left, Lou raised himself on his elbows and stared past me. "Give me the three of hearts," he whispered. Then he'd flopped back onto his pillow, and the rattling had resumed.

Laughter burst from a room at the end of the corridor. I snubbed out my cigarette on the floor and walked toward the laughter.

"Well, the gang's all here," Daddy said when I went inside. Mama and Nadine hugged me, and Luke shook my hand.

"Let's go down the hall and sing Christmas carols," Mama said.

"It's after nine," I said. "We'd wake people up."

"They can go back to sleep," Mama said. "None of them have to get up at six to milk cows." Luke and Nadine, less thoughtful than I, sided with Mama.

"I'll stay and keep Dad company," I said.

"Go ahead," Daddy said, perhaps aware that my company would consist of sitting in a chair and thinking about poker hands I'd misplayed that afternoon. Or maybe he wanted to get me out of the room before Mama suggested we wheel his bed down the corridor, too.

Outside a half-open door we began "Angels from the Realms of Glory," Mama singing soprano and Nadine alto. I resigned myself to following Luke's tenor, an octave lower, unless the room's occupant happened to be a bass who felt well enough to join in.

We sang "Joy to the World" outside the closed door of room 326. A card taped to the door read "Whalen, James." How insensitive, I thought. His door's closed because he's so sick he wants to be left alone, maybe dying for all we know, and we're singing about joy.

When we finished I heard a faint tapping, slow and rhythmic like a faucet dripping. It was coming from behind the closed door.

"What's that sound?" I said.

"Mr. Whalen is clapping," Mama said.

We began "Silent Night" outside Daddy's room. At "sleep in heavenly peace" my throat clogged and I stopped singing. I wanted the song to hurry up and be over so we could go inside and make sure Daddy was all right. Then, as the others gathered their breaths for the next verse, I heard his whistle. He was whistling the tune he'd learned from the meadowlarks that sang to each other across our canyons of bunch grass. His tune blended with "Silent Night" about as well as when I used to ride the school bus to football games, the girls singing "Sweet Alice Blue Gown" while we boys tried to drown them out with "Ninety-Nine Bottles of Beer on the Wall."

When we went into his room, Daddy was chinning himself on the trapeze bar that hung over his bed. "I could hear you clear down at the far end," he said. "You sounded like twenty voices."

* * *

Years passed in a blur of cards, thirty poker hands an hour, three hundred a day, ninety thousand a year. I became as stimulating a conversationalist as the other gamblers. "Read 'em and weep." "Cut the cards." "What's the bet?" On good days I basked behind towering stacks of chips, marveling at my skill. On days my billfold got a workout, I shook my fist at the ceiling and cussed out God. My income dropped the year the burly man went to prison, but climbed the following year as neophyte gamblers learned to cash their Friday paychecks at Shep's. I celebrated Good Friday every week, as long as I avoided the eyes of the silent women who waited in the doorway.

On a breezy Sunday morning when I was forty-nine, I stood on the sidewalk outside Shep's, counting my bankroll and wishing I'd quit at midnight. Far away a church bell began ringing, two peals close together, like the supper bell Mama used to ring when I'd wander too long in the hills. Suddenly I got the urge to hear her play again. I looked at my watch. Not enough time to go back to my apartment and shave before heading north.

I drove to the farm between hills of yellowing wheat that billowed in the wind as though crop-dusters were skimming the slopes ahead of me. When I turned into the lane, Daddy was hosing off his pickup's windshield, standing well back so mud wouldn't splatter his suit.

"I didn't think to wash the car before Lola left for Sunday school," he said.

After nodding to people I vaguely recognized, I settled into the back pew alongside Daddy. Strange sounds jangled up from the basement, jerky and halting. I adjusted my hearing aids until I recognized "Amazing Grace." Could one of Mama's pupils be playing the piano? For the next five minutes I watched the door behind the pulpit, where Mama would emerge on her way to the organ.

The heavy front door creaked, and the foyer doors blew open. Wind ruffled the hair of people alongside the aisle. Two candles by the altar flickered, then flared brighter than before. Mama stood in the foyer doorway.

She slid onto the bench beside us and gave me a hug, then leaned across me and hugged Daddy, probably feeling as if she were hugging mannequins. Daddy and I looked straight ahead with poker faces.

"Why aren't you playing?" I said.

"My arthritis got too bad." Mama gestured up front where Jeannie was smoothing sheet music at the organ. "Anyway, Jeannie's been waiting long enough."

"She could have waited a few more years," I said. "She's barely fifty."

* * *

By the time Daddy died, osteoporosis had shrunk Mama so small she had to peer between spokes of the steering wheel, but she still drove ten miles an hour over the speed limit. Drivers glancing in their rear-view mirrors must have felt like Ichabod Crane when he looked back and saw the headless horseman gaining on him.

One Saturday afternoon I sat alongside Spittin' Joe at the poker table, an ideal location to extract my share of his Social Security check. He held his cards in a shaking hand close to his face, like Daddy held a newspaper during his last years. Joe bet a purple five-dollar chip. Without turning my head I peeked at his hole cards, two jacks, which couldn't beat my aces. I raised him.

He dropped his last chip into the pot and turned his second-best jacks face up. I studied the fringe of white hair, the tiers of wrinkles, and Joe began to look like Daddy.

I pushed him the pot. "You win, Joe." I tossed my aces into the muck, face down, and cashed in my chips. As the house man counted my chips, I looked around the card room for the last time, at the cash register that had supported me for thirty-five years, at the halo of smoke that hung over the seven humped men. Then I drove to the ranch.

Mama was cutting gladiola stems by the porch. "I'll run these down to the church," she said. "Be back in a few minutes."

"I'll drive you," I said.

"Don't be silly."

I watched what appeared to be a driver-less car turn from the lane onto the highway, its right rear wheel dipping at the edge of the culvert. I paced for half an hour before I dug out my car keys. When I rounded a bend and saw Whetstone's houses, the ditches along the highway empty of cars, I relaxed.

I swerved onto the gravel alongside Mama's car in front of the church. Church? I stared at the building, disoriented, like a militant atheist who'd come looking for a church to bomb and got the directions wrong. "First National Bank" was etched in granite above the glass door. I had a feeling that if I pressed my nose against the glass, I'd see a couple of farmers talking crops in front of a teller's station.

Why was I seeing a bank? I'd helped convert this building forty-three years ago, after our old church had burned down, the one Daddy's Uncle Sam and Aunt Mary had built. Although I'd been only eleven, Ben Morgan had let me slip dynamite sticks into cracks in the concrete when we'd blown out a basement vault that was designed to hold money instead of the Beginners' Sunday school class.

As I sat in the car, I thought I heard organ music. I looked around. No other cars were parked near the church, which didn't make sense because Mama's arthritis had forced her to quit playing the organ long ago.

Were my hearing aids playing tricks on me again? I opened the big glass door and stepped into the foyer. Music seemed to come from everywhere in the church. Instead of the organ's strings and reeds, I could hear bees buzzing, water rippling, wind blowing through tree leaves. I pushed open the foyer's swinging doors. Red and yellow gladiolus sprouted from two vases at the foot of the pulpit. Because the organ faced the pulpit at right angles to the pews, Mama hadn't seen me come in. She was hunched over the keyboard, peering up at the sheet music, glasses teetering on the tip of her nose. She sat on the edge of the bench and pumped the foot pedals with her toes. A painting of the Last Supper hung on the wall behind the choir pews. Even at this distance I could make out Judas, leaning backward at the table staring at Jesus, his spoon upside down in his hand, wondering if he'd given up too much for his thirty pieces of silver.

I stepped to the right so Mama wouldn't see me and stop playing. I stood behind the back pew, our pew. It was drenched in a pool of golden light that streamed from the stained glass window. We had never sat in that light, for church was always held in the mornings. The sun shone directly behind the gold center design of the nearest window. I rotated my head slightly, and crimson, turquoise, violet dazzled in turn, like a kaleidoscope. Below the design was engraved "In memory of William and Ida Stewart." Daddy's parents.

I gripped the back of the pew and felt the sun warm my cheek as I listened to Mama.

She turned the last page. The whistle of the flute lingered, like a mourning dove's call. She lifted her hand, and the music stopped. She sat still, head tilted, as though listening for another sound.

I walked toward her. "That's the best I ever heard you play."

"Go on." She jabbed a finger toward one of my hearing aids. "Better get those things checked."

"I thought you couldn't play any more on account of your arthritis."

"It lets up once in awhile." She rubbed her knuckles.

"Why don't you play tomorrow? Jeannie won't mind. I'll phone her myself."

"Don't you dare. By tomorrow I won't be able to bend my fingers."

Two weeks later Mama dozed off and drove through a wooden railing on the way home from Walla Walla, finally stopping in Lloyd Dozier's wheat field. When Lloyd reached her, she was walking around the car, inspecting it, her right arm hanging limp and her nose bleeding.

"Hardly scratched it," she told Lloyd.

That afternoon the surgeon came out of the recovery room and said, "She'll never be able to raise her arm. Her bones are so thin it was like cutting paper."

After Mama came back from the nursing home, Nadine and I watched her pin gold braid to purple velvet on one of the Christmas balls she gave every year to her past Sunday school students, even the ones pushing fifty who couldn't have had much room left on their trees.

"Beautiful," Nadine said. "How can you make those tiny designs when you can't lift your arm?"

"Mind over matter," Mama said as she poked a pin through a silver bead on her third try. "I'm going to play the piano again, too, soon as my arm heals. And I'm going to drive again."

Nadine looked at me with her eyebrows raised. "How long will the car be in the shop?"

"A long, long time," I said.

* * *

It was November fourth, two days after a second operation on Mama's arm – she'd fallen against the bathtub – when Luke unbuckled his guitar case in her hospital room. All afternoon we had helped her try to walk, none of us wanting to believe that the weakness in her leg and the loss of range in her speech had been caused by a stroke. Now she lay with her eyes closed, sometimes responding when we asked her a question, sometimes not.

Luke strummed his guitar and started "Rounded up in Glory," singing tenor to Nadine's alto. Mama rasped the words in a monotone. I didn't move my lips, not having sung outside my bathroom for years. Mama tightened her fingers around mine. Her hand felt small, as my hand must have felt to her fifty years before when she would make sure she didn't lose me in the Walla Walla stores.

When the song was over, I said, "Sing something funny."

They did "Old MacDonald Had a Farm." When they got to "with a cluck-cluck here and a cluck-cluck there," Mama's monotone worked fine. She knew how to do Old MacDonald's animals; she had fed them, milked them, ridden them, chased them out of her garden. Rob and Nadine did an ordinary "nay," but Mama's "neigh-h-h" tailed off in a whinny.

After the last "eeyi eeyi oh," Luke leaned over and said, "What would you like now, Mom?"

Mama mumbled something I couldn't understand. Luke nodded, and they began "Precious Lord, Take my Hand."

From the corner of my eye, I glimpsed a figure in white standing in the doorway. A nurse, I thought, come to listen. But when I turned to look, she was gone.

* * *

Five days later we were all in church again. This time the church was packed. The afternoon sun poured through the windows, warming everyone to the right of the aisle. Nadine and Luke and I sat in the front row left, and sunlight had not reached us yet. I tried to persuade a drop of water to evaporate before it leaked out of my eyelid.

"Page thirty-eight," the minister said. Someone from the pew behind handed me a hymnal. I took it to be polite, although I did not intend to sing. "Amazing Grace" started as a whisper, not because the singers planned to build to a crescendo for dramatic effect, but because they didn't want to sing "that saved a wretch like me" with such fervor that they'd draw appraising glances. But when they reached, "I once was lost but now am found," their voices swelled, and the hairs on my arm tingled. Suddenly I wanted to sing, too. I searched for a bass voice I could hitch onto. A bass rumbled from my right, half a note flat. By the time I got my mouth open all I could hear was the melody, led by Luke's tenor alongside. I clamped my mouth shut, unwilling to mimic my own brother an octave too low.

"Was blind but now I see," soared through the church, almost lifting me off the floor, and I couldn't hold back any longer, I had to sing. I tried for low "G" but wobbled between "A" sharp and "B" flat. I groped lower, knowing "G" must be down there somewhere, and my voice warped downward like a phonograph turned off with its needle still in the groove. Luke's voice faltered, and I was afraid I would throw off the whole congregation. Then I heard the piano's hard clunk, and I aimed for its lowest note and hit "G" dead center. Following the plink of the piano, I sang, "And grace will lead me home," every note true, dipping to "C" sharp as if I'd been singing on key all my life.

It hit me that the church must have switched from the organ back to the piano since I was last here. I forced myself to look front right, past the table I'd been avoiding. But the organ was still there, and Jeannie was swaying and pumping into the last verse.

We sang, "When we've been there ten thousand years …" I heard the other bass again, on key now that he could follow the piano. And now I heard a quavering tenor and more new voices, way too many for this little church, and I realized we would be in trouble if a fire marshal walked in – if he could count all the singers.

I cocked my head toward the back of the church and fiddled with my hearing aids until I heard the other sound. It was coming from way in back. Not the sad whistle of the organ's flute, but the song of the meadowlark, the whistle of someone who was glad to have the piano back, its player too, and didn't care if he was a few notes off key.

RECITAL, EARLY APRIL

Christopher J. F. Martin

The end of middle school open house had been a tiresome affair: they show you to toy desks and you sit there while teachers show off their students' standout work. After that, you stand in groups, shaking sweaty hands, and interrogating the musky smell of obligation. When the teachers tire of this, they assemble you in the auditorium and the principal says a few words into a wired microphone. *Can people in the way back hear me? Then let me begin...*

Big Tom Redding had seen me from across the auditorium, caught up with me in the parking lot, and tapped my shoulder the way women sometimes test the sound of crystal-ware. His stature was short and incautious, that of the salesman—his back went diplomatically rigid and he looked straight at me. Then, as if by habit, his thick idling hand found the head of Tom Junior.

"What do you say? It's not every day my son gets to stay at the house of a world-renowned violin player, if you get my thinking," Big Tom said.

Next to Junior was my son, Louis. I sent him to the car, where I hoped he wouldn't be able to hear the exchange where I planned to break Big Tom's heart; but my boy rolled down the window, and my wife, Nancy Lynn, who was getting impatient, yelled out to ask if it was true, if Junior was going to sleep over at our house.

"It'd mean a lot," said Big Tom. "A whole lot to both of them. They could practice together and get real ready for the recital. I've never really known much about music, but then here *you* are..."

"If that would suit my son, I don't see why not."

"That's great! Tom's been wanting to spend time with Louis, and the wife and I want to get him out of the house. It's great they're friends, isn't it?"

Big Tom laughed to himself, giving his son a light push in my direction. "Get along, then, Junior."

Junior grabbed the guitar case and went past me to the car.

"When should I pick him up?" Big Tom said.

Instead of explaining that Louis had practice every morning, I merely informed Big Tom that we didn't live too far away and could drive him home early tomorrow.

"Fine with us. Hope it's not too much trouble for you," he said.

I explained: "I'm an early riser."

* * *

We rode the ridge's breadth to our street and pulled into the driveway. Junior kept asking me about my work, if I had been to Europe with the symphony—yes—and how many times—several—and to how many places—too many to count. Here're a few: Paris, Dortmund, Crete. It was as though he was gathering information, which he would no doubt forget in a few hours, but he kept at it, probing and pestering, his voice a Magpie's shrill song. He seemed to be able to read body language. As I exited the vehicle I closed my door too firmly, and he was quiet.

* * *

"Oscar," said Nancy Lynn with a muted urgency.

"You must excuse me," I bowed shallowly to Junior. "I don't usually discuss my work. It's nothing personal, but perhaps if you would like to discuss music..."

Louis, who had been quiet the whole ride back, suddenly elbowed me in the hip.

"Can you not be weird, please?"

"Again," I said, this time not bowing. "You must excuse me."

We went inside and after taking everyone's requests, Nancy Lynn phoned an order to a Vietnamese restaurant. Louis occupied his companion by showing him his room and offering him a soda. Louis takes after me in manner, but he has the blonde hair, brown eyes, and teacup chin of Nancy Lynn. (I have often lamented the fact that physical traits ennoble one's ignorance of manner; a disappointing, if unchangeable, truth.) Louis is a good boy, though. The kind who speaks only when there's the need, to perhaps say something beautiful with his music when he's older. He can recognize music the way I have taught him: the moderato of drizzling rain, the vulgar cuss of commuter trains, the softly swelling crescendo of summer sunrises. He understands the importance of sound, the importance of preserving it, of being able to imagine and create it.

When I got into our bedroom, Nancy Lynn took me aside. She was eight years my junior, very lovely, a former model. When Louis was born she did not return to the lifestyle.

"How did we end up with another kid?" she said. "What did you do? We're not prepared for sleepovers. After the doctor, I expected to get some sleep. Then the open house was unbearable."

I engaged her in a calm discussion of the appropriateness of outward, social appearances, but she was having none of it. She became defensive, incoherent, childish. Her eyes swelled, her shallow cheeks moved in as though to kiss her nose, her small mouth melted into a glassy frown.

Nancy Lynn got this way when made to take care of things that didn't belong to her. While I was abroad playing in Glasgow—we were still then in our honeymoon years—I sent to her a six-month-old miniature poodle named Gypsy. I received a phone call the next day, which, I must embarrassingly admit, I was unable to answer and went to the machine. On playback, the message said: "Gypsy is a horrible, horrible creature! I do not at all know what to do with it. I do not at all know what to feed it. I have given her some fruit and prosciutto. You would not believe the mess she has made." In that message, a hysterical series of more or less irritating sounds, she acknowledged that this deficiency had been unwittingly bestowed upon her by her progenitors— Mr. and Mrs. Koppel, professors of English at Montpelier, who considered our marriage a fortunate melody.

I must heretofore explain that my disposition toward manner was neither bestowed on my self nor taken from any other person. This methodology—one might call it—is utterly my own, having struck its chord in me long before my father, a union man in California working as a municipal electrical specialist, had even thought about abandoning this work for public relations. His decision to leave his beloved field in favor of a desk-and-phone job was for the paycheck, which greatly alleviated my mother's expanding household of four children, myself being the third. It was about this time that my father fell into a depression, brought on by the crushing defeat of Barry Goldwater. His inventiveness with tools began to leave him and he found the bottle. In my memory, he keeps appearing beside a bedraggled lampshade, silently poring over my report card, and in the recliner as my mother paced nursing my sister Anna and reading Tolstoy's Anna Karenina, and in the garage, slouching over a workbench, clutching a screwdriver in hand like a flashlight.

Toward the end of my discussion with Nancy Lynn, I was of the cooler and more reasoned head, and she assented to letting the boy sleep over.

I explained that I'd take care of them, that she could sleep, she could dream, she did not need to worry. Once out of her clothes and into her slip-on, she asked me if there was any other person I'd rather be with, and I said, "Of course not."

"I feel like I'm too much drama, sometimes. I'm too much Angelina and not enough Brad."

"I'm your Brad," I said to her. And this seemed to make her feel better, because she then turned over with an adagioed moan, a down pillow pinched between her long tanned legs, and quickly fell asleep.

* * *

When the food arrived, I dared not wake Nancy Lynn. I took the orders and gratefully rewarded the deliverer. The three of us ate from our boxes at the dining room table, occasionally sharing spoonfuls with the other when tired of our own. As Louis and Junior talked about the coming recital, I noted that Junior was nervous about playing in front of an audience.

"That's understandable," I said. "But it doesn't excuse bad playing."

"I guess." He thought a moment. "Is there anything I can do?"

"Concentrate on the music," I said. "That's all you can do."

The boys spent the evening in Louis's room, practicing. Louis played the violin, Junior the guitar. Louis played bits of Schubert, making him resonate in the porcelain vase and the floorboards outside the room. Junior played Kurt Cobain, which I guessed had been chosen for the anniversary of his death. For a while, they tried playing this song together. Louis couldn't keep himself from getting flustered, running the hair of the bow over the bridge, stammering it on the strings. His fretting was sloppy, his tempo was rushed, and I could tell that he didn't have his fingers firmly set.

The door opened and Louis came out and closed the door.

"What are you doing out here?"

"Listening. You were playing so well."

"I was playing too fast," said Louis reproachfully. "I couldn't hear myself over the guitar."

"You're right. It was too fast."

"Why can't you be honest with me?"

"I am being honest."

"Is Mom having another kid?"

"What do you mean?"

"I'm twelve, Dad. I notice things. She's been eating weird stuff. She's been sleeping a lot. She hums nursery rhymes to herself."

I made my finger into a shhhh gesture and led him into the kitchen. He sat on the bar stool with his feet dangling from the ground and torso just barely asserting itself over the counter. Through the window came a blue light. I filled a glass of water and handed it to him. He was waiting for me to speak. I gathered my nerve and said to him honestly: "It looks to be the case."

"Why didn't you tell me?"

"We didn't know for sure. I guess I was worried."

"Brother or sister?"

"It's far too early to tell that."

He drank from the glass, avoiding eye contact as though he were ashamed.

"Why were you worried?" he said.

"Many reasons," I said, but resisted the urge to go into any detail that my son would not yet understand. If he had asked, I would have had to admit what too many children did to my father, how he each day looked more frightened until his fright instilled in him the same look at all times.

Luckily, he did not press me any further on the matter.

"What does Mom think?"

"You can ask her tomorrow. Now run along. Be a good host. Are you being polite?"

"Yes."

"That's all that matters." I smiled and kissed Louis on the head, and he rolled his eyes.

* * *

I did not sleep well. If there was something I inherited from my father, it was this trait. I lay on my back, listening to cars droning and the distant snore of aircraft. Pre-dawn birds called out their impossible-to-anticipate meter. My hand found its familiar fretwork and moved in silent accompaniment.

It was nearly five when I rose from bed and from Nancy Lynn. At Louis's room, I knocked once, then again. And at the sound of footsteps I entered, hitting the switch, catching them rubbing their eyes.

"Up, the both of you, get your shoes, and come with me."

In their pajamas, they followed me down the hall, out the door, and onto the sidewalk. We went toward the ridgeline.

"Where are we going, Mr. Valentine?" Junior said, weak and hoary.

Our shoes pattered on the slab cement.

"It's late," Louis said. "It's too late."

I corrected him: "It's an odd time, Louis. Some things you can only do at odd times. Watch your step here, there's some glass."

He went quiet. The sound of understanding. How could I explain to him that the world is but a deceptive cadence, that the last chord progression will suggest a finish, but will not, itself, conclude? To successfully do it in music? But in life, it happens without forewarning, and all the time.

Tom Junior began asking, "When? When?"

"Tom," I said to him. "Had your father taught you the perfections of silence, you would be experiencing the most monumental swelling of voices. Can you not hear the birds' foreign melody? Can you not feel the Great Eye rolling awake?"

"Don't know," Tom Junior said, "what that is. But I think I want to know."

"Do you?"

I was brimming with enthusiasm. Perhaps there was promise in Junior, despite his father's ignorance of music. I thought of my own father, and pictured his down-turned head resting on his knuckles. After a while, my father found work as a contractor in response to the country's grab for energy. In doing so he quit his employ with the state, and sought out a private corporation. Though I could hear notes of doubt in her, my mother readily supported his decision. My father planned to develop a more efficient and durable four-way traffic light, to cover the California landscape with them, but there was concern over funding and the state abandoned this route. The rights to the new devices fell to the corporation and my father went to beg for his job back.

We arrived along the ridge, looking down from the hills of southern California, the red traffic light the only thing between us and an endless fretboard of sky. There, westward, was the Santa Monica Bay, and eastward, the rising redness, which, as it grew, played each building like a string of a different tone.

"Do you know what this time is called, Tom?" I asked. He did not answer. "It is the ostinato, and it lasts until midday, where it speeds up into a brilliant crescendoing, until tomorrow, when it repeats the same pattern. Do you hear it? Well?"

"Don't know," Junior said.

"Let's go home, Dad. It's too late. We're tired."

"If your father had taught you anything about music, you would hear it," I said to Junior, or perhaps it had been directed at Louis. Then I turned to Junior directly: "You have to allow yourself to be taken by the music. Now, if I may—" I lifted Junior into the air from under his shoulders. He showed no resistance, and set himself comfortably on my shoulders. Those magnificent sounds, now, with him: those cymbals and tom drums, those tubas and bassinets. "Can you not hear it beginning?"

The sun was rising.

"Don't know," Junior said. "But the city..."

"Yes, listen!"

Louis tugged at my shirt. "Dad! Please! Let's go back!"

"Not yet! It's almost time!" I said, directing Junior toward east just as light touched the buildings. "Listen! Listen!"

WHEN CAROL LEFT ME

Linda Griffin

When Carol left me, she moved into a small apartment across town, a funny little place over a converted garage. There were a lot of stairs, and I carried her sewing machine and her stereo and one of three cardboard boxes up them. Those boxes were filled with pieces of her life, of what was no longer our life.

Carol stood with her hands on her hips, watching while I hooked up the stereo. When I looked at her she smiled faintly. I think she was a little off balance, half charmed by my helpfulness, half annoyed by what may have seemed like indifference.

I was not indifferent. I felt that I was being adult about our separation, taking it really well. I didn't understand what Carol was feeling, but I admired her independence and determination. It takes so much sheer will just to overcome the inertia of our daily routine, and here was Carol moving into an apartment she had found all on her own. She had almost no furniture, and that made the new place seem so uncluttered and clean, like the new life she was going to make here. A fresh start is always invigorating, and I felt a certain enthusiasm for hers, almost forgetting that I wasn't going to be part of it.

When I was ready to leave, Carol said, "Thanks," and gave me a quick, casual kiss on the cheek, as between friends. She pressed a key into my palm, and just for a second I thought it was the key to her new apartment. It was instead her key to our place. I started to protest, to give it back to her, to remind her that she might think of other things she wanted to salvage from the wreck of our marriage. Such as me.

But no. We could at least be civilized about it. I said good-bye and left without a backward glance. I felt fairly upbeat, energized by the clear, purposeful tenor of Carol's new beginning.

It was only later, alone in our old place, in what used to be our home, that I thought to say, "Don't leave me." It was too late, and I was faced with my own future, with all the lonely, echoing emptiness of my days. I imagined Carol busying herself with her new life, making herself at home above the garage, running up nice little curtains on her sewing machine. I got myself a beer and slumped on the couch in front of the television set. There was nothing on. It was a long night.

The next day at work, in the middle of selling a guitar to a hesitant customer, I had flashes of memory of that small apartment. The stairs rising alongside the old garage. The new rectangular tiles in the tiny kitchen. The square windows, bare but inviting with their clean glass and deep sills. The door to the bedroom I had no reason to enter. Cardboard boxes filled with trivial possessions.

At odd times during the day, those memories would replay themselves in my head. It was like a secret to be cherished—the knowledge that there was another place that was not home, but where my heart was engaged. It was the same way when we first met, when she still lived with a roommate several blocks away, and I didn't see her sometimes for days. I knew she was there, in that special, separate, unfamiliar place that I yearned toward every night in my solitary bed. Now it was solitary again, and if I couldn't sleep I would no doubt be yearning again. I had not expected that her leaving me would feel so much like our courtship.

I got through the day and I went home, and Carol wasn't there. I made myself a sandwich and I didn't miss Carol's cooking, but I missed turning to her with every stray thought that came to mind. Would she have smiled about the customer in the awful hat? Would she have commiserated with my distraction? Why was I distracted? Because Carol left me.

I could remember, much more clearly than I had for years, everything about her that first attracted me, that set her apart from all the other pretty young women in the world. How had I lost all that? How had it slipped through my fingers? Her eyes were gray, and she had a silvery, infectious laugh—I never heard her laugh anymore. When had she stopped laughing, or at least sharing it with me? Her hair was curly and fine and the color of summer wheat fields. She wore it a little longer now, but it was still as pretty as ever, and somehow I had forgotten to notice that or tell her that I noticed. How she had filled my dreams in those early days! I remembered her laughing, standing easily beside me on a bridge–where had that been?–leaning on the railing and running her fingers through her hair. She still did that, didn't she? How had such wonder become commonplace?

I was conscious all the time that, while my daily routine was unchanged, my reality had altered forever. At work I remembered how amused and mystified Carol had been by my job when we first met. The very idea that there was a store that sold nothing but guitars had seemed strange to her. She couldn't believe that I could make a living at it or that I enjoyed it. Now I supposed she took it for granted. I had taught her to play and had been proud of her efforts. How long had it been since she picked up her guitar, except to dust behind it?

On the third day, Olivia, Carol's former roommate and still one of her best friends, came into the guitar store, apparently just to confront me. "Why did you let her go?" she asked. This from a woman who had objected several times in my hearing to women saying their husbands or boyfriends "wouldn't let" them go back to school, cut their hair, or buy new slipcovers. "You don't need his permission," she would say. "How could he stop you?"

"How could I stop her?" I asked.

Olivia gave me a dirty look. "Why did she leave?" she asked. I was surprised that she didn't know, better than I could. Didn't women confide such things to their friends?

"I don't know," I said and realized for the first time that I really didn't. Did she stop loving me, or did we just stop communicating? I had known she was unhappy, but there didn't seem to be anything I could do about it. Inertia again.

"You are such a jerk," Olivia said and walked out. Was I a jerk? Did Carol think so? Did Olivia even think so, or was that just her charming way of ending a conversation she had no business beginning?

That night I sat on the couch with Carol's guitar–one of the many things she hadn't taken with her, left behind like a discarded husband. I tried to remember the first song I had played for her and the easy ones I had taught her. I remembered the way she used to hold it, how her fingers had looked as they moved across the strings. I remembered her hair falling across her face and her little frown of concentration and the smile when she got it right.

I missed Carol. I missed her footsteps, her laughter, and her subtle fragrance. After a while I even missed her bad habits. She used to leave the cap off the toothpaste in the rush of getting ready in the morning, although she always remembered to put it back at night. Half a bad habit. When we were first married, I was so crazy about her that I found it endearing.

I called Carol and told her Olivia had dropped by the store. I didn't tell her what she'd said. I casually suggested that we get together and talk about things. I could go to her place or she could come–I wanted to say "home," but settled for "here." Carol thought not. I suggested we just meet somewhere for a cup of coffee and, after a moment's hesitation, she agreed.

I was as eager and anxious as I would have been if it was our first date. I went to the florist down the block from the guitar store and hesitated over the roses. A dozen would be too obvious, a single bud too precious. I settled for four, hoping that would be lucky, like a four-leaf clover.

We met at the coffee shop where we used to have lunch together when we were both working downtown. It had booths next to the window where you could watch people go by, and we used to laugh a lot and feed each other bits of fruit or pastries. When I walked in I looked automatically at our favorite booth, but Carol had instead taken a small table near the kitchen. She was wearing a light blue sweater, and her hair was brushed and shining. She looked great, even though she was frowning and tapping her fingers on the table.

"Hi," I said breezily, wondering if I should try to kiss her.

"You're late," she said, although I wasn't, or just barely. I held out the roses, hoping for a smile or at least a softening of her stern expression. She seemed mainly puzzled by them. "Thanks," she said and laid them on the table.

The waitress came, and we ordered coffee, and she gave us a resigned look and went away again.

"What did you want to talk about?" Carol asked. I realized she was nervous, that she had probably been dreading this, thinking I was going to bully her in some way.

"Nothing in particular," I said. "I just wanted to talk to you." I started to say I missed her, but decided it would be a mistake. She was like a bird that could be easily startled into taking wing.

"Oh," was all she said. The waitress came back with the coffee and asked hopefully if we wanted anything else.

"No," said Carol, and then, obviously on impulse, she picked up the roses and handed them to the waitress. "These are for you. Put them in water, or they'll droop."

The waitress seemed puzzled too and then she looked at the roses, and her face softened as Carol's had not, and she smiled and blushed a little and said, "How sweet. Thank you."

I should have been annoyed–I had bought the roses for Carol–but I wasn't. It was somehow appropriate to the occasion and it was very much the Carol I had known and loved, full of surprises and generous impulses.

"Listen," I said into the silence that fell after the waitress left. "Would you like to go to a movie?"

"Now?" Carol asked rather blankly. She knew I had to go back to work.

"Tonight," I said. "Or tomorrow night. Whenever you like. You can choose the movie. I just want to sit in the dark and eat popcorn." And hold hands. When had we stopped holding hands in the movies? I knew which movie she would choose; she had been wanting to see the new Christian Slater film.

"I don't think so," she said. She was rejecting me and Christian Slater both, apparently without a qualm.

"Carol," I said, "Please talk to me. Tell me what you're thinking."

"I'm thinking I don't want to do this anymore," she said.

"This?" I gestured at the coffee cups.

"This," she clarified, indicating the two of us. "I'm tired. I just want to be left alone."

Which was exactly what I did not want. She had left me, and I was alone in a way I had never been before we met.

We didn't go to the movies. We didn't really talk.

A few more days passed in which I had no contact with Carol. Inertia kept me from even trying to call her. What would I say? She was tired. She wanted to be left alone. Tired, apparently, of me.

Ten days after Carol left me, a very young, newly-engaged couple came into the guitar store. He played and was fairly savvy about frets and amps and lacquer. She was a novice, overwhelmed and a bit worshipful. Their situation might have reminded me of myself and Carol, but it didn't. They were younger and more self-absorbed than we had ever been. This little girl lacked Carol's intelligence, humor, character. She was a pretty young thing, but Carol had been, still was, beautiful. It wasn't his teaching her to play the guitar, as I taught Carol, that caught my attention. They were giggling over the prospect of being able to play "their" song together.

I tried to remember if Carol and I had had a song, but nothing would come to mind. I remembered her favorite song, but not whether we had ever referred to it as "our song." In the early days, when we were so thoroughly infatuated with one another, I had gone along with everything she liked.

It was not until the young couple had proudly charged their chosen instrument on her father's credit card and gone out clinging and whispering that it occurred to me that I was still acceding to Carol's wishes, going along with the separation with hardly a murmur because it was what she wanted.

Maybe it was time for me to take a stand.

That evening, I picked up Carol's abandoned guitar and strummed it experimentally. If Carol and I didn't have a song, maybe I should write one for her. I did write songs when I was young and foolish and thought they would someday make my fortune. I had dreamed of the Rock and Roll Hall of Fame and Tony-winning musicals. And what had Carol dreamed of? I idly considered writing her a shamelessly romantic love song, but feared I wouldn't be able to play it with a straight face. I was too old for idealism and too young for nostalgia.

It was mostly curiosity that prompted me to dig out my old sheet music. I couldn't remember who I had been in those days, or what sort of junk I had been writing. I found those lost masterpieces at the bottom of an old trunk in the back of a little-used closet. Most of them were, as I had suspected, junk. What impressed me was not the few hints of talent or creativity, but that I could now see so clearly where I had been wrong and stupid and trite. With the objectivity gained by time or maturity, perhaps something could be salvaged. Dreams of glory were no longer important; the work itself intrigued me in a way I could not remember experiencing before.

I was up half the night, filing page after page with notes, trying out melodies on Carol's guitar, drinking coffee and forgetting that morning would come all too soon. When I fell into bed, too tired to sleep, I decided that I would put the pages away again at the bottom of the chest and leave them for awhile. When I looked at them again, with calmer, more objective eyes, perhaps I could judge whether they could be improved still further or should be discarded altogether.

In the morning, feeling rather hung over, I rushed around trying not to be late, and yes, I left the cap off the toothpaste. I had shoved the scattered music paper into one disheveled pile on the table and at the last minute I grabbed one sheet and took it with me, thinking that it still promised something I might tinker with during the day.

It was a terrible day, unproductive and frustrating, without a single one of the compensations that usually allowed me to enjoy my work. I was tired from lack of sleep and feeling rather foolish about my enthusiasm for what would probably turn out to be dross. To cheer myself up, I went to the coffee shop for lunch and sat in our favorite booth. I took the sheet music with me, but what I had seen in it that morning now eluded me, so I sat watching the people walk by as I ate my cheeseburger and fries. A beautiful young woman hurried by as if she was late for something. I knew objectively that she was beautiful, but I was not in any way attracted to her, just because she wasn't Carol.

And just like that everything about Carol that made her beautiful to me, every single thing I loved or admired about her, was suddenly as clear to me as the lettering on the window, and I knew exactly what it was that this single sheet of music was intended to become.

It was Carol's love song.

I was late getting back to work, and the day only got worse, but now I had something to show for it, something real. Was I kidding myself, I wondered? Was I just sleep-deprived and irrational? No matter. Sometimes you have to take a chance, as Carol had when she left me.

I didn't call her. I took the chance of finding her out or with company. For some reason I had taken it for granted that there was not another man in her life, but I could be wrong. It would be even worse if she had female friends over, especially Olivia, who would delight in my embarrassment. I went anyway.

Carol was home; there were lights behind the curtains. No unfamiliar cars were in the driveway. I stood at the bottom of the stairs and called her name like the lovesick fool that I was.

Carol opened a window and looked out. She was annoyed, and I'm sure she wondered why I hadn't just come to the door. Why was I standing in the alley like an idiot, holding a guitar?

I played the song and I sang the words I had scribbled in the coffee shop in my mediocre tenor, and other windows opened, and the neighbors gawked, and a dog barked, and Carol frowned, and I didn't care. The song was shamelessly romantic after all, but it was also pretty, like Carol, and clever, like Carol, and sweet, like Carol. I sang it twice, and the neighbors closed their windows, and I felt as if I had staked my entire life on the lamest idea I had ever had.

And then Carol laughed.

She laughed and she was leaning on the broad sill, framed by curtains she had stitched herself, and her hair was loose and shining around her pretty, pretty face, and she was laughing at me and with me, and I loved her so much I didn't care what the neighbors thought, and Carol was laughing because she loved me too.

That's how my life really began when Carol left me.

SMALL COMFORT

Aaron Beyer

Piazza Navona, Rome, August, 7:30 pm.

"Sir, may I ask you a question?"

A nervous glance but no answer. No, not nervous, fearful. He keeps walking away at a steady pace. His head turns to where the sun has hidden behind buildings, as if looking for something there.

"A hug then, no questions asked."

He lowers his head, stops, turns, and looks. Blue-grey eyes. Straight, slim nose. Brown hair. A smile that reveals pain or oldness in the eyes.

"No hug for me, thanks."

American.

"Just a question then."

He wants to leave. He waits.

It could go either way. If he is defensive and feels cornered he could tell me off. He could yell. I cast my face down and look up between brunette bangs. Innocence, I implore. "Why?"

The center-fountain trickles time. I imagine that moment caught between the fingers of God and Adam on the ceiling of the Sistine. That moment is all the world.

"I don't do hugs. Sorry." His apology has a question in it. His words wonder if they hurt. So I pout. I have good lips for a full pout.

He smiles with his teeth this time, and they are straight and big, and very white. They are not old teeth, but his eyes still tell black-and-white stories. I have him now for another moment. Who knows how long before he is gone and forgets me, and then I forget him, and then the world forgets us both.

"Never?" Extra accent.

He looks up at the sky, down and left to the fountain. It smells like beer and chlorine near the water. I wonder where he was going. He groans in what I think is supposed to be a comical way, so I smile a little and push my lips together, as if sharing a joke while waiting for a real answer.

"Not never. Just not strangers."

I see an open door, and I am a thief sometimes, like now. The pie is in the oven, and I want it, but if I try to reach it I will be burned and the pie will be ruined, and the house might burn down, and the world might end. It always might end.

He is looking me in the eyes, so I risk topics that usually hide goodbyes. "What is your name?"

He tells me in a word, and so I tell him mine in four (the last two share a hyphen and a hymen). Now my accent makes him smile again. He knows my entire name, and that is privilege and power, and I tell him so. He repeats some of my words in his head, I know, so he can think about them later.

"Nice to meet you, and now I am not some stranger," I say, cocking my head in a very small admonishment.

He shakes his head no.

Before he stops shaking his shiny hair, I put my pointer-finger on my lips for silence, and close my eyes. This will always buy some time no matter what. I speak without knowing what I am going to say.

"I am going to walk toward you, but I promise I will not hug you."

I can feel his heart tell him that this is getting more serious than expected. His heart is my friend, and will not let him leave. Another's heart is always a friend. It beats for a moment only, and knows it.

I walk forward until a pigeon could only just squeeze between us. I whisper. "Close your eyes and whisper with me." My nostrils flare when I look at him, and I blink fast twice. "Please."

My lips are as tall as his collarbone. He closes his eyes, and I imagine his world going as dark as mine does, when I close them. "Whisper." My tone hints at pleading, so he knows that whispering is a rule. Now we are both in the kitchen, figuring out how the oven works.

"What are your parents like?" I want to picture old people with pitchforks.

"Nice. They're good people. My dad is a mechanic - builds cool old cars - and my mom does book-keeping. We grew up in Ohio, in a small town, and everybody likes them."

"What do you call them?"

He laughs out of his nose once. Surprise. "Dad. Ma."

"Are they married?"

"No, not for years. They got a divorce when I was young." Dangerous territory. I open my eyes, to see him doing the same.

"Don't peek!"

"Sorry!"

Closed eyes again and smells of touristy restaurant bread, wine, slight sewer.

"My parents are old and funny. My mom makes the kind of food that makes it hard to leave home. My dad owns olive presses, and I think he is made out of olives. He tells the same jokes and stories now as he always did, but we drink good wine at home so they are still funny. Our house is old and has cracks, and I know every crack in the house, between my parents, my brothers, and on their faces, their hearts."

He breathes, and I think he smells my hair. I use shampoo with apricot and honey in it, and the sun baked my black hair earlier today.

"Are you Italian?"

"Does it matter?"

"No, I guess not," he laughs and I know he is peeking again, but I don't. I know he will come back, and he does, closing his eyes again, leaning his head down.

"Did your parents hug you?"

"A lot. Every day."

"Do your friends hug you?"

"No. Well. Girls do, sometimes, but I try to avoid it, and guys have a half-hug they do."

"Why?"

"Which one?"

"Both."

"Women can hug because it's more accepted. I mean women can hold hands and walk down a street. Guys don't get that kind of leeway. We always have to show how manly we are."

"No you don't."

"You wouldn't know."

"I think hugs are good no matter what. It shows how open you are."

"I think it's too intimate. Hugging is beyond kissing to me. It's touching someone with your whole body. "

"Even if you are hugging family?"

"No, no. That's more like accepting them. Showing togetherness."

"What if you hugged everyone like family then, to show togetherness. It wouldn't be intimate then."

"But not everyone is family."

"No?"

"No."

I sigh. I know what it will take. I have to.

"Then I will show you something different. Are you married?"

"No."

"Girlfriend back home?"

"Does it matter?"

I open my eyes and squint at him. I look to the buildings where the sun is hiding. I look to the fountain of time. I look to the sky. His eyes stayed closed.

"Marry me," I say.

"Right now?"

"Yes."

I want him to hold me close, as a stranger, as a friend, as a lover, as family, as all of that in one. To know that it is possible. I tell him so. We both open our eyes and look far inside the other, past bones and memories. The fingers between Adam and God tremble, move closer, but not so anyone else can see.

He grabs me around my waist, and hugs me tight against his chest. His breathing is big and steady. He picks me up, gently, and sets me down beside the fountain. He sits down on the side of the fountain, and we are the same height. He draws me close and holds me there. The sun finds other lands beyond Italy. The glowing night buzzes above and around us. It is the longest embrace of my life. It has to be that for him too. It stays an embrace, for hours. No kissing, no questing hands, just a hug.

Then there are sounds of tables being broken down and chairs stacked, and doors being closed. Everything gets quieter. Still we remain enfolded, as a single knot of perfect temperature and poise.

The night grows old, and dew licks at stones and trees. The glow of the sun returning for another day makes everything purple and luminous. Streetlights add orange until they flick off. I fall asleep. When I wake he is gone and I lay beside the fountain.

Mother, Father, I married again, and though it could not last, it was perfect.

THE ORAL TRADITIONS OF ELEPHANTS

Seth Marlin

They came in the night, bearing arms and floodlights, working in tandem to frighten the clan with numbers and sound. A young mother – she was Swayer Of Lions – had just returned from the riverbank, and found herself separated from her calf and family. She was no match against the weapons of the poachers. Her song is silenced now. She lies upon the hard-baked dirt of the Veldt.

When a song is ended, the other clans for miles around always know. Perhaps it ends in the way of the elderly: a disharmony that twists and weakens for a season before finally guttering out. More often these days, it is more abrupt – a crescendo, a panicked cry for help amidst the final killing-strokes – and thus it was for Swayer of Lions. The hunters shouted and flashed their lights, fired their weapons into the air and there were none amongst the clan who dared intervene. Legend says the Two-Legs are collectors from the Other World, that place where all elephants go when they have quit of this one. To challenge the Two-Legs is to risk collection oneself.

Now Swayer Of Lions shares the fate of so many: to lie and wither beneath an uncaring sun, skin shrinking against bones as the flies lay eggs in her meat. At night the jackals will howl her lullabies; their eyes will shine in the dark as they tug at what parts the bigger scavengers deemed unfit. They'll bound off yipping with these spoils, snarling and fighting over her scraps. And when the day breaks and the vultures circle in to perch, they'll fan their wings and give shade to what little of her remains.

These things will come, as they come all who die on the Veldt. But not tonight. Tonight the clan is with her, singing songs to bid her sleep, and so they stand, shielding her memory from the sad truths of mortal flesh.

* * *

On an early dawn two days into the funeral vigil, one of the survivors leads her dead sister's calf down to the river. She is Brings None Forward. It is the dry season, and the river is a goodly walk, but a trip past due for both of them. There's been little rest, and with all the flies these last few days she feels tired, sore, unclean. A bath will be good, she thinks – cool and refreshing, good for the spirit. The noise from their kin filters down over the ridgeline as they bathe. The marsh birds upriver barely notice, but Brings None Forward surely does. She feels it in the water submerging her shoulders, feels the movements of her clanmates in the mud beneath her feet. She hears that infrasonic moan, rumbling in her bones, rumbling into the earth itself without end – the voice of her mother.

They finish their bathing and she spurs the calf up the bank. They take their time, allowing the calf to nose about and tug up tufts of grass with her trunk, which she deposits into her mouth, chewing slowly. This act of feeding is still a new thing; had all this happened before the weaning-time she might be dead now. Still, she's healthy, going on four years old, and the reality of her situation has yet to sink in. The rumbling grows as they return to the gathering. They find the others assembled much as they left them, all bunched in a semicircle, flanks pressed against flanks. The air smells of decay and sorrow, and at their center lies Swayer of Lions, crumpled motionless upon the ground, while standing over her is their mother and clan Matriarch – she is Walks Upon Stones. Her daughter does not move, and what used to be the younger cow's face is now missing.

The rumble is Walks Upon Stones' bereavement cry, a wail of mourning deaf on most ears but loud enough to frighten the hyenas some ten miles distant. She trails her trunk across skin grown dry and stiff in the night, caresses a brow now cloven by the saw. Her daughter's tusks are removed and her trunk lies discarded to one side of her body. The old mother pours her cries into the earth, beyond hope, beyond all reasoning, while behind her the others flinch and draw back. She is their leader, their anchor, and seeing her behave this way frightens them. She has wailed unabated for two days now, more than any mother should or has any right to, and though she moans and nudges her daughter's carcass with a foot the flesh doesn't give, nor show any sign of stirring.

She was their mother's favorite, a healthy breeder and the desire of all the bulls. Brings None Forward has had no bull. Nearly ten seasons now since her first stuttering estrous, her first and only, and since that time her womb has been silent. No male has sought her out in the *musth*.

The lamentations continue. Brings None Forward feels her niece huddled against her leg, and this is hard, she realizes. The calf has never known a death, much less of a parent, much less so young. It is just as hard for Brings None Forward. It was she their mother first chose as nurse, she who taught her sister to paw and stamp at the crocs down in the shallows. Now her sister is gone, and their mother can see nothing else.

In the distance beyond the tablelands, heavy clouds rise and thicken. She makes to approach, but hears footsteps behind her, stops, tastes the air. She glances back with an eye to find a single clanmate standing back of the crowd, an aunt, Slow Like The Rock. The older cow snorts, wards her off, but with dark eyes that also blink with deep understanding. Cracked gray lids and wispy lashes enshroud the long wisdom of age; their message is clear. *Leave her be.*

* * *

There is an idea in elephant culture. In the mind of Walks Upon Stones it has no name, no word, only a sound – a *resonance*. It is a single clear note deeper than stone, deeper than blood or bone; it says that *every mother is every daughter is every sister*, with voices that drone as one all the way back to First Elephant, and even unto whatever it was that came before Her.

Most would understand it thus: *We sing together.*

There are songs among the Matriarchs – such few as are left – that sing of evening and fresh grass and the light acrid tang of acacia. They sing of high rivers, of dust and manure and the heavy sweet musk of courting bulls. There are no stillborn calves in these songs, no hunger-pangs or water-ache, nor any hunters with weapons to steal the souls of young mothers then deface their bodies when they have gone. Once these songs could be trusted; now they're just fragments, bits of verse whose choruses are long since forgotten. The younger cows don't know them, but the elders still do. They know and guard them, as they guard the memories of their own dead mothers. The Matriarchs would expect no less. It is their Way.

How long does one lament the history of a people? Is any time enough? These songs were comfort for the aged, instruction for the young on what it meant to *be* elephant. Now they're fading. When Walks Upon Stones was born, before any even knew her by that name, she emerged as all calves do blind and slick and unable to stand. The earth she knelt on cut like shards, and the air was cold and foreign, filled with frightening smells. As to rabbits on some distant shore, the world was a white blindness, pouring all the pain of life into her eyes. Her heart raced and she shook her head, tried to bellow but only a halfhearted squeal came forth.

These were her first moments: light and cold and fear. But then there came the shadow, the footsteps on gravel, the trunk brushing its tip across her back. It was joined by another, and then another, and still another until soon there were a dozen trunks caressing her, laying hands as their shadows blocked the sun and a rumbling shook the very earth itself. She'd first heard this song inside the womb, joined to the firm deep *thump* of her mother's heartbeat; now she knew it as the voice of her clan, the voice of safety and comfort, singing for joy, singing for thanks and praise to bid her, their newest member:

Welcome.

Once, she sang this song for her own newborn daughters. Now there is no singing. There will be no singing again.

* * *

The morning draws full, a long night warded off by the harsh vigilance of the aggrieved. The sun rises and in the east the clouds move on, taking with them promises of rain, promises meant for places that *are not here*. The clan has lingered for a day and a night now, but as the new dawn swells they grow restless. Now is the time when all elephants look to their Matriarch, look for solace in the wisdom of the ancient rituals. It is *the burying time*. Still, though some huddle and wait, Walks Upon Stones refuses to move from the body. For an hour after sunrise they linger, but not knowing what to do, a few soon drift toward the river, or to the stands of trees to their west. Slow Like The Rock takes watch of the calf, and free to wander Brings None Forward paces the ridge overlooking the riverbank. Back at her sister's body, their mother remains disconsolate.

The day comes into bloom. The grasses are still pregnant with dew; a few scrub trees perk up with competing trills of birdsong. A million creatures, tiny lives each smaller than a toenail, emerge from the brush and set the ground-cover alive with their skittering. A breeze drifts in and what little moisture it carries speaks to that most outlandish of elephant legends: that somewhere beyond the horizon lies *the place that is only water*, with more lives beneath its surface than there are even stars in the sky. Brings None Forward thinks upon these tales, wonders if such souls know what it is love, to lose.

The sun casts blue shadows across the Veldt, reduces the mountains to orange and crimson silhouettes. Members of the clan lumber up the riverbank with shining wet hides; others graze from low standing branches with their trunks. Every so often one or two wander back to the carcass, carrying bundles of foliage, clumps of dirt, bits of grass with which to cover their fallen clanmate. They hold these burdens and watch their leader at a distance, but after several moments spent shuffling from foot to foot, they each eventually lose hope and trundle off. Something in the Matriarch's scent, one thinks, a foreboding that speaks not merely of grief but of something darker. Time has passed and they should bury the body, but as long as the old Matriarch stands fast there will be none who dare attempt it. Walks Upon Stones is loved and respected, but also feared.

For a long time Brings None Forward watches. Her mother's wailing has finally given out; now it persists as a protracted sigh, a song of too many days and too many deaths and too many afternoons praying for rain. She longs to approach, longs to meet her mother's gaze in a way that will say *I am still here*, but when she tries her mother's song changes – a shift, a note that insists in its elephant way that *You can not understand*. She sings this without turning to look, and the presumption makes it all the more painful. Brings None Forward moves no closer, her music not of the dead nor of the bereaved, but of the neglected living.

* * *

Morning gives way to afternoon. The day grows high and the heat sets in, bringing all the Veldt to a slow relentless bake. In the grasses the choirs of locusts fill the air with chanted prayer in their millions.

Walks Upon Stones mourns. The rest of the clan stays at a distance, or retreats to the shade of nearby treestands. The dry season is setting in, and the clan should move on to other feeding grounds, but there can be no moving on without a proper burial. In the rainy season these wakes might last for days, but in the heat of the lean months such dallying is suicide. The flies and the smell will bring scavengers, and with them larger predators. The Two-Legs have been here; they will be here again. There is a calf to think about.

Brings None Forward wanders, paces the circle which none dare enter. Here and there are yet more piles of debris, burial-offerings all denied and dropped. Her mother does not notice, indeed does not notice anything. She refuses to acknowledge the death, as though such things have never happened before or will not happen again. There is a new rumbling within the clan, quiet and insistent. Some have come to doubt the old mother's judgment.

Brings None Forward grows weary of the heat, weary of the smell. Confused, hurt, irritable. She is torn between the bonds of clan and clan-mother, a pain which every grown daughter must one day face but which still the knowing cannot assuage. She wanders the edge of where they camp, meets the sun where it begins to sink. A breeze kicks up hot and stale, bringing with it a faint smell of her sister.

For a long time she stands without moving, stares at the western horizon toward the mountains and the sweet-smelling earth that carpets those slopes. Such soils would nurse good grazing, she thinks, but the walk is far and the slopes are high. Out of their territory. Out of reach.

She rouses to loafing footsteps behind her, and a great thunder of flapping ears. She glances back to find Slow Like The Rock come to join her. Her aunt nods and snorts, drawing up beside and staring out at the same vast horizon, and this pleases her. More than the others, this eldest of her aunts – childless, unconcerned with Matriarchy – always seems to know.

They face the sun and their grief, and look out upon the great endless sweep of the Veldt. A breeze kicks up, and with it again the smell of kin. The old cow clears her throat, smelling of resignation, and Brings None Forward understands her to mean that *This is the way of things*. The sun glimmers on the grass and stones and loose bare clumps of earth; on the ground at her feet Brings None Forward notices a pile of dung, two days old, baked by the sun but still smelling unmistakably of her sister. She moves to examine it, tests its firmness with her trunk. She breaks off a portion – still moist inside – and places this slowly into her mouth. She chews. Her sister's last grazings had been dropgrass and commiphora, standard dry-season fare, but the elephant that ate it was happy, a young mother with a healthy calf, in good spirits and part of a clan that loved her. Her aunt sighs, long and deep like the wind, and Bring None Forward reflects on what has just been said. She feels better.

* * *

Where are the songs for these times, the songs of mourning? Walks Upon Stones knows they exist. They are old songs, full of heartbreak and death and grass so dry it crumbles to dust, and once there must have been many such songs but by the time she was born they had been forgotten and so her people became complacent. They remember only the good songs, the songs of fat years, and even those bits too are broken and dying with them.

Theirs has been a proud nation, a prodigal nation, who have forgotten the old ways and so invited ruin. Why else would the world visit such cruelties? Why else would the Other World claim one calf of every two born, then come for the mothers that bear the strongest young? It is a sign. This blight will see them cast from the earth, into a day when there are no daughters left to roam the land. It is her punishment, the punishment of all the Matriarchs. To outlive one's healthy daughters, and then see the ones who live struck barren? The Veldt is inscrutable. The Veldt transcends questioning.

The sun sets. This heap of bones grows withered. There is no more life here, so why does she persist? No matter where she leads, they will find only starvation, predation, disease. But what is left to go back to? There can be no going back. Her body aches; her sisters speak of leaving. So it shall be. In the dawn they will come to bury her daughter, and she will be gone. She will go into the desert, follow the sun until she arrives among the bones of her mothers. She will go, and thirst until she thirsts no more. She will lay herself down for the vultures and the maggots. She will offer herself up to the Other World.

* * *

It is evening when the Two-Legs return. The clan hears them, smells them long before actually seeing them. It is the odor of their fourbeasts, a burning miasma that waters the eyes; it is the growls the fourbeasts make, a song that is not-song, their eerie glide a *not-walking* on *not-legs*. They are so like the People of the Tusk, and yet also like their neighbors the rhinoceros, the People of the Horn. But what they are is hideous. Wrong. A fell sign of the Two-Legs' coming.

There is only one this time, the same dead dun-color as the high grasses of summer. It glides to a stop on a hill just south of where they camp, and from its plated folds emerge a group of Two-Legs – some pink, some as dark as the river bottom itself. The clan rises, and there comes a chorus of shuffling and low groans as the clan seeks to secure the calf. The calf rushes to the side of one of the aunts, brushing against the old cow's leg and squealing. Her steps are awkward and shuffling in that way so typical of the young, and once again Brings None Forward feels that mothering-drive, that need to aid the small and helpless among them. Such need is pointless – she is barren. Cursed. Even her own mother will not see her. A flush then in her ears and behind her eyes; instead of joining the others she stands her ground.

For a time there is only silence. The clan stands mute. They cluster not far from the carcass, and though one lone aunt attempts to rouse the Matriarch, she does not budge. Something is wrong, her daughter realizes – a sense of defeat, a collapsed will she associates only with the dying. She turns to the Two-Legs now and tastes the air – these ones smell not of the killing-urge, but rather of a dull animal curiosity. They point and chatter, and she understands then that they are being watched.

The clan paces, marching a broad circle around where their leader still stands grieving. Brings None Forward watches the Two-Legs, notes their eerie behavior. It isn't natural to be observed so closely by predators; even the lions ignore unattended calves when not hunting. It is a necessity of daily life, the shared etiquette of the watering hole. But these Two-Legs don't observe such etiquette. Instead they stand and stare, crane their necks and foul the evening air with their meaningless gibber. They violate the rituals they themselves made necessary, and yet still they watch.

Brings None Forward blinks to clear her vision; behind her the footsteps of the clan slow and stop. The rumbling returns, but it is not in the voice she expected. It is her own. These Two-Legs are all that she sees. Not her mother, not her dead sister, not her ragged clan of elderly cows and their one sad calf; only the Two-Legs with their bloodlust and their fourbeasts and their beady staring eyes. They kill, they butcher, and then they come back in to watch, like the vultures but lower, for even those disease-ridden pests have the meager sense to wait until the grieving time is done. The rumble from her throat grows louder, and though a flock of marsh birds fly up panicking the Two-Legs stare as if she had said nothing at all.

The legends have all been wrong, she thinks. The Two-Legs are not of the Other World. They are not gods, not even People. The rumble builds in her throat so that even her kin in the mountains give pause at this rage, and when still the Two-Legs do not move she nods and flaps, raising her tusks in the way she has seen the bulls often do. She fills her lungs and shifts her voice into a register she knows they will understand.

She trumpets and charges.

Chaos. Behind her voices shouting, calling her off, urging her away from this course toward reason and calm. She does not heed them. Instead she lowers her head and musters her great bulk forward, loping at speed toward the fourbeast and its riders. The Two-Legs scramble, duck into safety like baby crocodiles into the mouth of their mother. A growl sounds, and then the fourbeast is turning, fleeing whilst on its back a pair of Two-Legs shout and raise their weapons, firing into the air. She keeps charging, resolves that if she can just get close enough she might flip the beast, gore it, stomp it flat until the growls cease and the Two-Legs lay pulverized in the grass. She trumpets, but the fourbeast is too fast and soon it's pulling away. It disappears in a cloud of dust, and when she at last grows tired of chasing it she draws to a stop, panting. The fourbeast races off, and watching it flee she draws a deep breath and trumpets. Then she trumpets again.

The clan is silent as she returns down the hill. She does not approach them but instead goes straight to the river, splashing to her shoulders, groaning, pulling deep with her trunk and spraying herself. This water is good, she thinks, cool and refreshing, better in fact than it has ever felt. More than at any time in the last two days, Brings None Forward feels exhausted, cleansed, relieved.

They stare as she climbs up the bank, dripping. Slow Like The Rock and the calf are among them. Brings None Forward brushes past the others and approaches her mother; she looks on the remains, clotting with flies, and then butts heads with the older cow. She snorts and uses her trunk to touch first her mother's tusks, then her cheek, then her forehead just aft of the snout. Her mother blinks and a dozen mysteries swirl behind her eyes. She nods and in a move that surprises everyone she returns the motion, reaches out and entwines her own trunk with that of her daughter. In keeping with the formal gesture, the heat of their shared breaths flows between them.

* * *

The clan sets out the following morning. Behind them lies Swayer of Lions, buried beneath a coat of dirt, grass and torn-down branches. The branches are as much a symbol as a cover – their leaves the choicest, the most succulent, an offering to sustain the soul on its way to the Other World. Now they move, the calf in tow, and at the front of the clan beside her mother walks Brings None Forward. Her skin is coated by dust in the style of a new Matriarch, and though Walks Upon Stones still leads, the future will lie not with her, nor with her sisters, but with this new generation. There will be new songs now. New traditions. New teachings by which to instruct the growing calves. The way forward at last lies open.

They walk across the Veldt, past the mountains, past the blinding snowcaps and lush green hills of their forest relatives. They head to where the rain clouds gather, seeking green shoots and fat moist leaves. The clan is alive with rumor and jokes and isolated bursts of song. Though the clan has suffered, and will yet suffer again, they are for the moment happy.

In the afternoon they stop to find the earth filled by a great new rumbling. In the foothills east of them a related clan has given birth to a new calf, singing praise so that all for miles around might hear. Brings None Forward listens, smells the air, and then finally joins her voice in song to theirs. Her mother follows suit. The other members of the herd join in one by one, and so in unison they send their voices deep into the earth.

They sing together.

THE FIRST KEY

T.D. Johnston

They say there's a good way and a bad way to learn a lesson. I guess I learned mine the good way, but I was lucky. Damn lucky, you ask me. So pay attention.

I was only three days on the job, see, and already I was late for an appointment. Hell, I was young in those days, but like I told you already, that's no excuse. The alarm buzzed at six, but I smacked the snooze button nine times after. *Nine times*, like I had all day. My dad would've called me a lazy nimrod. That's what he always called me when I slept in on Saturdays. Anyways, by the time I got out of bed it was seven-thirty, and I was supposed to be at this municipal government office by eight. God knows I still hate even thinking about it. I raced through the shower, all kinds of mess going through my mind. Second chances, wasted opportunities, shirked responsibilities. Unemployment. Death, of course. But that goes without saying.

My shaving hand was shaking, out of control. I could practically see the boss in the mirror. Mr. Bucci had spent a whole entire day training me on the "Five Keys to the Door of Success." The first key, he said, and the most important key, was Punctuality. "Sal," he said, "how can a man finish first if he always shows up last?" Then he looked at me for about ten seconds. I could see it meant a lot to him, being on time and all, so I wrote it down in my new daytimer. But I have to admit, I was young, like you, and I wrote it down mainly so he'd think I was paying real close attention.

Punctuality. I was at Clausen for what, six years? Six years, and nobody ever said anything about Punctuality being the first key to some Door of Success. They didn't teach us squat about business ethics, you see. Too busy telling us what to do.

But you should've seen me shaving. Miracle I didn't cut myself to hell. So anyways, here I was about to disappoint my new boss on my very first appointment. Mr. Bucci had even gone to the trouble of setting up the appointment, and was going as far as making the introductions for me. But he was real clear with his last words, the night before on the phone. "Eight sharp. Remember the First Key."

Christ, I could throw up even now, just thinking about it.

So there I was, pulling into the office parking lot at eight-fifteen in my old broken-down seventy-five Volvo, the one my big brother the banker had until the heart attack. I could feel my heartbeat thumping everywhere. I mean *everywhere*. Temples, ears, cheeks, especially my gut. It was a good thing my stomach was empty, or I'd have launched for sure.

What the hell are you looking at? There's nothing out there but concrete, boy. I told you to pay attention.

So I'm walking across the parking lot, thinking to myself, "What if this guy's a hardliner, a stickler for punctuality, this guy from Municipal Projects?" It was messing with my coordination, thinking about being dumped by Mr. Bucci on my third day, and I almost tripped when I missed the rhythm of that big revolving door going into the office building.

You follow what I'm saying, don't you? This guy from Municipal Projects? If his Five Keys are the same as Mr. Bucci's, I'm a dead man.

When you were a kid, and the teacher made you get up and make a presentation or a speech to the whole class, do you remember how hard it was to breathe? You figure everybody can see your paper shaking, watch your heartbeat on your face? Well, that's what I was like when I reached the elevator. For good measure, it was the kind of elevator I've always hated -- the glass kind, with the curved glass walls so everybody yakking in the lobby can watch you on your way to screwing up your future. Or coming back down without one.

I pressed the 'Up' arrow. Big, round button, and I almost missed it, my finger's shaking so bad. *Look* at me when I'm talking to you. I'm explaining what you're doing here. God *damn*.

So then I'm thinking, I'm thinking, I'm thinking, what are the other Keys to the Door of Success? The Man had just taught them to me, for Christ sake. Even gave me a memo sheet with bullet points. The works. And I remember one of them, like God put it there for me to remember.

Hope.

Maybe he's still there, this guy from Municipal Projects. Maybe. Oh, God, please let there be a maybe.

Yeah, I thought. And "maybe" he'll say, "Okay, Bucci, I gave you your chance to make a competitive bid. Didn't have all day to wait on you and your boy."

I kind of mumbled that last part out loud, so I was real embarrassed when I discovered that I wasn't alone waiting for the elevator. This older fellow, about sixty or so, dressed like a college professor, old-fashioned bifocals, tweed jacket, is standing there right next to me, reading the sports section. I can still see the damn thing, folded in half, a USA Today sports page. Funny how things stick in your mind. I remember thinking how wonderful it would be if I were actually five minutes *early* and had the luxury of studying last night's Cubs boxscore on a leisurely ride up the elevator.

I wanted to trade places with this old man real bad. *Real* bad. He looked so damn comfortable, like he'd just finished his eggs and coffee and was going back to his office to stretch out nice and easy before the masseuse arrived.

Then the elevator bell tinkled -- dinged -- whatever you call it, and the glass door was in front of us. This fat middle-aged lady in a mink coat and hat comes out, no doubt on her way to a pleasant day uncomplicated by the Five Keys to the Door of Success. This old tweed guy says "After you," really pleasant. He kind of waves me in with the sports section. So I enter and press the fourteenth floor. The old man comes in and says, "Fourteen, if you don't mind."

At first I don't realize that the man is speaking to me. The door swishes shut, and I turn around and see that we're the only two people in the elevator.

"Pardon?" I whisper. I'd meant to use my vocal chords, but they failed me. I was that scared about the First Key, you see.

The guy looks up casually from his paper. "If you could hit fourteen I would --- oh, it's already lit up. Sorry."

I cleared my throat. "That's okay," I said. It felt good to speak, sort of like talking to a priest before your execution. It may not change anything, but it feels better than the facts. I decided to relieve some of my anxiety by speaking again.

"You work in this building here, sir?" I was such a moron. What difference did it make? Still, I breathed more easily.

"Just until tomorrow, yes. I'm retiring, and I'm delighted to say it."

"I see." *Go ahead,* I think to myself. *Blow some steam.*

"Retiring from what, if you don't mind my inquiring?" I said "inquiring" because it was polite vocabulary. Mr. Bucci had made a special point of teaching me that the right vocabulary assists the good businessman in getting the customer's guard down. It isn't one of the Five Keys, but it certainly helps turn the knob.

The old guy looks at me and smiles. "I work in Municipal Projects. Fancy name for 'Stuff the City Does to Waste Tax Dollars'." He chuckles sort of self-deprecatingly.

Well, I've got to tell you. What a small world, I thought. You see, Mr. Bucci and I were going to the same department. Municipal Projects. Nineteen floors in this building, and this fellow and I are headed for the same place. What were the odds? So I say--

Okay. Nineteen to one, I guess. Wise guy. Or maybe eighteen-to-one if they got no thirteenth floor, and I really don't remember and we're getting off track. So shut up and let me finish. The point is we're going to the same department.

"No kidding!" I say. "That's where *I'm* headed!"

The fellow smiles again, but like he's tired or something. But he's nice. Very nice. Says, "Isn't that something. Small building, eh? Who are you going to see?"

"The head of purchasing and estimating. Guy named Telder."

The fellow frowns for a second, then goes back to smiling.

"You must work for Paul Bucci. I'm, I'm Frank Telder. I must confess I'm relieved that we're both late. Was having breakfast across the street and lost all track of the time." He shakes his head like he thinks he's an idiot or something. "Sometimes I get going on the sports page and - poof! - there goes the time and I'm late."

Now, this guy looks like he hasn't made a mistake since he was in grammar school, yet here he's done the same stupid thing I have. We're both late, though Mr. Bucci's only going to be miffed at me, as you of all people can imagine. So, I smile back at him and say, "I'm as relieved as you are, Mr. Telder. I just started working for Mr. Bucci, and I overslept. On the third day of a new job. Can you beat that for being a schmuck?"

The old man just laughs and adjusts the lapels of his tweed jacket, and the elevator stops and dings. I shouldn't be feeling better, just from a thirty-second conversation, but I am.

"Here's fourteen," the guy says, and he waves me through the door. I stop and stand on the gray carpet in the hallway, looking in both directions for Mr. Bucci.

The old guy walks on down the hallway on the left, and-- *Listen*, if there's something interesting out there, I wish you'd share it with me...

I didn't think so.

So the guy from Municipal Projects walks on down the hallway on the left. He turns and says, "Are you coming?" He holds out the newspaper like he wants to wave me ahead. I think to myself, "He doesn't seem very worried." I figured that was because he was on his own turf and all.

"Actually, I'm supposed to meet my boss here in the hall," I say, and it's true, and I'm shitting bricks, because I know how miffed the Man is by now. Probably he'd been standing there outside the elevator, looking like a jerk, for fifteen minutes waiting for my sorry rear end. Went looking for me, most likely, or was calling my apartment.

The man from Municipal Projects jingled some keys in his right pocket.

"Well, do me a favor before you come in, okay?" he says.

"Sure," I say, though naturally I don't really mean it at this point.

"Tell Paul that I really don't want to hear any new numbers today. The bids are sealed, and I'd like just once to do this right. Retire with my head held high. He should be able to understand that. Don't you think?"

I think to myself, "Whatever." But I remember what Mr. Bucci said in that first training session. Never let a customer know what you're *really* thinking. Unless you're discontinuing the business relationship, that is, and that should *only* be when the relationship is no longer profitable. The true one-minute manager knows how to stroke. The hell with sincerity. The Man always said there's only one synonym for ethics: The Bottom Line. That's the only ethic in business, and the only reason for learning the Five Keys.

So I say, "My pleasure." And I smile real big so he knows I mean it.

He raises his sports page to me and says, "Thank you," and continues on his way.

I take the smile off, and my heart starts pounding, because I'm so late and Mr. Bucci has left. At least that's what I thought. But then the elevator dings behind me, and I turn around in time to see the door slide open. And there he is.

And he's miffed. Christ, he's ticked. Asks me a rhetorical question about why the hell I think he took the time to teach me the Five Keys to the Door of Success. He doesn't let me answer, just waves his hand like I'm a nuisance, and I guess I was, violating the First Key and all.

But like I said, I was lucky. Luckier than you, anyway. We walk on down to Municipal Projects, and Mr. Bucci tells the secretary we're here to see Mr. Telder. Telder comes out of his office and says, "Come in, gentlemen," and tells his secretary to take a coffee break. We follow Telder into his office, Mr. Bucci first, then me. Telder closes the door, and the whole atmosphere changes.

"Listen, Paul," Telder says, standing in the middle of the room. I guess not offering us a seat was his way of saying it would be a short meeting. "I'm not buying today. I thought that was clear on the phone. I want to retire on a clear conscience."

Mr. Bucci just folds his arms, cool as an October breeze. Doesn't say a word. Sure enough, the customer fills the silence, just like always.

"What I mean is, Paul, I can't give you the contract on my last day." And Telder folds his arms too. Battle of the folding arms. Two old veterans.

Well, I knew it was over when Mr. Bucci smiled and stuck out his hand. Telder shook it, and seemed truly relieved that there would be no argument or haggling on his last day. And I was relieved as well, because it meant I'd finally get to do my job, and because it meant my being late hadn't cost Mr. Bucci this opportunity to discontinue a business relationship.

Mr. Bucci says, "Frank, I don't know about your conscience, but I would indeed feel terrible if this wasn't your last day." And he looks at me. And that's it.

I pull out my .44 and whip Telder backhand across the face. I guess his face is old, because his left cheek flaps apart like a peeled banana. He flops down on the floor, tries to fold up like a ball. But Mr. Bucci had said before that the guy from Municipal Projects needed a lesson in business ethics, and he wanted the lesson taken like a man.

So while I pull Telder up, him bleeding and spitting and wheezing, Mr. Bucci gives him the lesson. I still remember every word, all these years later. He started right after I brought a knee to Municipal's middle.

"You see, Frank, a business relationship is based upon features and benefits," the boss says, and begins to pace like a professor in front of a class. "The feature is just a description. The benefit is the *explanation* of what's *good* about the feature. A feature without a benefit is like food taken intravenously. You don't know it's good until you *taste* it." He pauses as I break Municipal's teeth with my elbow. I probably shouldn't have done the teeth like that, because the old man's gurgling forces Mr. Bucci to speak louder. But Mr. Bucci adapts and continues the lesson.

"In our bid, the feature was filled potholes. The benefit was five grand in your pocket. But Frank, on this day you ignored the Fifth Key to the Door of Success. Consistency. How many deals have we made over the years? And now, you choose to become inconsistent, violate the Fifth Key. That's bad ethics, Frank. Inconsistency is hell on a bottom line, my friend."

I think Mr. Bucci allowed himself a sigh when Telder spit out some teeth and tried to mumble something about the Right Thing.

"Frank, Frank, Frank....." the boss says, shaking his head and standing over the defeated bureaucrat. "Let's look at the Five Keys, shall we? And then you tell me about ethics. First, we have Punctuality, my friend. Did I violate this ethic, this key to good business, this first factor in making the sale? No. You did. Today and many other days. So did my new subordinate, who will be lucky if the bottom line allows him no, ah, reprimand." Of course, I look away when the boss says this, but I think he was looking a hole right through me. As a matter of fact, I think he was really talking to *me* the whole time. It was *my* business ethics he was talking about. Telder was just a prop for the lesson.

"Second, Frank, we have Anticipation. The good salesman *anticipates* the customer's objections. I anticipated yours today. Did you anticipate mine? I think not. Again, on your last day, you flatulate in the direction of the Five Keys." The boss reaches down and pulls Municipal's head up by the hair.

"The Third Key, Frank, is Perseverence. When you said yesterday on the phone that you were retiring and hence would award this contract to another of the sealed bids, did I accept your lame excuse and go meekly on my way? No. I insisted upon this appointment, until you agreed to host Sal and me so graciously and, I must say now, quietly. The man who observes and respects the Five Keys is standing, while he who spits on them now spits teeth."

The boss drops the head like a bowling ball.

"The Fourth Key, Frank, is Thoroughness. The old follow-through. We could leave you here to think about the Five Keys, but that would not be thorough. Once a man has lost his ethics, he is not to be trusted. Sal, please be thorough."

I step forward and put two bullets in Municipal's brain. Mr. Bucci leads me out to the secretary's office, and we sit while he talks about the close relationship between the fourth and fifth keys, Thoroughness and Consistency. After ten minutes, he suggests that perhaps there should be six keys to the Door of Success. I ask him what that should be, and he looks at his watch, smiles, and says "Patience."

The door from the hall opens and in comes Municipal's secretary. She's got a green coffee mug in her hand. I can still see the thing.

The boss says to her, very politely, "Excuse me, but do you know who I am?"

She studies him for a second, then looks at me.

"Why, yes, Mr. Bucci. But I don't know your friend."

The boss stands. "Did old Frank let you know I was coming this morning, by chance?"

"Oh, no, Mr. Bucci. He prefers that your meetings are kept confidential."

"How anticipative of him. Sal, please make sure today's meeting is kept, ah, confidential."

So I get up and remember the fourth key. Two in the brain.

Thoroughness, my friend. One of the Five Keys, never to forget.

I asked Mr. Bucci if it was okay if I grabbed the sports page from Telder's office, and then I went in, found it folded on the desk with a smidgeon of blood on it, wiped it against Municipal's pants, and we left. All the way down in the elevator, I could see Mr. Bucci was still miffed, but it was okay. The Bottom Line, my friend. The ultimate ethic.

I got to tell you, though. It feels *good* when you think you've screwed up, you're late, missing the First Key, your life's about over and then, *voila*, everything's fine.

So maybe it was a miracle. I don't know. But I learned my lesson, the good way, and I was lucky.

Anyways, I tell you all this because the *best* way to learn a lesson is to listen to people who know what the hell they're talking about. The ones that have been there. You didn't listen very well, and you weren't lucky enough to fill up the bottom line.

Pop quiz. I lied about one of the Five Keys. If you can tell me which one was a lie, this won't be your last day. I'll give you ten seconds...

Well, I'll be damned. You were paying attention after all. Hope. You're right, of course. Hope is not one of the Five Keys to the Door of Success.

Funny you got that one right. Okay, you're luckier than I thought. Let's go get a beer, and I'll show you how the Man liked it done. Fix your bottom line. God rest the old man's soul.

AMERICAN MONEY

Ray Busler

The women must think I am deaf, or a child. They say my granddaughter will marry a white man. When the pain goes away, I will rise and kill them both. Better for her to be dead, and it is a long time since I killed a white man.

The French priest comes by every day now. He brings medicine. He reads from the black book, and I sleep. I do not think I ask for his medicine, but I am no longer sure.

I was a man once. Now my belly grows like a woman with child. I travail like a woman. I lie here listening for the wagon that brings the priest and the medicine.

A guest, Crooked Nose, has come from Ft. McLeod. This will end soon; he would not have come otherwise.

"Can you see?" Crooked Nose raised the lamp wick until it smoked, and then lowered it a little. He pulled a tobacco sack from his pocket and emptied it into my hand.

"What is this? What have you given me?"

"A piece of money, but not from Canada. Look, American money, new money, a new thing."

There was a buffalo. I had not seen a buffalo in many summers. "*Tatanka,* in your father's time they covered the Earth, the dust of the herds put out the sun."

"Yes, yes I know all this. The buffalo is good medicine, but there is better, turn the money over. Tell me what you think."

"One of the People, an Indian."

"Look closer at this Indian."

"It cannot be."

"Look again, and tell me that!" Crooked Nose ordered.

He looked older than I remembered. His fierceness vanished into stiff dignity, like those reservation Indians who stayed in America and posed for any photographer who offered a drink of whiskey, but it was him. I was certain it was him. "Two Moons. This Indian on their money is Two Moons."

A grin broke across Crooked Nose's face and he laughed. He held my hand and laughed until I forgot the fire in my belly. I joined him; I was, for a moment, once more a young man. I felt summer heat; I heard blood sing in my ears; a taste of iron filled my mouth; and all that was became now. I saw the sloping hill above the Lakota village on the Greasy Grass River, the waters white men call the Little Big Horn. I saw horses, blue shirts, and arrows. I watched Two Moons raise his arm, bloody to the elbow, high above his head.

I saw the yellow hair in his hand.

"May I keep this?" I asked Crooked Nose.

He put the money back into the tobacco sack and tied it around my neck with a leather thong. It was a good sign that he came to see me. I no longer think I asked the French priest for his medicine. I do not think I have ever asked a white man for anything.

BOX OF LIGHT

Warren Slesinger

Late in the afternoon, he drummed his fingers on his desk, and placed his hand against the wall. He liked his little cubicle and felt safe inside it. He liked the size and weight of the filing cabinet because he could rest his arm on top of it. In fact, he liked the office life because it was predictable.

With each tick of the clock, he followed a routine from the staff meeting in the morning, to lunch in the cafeteria, to beer with the boss after work.

He watched the woman who plopped a folder on his desk and walked into the office across the hall. She looked like his ex-wife, and he was glad to see her go.

"She shopped," he thought, "while I fought."

Even so, he tipped back in his chair, and told himself he didn't care about the baby and divorce. The point was self-protection, and he got it on the job.

Each day, he came to work on time, stayed at his desk, and did what he was told. His boss had given him a good evaluation, and his boss was another vet.

So he was not worried when his boss walked in with another man until he said,"He wants to take a second deposition."

"Why?"

"To solve the case."

His boss rolled his eyes, and looked at the clock. It was after five. He heard a chair bump against a wall, someone rummage in a drawer for keys, and the laugh of the woman when she left the office.

* * *

There was cunning in his coming as it was getting dark. The office closed with the man standing in his personal space. He switched on the light. As soon as the man came forward, he knew that he was not looking at another empty suit from the same department because he moved with a surprising quickness for a big man, and stared with an intensity that made it hard to hold his gaze.

"You're divorced."

"That's right."

"Whose fault: yours or hers?"

"Depends on your point of view."

The man dragged the other chair across the carpet, and placed his hard-knuckled hands on the desk.

"What was the problem?"

"We fought."

"About what?"

"I had a hard time sleeping."

And that was the problem before the divorce. His wife would turn out the light and tell him to settle down, but he could not go to sleep. Even the soft bump of her behind would make him mutter, jab the pillow with his elbow, and move his feet as if to find more solid footing in the sheets, and soon they were arguing in the middle of the night about his "inability to adjust to civilian life." He was easily startled by the creak of a board when his wife went to the bathroom, and when she came back to bed. He would lie in the dark, and listen as if something intangible were there.

One morning, she slammed a drawer when he came into the kitchen.

"A drawer of knives," he thought.

She faced him with an exhausted look.

"Another one of your damned nights!"

"I'm afraid so."

"What about me?"

"I'm sorry."

"Me too!"

The high pitch of her voice came down hard on his nerves, and he raised his hand, but his threat was met with sarcasm.

"What's that?"

He made a fist, and lightly tapped her on the chin with it.

"You'd better not," she said, and went into the bedroom to get dressed.

* * *

The man waited for him to come back to the present moment in the office, and met him with a curious smile.

"You're not hard of hearing?"

He shook his head. The man sat back and studied him.

"And you live alone?"

"Now and then."

The man moved close enough for him to smell the tobacco on his breath.

"Which is it?"

"Not if I find another woman."

Of course, he could. The last woman that he brought into the bedroom only laughed when he locked the door, and asked him if he expected someone else.

While she undressed, he looked out the window at the street. That was when he knew it wasn't a woman that he wanted, but a safe place to sleep.

And it wasn't going to be easy to find it, if the man made it hard to forget what happened. The man kicked back the chair, and stood up.

"You said that you had a hard time sleeping, but according to the other deposition, you slept through the beating of Sgt. White."

"I didn't sleep through it, but I didn't see it either. It was dark, and I was too damned tired to get up."

"And you didn't hear a thing?"

"I heard the shovel hit something -- someone, and then a body in a sleeping bag dragged through the sand."

The man's eyes moved to the ceiling as though going over the same old ground.

"What else?"

"In the morning, I saw blood on the shovel."

"And?"

"That's all I remember."

But he remembered much more: the weight of the body in the sleeping bag, and the sound of nylon as it slid through the sand; the sand in the shovel,the heat of the mid-morning sun; the blood that seeped through the bag; how the handle of the shovel was wet with sweat when they were finished.

"What happened to the shovel?

"We buried him, and left it on the ground."

"With all of your fingerprints on it?

"Yes."

The man stepped back from the desk.

"Would anyone in your platoon want to kill him?

"I don't think so."

"Why?"

"He was from another unit."

The man seemed to measure the distance between them.

"Think he had it coming?"

"I wouldn't know."

With that the man moved toward the door, and stood for a moment as if confronted with something he couldn't leave behind.

"Think about it."

"Are you coming back?"

The man smiled as if amused with himself.

"Perhaps."

* * *

Left alone, he felt no compulsion to go home to an apartment that was furnished with what his ex-wife hadn't wanted: a formica table, shag rug, and a sagging bed. So he stayed in the office, and drew on a piece of paper, a diagram of what happened in the sand.

* * *

That night he lay down late and did not dream until the early morning.

He had pushed his unmade bed against the wall, and once again, a heavy chair against the door. He lay on his right side like he did in the service, and closed his eyes against the growing light. He saw himself inside a house with bars on the window and a bolt in the door. It was on a hilltop without a tree or a bush to block the view. He would take up a position on the rug in the living room with his rifle in the cradle of his arm, and wait for whatever came his way on the only road.

CONFIRMATION

Tim Plaehn

Thomas had never been in a funeral parlor. At twelve, he did not know what to expect or how he should act. Richardson's Funeral Home looked like a mansion to him. With its four pillars and its immaculately cut grass, it could be the entrance to heaven.

But when he went through the front door he stiffened. He picked up a scent of something like dirt or clay, but a bit smoky, something he could not quite place. This smell may have been mixed with flowers and perfume and pleasing aftershave, but Thomas recognized a depressing finality to it. He wanted to leave.

He stood in a hand-me-down suit on the threshold of a room crowded with men and women. They were all around his father's age. The room itself was adorned with paintings of distant mountains and clouds that did not threaten.

"Here they are," he heard someone say, and people turned to look at him. Thomas waited for his mother and his brothers and sisters. His family passed him and exchanged greetings and hugs, accepted heartfelt condolences, and made their way to the far side of the room. His mother received many people at once, thanking them for their concern. Thomas took a step or two and then stopped. He looked down at the carpeting as thoughts of blood overtook him.

"Thomas."

His own name startled him.

"I am so sorry, dear." The woman wore a shiny purple dress and a pinecone brooch that scratched his face when she hugged him.

"Thank you, Mrs. O'Donnell."

"Are you being strong for your mother?" She brushed a blond hair from his eyes.

"I'm trying."

"That's a good man. And look at you, your freckles are fading. You really are becoming a teenager before our very eyes."

"Yes, ma'am."

Mrs. O'Donnell turned from him after one last hug. She made her way to William, Thomas's oldest brother, and Thomas heard her ask him the exact same question. Other adults offered him more of the same, and he desperately wanted to escape. The casket offered the only refuge, but as Thomas made his way to his father he avoided looking directly at the body, concentrating instead on the family photo placed to the left. He studied that picture as his family continued to make small talk. In this crowded, suffocating room, Thomas had a moment to himself. The photo was taken on a blustery day at the beach the previous fall. His father's green sweater gave the picture its only vibrancy. The ocean, stilled by the camera, seemed only a prop next to his father, but Thomas remembered the powerful surf had forced them to yell, that the stranger wouldn't take the picture until he had heard "cheese" from each of them. He looked at the picture and tried to remember what his father's last words were.

"I think he looks weird, don't you?" Katie O'Donnell, one of his classmates at St. Paul's, had come up behind him. Thomas was sure she'd never been to a wake either, but Katie never wanted to let on that she was unfamiliar with anything. Katie was always in charge, always a little ahead of the rest of them.

"His face is all weird. Like a peach fruit roll-up you leave in your bag and don't find until a few days later."

"Yeah."

"I've been staring at him trying to figure out just what he looks like. I've come up with a bunch, but all the other ones were gross."

Even as he stood in front of his father, Thomas had yet to look, but Katie left him no choice. The glimpse stunned him, and he quickly turned away. "Weird" was all he said. He compared his father's face in death with his face in the picture. His smile at the beach jumped out at Thomas, but he couldn't help but think that his father—or his father's body perhaps—knew what was coming, knew what the next six months would bring.

"He's got no color, even with that make-up. It's because they take all his blood, y'know."

"I know," Thomas muttered. He always had trouble talking to Katie, and Katie was always talking. Sometimes she said funny things and sometimes she said mean things and sometimes she seemed to talk just to have something to say. One time, however, Thomas saw her crying, and what she said that time struck him as scared—and that Katie O'Donnell felt scared left him in a kind of shock. At Jacob Evans's birthday party, a game of spin-the-bottle had broken out in the basement, and everyone was doing it. Thomas made for the sliding door, telling everyone that his dad was picking him up early. Some of the kids laughed and made fun of him, but Katie came to his defense. "You guys, shut up. His dad's totally on his way. Don't be such jerks." With that she turned and announced that she would wait with Thomas.

Outside, Thomas saw her eyes beginning to well. He didn't know how to comfort her. He didn't even know what was wrong. A couple of tears dropped before she said anything. "Oh, they're mature. Yeah, that's what older people do. Please, y'know. "

"Yeah."

Thomas thought of that moment whenever Katie acted older or bolder than she really was. He glanced up at her as she continued looking at his father. She had on a gray skirt and a white blouse—it may as well have been her uniform, but Thomas thought this blouse seemed different from the school ones. He could almost see through this one.

"And then they staple his mouth or something." She turned to Thomas, and he averted his eyes. "What did your family do with the blood? Did you donate it or just pour it down the drain?"

"I don't know." His thoughts rushed to an image he'd been trying to cleanse from his mind for two weeks: his father's vivid blood coagulating in Coca-Cola. He had cleared a glass from his father's bedside then had to run to the bathroom. He knelt over the toilet for ten minutes but was unable to vomit.

Thomas looked at Katie to excuse himself. "I have to say a prayer." He knelt down before the open casket—without looking at his father—and began to bless himself. Katie made for the closest chair and bowed her head. She finished quickly and kept her eyes on Thomas.

"Please accept my father into heaven; forgive him his sins," Thomas whispered into his hands. He raised his head. "Not that he had many." He bowed his head once more. "And bless my mom and help her through this. She needs—" Wait a minute, Thomas thought as he again lifted his head to his father's body. But it wasn't his father's strange face that he focused on. He was much more concerned with the flowered print tie he was just beginning to recognize. "Why'd she put him in that?"

He began to say a Hail Mary, but the tie made him frustrated or angry—to the point where he stopped after "among women" and rose from the kneeler. Dad doesn't want to be buried in that, he thought. Forgetting about Katie O'Donnell, Thomas surveyed the room until he spotted his brother John, who was eight years older. John always knew what to do.

He came up behind John and waited impatiently for his conversation with an older couple to reach a natural conclusion. "They said I could take my exams during the summer," he told them. "They're being very understanding."

"Well, your father was very proud of you, John."

"Thank you, Mr. Raymond."

"Not a day went by where he didn't talk about your classes or the team or who the latest flame was. You were the talk of the office."

John laughed somberly, "Things were always pretty slow down there, but that's a new low."

"No, no, no," insisted Mr. Raymond. "Your dad couldn't tell enough John stories. He said that on the day your coach switched you to third, you told—"

"Johnny!" Thomas tugged at his brother's suit jacket. "Johnny, I have to tell you something."

Anguish appeared on those older faces as the Raymonds looked down at Thomas. On Johnny's face, however, Thomas saw only surprised embarrassment and impatience. "Tommy, have you said hello to Mr. and Mrs. Raymond? Mr. Raymond's pretty much been doing the work of two men since dad got sick."

Thomas absorbed his brother's scolding tone and said a quiet hello. He then ignored Mrs. Raymond's question—"How you holding up, honey?"—and navigated his way to the bathroom. It was a small room back by the front, and Thomas locked the door. He knew Father Bradley would be starting the rosary pretty soon, but no one would miss him. Thomas pooled some water from the faucet, and he slurped from his cupped hands, drinking enough water to fill two glasses. He then sat on the toilet seat and put his chin in his hands. The maze-like pattern of the wallpaper held his attention, and Thomas let his mind wander all over it.

On cream paper, blue and red flowers stretched vertically, their stems veering left and right with every new flower. Thomas followed the green stems upward, learning quickly that every blue flower led to a dead end—it was the red flowers he could follow to the ceiling. He eventually grew bored with the pattern and dismissed the wallpaper, along with his father's flowered tie, as worthy of nothing. Plain ugly, he thought. Who would pick this stuff out? Thomas wondered if the funeral director or whoever decorated this bathroom had the last say in what his father wore to his grave rather than his mother. He imagined his father spending eternity in that tie, of him walking on puffy clouds towards the gates of heaven, of St. Peter grimly informing him that there are no white flowing robes—people wear what they have. And then St. Peter snickered. God himself would be struck by the dull colors and the clutter of the pattern.

A soft but rapid knock brought Thomas back from the heavens.

"Tommy? Tommy are you okay?" It was Katie O'Donnell.

"Yes," he asserted. "I'm fine."

"You've been in there forever," she whispered. "What are you doing?"

Panic quickly followed Thomas's realization of what Katie must be thinking.

"Do you feel okay?" she persisted. "Do you want me to get your mom?"

"No!" Thomas looked around. "I'm . . . I'm just fixing my shoelaces." He then heard her say, "Hi, Mr. Hughes . . . No, sir, I'm not in line. Tommy Fitzgerald's in there." And then, more quietly, "I think he has an upset stomach."

His mouth dropped. "Okay, okay, I'm coming out." Thomas checked himself in the mirror. He wiped his eyes clear and flashed his braces before setting his mouth tight and grim. He told himself to look her in the eye and pretend it's no big deal. Emerging from the bathroom, however, he faltered; her green eyes were too big for him, too pretty, too demanding. His gaze settled on her black shoes. Katie's right foot twisted to the left and right on its heel, giving Thomas the impression—that he quickly dismissed—that she was nervous.

"Are you okay?" she finally asked.

"Yes."

"You practically ran out of that room." She motioned with her head, and her face winced in understanding. "I didn't know what I was saying—"

"I don't want to be there," Thomas interrupted. "This whole thing is stupid."

"Yeah, it is," Katie confirmed. "And the people are so fake. Like when they say, 'I'm sorry' or 'Be strong.' Those are just clichés, y'know. I mean, what can anyone really say?"

Thomas watched her mouth as she spoke, becoming entranced by the droop and the fullness of her lower lip. When she stopped, Thomas realized he was staring.

"And what's with that tie? I mean, your dad's dead. Can't he just rest in peace or does he really have to wear that ugly tie?"

Thomas heard the other room go quiet, and he heard Father Bradley's voice leading all the mourners: "In the name of the Father, the Son, and the…"

"We should get back in there," Katie said, but Thomas did not move.

"That tie is so stupid. My father never even wore the thing." He could feel an emotion in his throat—he didn't know exactly what it was, but it wanted something. It was making him talk, rapidly and to Katie O'Donnell. "The thing's so ugly. Those stupid flowers are just huge, and the colors on it are supposed to make it like jump out at you or something but they're really dull. If he had known he was dying, he would have made sure to pick out his clothes—there's no way he'd be buried in that thing. My father never even wore it. It just hung in the back of his closet." That emotion had made its way to his eyes, but Thomas pushed back the tears with a shrug. "I gave it to him like five years ago on Father's Day—one of those times where your mom takes you out, y'know, and you point at what you want to give your dad—no big deal. He wore it maybe once. My mother even made fun of it on the day he had it on and now she's gonna bury him in it. It's just a stupid tie."

When he finished, Thomas noticed that Katie was close to crying, her eyelashes wet with every blink. And just like on that night with spin-the-bottle, he quickly looked away.

"I shouldn't have . . ." Katie stopped. "I mean, it's what I should have done—that's what I'm sorry for." She began crying in earnest, and Thomas searched for the right question to ask, but Katie ended the conversation abruptly, saying, "Sometimes I hate being a kid," as she turned and walked away.

Both of them were late for Father Bradley's blessing. Thomas sat down next to his mother and again clasped his hands in prayer. Whenever he raised his head, he'd look at Katie O'Donnell and follow the gaze of her green eyes to the casket.

* * *

The next day Thomas attended the funeral and burial of his father. He was numb to it all—to the homily about his father's virtues; to his own singing on "How Great Thou Art"; even to the dirt he threw down on his father. A bagpiper played on a hill over one hundred yards away. He couldn't believe how far the music carried.

Mrs. Nisbet's Swedish meatballs and Mrs. O'Connor's chicken casserole drove much of the discussion at Thomas's house that evening. The formal mourning over, friends told the stories about his dad they'd been thinking about for days. Thomas stayed in the den until the drinking and the laughing became too much for him. He escaped the crowd and grabbed a bag of pretzels from the kitchen, dodging mourners as he went. His room would provide the solitude missing in this long day, but he didn't notice Katie O'Donnell following him.

She called up the stairs before he had opened his door. Thomas turned to see her and felt a spring in his stomach bounce something from his spleen to his liver to his kidneys to his heart, finally getting whatever it was lodged in his lungs. He couldn't even gasp. She wore a black dress, and she had her brown hair pulled back. He motioned to his room.

In his room Katie seemed a bit lost, stripped of the rambunctiousness she usually possessed. "I feel," Katie began awkwardly, "like you want to be alone and here I keep showing up to bug you."

"Nah. I just don't want to be with all those people."

"Me neither." She stopped talking but kept looking at him, causing even more inner turmoil. The numbness with which he went through the day had fled, and his senses were all on the highest of alert, ready for what was next.

"Do you like pretzels?" he asked. Katie nodded. "Do you want to go on the roof and eat pretzels?"

"Sure."

Thomas led her out his window onto the roof of his garage. From there they climbed to the roof of the house and sat down near the chimney. They ate pretzels and watched the sun sink before them. Katie liked to eat a pretzel around its edges, trying not to break it into pieces before she had made it all the way around. Whenever she messed up and bit through, she'd toss the pretzel down to the gutter. He noticed how she bit her lip with each disappointment.

They ate in silence, but were aware of a communion of sorts. They even began holding hands once they finished off the pretzels. The sky glowed as if the heavens were there to bear witness, to behold these hands. Thomas turned, and saw Katie's front teeth biting down on her bottom lip. Her eyes blinked once and then she leaned toward him.

Her lip—suddenly released—became the most beautiful red he had ever seen.

UNDER THE HOOD

Jonathan Sapers

It was dark when they got into the car and there was rain on the windshield. Just the slightest sprinkling, moistening the lens. Tincturing. She thought: This could be what love is like. Like this. The world looks like this on love. In love.

She put her hands on the steering wheel. She felt goose bumps on her arms. He got in beside her and shut the door.

"Can I drive?" she asked. She was glad. How nice that word was to think of. Glad. She was happy. Good dinner. Good wine. Nice boy.

"Can you drive?"

"I want to drive."

"Sure."

"You rock my world!" He did. So far, he did.

"You realize, if we get caught, we could end up going to jail. You will never get your license and I will never be able to drive again."

"Yes."

He reached into his pocket and gave her the key. She started the car. She had seen her father do this. Seen him do it. Seen others do it. Just like this. Just like this. Just like this. You could have a style of starting a car. She would. She stuck the key in. She shivered. The car roared to life. She felt as if she were sitting on top of a large animal.

"I can do this," she said. She put the car in gear. She would have to drive as if she meant it, as if she were legitimate. As if she had a right to.

She pulled out of the restaurant parking lot. She could hear the sound the tires made on the cement. She could feel the way the tires were moving. She – She would have to stop thinking about the tires.

In a turn or two, they would be on the highway. Now they were. Now it was just a matter of settling in. Keeping to a pace. Sticking to it. Music would help. She reached for the radio dial. Who drove this way? One hand on the wheel, one on the tuner? A boyfriend she had known once, who had not turned out well. Had bad taste in music. Or the kind of taste one really shouldn't be compulsive about. He was unsure of his taste. He would start playing a song, play it long enough for her to decide she liked it, then he would say it was really a bad song and he was tired of it. It wasn't taste at all. Just indecision, or cruelty. Or indecision resulting from cruelty. Luckily she'd dumped him.

Wow! That was close. She smiled and looked over at him. He was not like that. He did not care what was playing on the radio. He did not care — there were red lights in her rear view mirror. She could see, due to a certain way the road turned here, the cars going the other way very clearly. This was something she shouldn't be watching. She looked back at him. He was looking ahead at the road with a kind of bemused expression on his face.

This was nice, but it could also mean a whole host of unfortunate things. What if it meant he was suicidal and that he let her drive because he wanted them to die some ridiculous, glamorous death together? Or maybe the whole thing was a dare. A sexy way to show he trusted her.

She preferred this idea and adopted it. The way she'd adopted him. On their way to a party, on the street. She'd put her arm through his and they'd pretended they'd come together. No one could understand how they'd met; they kept changing their story. It was a party for a mutual friend. The friend was graduating from a program in something —

It was all very good to be reviewing her life story here, but she needed to be paying attention. Not too much attention because she didn't want to look like she was watching for cops. Yikes there's one now! Steady, steady. As if you've seen nothing as if —

Was she crazy? If so, it had started this morning, when she had woken up with a start. From a dream in which she was stuck in a revolving door. The door started turning on its own. Faster, faster. She was carrying a dessert. If she dropped the dessert, she understood, she would be killed. Still holding. Still holding. She screamed and woke herself up.

The cop had not noticed. They were safely past. The way to do this was not to think about it.

"Did you see what you just passed?"

"Yes."

"You're incredible."

She looked over at him. He was smiling. He seemed sure of himself. Too sure. She would not, she suddenly realized, be able to depend on him. This was not new. There wasn't really anyone she could — well wanted to — depend on. She was almost on her own. This made her tired to think of. It would turn out wrong. He was supposed to say no, she couldn't drive his car illegally, and they were supposed to fight about it and he was supposed to win. But he didn't care about it at all. Maybe he was suicidal. How could he be suicidal after a night like this? It had been a nice night. Funny. And he was so cute.

Had she really thought that? Was she some kind of moron? She needed to concentrate. Be serious. On the world outside her window. Traffic was stopped or slowing ahead: red lights in lines into the distance. Why were there so many red lights? She braked suddenly, jerkily, just in time.

"Rubberneckers," he said.

She thought of this expression, which seemed both so apt and so unpleasantly physical. As if the cars were inhabited by dolls with melted necks. But what were they looking at? She turned too.

On the side of the road were three cars, one mangled, the other two stopped at odd angles. Two people stood looking at each other between the two cars. A third spoke to a policeman. They were — they were all slowing down to see if they could see death.

She did not want to see death. She thought of it too much as it was. She did not want to be one of those people who constantly thought about the end of things rather than the beginning.

The traffic began to thin; the cars ahead of her picked up speed. She followed suit. The wine had probably worn off by now. "So, tell me about your life," she said.

He was quiet. He had fallen asleep. It was like a boyfriend to do this. She was just sorry. Boyfriends were often disappointing. But this one had so much promise. He was smart. His jokes were funny. He trusted her to do what she was doing now. But he didn't care whether he lived or died.

This would not do. He wouldn't pass muster with her mother. Not this one. Not this one either. Maybe the answer was to pick someone who didn't. Stop trying to predict. Give up on her mother. Her father didn't care. Why should the fact that her mother did give her mother some kind of special status in the approval department?

She would keep him, though, for now. He liked to have a drink and a laugh; tonight they had had a lot of both. They had gone on from the party to lots of nights like this one. Dinners with a lot of laughs. Followed by his place, because hers was too small. Restaurants were hers though — she found them. She had developed an ascending scale of favorites. Tonight's was at the top. A place in the suburbs where she could just walk in and say, "Muscles, please" and they knew what she meant and brought them to her the way she liked. This was carving out a life.

But what had she earned? Good taste was not a career. Having boys like this was not having relationships. This was her mother speaking, or the admittedly unfair version of her mother lodged so firmly in her head. She disagreed, but this was the problem when one's parents still walked the earth while one tried so hard to come into one's own. Her mother's generation — maybe just her mother — was always claiming credit for things. And demanding appreciation. But, she was sorry. She had the right to enjoy the freedoms that had been won for her and she should not have to win them again from her mother. After all, the idea that a young woman could not live on her own was outrageous, could not choose her own restaurant, insane. These were rights that seemed so fundamental it seemed ridiculous any one should ever have had to fight for them — and yet the older generation was not happy, relieved, or even proud to see their children exercise them. So why weren't they happy? They were just annoyed. Annoyed to see how easy it was for them. Easy? Of course not. Life is never ever easy. Even she knew this.

Another dream: She has been told she has to lead a group of camels across a desert. First she must feed them. One of them is sick. It keeps throwing up. It appears there is no way to help it. Then, she is given a medicine she is told will make the camel better. She gives it to it and it drops dead. She thinks she is supposed to learn something from this dream, but is not sure what. That she should be more caring? Should only travel alone? Should not consider a career in medicine? Should think twice about having babies?

Recently, she and her mother had gone to a party at the home of a rich family friend. On the way home, she had joked that she could get used to living like that. Her mother had said, you know, you may be a little too difficult to please. And she had smiled and said, isn't that how you taught me? And her mother had frowned at her, misunderstanding. She had meant it conspiratorially, but her mother had refused to join in. She had meant it — it was a perfectly accurate comment — but she was pathetically heartbroken to discover that her mother had begun disassociating herself from the parts of her daughter — even the smart, funny parts — that she now felt were the cause of her daughter's life problems. It was wrong. It was inaccurate to pick out some parts and not others. Her elbow would not find the perfect man only to be turned down by her knee.

The thing about men was that unlike her mother, she had grown up in a time when women could know everything there was to know about men in advance. In graphic detail. Why shouldn't she choose her boys like cars and discard them when they failed to live up to dealers' descriptions? These days the dealers' descriptions were pretty accurate. But what about the mystery? Her mother would say. Fuck the mystery. She wanted facts. How had the mystery helped her mother with her father? But that was hitting below the belt. The point was, she did not agree that her father was a bad choice; only that her mother had guessed based on inadequate information. And she, an only child, had been left to pick up the pieces. Or piece through the pieces. Or maybe they had left her in pieces. Did she care? Anyway, now she had to learn how to feed camels.

She pumped the gas pedal. She had better get on with it. It was time to get Mr. Rock My World home.

* * *

By the time they reached the outskirts of the city, she was, she told herself, no longer drunk. Just tired. There was no one on the streets. A long time back, he had woken up again and lit a cigarette and for most of the ensuing trip, they had not spoken. She thought that this outcome was so obvious her mother could have predicted it. And so the next obvious question was, Why hadn't she?

She took a drag of his cigarette. Cigarettes were so ten years ago. She imagined the myriad ways he could permanently ruin his health. He would drink too much or rarely exercise. When he was older, he would look back on this night that wasn't with regret. He didn't look like it though. He didn't look like he was planning on regretting anything, she thought, with a pang. It wasn't the sex. They had taken care of that. And if they hadn't, she could have trapped him. Pulled over to the side of the road, and while he was still sleeping, done any number of things to him. But that was the preliminaries. And the preliminaries weren't the problem. It was what came next. That was usually where she failed. She wanted to get further along in the relationship, where people learned to overlook failures, or grew to live with them, saw them as necessary evils. She wished she knew more about further along; she didn't get there much. Perhaps it was her fault. She who caused the trouble. Had the most fences. Because she kept wondering whether she'd missed something. Checking under the hood, which, since they were often stark naked at the time, was perhaps too accurate a metaphor and was furthermore distracting. But tonight she had felt as if — she had been on the point of blurting out that she thought he might be the — and then —

Still, he wasn't running. He was waiting for her now, to say something? It was after all his car.

She had parked outside the apartment he was renting, where she had been staying off and on. What she really wished to do was to leave him off. Take the car and leave. It hadn't been him after all, it had been the car she'd been after. And now that she had it, she would simply toss him from it, like a pit from a peach. And yet she didn't want to leave. She wanted to stay. And he didn't seem to be leaving. He seemed simply to be sitting in the passenger seat. It was time to get out. She opened the door and stood up. The night air was fresh and cool and wet. Standing up, she realized she was not as sober as she had thought. She stumbled a step.

"Wait," he said and scooted after her, over to the driver's seat. She lurched forward and steadied herself on the front light. She looked back at him. He sat leaning forward, hands on the steering wheel. She had the feeling just for a minute, that she was being hit by a car in very slow motion. Simultaneously, it occurred to her that this story did not have to have a sad ending. She maneuvered herself around to the other front headlight and paused, just for a moment. What would her mother think of her if she saw her like this, wrapped around the front of a car? Her body spasmed and she leaned over and threw up on the street side of the right fender. Maybe, just maybe he had been looking in a different direction. What had she eaten? Whatever it was, there was apparently a great deal of it. Again, again. She felt hands on her shoulders and someone holding her hair back.

"If you get drunk and throw up, always remember to have someone hold your hair back." Had her mother really said that to her, one night, a long time ago?

Yes, she had. The night her father had left them. Stormed out. Actually, he hadn't stormed out, but he had left, gradually over weeks and weeks, her mother having a little more wine each night without meaning to, or at the very least without counting. She could think this now but then, she really hadn't understood what she was seeing when she saw her mother stumble a little more each night on the way past her room to bed, as it became more and more clear he wasn't coming back. She hadn't understood enough about heartbreak, let alone drinking, to expect her mother's wrong turn, right, after her door, to the bathroom, instead of left and on to bed ("Mom!" she had called out, "It's the other way!"). She had heard her mother mumble something and then the sound of her vomiting. She had gone in sleepily and her mother had showed her, between heaves, how to hold her hair back so she could throw-up in a ladylike fashion. At the time she had thought it was the ultimate in hypocrisy. Could you kill someone politely? Steal fairly?

Now that she had stopped, the hands gently lifted her and helped her back to the passenger seat. And, with a hum, lowered her seat so she was in a sleeping position. The hands closed the door behind her and disappeared. Now what?

The driver's door opened. "Where to?" a voice said. She heard the key turn in the ignition.

ARBOR DAY

Manuel Royal

Every time we got together, my skinny grandfather showed me that last picture of his son, my father. It was a stranger with my face, surrounded by woodworking tools in his workshop. Calm on his last day, age twenty-five.

I was older than that, now. It was a sunny April morning, and the little graveyard made a pretty sight. Rows of white stones sunk in green turf, scattered around the big spreading oak. Shady, peaceful.

Chock full of my dead relatives. Dead, silent, and out of my hair, which suited me. Especially some of the great-aunts. I never visited when we weren't burying somebody.

But there I was, along with my still-living, talking, in-my-hair Gramps. He'd called me away from my endless waste of time and money at Northwestern, claiming urgent business at the family boneyard. Like an idiot, I'd gone ahead and put on my funeral suit and good shoes.

Gramps and I got out of his old pickup and he leaned back against it, pulled a pack out of his jacket and lit an unfiltered Pall Mall before speaking. "Harv, I got nut cancer." I waited while he sucked down some smoke. "Nut cancer, ass cancer, who knows what else cancer."

"Lungs?"

"Nah."

"You're kidding. Two packs a day -- you dodged a bullet."

"Guess so."

"Lucky sonofabitch." Damnit, I'd miss the old guy.

He didn't crack a smile; the man had no sense of humor. He spit instead. "Kid, you oughta have knocked up that Danielle girl sometime in those three months you was married."

"Okay. Whatever you want to talk about."

"If you're not gonna have kids, it's all up anyway, family's over."

"Fine, sorry I used those condoms."

"Jesus God, Harv, you think your dick's just for fun? It ain't."

"Sure wasn't with Danielle."

"Christ knows your homo cousin Reggie ain't having kids. You gonna make some babies or let your whole family just die out forever?" He ran out of breath and bent forward, his hands on his knees, face red.

"Jesus, Gramps, okay, I'll have some stupid kids. Whatever."

"With a woman."

"Sure, why not."

"Don't have a test tube baby or some goddamn thing. Stick it in a woman, Boy. Make it count."

"You should write those Hallmark cards, Gramps."

"Look here." He straightened up, went around to the back of the truck. He opened a toolbox, pulled out a tubular steel implement and held it up. "Increment borer. For dendrochronology. Got it?"

"Absolutely. No idea what the hell you're talking about."

Gramps stumped off toward the oak tree, lighting another butt. "Help me get a core from the tree. Grab the straightedge level from the box. And the 3-in-1 oil."

We walked on soft grass between my dead aunts and uncles, my dead dad and all the other dead Dwyatts. There was already a stone in place for Walter Jefferson Dwyatt, aka Gramps. The stone lacked only the second date. My own stone was in storage, ready for the big day. I could remember picking it out on my tenth birthday.

Gramps walked past his plot, into the shade under the spreading branches. He set the borer against the trunk and got it started, then leaned against the tree and nodded at the tool. "Steady and even. You work, I'll talk."

"So we'll both be boring." I took off my jacket and draped it over a marble angel. (One of my siblings, I think. I'm the only one made it past infancy). I grabbed the bore handles and twisted.

Gramps got another good lungful of nicotine. "Keep putting some oil on it as you go. Okay, now. Remember in my will, where it says you got to take care of the family tree? This is the tree."

"Seriously? Of course you're serious. I thought that meant Mom's genealogy charts." I looked up through the branches. The live oak was a good forty feet high.

"Now why the hell would I care about a bunch of Vicky's family crap? Your mother was a good woman with a nice can, but that bunch of halfwits on her side aren't blood kin."

"They are to me. How far in do I go with this?"

"Up a few inches short of the handle. Keep 'er straight in to the core. Oak tree's exogenous."

"It grows outward."

"Right, college boy, it grows outward. Living on the outside, dead in the center."

"Like my ex-wife."

No sense of humor. "You only want to do this every few years. Okay, deep enough; let's get the bore out."

A steady pull brought out a pencil-thick, foot long cylinder of wood, striated with sections of the growth rings. Gramps took the core from me, holding it gingerly. He peered through his trifocals at the piece of wood, sliding his tobacco-stained thumbnail along it from the bark inward as he counted rings. He nicked the wood with his nail.

"Right there, that ring or close to. That's your great-grandmother Lucille. My mother. You never met her." He mused for some time, spitting twice. "Shrieking harridan, in fact. Sick in the head."

"So, that ring marks the year she was born?"

"Why the hell would it?"

"I thought you were trying to make a point about family tradition. So, what, it's the year she died?"

"Just after. Jumped off a bridge, and my old man had to bribe the coroner to get the body away in time for planting, over there." He pointed to an oblong marble stone, where I could just make out "LUCILLE DWYATT".

It struck me just then -- for the first time, honestly -- struck me that, if I were a stranger, stopping by on a warm spring day to relax in a little country graveyard, I'd be wondering why all the stones were facing the oak tree. Why they were laid out in rough concentric circles, all turning their carved stone faces to the tree like an audience. I don't think most cemeteries are arranged that way.

Under Lucille's name was something else, a carved image; I remembered now. "Damn, I always wondered why there was a picture of a bridge carved on there. Does that mean Uncle Gary shot himself?"

"Yep. Right in both eyes."

"How'd he -- never mind. What about the skull and crossbones over there on Aunt Hedda's stone?"

"Rat poison. She had the stone carved a week before she did it. She's about here." He nicked another spot on the rod of wood. "You see why this tree has got to be taken care of."

I didn't, particularly. "Fine; tradition. You can mark everybody's death on the growth rings. Some people use calendars, but what the hell."

He stared at me, for a moment looking confused and close to his limit, not the hard old bastard I knew. He pointed again to the first nick. "Clean the shit outta your ears, boy. *This* is your great-grandmother Lucille. That ring right there. Her soul's grown into the wood. They all are, alla them bygone Dwyatts. They live in the tree."

I couldn't think of a good response. "Our dead relatives live in a tree."

"Only the direct descendants of Augustus Dwyatt. Every soul buried here, man or woman, is a Dwyatt by bloodline."

"And they're dead, but they live in this tree."

"That's the fact."

"Are they baking chocolate chip cookies in there?"

Gramps grabbed my shoulder. "A person's soul stays with the body for a little while, a day or two."

"Okay."

"Why'd you think I made it look accidental when your dad killed himself with the table saw? Just for fun?"

"No idea. I do remember you sitting me down and making sure I understood Dad killed himself on purpose, so thanks again for that, old man."

"Had to put him in the ground the next day; no time for an autopsy and inquest and all."

"You said we'd see him again."

"You will. You'll talk to him, Harv."

"I thought you meant, like, Heaven."

For once, Gramps laughed. "Ain't any phony-baloney heaven and angels. We got this tree. The roots spread out, see, into every one of these plots, clear across to your worthless Uncle Spence over by the wall. You put a Dwyatt in there and the roots extract his soul, draw it up like water and it just soaks into that year's growth ring, settles down into every little cell."

"Like, where? The chlorophyll?" Do you go along with a delusion, or argue?

Gramps spit and snorted simultaneously. "Jesus, Boy, what're they teaching at that school? Chlorophyll's in the leaves. Why the hell would my mother be in an oak leaf?"

"You're right, that makes no sense."

"She's in the wood. That's the part that lasts. Cellulose. Tracheids, vessels. Porous wood." He lit a match with his big yellow thumbnail and sparked another Pall Mall. "That's how come we don't lay our people in coffins. Gets in the way. Got to let the roots poke in there."

"And it saves money, I guess."

"Saves some money. Give me that." He carefully slid the bore back into the trunk and tapped it in place. "More of us in the old tree than out, that's for sure. My time's comin', just around the corner -- God, boy, damn it all, you got to get some damn kids, or else you are the ass-end of the Dwyatt line."

"Ah, Jesus. I'm gonna sit down for a second." My knees weren't feeling too solid; I let them fold and dropped down on my ass, back against the live wood.

A lifetime of casually observing my family's little quirks was coming into focus for me. The social isolation, the annual rehearsal funerals, the tendency to suicide and unlikely accidents. The family legends. ("Legend" means "surreal, pointless anecdote ending in abrupt death".)

And the business, which I wanted nothing to do with. There's nothing wrong with manufacturing veterinary enemas, but it doesn't excite me as a career.

Everything I'd always wanted to get away from. Almost seemed normal now, compared to this revelation.

Gramps took my arm, practically hauled me up. For a dying old crazy person, he had a good grip. "Augustus Dwyatt disappeared in

1851, declared dead in 1858. Last time anybody saw him, he came out here. Said he was going to cheat death and then go into town for some tobacco. Never seen again. I figure he's inside the trunk, maybe in that bole where it divides."

I looked up at it. "What -- what do you think he did?"

"You can ask him yourself some day. Spend a few nights out here by this tree, you'll hear 'em all right. God damn, Harv ... they don't stop talking. Once you start hearing them."

He took a last drag on the butt, burning it down to his fingers, and flicked it away. "You won't be lonesome."

"Gramps -- " I found myself with literally nothing to say except, "How many?"

"Seventy-three Dwyatts, plus old Augustus makes seventy-four. Big oak like this's got another five hundred, maybe a thousand years in it, if it's took care of. That's you, Harv. You have got to carry on the line, make sure it's done. It needs to be a direct descendant. Has to be. Listen."

"Still listening."

"One, get a woman, two, knock her up, three, keep this tree alive."

"Gramps, has it ever occurred to you that maybe you're just an insane old man?"

It hadn't.

Long story short, Gramps got his promise out of me. When badgering didn't work, he brought up his ass cancer. Then he showed me his latest will, and the black and white figures with their little conga line of zeroes. Those zeroes sealed the deal.

After that, the old man must have felt he could let go, because he was dead inside of a week. My guess is he induced a coronary somehow, but there was no autopsy, and I got him in the ground the next day.

There was nobody to contest his will, and a vague "take care of said tree with his own hands" clause is hard to enforce. The figures were rock solid, though.

I did my part. For a while. Ten years. Pruning, guarding against root rot and gall incursions, maintaining the right soil moisture. That tree and I had a longer, more nurturing relationship than I ever managed with a woman.

Another marriage, just as childless as the first but even more expensive. I sat in a big house and drank expensive booze, trying and failing to picture a child with my eyes. I didn't want to look into those eyes. In a rare decisive act and with some Dutch courage I got it taken care of. (They're not supposed to perform a vasectomy on a guy who just wanders in drunk, but enough cash at the right clinic gets results.)

After I sobered up, I reflected on how my entire life had consisted of waiting to die. It was time to get out of the family psychotic delusion business.

I rented equipment and went out and took the oak apart in sections. With a week's hard work I cut, burned or blasted it all. The roots would die and the remaining bits would rot.

I sold the Dwyatt house and the Dwyatt land, and anything else that reminded me of my crazy family, my family tree, craziness in general, families in general or trees in general. Walked away and pre-arranged for cremation.

When somebody asks about my "people", I say I put the family tree through a chipper. That goes over well with the damaged women I briefly attract.

I did keep one little piece of the past. It's a strange thing. An object I found when I was splitting the trunk at its juncture, wedged inside the bole. Somebody's jawbone. Three gold teeth.

Did Augustus Dwyatt have gold teeth?

Who can I ask? There's no one.

KAREEMA

Craig Murray

The screams ripped through the morning air, sounding in many ways louder than the previous explosion. Figures appeared through the haze of dust and smoke. Some stumbling, babbling incoherently, others silent, wraith-like ghosts, too shocked to even react to the horror that wrapped about them in death's shroud.

There was a pause, a preternatural moment of silence, and then the screams began again. The wailing, pain-filled shrieks of the injured and the terrible raw cries of those desperately seeking loved ones.

The house of Kahlil Marek seemed to take the brunt of the explosion. Where moments before, family and friends celebrated a wedding, now there was little left but rubble and smoke. Kahlil had been standing on the street speaking with friends, when his world was shattered. Suddenly he was airborne, tumbling through a dark cloud of debris and noise that had once been his family.

Neighbours and friends rushed to the ruins and quickly started to help. Shattered walls were lifted brick by brick in desperate hope of finding anyone alive. Kahlil was propped against a wall gazing in disbelief as the bodies were removed and stacked like so much dead wood near the road. He felt nothing, not the pain from his broken leg or torn skin, not the pain of watching his family lying on the street.

Kahlil was drifting in and out of consciousness when a great cry arose from the rescuers. A section of the upstairs floor lay propped over some shattered furnishings. The crowd surged towards it and the last thing he heard before passing out was "She's still alive".

"You are very lucky to be alive, Kahlil," said Ahmed. "Your leg is healing well, you would hardly know..."

"Know my whole family, everything I owned, almost everyone I know is gone?" he asked.

"You have Kareema, your sister's daughter. She is a gift from God," said Ahmed.

"A gift from God? Everyone is dead except one girl, and not even my child! Why did God leave me like this?" said Kahlil.

"Lower your voice my friend. She is in the hallway waiting," Ahmed said.

"And now I am to raise this child?" he asked.

"As your own for, like you, she has no one else," replied Ahmed.

* * *

"Well I am glad to know that you are well, and the girl?" asked Tariq.

Kahlil paused for a moment, his brow furrowed as he thought.

"She is a very quiet and well-mannered child. My sister did a good job with her. I have had much help from the women in the neighborhood. They come to see we both are fed. They know that raising a girl is not a man's task."

"Well that is good. These people, all of us have suffered greatly, especially you. It is right for us to all join together," Tariq said.

Rising, he grasped his friend's shoulders and kissed both his cheeks. Kahlil smiled and yelled over his shoulder. "Kareema, come here and say goodbye to Mr. Haleel."

Kareema appeared and bowed, her hands clasped together, eyes lowered as she spoke.

"My uncle speaks often and fondly of you sir. Thank you for visiting."

Tariq smiled at his friend, his face displaying his surprise at the very formal manner of speech.

"You are welcome, young Kareema. Listen to your uncle and be a good girl," he admonished before moving to the door. He had just stepped through when Kareema's voice cried out. "Wait! Wait!"

Tariq stopped, surprise growing as the young girl raced forward and hugged him.

"You are loved and will be greatly missed, Tariq Haleel," she said before bowing once again and running from the room.

Tariq looked curiously at the retreating figure before turning back to his friend and shrugging. Kahlil dismissed the girl's behaviour as nothing more than a side effect of the tragedy.

The following day as he walked along the street, he heard a voice calling.

"Kahlil! Kahlil, wait."

Kahlil's smile faded as he saw the look on his friend's face.

"Ahmed, what's the matter?" he asked.

"Oh it is so terrible, so terrible. You were friends with Tariq Haleel, were you not? Well last night, near seven o'clock, he was hit by an ambulance. He is dead, my friend," said Ahmed. "He was loved and will be greatly missed," he continued.

Kahlil's heart lurched as Ahmed said the last part, and he found himself leaning heavily on the wall.

"Oh I am so sorry, so terribly sorry. I had not thought, I mean, so soon after..." he said.

Kahlil shook his head and straightened himself up. "No, I'm alright."

The girl said that. Did she know? How could she have known? he thought.

Pulling himself upright, he stammered a goodbye and continued walking. Ahmed said some small apologetic words that Kahlil never heard. Inside his mind was a storm of conflicting thoughts.

The days passed and soon enough he had put it all behind him. Kareema's words, he decided, were little more than coincidence. It was a blazingly bright Thursday as he walked along the street towards the house he now shared with Kareema. Turning the corner he saw a scene of pandemonium. Ambulances, army, police and the ever present crowd of onlookers milled or rushed about in front of his neighbors house. Immediately his thoughts turned to his niece. This was where she stayed while he worked.

Rushing forward, he pushed his way until finally he spotted Waheed.

"Waheed! What has happened? Where is Kareema?" he asked.

Waheed turned with a grimace towards Kahlil.

"She is fine. She is safe; no one else is," he said grimly.

"What..." stammered Kahlil.

"There were ten children my wife watched. Never did Allah bless us with our own but always our house was filled. That will be no more," he said.

"Tell me what has happened," begged Kahlil.

"The Coalitions were giving out candy to the children. Just behind us, by the school. The children begged my wife to let them go, and she did. A mortar bomb fell in the midst of them. They are all dead, all except that girl because she refused to go."

"Why?" Kahlil asked, a ball of ice forming in his stomach.

"She just refused. She said nothing else other than to the other children," Waheed said.

"What...What did she say?" Kahlil asked.

"She took each by the hands and said 'You are loved and will be greatly missed.' And then she sat and watched until it happened."

Kahlil felt as if a train was racing through his head. The world spun and he staggered and lurched into the arms of Waheed.

"She cannot stay here anymore. My wife collapsed, they have taken her away. Never again shall these walls echo with the laughter of children," Waheed droned.

Kahlil moved mechanically towards Kareema. Without a word being said she rose and fell in behind him. They walked silently into the house and silently into the sitting room. Kahlil dropped himself into a chair and sat in stunned silence.

"Uncle, are you mad at me?" the little girl asked.

Kahlil took a moment to respond. "Should I be?"

"No uncle, I have done nothing wrong."

Kahlil tried to force the thoughts out of his head, tried to dispel the ghosts that seemed to scream at him. *She is possessed*, he thought. *Everyone died and she didn't have a scratch. I know now what happened. The girl died as well but there was a demon waiting for a body to claim.*

"Kareema. How did...What you said to Mister Haleel, what you said to the children..."

"I only said goodbye, uncle. I said goodbye as one day I must say goodbye to you," the child responded.

Kahlil's skin grew cold and he felt icy fingers creep across his skin. He had no doubt now. No questions. He also had a plan. In his most forced and friendly tone he spoke.

"There has been too much death here. Too much sadness. I think we need a vacation, a chance to get away. Quickly now my niece, upstairs and gather your things. I shall get the car."

"Where are we going, uncle?" she asked.

"We shall drive to the coast, see the wide waters, the deep blue waves and get away from this place. Now hurry, get your things."

Kareema rushed upstairs and quickly packed all of her meager belongings. Outside she could hear her uncle's car starting. She paused before a full length mirror and brushed away a tiny tear. Wrapping her arms tightly about herself she said, "Goodbye Kareema, goodbye. You were once well loved, but you shall not be missed. Goodbye."

THE DESK

B.F. McCune

The desk is not the main topic on the agenda, but it consumes most of the time at the January meeting of the Cultural Organization of Women. Milly Stone, one of "our senior members," mentions the desk first.

She stands and smoothes her flowered print dress over her cushioned front. "I would like to propose that we sell the desk in the upstairs room and use the proceeds for establishing a scholarship fund for new artists," she says.

Heads turn around the room, and chatter stops. A bite of cake falls to the table from Barbara Bigosh's fork. She quickly brushes it under her plate.

Hazel Foresythe can be counted upon to oppose any of Milly's suggestions, even though they are best friends and were widowed the same year.

"That desk was willed to us by Catherine Grant," she says and bows her head reverently for a moment. "I really don't think we have the right to sell it. She did some of her finest work for this organization at that desk."

Milly sniffs. "I doubt that very much. The thing is totally unusable. You have to open the top to reach the typing area. Then, if you reach for the bookshelf, you knock all the folders off the section next to the typewriter. When the desk is completely unfolded, there's no space in the room to move. When it's closed, you can't get to the storage."

"It was custom-designed for Caty," continues Hazel, ignoring the interruption. "It's made of mahogany. There's only one other like it in the world."

"Then that's two too many," Milly snips. "I knew Caty. In fact, she palmed the desk off on me originally. We tried it in every corner of my house. We dragged it into the biggest room there, and it still stuck out like a wart on a hand. That's when she decided to donate it to the club. Caty would have wanted us to sell it if we could use the money in a better way."

Barbara raises her hand. "I don't understand. Who would buy the desk if it's so terrible."

"It's an antique. Valued at $1500," answers Milly. "Even if we get only part of that, we'll have a decent sum to start the scholarship fund."

"How will we continue the scholarship?" asks the woman to Barbara's right. "A scholarship is all well and good, but we can't just give it once. How will we raise the money every year? Continue selling all the club furniture?"

A member across the dining room jumps to her feet. "I agree! We raise about five hundred from the annual garage sale. Our lunches pull in some, but expenses to maintain the clubhouse take almost everything."

A woman in a charcoal gray, pinstriped suit who directs public relations for the school district, speaks up. "I'm sure we can co-sponsor an event with the Exeter Corporation. They're trying to improve their image by getting involved with the arts. I know they'd put up seed money."

"Ladies, ladies," warns the president. "We're getting off the subject. The desk. I agree with Milly. Those of us who have tried to work upstairs know the desk is totally wasted. It's an eyesore, it's bulky, it's in the way. I knew Caty, too. She supported our commitment to the arts and would not disapprove of the proposal."

And she probably hated her own desk, thinks Barbara. Once she had the monstrosity, she didn't know what to do with it, so she foisted it off on us.

"Isn't there somewhere else we can put it?" asks Hazel. "Store it in the basement, or put it in the entryway?"

Cover it with a tablecloth, plaster it with corkboard and use it for messages? wonders Barbara.

"I move we table the desk, appoint a committee to look into alternatives, and reconsider the idea at the next meeting," says the business-suited woman, who has had some training in parliamentary procedure.

"Is there a second?" asks the president. "All in favor?" Several murmurs are heard, and she bangs the gavel. "Any volunteers for the committee?" No hands raise in the air, so she points to three or four members or their neighbors, no one is sure who. "You, you, and you. Get together after the meeting and report back next month."

Barbara is one of the unlucky ones who feel obliged to take on the task. She dutifully waits after lunch to meet with the committee—Milly and the business-suited woman, Janine Taylor. Ever-alert Hazel lurks in the background pretending to clear dishes while she eavesdrops on the conversation.

Janine takes charge. "The first thing we need to do is determine the actual, salable value of the desk. I know a reliable antique dealer who will give us a quote."

"In my opinion, which probably doesn't count for much, I think we should offer the desk to club members first," Milly says. "Maybe someone would want it for sentimental reasons, although God only knows why."

"But we won't know what to ask," Janine replies, patient in the face of illogic. "Once we know the value, we can establish an asking price."

"We know the value. Fifteen hundred. The insurance man told us that," says Milly.

Janine looks at her watch, evaluating how much time she has before the two o'clock school board meeting. Time enough to convince a stubborn old woman? "He's not an antiques expert," she explains.

"I've never seen the desk," Barbara breaks in. As Janine and Milly turn shocked faces to her, she amends, "I mean, I've been upstairs. But I've never unfolded the desk. Can we go look at it? Then we might be able to tell if we can use it somewhere or what kind of person might buy it."

The three troop up the narrow staircase followed by Hazel who has dropped her pretense of dish-clearing and begins to bristle like a wary squirrel. The group crowds into the upstairs room, one of a set which overlook the dining area below. Filing cabinets line one wall; in another corner a battered armchair rests underneath at least two hundred framed photos of former club presidents and certificates from civic organizations attesting to the valuable work of the organization. The door and additional framed documents occupy the third wall. The fourth wall is the home of the desk.

Large, black and boxy, it extends half-way into the room. Strange cracks run horizontally and vertically to indicate doors and drawers. Barbara touches the top with one finger. It doesn't move. She pushes with more pressure, and the top leaps up to reveal a dark void underneath. Envelopes, sheets of paper and membership applications bristle from side sections. Barbara moves the two sides, and a file-sized drawer springs to life under her left knee, knocking the sensitive kneecap into total immobility. Barbara falls in love with the desk on the spot.

"It certainly is...large," Barbara says, moving the file drawer back into place. A chain reaction forces the lower side wings out, one of which hits Milly who falls back against Hazel, who then bumps some of the framed documents askew. Milly pulls Hazel upright and glares at her.

Barbara runs her hand along the revealed writing surface. She wipes dust on her skirt and continues to poke her fingers into various cubby holes. A penny falls from one. Another contains stubs of dozens of pencils, all gnawed and chewed by the now-departed Caty in the throes of creative energy.

Efficient Janine points out, "There's no room to move in here." The group looks around. That statement certainly is true. With the desk fully extended, filing cabinets can not be opened and only a midget could sit in the chair.

Hazel proposes, "Check the next room. It should fit there."

"We'll check the next room," emphasizes Milly.

The group inches its way out of one room and into the second. It is, if possible, in worse shape than its twin. Someone has attempted to create a display of the club's collection of books, art and music recordings, but the accumulation has outstripped storage areas. On a sadly moth-eaten sofa nest stacks of books (most autographed, Barbara sees as she checks the fly leafs), threatening to tumble to the floor. Unframed sketches and oil paintings lean against several small side tables. An enormous bronze creation (a long-forgotten, revolving, achievement in the arts award), which consists of flying buttresses and cubes, takes up a corner and flaunts old tablecloths. Every inch of wall space is hung with crammed book shelves.

Janine shrugs her shoulders. "The entry hall," squeaks Hazel and leads the way downstairs. She stands in the dark hallway, arms flung dramatically to their widest to demonstrate that the desk would indeed fit there. Milly turns sideways and opens her arms, touching both walls, showing that the desk could not be opened.

"There must be somewhere," Hazel moans.

"Where? The patio?" asks Milly. 'The fireplace would be the best location."

Janine ignores the squabble. "I'll call the antique dealer. Then at our next meeting, we can report. Perhaps it would be best to offer the desk to our members first."

The group goes its separate ways, with Milly and Hazel glaring at each other as they climb into the same car.

Visions of the desk cloud Barbara's mind as she drives home. It reminds her of a big, black dog that nobody wants. She sees it crouched in the dark clubhouse mourning its lost owner, distressed over the slurs cast upon it by uncaring people.

Even through dinner preparations, Barbara grieves for the desk. She's always wanted a desk of her own. She works now at a rickety card table, lame in one leg, in the family room. Letters to be answered stacked on top of minutes from the PTA, bills in a manila envelope, pencils in a cup with a broken handle. On one corner, carefully preserved in an expanding file, travel brochures (Europe, India, Mexico), flyers about adult education classes, sketches for home improvements. Barbara thumbs through the slowly deteriorating papers once a year. Her older sister's discarded and outdated laptop is shoved under the table until someone needs it.

Barbara carries a load of folded laundry from the back porch to the family room. Pushing Kevin's scattered train set with her foot, she opens the door of the buffet with her elbow. As she stoops to put the tablecloth and napkins inside, she looks at the card table next to the buffet. She straightens, walks over to the table and holds out her arms. The desk would fit! Right there! But fifteen hundred dollars? Fifteen hundred dollars would pay for braces for one of the kids. Or insulation for the house. Or a summer vacation. Mentally filing the wish along with a recipe for stuffed filet of beef she always wanted to try but never could afford, Barbara starts dinner.

At the February meeting of the Cultural Organization of Women, the director of the All-City High School Orchestra tries his bland best to convince his audience of the school district's excellence. "These young people are examples of the fine job which our public schools are doing," he drones. "After years of dedication and practice, their skills can match and beat any school system in the country, private or public."

Barbara stirs her coffee when a movement at the back of the room catches her eye. Janine has just come in clutching a sheaf of papers, her report on the desk. A polite round of applause ushers the speaker from the podium.

The president stands. "We have one item of old business," she says. "Catherine Grant's desk. Janine, will you report?"

Janine walks to the front of the room so everyone can hear her. "The committee met and reviewed the situation. After considering all options for relocation, we agreed that we have no proper setting for such an unique piece of furniture." A murmur rises as those who favor keeping the desk complain to their neighbors. Janine holds up a hand. "I contacted an antique dealer who estimated that the desk is, indeed, worth $1500." A competing murmur beats against the first, like waves against a shore, from members with visions of wealth and greater club glory.

"Unfortunately, the dealer said a great many repairs need to be made to the desk before we can hope to get that figure. In his opinion, a qualified woodworker would charge about $500 to match the missing trim and complete other work."

Milly Stone jumps to her feet. "I say we do it! We'd still make a thousand."

Hazel looks up from her seat. "Now, Milly, you know we don't- have five hundred in the treasury."

Janine interrupts. "The dealer advised us to sell the desk for what we can get without repairs. I so move, and add that we advertise within our membership first."

Barbara seconds the motion. As the vote is taken, twenty-six ayes and fourteen nayes, she thinks she wouldn't care if woodwork is missing. She covets the desk, lusts after it, as if it were Tom Cruise or a triple-dip ice-cream cone. She even prays no one will bid on the desk, that all will remain as indifferent as they have in the past.

At the dinner table that night, Barbara mentions the desk and its price. Don doesn't blink an eye but just keeps chewing his chicken chop suey very thoroughly, testing for bones that always sneak in.

Kevin, however, is delighted. "I think that's a great idea, Mom. I'd be happy to give up my braces so you can buy the desk."

Nell objects violently. "That's insane," she shrieks in her usual immoderate, sixteen-year-old manner. "I could buy a complete wardrobe for a thousand dollars."

The other three kids say nothing. Jesse barely can talk and voices her opinion in other ways (screaming, throwing things), but only when they affect her directly. B. J. is more interested in hiding her unwanted mushrooms under her rice, while Mark bounces an imaginary basketball on the floor next to his chair in rhythm with his chewing. Barbara suddenly realizes that if she didn't have so many children, she could easily afford a desk. She squelches the thought immediately with other disloyal urges, like her occasional desire for time to herself.

"Actually, I think I could talk them down to five hundred," says Barbara. "They might not get any higher bids," She twirls the bean sprouts around her fork and holds her breath.

"Five hundred we might be able to swing," says Don. "We have three hundred coming back from taxes. With one hundred from savings and fifty a month squeezed out of your paycheck, we could do it. Why don't you see if they'll accept that figure?"

Barbara lays down her fork and beams. "I will. I'll write the club tonight with my offer."

After dinner Barbara sits at the card table and composes her letter. She stuffs the paper in the envelope, licks the flap to close it, leans back in the folding chair. Soon, very soon, she might be sitting at her own desk. She closes her eyes and runs the palms of her hands over the top of the table. She can feel the silky smoothness of the desk's wood, so unlike the pebbled plastic roughness of the table.

Several weeks later, the committee gathers to open bids. They sit in the central clubroom. Janine fans three envelopes in her hand and waves them in the air.

"Now comes the crucial point. Has anyone offered enough to make our task worthwhile?"

Millie reaches out to stop Janine's hand-swing. "What if all the bids are low? Do we still sell?"

"Of course," says Barbara. "We already agreed on that." She can see her desk slipping, slipping away from her.

"No, we didn't actually," replies Janine. "Perhaps we'd better clarify that now." She puts the envelopes on the coffee table in the middle of the committee. There they lie containing what figures only they know.

"I think we should accept nothing less than one thousand," says Millie. "Obviously we would take anything higher."

"But isn't something better than nothing?" asks Barbara. "Even if we don't get the full amount? We can't just throw that away." In her anxiety, she leans forward till she nearly touches the letters.

"Yes, but the purpose of the original donation was to benefit the club. Either by alleviating the need to purchase a desk. Or, I'm sure, so the club could accrue a profit. There would hardly be any profit if we made a minuscule amount," argues Janine.

"I think seven hundred fifty is definitely the lowest we should go," says Millie. With pursed lips she dares Barbara to challenge her seniority.

Barbara turns her head back and forth between the two other women. "Since I am one of the people who has bid, I can hardly insist, but...."

Janine gasps. "You have bid! Then by all ethical dealings, you should withdraw as a member of the committee!"

"I should?"

Both women nod. Barbara stands, bends to pick up her purse. "In that case, I'll leave you to your deliberations." She turns to leave, hair, purse and coat swinging after her.

"Don't be upset," calls Janine after her. "We'll consult with the members of the Executive Board if you have the high bid. And we won't bias them in advance." Her raised voice follows Barbara's trail.

A horrendous journey to the supermarket caps Barbara's afternoon. She battles a store full of mothers with wailing young children and an ill-tempered checkout clerk who insists apples are selling for one-eighty-nine cents a pound, not one-fifty-nine. The phone is ringing as she struggles with the door key, and the bag she carries rips, strewing cheese and bread on the floor.

"Hello?" she gasps into the receiver.

Janine's smooth, calm voice greets her. "We opened the bids after you left. Yours was the highest."

"Does this mean I get the desk?"

Janine will not be hurried. "We consulted with the Executive Board. Three out of four of them favored taking any reasonable bid. We have decided to award you the desk."

Barbara leans against the wall next to the phone and exhales. The desk is hers. It will live in the family room between the fireplace and the buffet. It will grow scratched and dented, push down the carpet. She will lose notes to herself in its cubby holes, stub her toes on its leg. The travel brochures, plans for house improvements, flyers on classes, articles on successful women over forty will fill its bowels, waiting the time when she can do something with them.

That night Barbara dreams of organizing the contents of the desk. Things categorized-- recipes in one file, newspaper clippings in another, baby books stacked on a shelf. There is none of the frantic terror or physical stress of a nightmare. She moves smoothly, ponders long.

"Mom, there's something wrong with the toilet." B.J.'s voice wakes her early, before she can finish her dream task.

"What did you put in it?"

"Nothing! You always say I did something."

Delaying the inevitable rising, Barbara turns her head out of the pillow. "Well, jiggle the handle."

"I did. It just....gurgles."

Barbara pokes Don with her elbow. He grunts. "Go see what's wrong with the toilet," she tells him. "B.J. says it's broken."

Don staggers down the stairs pulling his tiger-striped bathrobe around him. Five minutes later, his voice drifts back up. "There's something wrong with the toilet."

Barbara gives up and rolls out of bed. "What can I do?" she mutters.

"Can't anyone function without me?"

The family is gathered in the bathroom. Kevin jumps up and down yelling he has to go and would everyone please get out. Nell cranes her neck to look in the mirror, eyebrow pencil in hand, one eyelid blue, the other its natural color. Don crouches by the toilet, head downward, jiggling the handle with one hand, its mate stuck deep in the tank, damns floating from the vicinity of the seat. Jesse sits in wet diapers on the potty chair singing "Jesus Loves Me." B.J. swings a plumber's helper from hand to hand, narrowly missing Mark who has plugged the blow dryer in the hall but has stationed himself in the doorway. As one, they turn to Barbara.

"Kevin, go in the backyard in the bushes," Barbara commands.

"Yeeech," says B. J.

"This once won't hurt. Jesse, let Nell change you. B. J., you can wash in the kitchen sink."

The bathroom finally clear, Barbara looks in the tank. Despite rust and slime, the bulb is in place, the tank is full. Everything looks in order. She flushes. Immediately, the toilet starts to fill, to climb higher, to overflow. Hastily she lifts the handle to stop the flow. Must be plugged. Plumber's helper next step. Chulunk, chulunk, up and down. Flush again, overflow again. Chulunk, chulunk, up and down. Flush again, overflow again.

"This is ridiculous," Barbara mutters. She repeats herself as Don comes in dressed for work. "This is ridiculous. Can't you do anything?"

"I tried," replies Don, looking in the mirror and combing his hair. "I'm late now. You'll have to call the plumber."

Barbara walks into the kitchen, pulling her robe tighter around her waist. She sees the remains of several breakfasts heaped on counters and table--congealed egg yolk, crumbs from one end to another, cereal packages. Jesse sits in her high chair poking pieces of cereal in her mouth one by one with chubby fingers. "Ridiculous," Barbara says to Jesse.

Barbara stops at the kitchen sink. Dirty dishes float in several inches of gray water. Rings marching up the side of the sink show the water's previous levels. It slowly recedes like a flood in a canyon. Barbara gets a hint that something is seriously wrong with the water system.

"Ridiculous," she says again to the baby. "Reee-dick-you-us," Jesse answers.

Dinner is chaos. No water to cook with unless hauled from next door in pitchers. Paper plates to avoid washing dishes. Every time someone needs to go to the bathroom, he squats on the Ti-dee-Camper ferreted out from the basement where it has gathered cobwebs since the last attempt at family camping two years ago.

Barbara spoons out canned spaghetti and franks. Kevin methodically picks out all the franks while Jesse eats only the spaghetti and throws the franks on the floor where the cat gnaws daintily.

"Betty Jo, you have to eat something. I don't care if you're on a diet. And the plumber said the whole system is clogged up. Roots growing everywhere," Barbara says. "They'll have to go in from the backyard. Jesse, no! Those are to eat, not throw." Barbara picks up a piece of frankfurter and offers it to the baby who shakes her head violently back and forth.

"How much?" Don asks. He clears his throat, raises his voice. "How much?"

"Six or seven hundred."

"You're sure?"

"I'm sure."

Don lays his fork down. "Well, it's got to be done. The tax refund, a little from savings."

"But that was for my desk," Barbara whispers. Along the table, chatter quiets and heads turn toward her. She stares at her plate. "That was for my desk," she repeats louder.

"Wouldn't you rather be able to go to the bathroom than have a desk?" asks Don.

Barbara doesn't answer. She has visions of digging a hole in the backyard, constructing an outhouse, the family lined up in the snow for turns, B. J. jostling with Kevin with Nell with Mark in the midst of a sink of dirty dishes to wash their faces. "I guess so," she says slowly.

"Well, Mom, you know what you always say. You can't always get what you want. Adversity builds character." The clichés fall from Nell's mouth like spit. With a flip of her hair and a sly smile, she leaves the table.

It's not fair, thinks Barbara. "It's not fair," she says to those left at the table.

B.J. catches her mother. "To quote you, 'Who says life has to be fair?'"

Sometimes, thinks Barbara, it's not worth it to be the adult. Then she files the desk away in her mind along with dreams of travel, a remodeled kitchen, a degree in French, and begins to clear the dinner dishes.

THE END OF BASEBALL
A Story
Richard Hawley

When you are a kid you never think about things suddenly changing. Maybe you do if your mother dies or if you are jarringly relocated to a different state, but usually you just wake up in the morning and expect things are going to stay the way they were when you went to bed. But in the summer between fifth grade and Junior High, something, what felt like the biggest thing in my life, came to an end, and only now, in the declining years of my life, have I begun to find words for it.

That summer there were no words, just sensations and urgent impulses. I would awake to a flash of sky and sun, my eyes barely open before I could feel myself pedaling my fat tired bike to the park where there would still be dew on the infield grass and the faintly sweet, faintly sour smell of the mustard colored dirt. The airless necessities of school had at last opened up into summer, and summer was baseball.

Baseball was not a game I played. It was not a diversion or even a vivid preoccupation. Baseball was an enchanted realm in which I was at once eager explorer and captive, a realm as numinous and charged with feeling as Pan's Arcady or the Garden of Eden. By the time I was eight I was held fast and rapt in the rhythms and textures of baseball—the smack of the ball in the oiled pocket of my mitt, the dink, pop, or crack of the bat striking the ball, the dark dot of a fly ball's arc against sky as I braced to sense its trajectory and took off to get under it, the target, the orange pancake target of the catcher's mitt behind the plate, and I, squinting down from the mound at that target, fingers caressing the raised seams of the ball, savoring, like an assassin, the pause before rocking into my windup.

That summer between fifth grade and junior high would mark a change in all of this, a world opening up to still greater worlds as my friends and I advanced from Junior Little League to the Ten-to-Twelves division—Little League itself. This meant you got to play on the good diamond, which had lights at night. You also got full uniforms with white or gray jerseys and pants, long socks with a loop on the bottom that went over your other socks, and a hat which was just like the real hat of a major league team.

There were try-outs for the ten-to-twelve teams, and the managers picked you. All the teams were supposed to be equal, but they really weren't. The Indians and the Cubs were the best teams every year, because Mr. Hightower and Mr. Spinks were the best managers, and they always knew who the kids were and who was good, and they always ended up with the best players. I wanted to get on a pretty good team, but I didn't care too much which one, except the Padres, which had the worst uniforms. I was one of the best players in the eight-and nines, but I was a pitcher and also one of the smallest kids, and the pitching rubber in ten-to-twelves was ten feet farther away from the plate and it was up on a little mound.

The tryouts were on a really hot Saturday morning. The managers got everybody signed up for their positions and then had each group go out to a base or to the outfield somewhere and take turns fielding balls. I was with the pitchers and catchers, and after we warmed up for a while, I got in a line behind the pitcher's mound and waited for my turn to pitch to a catcher behind the plate. One of the dads stood in the batter's box, but he didn't swing.

Mr. Hightower, the manager of the Indians, was in charge of the pitcher tryouts, and I was nervous waiting for my turn, because he had a voice like someone with laryngitis, and I thought he might turn out to be kind of mean. "Okay, Force," he said, when it was my turn. He already knew who I was. "I hear you're the strike out king. Let's see what you can do." The mound on the good diamond was built up on a little hill, so you actually looked down at the batter and the catcher. Something about it made the catcher's mitt look really far away, not just ten extra feet.

I threw a pitch, and it was pretty good. It made the right kind of smack in the glove, and I started to feel better. Mr. Hightower said, "That's good, now see if you can bring that down a little bit, right at the knees." I was starting to like the way he talked, and I liked that he thought I knew how to throw my pitch a little lower. I threw the next pitch as hard as I could, and it was lower, but right over the plate. Mr. Hightower didn't say anything for a while, and I kept pitching to the target. Wayne Stegner, my old eight-and-nines coach, was standing behind the backstop, and he was shouting things like, "You're throwing smoke, Lefty, you're burning them in." I didn't look up at him, and I really wished he would go away.

After I had thrown a bunch of pitches Mr. Hightower said, "Nice job," and asked me if I had any other pitches. I said I did. I had a curve, which my father taught me how to throw by putting my first two fingers right next to the seam, and then twisting my wrist as I let go of the ball. I thought my curve was amazing because it would go straight, but with a funny spin on it, until about ten feet before it got to the target. Then it would seem almost to stop in mid air and float over to the right. My father laughed when he caught my curves. He said I had "a big hook."

I actually wanted to show Mr. Hightower my curve, but I had never thrown one with a batter standing there. The dad was batting on the left side of the plate now, and I was trying to figure out where to aim in order to make my curve to end up in the target. I decided that if I threw it toward his hip, it might end up over the plate. I tried it, and for a second I thought the ball might actually go behind the batter's back, but it kind of hesitated, the way I hoped it would, and started floating over to the right. The extra distance from the new mound made it curve even more than usual, and the ball went from almost behind the batter's butt to the front of his pants and then over to the far side of the plate. The dad batting laughed and said something, and behind the backstop Wayne Stegner shouted, "Hey, Lefty, where'd *that* come from?" Mr. Hightower said, "That's a helluva hook," and let the next kid in line pitch.

That night after supper, some kids called me up and said they heard I made the Indians, which made me feel excited but also nervous, and then Mr. Hightower called up and told me I really was on the Indians and that I was going to be the only ten-year-old pitcher. I had a funny feeling about being picked for the Indians. I knew they were the best team and they had most of the best players, but when I pictured those kids in my mind, they were all big kids, and I didn't know them very well. I pictured the best pitcher on the Indians, Craig Cummerford. He was twelve and really big. The kids said he was five feet nine. His legs and arms were at least twice as big around as mine. I wasn't even five feet yet.

Later, when practices started and I came up to bat against Craig Cummerford, his pitches would seem to hiss past me before I could even think about swinging. They cracked into the catcher's mitt with such force I felt jittery in my stomach. I couldn't stand to think about what it would feel like if one of Craig Cummerford's pitches hit me. My father would always tell me that the worst thing in baseball was to be afraid of the ball. When I stood up to bat and Craig Cummerford was going through his wind up, I tried to squint back at him and tighten my grip on the bat like I was ready to take a big swing, but I knew I wasn't going to do it. I wanted him to throw balls and walk me. The truth was that I didn't want to get hit. He was a really good pitcher, and he almost always threw strikes, so I knew I had to swing, but I also knew I could never hit a pitch from Craig Cummerford. From the dugout Mr.Hightower would say, "You're late, you're swinging late." From behind the backstop my father would call out, "You're waving at the ball," and I was.

The kids in my grade I played baseball with were kind of jealous that I got on the Indians, but for some reason I wasn't that glad about it. I was pretty excited before the first game, mainly because of the new uniform and the way INDIANS was written in orange and black letters across the chest of the jersey. Also, my father took me to the sporting goods store and bought me a pair of spikes and a leather pitching toe that screwed in over the front of my left shoe. The smallest pair of spikes they had were one size too big for me, but my father bought them anyway. He said I would grow into them and that we could stuff some cloth up into the toe area where the extra room was. I was glad they were too big, because they made my feet look bigger.

Even when we were warming up before our first game, I could tell something was wrong. I didn't really know the other kids on the Indians very well, and the one kid I did know, Gary Spender, wasn't much fun to be around. He was also the worst player on the team, and the only reason he was on the Indians was because his dad was one of the managers with Mr. Hightower. Just before the game started, Mr. Hightower called us over and read out the starting line up. It was the opening game, and I knew Craig Cummerford was going to pitch and that I wasn't going to be playing any other position, but it still surprised me for some reason that my name wasn't called and I wasn't going to play. I felt like I might even cry, which would have been really embarrassing, so I started walking fast out toward the outfield.

Maybe my face looked funny, because Mr. Hightower called after me and said I was going to be his fireman. I asked him what that was, and he said fireman was a name for a relief pitcher, a pitcher who came in and put the fire out. I liked the idea of being a fireman for the Indians, but after the game got started, I realized that there wasn't going to be any fire. Craig Cummerford was striking out just about every batter, and the Indians were getting a lot of hits and scoring runs in every inning. The games were six innings long, and by the fifth inning the Indians were winning by about sixteen to nothing. There was no reason for Mr. Hightower to take out Craig Cummerford and put me in, but I wanted him to do it anyway.

I started to make a plan to slip away behind the bench and go home, but I knew my father was somewhere in the stands watching the game and that I would really get it if I went home without him. When it got to be the last half of the sixth inning, Mr. Hightower decided to put in a lot of subs. I was sent out to play right field, and Gary Spender was put in center, which made it worse. It was practically dark, and I'm not sure I would have been able to see a ball if it came out to me, but I could see Craig Cummerford winding up and then hear the ball smacking into the catcher's mitt. When the inning was over, I hadn't even moved. As I ran back to the bench, I saw that our team was forming a big huddle. They started the cheer, "Two, four, six, eight, who do we appreciate…" and I ran right past them into the parking lot to look for our car. I felt really terrible, and I hoped my father wouldn't make me talk to him, because I didn't want to start to cry.

A few games after that, Mr. Hightower told me I was going to pitch against the Dodgers. It was going to be a Saturday afternoon game, which felt to me less important than a night game, because there wouldn't be the fuzzed, golden look of everything under the lights. The Dodgers were supposed to be a pretty crummy team, but I kind of liked them because of the bright blue color of their hats and letters. Also, some of my friends from school were on the Dodgers. As soon as Mr. Hightower told me I was going to pitch, I started making pictures of myself up on the mound against the Dodgers on a bright, hot Saturday afternoon, but I couldn't make the pictures seem any good. I knew when the time came I would probably go into my trance, but when I thought about the game in advance, it just seemed like a lot of effort to be throwing all those pitches.

Even so, the night before the game, I did not sleep for one minute. All I could do was make pictures of myself going through my wind-up on the mound and throwing toward the target, but every time something was a little off. I wouldn't shift my weight forward enough, so I would be off balance when I let go of the ball, or I'd be so off balance at the end of my wind-up that I couldn't throw at all. I wondered for a while in the dark whether I might completely forget how to pitch. I pictured myself being totally wild, throwing the ball way behind the batters' backs and over the umpire's head into the backstop. As it was started to get light out, I could hear it begin to rain. At first there was the tapping and hissing of a drizzle, then the splat of the big drops. I really didn't want the game to be rained out. I wanted to be able to stop picturing bad things.

It stopped raining by the middle of the morning, but they sky did not clear up. When I went over to the park at noon to warm up, the light outside was so strange, it almost didn't seem like the regular world. The clouds overhead were black and purple, making the sky look more like night than day, but it wasn't dark at all on the field. In fact, everything kind of glowed. The dirt of the infield, which was usually just dusty and gray, was moist and black, and the wet grass beyond the infield was a sparkly green. The white in our uniforms really did glow in that light, and the color of the letters and numbers—bright blue, black and gold—flashed in your eye the way bluebirds and orioles look in the woods. I had thrown plenty of new baseballs before, but I had never seen anything whiter and redder than the leather and the stitched seams of the ball they gave me to warm up with.

Warming up was nothing like my night pictures. My wind-up was fine, and each white pitch went right into the target exactly the same way. I wanted to relax into my trance, and I'm sure I would have, but Mr. Hightower and the other managers kept talking to the umpires about whether we should play. They thought there might be a storm, but finally, because there was no lightning or thunder, they decided we could play the game.

We were the home team, so the Dodgers batted first. Because of the dark sky and the glowing colors, I went into a different kind of trance than usual. I wasn't thinking or planning at all, and if somebody had spoken to me or asked me something, I'm pretty sure I wouldn't have been able to answer. My warm up pitches were just like the ones I had been throwing on the sidelines, right in the target, hitting the catcher's mitt with a terrific *smack*.

Then the first hitter came up, Russell Weeks, a kid from my class. He was tall but skinny like me. He stood up straight in the batter's box and looked out at me with an expression that let me know he was never going to hit the ball. I threw three identical strikes to him, and he struck out, swinging at the third one, actually just waving at it. The next two batters also struck out. Mr. Hightower said nice going, and I stayed in my trance while we batted, then I was up on the mound again under the dark sky in the glowing light. I knew most of the other Dodgers. They weren't that good, and they didn't look as if they thought they would hit the ball. This was probably because the first three kids struck out. The next two kids did too, and it felt a little like pitching in the eight-and-nines, except the sixth batter swung and hit a ball pretty hard which bounced chest-high into the glove of our first baseman who trotted over to his base for the out.

When we were up again, I got to bat and walked and then scored. We were winning, but it never occurred to me that we wouldn't be. Then, in what seemed like a second, everything changed. The swollen dark clouds moved on, and they sky was just gray. The color of everything faded back to normal, and when I got back up on the mound to pitch again, there was a wind blowing into my face. I know you can't blame something like the wind, but I remember getting mad at it, because now it seemed like there was something in the way between me and the target.

The first batter of the inning was a big fat kid named Stu Freyberg, another kid from my fifth grade class. He acted big and tough, and some of the dads thought he was really good because of his size, but I knew he wasn't that good, at anything. He was making a fierce-looking face at me, and he twirled his bat in little circles as he waited for me to pitch. I felt myself getting mad at the expression on his face, and I was already mad at the wind. I threw a pretty good pitch, and Stu took a big swing and hit it really far down the third base line. It went foul, but his hitting it like that all of a sudden made everyone on the Dodgers' bench start yelling and cheering. This made me mad too. I wouldn't have minded throwing one right into Stu Freyberg's fat stomach, but that would have been bad sportsmanship, and I wanted him to strike out.

He hit the next pitch even harder, and this time it was fair, into left center field between the two outfielders, who had to chase after it. It was a triple, and it probably would have been a homer if Stu Freyberg wasn't so fat and slow. The kids on the Dodgers bench and now a lot of the dads were whooping it up, and I started to feel really bad, a combination of still being mad and being ashamed that a kid like Stu Freyberg got a triple off me. Then I walked a kid, and the people on the Dodgers side started yelling and jeering. The next kid up was left-handed, and I knew a left-handed kid would have a hard time hitting my curve ball. So I threw one, and it was perfect. It started off headed straight for his butt, then it did its little wiggle and started floating to the right. It ended up right in the middle of the target. The umpire called out, "*Ball!*" I felt an electric shock behind my eyes. It wasn't a ball. I walked toward the umpire and said, "That wasn't a ball," and our catcher, Steve Minz, was standing up saying the pitch was right in there. But the umpire shouted right back at me. He said the ball was inside when it passed the plate and only ended up in the target. I looked up at him in a way that I hoped would let him see how mad I was, and as I was walking back to the mound, he came out after me and grabbed my shoulder and said, "What did you say, young man?" I told him I didn't say anything. I did say "total jerk" to myself, but without making any sound. He said he heard me say something and that I should watch my mouth. Then he told me again how my curve was inside when it passed the plate.

Now there was just crazy yelling and the wind and names I was saying to myself inside my head. I threw another curve, which started off toward the kid's butt, which I wouldn't have minded hitting, but then it floated even farther to the right than the last one. Steve Minz had to move the target outside to catch it, but I was pretty sure it was a strike when it crossed the plate. The umpire said, "*Ball two!*" I said, "*What?*"--I didn't plan it, it just came out. The umpire said it was a ball, outside, and that I better watch my mouth or I could watch the game from the bench. Mr. Hightower came out to the mound and squeezed my shoulders with his hands. He said to cool off. He said to just throw strikes. I couldn't think. I decided to pitch as hard as I could and not say anything. I threw the next pitch at the left-handed kid's butt, but I forgot to make it a curve, and it hit him. I pretended to be really calm. I walked over to the kid I hit, who was sniffling a little, and I said I was sorry and that I didn't mean it. He was okay, and when he went down to first, all the Dodgers people cheered.

Now the bases were loaded, and Russell Weeks was up again. My first pitch missed the target, and then I threw two good strikes. The next pitch was going to be a strike too, but Russell swung and hit the ball over the shortstop's head into the outfield. The Dodgers were scoring runs, and I went back into my trance, but in a different way, because now I was secretly crying the whole time. I didn't say anything bad. I watched my mouth and threw pitches, but my trance didn't work anymore. The Dodgers kept getting hits off me, and Stu Freyberg got a hit every time. The kids coming up to bat, even quiet kids like Russell Weeks, weren't afraid of the ball. They looked like they wanted to hit it, and they did.

I pitched the whole game, and we lost, nine to four. I knew I wasn't going to be amazing on the Indians. Something final had happened when the field stopped glowing and the wind came up. Mr.Hightower said I could be his fireman again, but I only got to pitch when we were way ahead, usually for just one inning. He also let me play right field a few times, but I almost never had to make any plays. I just stood out there, picturing things, like the night my father taught me how to catch fly balls.

Nobody my age could hit balls like that yet, but one night after supper my father got a bat and sent me down over the slope of our yard, through the bushes and scrub and up over the far side onto the flat place on the Metzger's vacant lot. We were so far away from each other that I could barely hear what he was saying. He would toss the ball up with one hand and then hit it way up in the air out toward me. I didn't get it at all at first. I just stood there trying to track the black dot of the ball against the sky until it thudded down somewhere, and I would run and get it. I could hear my father shouting at me. He said, "*Get under it! Get under the ball!*" He was getting mad, but I saw what he meant. I got so I could get under where the ball was coming down, but I had a feeling that because it was coming from so high up and so far away, it would have a terrific force behind it, and it would shatter my hand inside the glove. When I got under one of the fly balls, I would offer up a stiff arm and make a tight face. I kept missing, and then I saw my father walking down the lawn toward me holding the bat. I started to feel the can't-do-anything feeling, and I thought I was going to get a crack in the head.

But my father wasn't even mad. He talked to me in a slow, nice way. He said that catching a long fly ball was the same as catching a pop up. I just had to keep my eye on it, get under it and gather it in. When he said "gather it in," he showed me how to bring the glove down into my body as the ball fell into it. He showed me what I was doing with my stiff arm and how that didn't work. I had to gather the ball into the pocket and seal it with my other hand. He made it look slow and smooth and graceful. He said to imagine that it was a bird I was taking into my glove. I should take it in firmly enough to keep it, but not to hurt it. He threw me a couple of pop ups to let me get used to the bird idea, then he walked back over to our yard and started hitting me long flies.

After one or two, I got it. I heard the pop of the bat against the ball and tracked the dark dot. I ran a few yards to my right, got under it, and gathered it into the pocket of my glove. The ball made just the right smack in the mitt, and it didn't feel any harder than a pop up. I heard "*Atta boy! Atta boy*"*!* and I couldn't stop the waves of tingling in my neck. I caught all of the next ones, and in a few minutes I couldn't wait for my father to hit the next ball. I was tracking and getting under everything, including a few that started going way over my head. My father shouted, "Wait a minute!" and went inside the house and got my mother. Then he was hitting me more balls, and I got under them and gathered them in. I knew where the ball was going the second I heard the crack of the bat. I was talking to God out loud, saying please don't let it get dark.

I am not sure those were my precise recollections as I idled in the right field twilight during those seasons with the Indians, but I remember the feeling of being out there, alone and distanced from the action, half fearing and yet desperately wanting to get back inside the bright, pulsing baseball world that had held me in such thrall.

It would not happen. I suppose I became a serviceable player in the summer leagues and then, for a while, in high school. I had gained what I suppose was necessary perspective. I had a pretty clear idea where I stood, what I could contribute. But although I could not have articulated it then, I felt *diminished* when baseball came to feel like another thing I was expected to do, like taking piano lessons and serving as an acolyte at the early service once a month.

But while I hardened and distanced myself from the game, I did not grow out of baseball—I forsook it, or perhaps just lost it, lost access to its mythy tug. But there had been that tug, that realm. Its intimation has not dimmed in the slightest. At my advanced age I am open to the possibility that its beckoning insistence may be more than baseball, that baseball may have been a mere vestibule to another, still greater world, but it was in baseball that I sensed and for a time dwelled within that world. Far from relegating it to a faded preserve of my boyhood, I find myself coming back to baseball, to what it was trying to tell me, to that time, like the darkening evening in our back lot when my father hit me fly balls and I was talking to God out loud.

WHAT JOHN DREADS

Johanna Miklós

The instant coffee smells like dirty laundry. I dump it on the burnt pepperoni pizza in the sink. The whole house stinks.

I stare out the window as I did when waiting for Sue to come home. The wind blasts the school bus with snow from the weeping birch. Sue's father planted that tree when she was a little girl.

Bobby's going to nag about the burnt meal and the three weeks pocket money I owe. Not like when . . . He kicks the gate and chips the Bahia-blue paint Sue picked out last summer. "It's one step closer to our dream trip to Brazil," she said.

I grab a beer. I keep them in the fridge, all the way in the back, behind the milk cartons and the peanut butter he's not eating 'cause I didn't get the right kind.

I pop the lid. The kid stomps through the snow in boots that don't fit right. He's dragging the knapsack. Says he can't put it on his back 'cause the straps are broken.

I take a cool gulp. He'll walk in and pull off the fuzzy wool cap Sue gave him for Christmas. He's got black curls just like his Mom's. He'll leave the knapsack on the floor that hasn't been washed since the funeral and whine that he's the only kid who's not going on the fifth-grade ski trip, he doesn't have a game-boy, his parka's too tight and we're out of toothpaste.

The kid and the wind open the door. Blue specks swirl in the snow under Sue's tree.

"Mom didn't want you drinking," Bobby says.

PENANCE

Jess Harris

My eyes open in the pre-dawn darkness and I seek your hand, surprised when you aren't there. Then I remember.

I retreat to the back yard and lift my face to a thick, black sky. I try to inhale but my throat refuses the grit and miasma.

Eyes closed, arms stretched heavenward, I whisper, "I'm ready," and stand motionless until my hands drift back to my sides.

I spread peanut butter on dry bread, remove bottled water from a dwindling supply, and leave for the office. The dust that hid the stars should throw morning rays across the horizon in blazing orange and red, but I perceive only shades of gray as I hurry off to work.

The few vehicles on the freeway head the opposite direction, out of the city. When my mind wanders toward the decaying wreckage by the side of the road, I bypass it with premeditated indifference.

The skyline is a gap-toothed grin of untouched buildings standing among the ruins like shell-shocked soldiers.

Fragments of masonry and derelict cars litter the streets downtown, where tattered clothes hang from the backs of the blank-faced people who bear them; all are gray with dust. Empty stares pass through me, and I wonder if these are ghosts.

I navigate the unlit parking garage beneath my building until I reach the stairwell and ascend, step after step, to the top floor where gray cubicles stand in rows like headstones, nameplates identifying the departed.

I can't bear to turn the silver-framed photo in my office on its face, so I avert my eyes from your smile.

My fingers pass over desk and chair, seeking the warmth of hand-rubbed mahogany and the caress of soft leather, receiving neither. Familiar furnishings envelop me, and I reflexively reach for the computer's power switch. The dark screen reminds me that there are no more emails or electronic documents. I pull hard copies from filing cabinets, read reports, tally invoices, cross-check spreadsheets; the company was thriving when it died.

At midday I descend the stairs with the water and sandwich, creating no echo of footsteps in the concrete stairwell or off the marble walls of the empty lobby.

The park is desolate. That sculpture you liked with the woman and the birds is still there, but the horse and rider have fallen.

At the bench where I so often took my lunch, I wait for movement from the pile of newspapers and gray-brown rags that now occupy my former refuge. When dark eyes peer past the irrelevant headlines, I present my offering. Believing and unbelieving, boney hands stretch out, hesitating as if expecting the provisions to vanish. I persist until the gift is accepted and withdrawn into the bosom of rubbish. Muffled slurps and chewing sounds emanate, no thanks given or expected.

I return to my office to pull hard-copies, read reports, tally invoices and cross-check spreadsheets, remembering that sixteen years, two months, and three weeks ago I vowed to someday occupy a top floor office with a view of the park. Did you count the days? How many nights did you lie sleepless, alone?

I work until my vision dims, then slip past the workstation graveyard, down the stairwell to the parking garage. Nothing to carry, I emerge in our kitchen. I turn away from the missing wall to see Rascal dancing on his hind legs, whirling, eyes sparkling, pink tongue flicking in and out in time with happy panting. For a moment he is with me, and then I am reminded that his body accompanies yours in the detritus that used to be our bedroom, and he fades from view.

If I had believed the sullen predictions of destruction I would not have worked so late the night our home was cut in half; I could have been here when you died. But my bones molder alone in the wreckage of the car, willfully ignored along the side of the road.

Eyes closed, arms stretched toward a thick, black sky, I whisper, "I'm ready," in voiceless words that might be the wind rustling dry leaves. I am motionless until my hands drift back to my sides. Nothing changes.

Nothing follows.

A MORNING ALONG THE WAY

T.D. Johnston

Dawn brushed its vague light along Shenita Tabor's eyelids with just a suggestion that she forgot to set her alarm.

Shenita's eyes flung open. It was the first day of school. Day One of her senior year. She *would* go to college. She would *go* to college. After all, her big brother didn't go, and somebody in this family had to pay attention to better things. But first she had to shower, dress and eat breakfast.

Mama was already gone to the drycleaners. There was a little bit of skim left in the fridge, just enough to make the Life soft and spoonable in the purple bowl she preferred because it wasn't part of a set.

She got to the bus stop with a few minutes to spare, Barry's old backpack clinging to her left elbow with five spiral notebooks and a blue Roller Ball pen hiding at its bottom. As the bus came into view from the south end of St. Helena Street, Shenita risked a glance at one of the boys waiting at the curb. His name was Robinson. She didn't know his last name, but his first name was Robinson and his shirt was tucked in.

She wanted to sit next to Robinson. She wanted to sit next to him on the bus. She wanted to sit next to him in class. She wanted to sit next to him at lunch. If he wasn't on the football team, she wanted to sit next to him on the bus ride home to St. Helena Street. If he *was* on the football team, she wanted to do her homework in the stadium stands and catch a ride with Robinson's carpool after practice.

If she could sit next to him on the bus this morning, she'd know if he was on the football team by the time they got to school. She thought she knew the answer already, because his shirt was tucked in and they weren't even at the metal detectors yet. But sitting next to him she could be sure about the afternoon bus ride. She could be sure.

She needed to be sure.

Robinson looked like he was going to college.

As Robinson stood waiting for the bus to pull up, he spoke to no one, looked at no one. His backpack was actually on his back. It was full. He ignored the two guys behind him who thought something was funny about calling each other the n-word at the beginning of each sentence. Shenita could hear them because she was fifth in line and they were tied for second.

The yellow-and-black school bus slowed in front of them, its stop sign out and red lights flashing. The door folded open. Robinson, first in line, hefted his backpack higher onto his shoulders and prepared to step up.

"Hey, *college* boy! Get your *Obama* ass up them steps so white boy can drive us to school," came the loud instructions from one of the pair behind Robinson. Shenita drew her breath sharply and looked at the back of Robinson's head. He proceeded directly up the steps, apparently not having heard the dreadlocked boy behind him.

Shenita watched Robinson turn left at the top and disappear into the torso of the bus. The driver, a middle-aged white man in a royal blue golf shirt and dirty yellow baseball cap, stared straight ahead, his right hand gripping the handle of the old manual door opener. His knuckles looked as white as Wonder bread.

When Shenita got to the top of the steps, she tried to look casual as her eyes searched for Robinson. She found him quickly, halfway down the aisle on the left. He was seated in an aisle seat, with nobody sitting at the window. The bus was about a third full, with two more stops on the way to school. She couldn't quite make a crowded bus her reason for sitting next to Robinson, and unfortunately the aisle seat across from his was occupied by William Smalls, who lived three houses down from Shenita and wasn't going to go to college because he wanted to work on the shrimp boats like his dad and his uncle.

Robinson wasn't going to work on the shrimp boats. His shirt was still tucked in and his backpack was still full, and he didn't pay any attention to losers who said nigger.

She had two or three more short steps to find an excuse to sit next to him. She decided to be direct, and stopped in front of him.

"Hi, Robinson. Can I sit next to the window?" Shenita smiled and held her backpack in front of her apologetically, like she had no choice in the matter and the backpack really just wanted to sit there.

Robinson looked behind him, and then back at Shenita. Saying nothing, he moved his knees to his right, and Shenita said thank you and shimmied past him and sat down on the window side of Robinson with Barry's old backpack in her lap like a dog.

She couldn't think of anything to say as the bus pulled forward and continued its trek along Helena Street. She concentrated so hard on coming up with something that she almost missed his question.

"You're Barry Tabor's kid sister, aren't you?"

He wasn't looking at her, but she wasn't looking at him either so that was fair. She answered while examining the left front seam of the backpack.

"Um, yes. Did, did you know my brother?"

An outburst behind them delayed the response, and then Robinson reached out with his right hand and touched the seat in front of him, still looking straight ahead.

"Yeah. I knew him. I'm sorry about....everything."

Shenita found another seam to examine. This one had a tear in it, the red canvas separating for several inches along a plastic groove.

"That's okay, Robinson. I'll bet Barry liked you. Were you….friends?" She inserted her right forefinger into the torn section of the backpack, and felt one of the spiral notebooks. She pushed the finger in between the metal spiral of the notebook's spine.

"Kind of. But we didn't really, you know, hang with the same people. Um…."

Shenita listened to Robinson's voice trailing off as if it were hiding behind a tree in back of her. She was sure his voice wanted her to come and look behind that tree.

So she did.

"Tell me what happened, Robinson. I miss my brother. Tell me what happened. Please?" Shenita tried to make her plea both plaintive (a new vocab word last year in Mister Swilling's English class) and coy (a new vocab word also in Mister Swilling's English class).

Neither worked. Silence broke through the riotous cacophony (Swilling) in the rows behind them as Robinson inhaled and slapped his palms on his bookbag, turning to look at Shenita.

"Why do you have to ask that? You think the cops didn't ask that a couple of million times? I'm never telling anybody what happened, even if you are Barry's sister." Robinson's voice shook almost imperceptibly (Mr. Swilling would have liked the context here, she thought) as he stumbled through the vowels and consonants of 'sister.'

"Sorry," Shenita said. She wrapped her finger around the metal spine of the spiral notebook and squeezed, not knowing what to say, certain she'd blown it. After all, she already knew what happened. But she didn't know that Robinson actually *knew*. She'd just thought she could earn a little sympathy by asking the question plaintively, and maybe earn a little interest by mixing in some coyness.

"Really, I'm sorry, Robinson. I see it's personal for you too. It's just that, well, when your brother commits, you know, it's, like, hard. I miss him, Robinson. But I know what happened, and I'm okay with it now. It's important to be strong, isn't it?"

Robinson's face was blank.

"I'm going to college," he said.

"I know you are," she said. "So am I. They can't stop us, Robinson. Can they?"

Robinson reacted when someone toward the back yelled an expletive at the driver to get a blanking move on, but then returned his attention to Shenita.

"They stopped Barry. What makes you think they can't stop us?"

"Who stopped Barry? The cops?"

"Hell, no." Barry looked behind him again. "*They* did."

Shenita peered toward the back rows of the bus.

"*Who* did, Robinson?"

"They did. They stopped him. And they want to stop me."

"What in the world are you talking about, Robinson? Barry killed himself."

"Every day, every damn day," Robinson said as if he had not heard her, "they call me Obama Ass. Every day they tell me I'm an uppity Obama-ass nigger and to watch it or they're gonna pop a cap on my head. They tell me that in the hall, in the bathroom, on the bus, in the--"

"Robinson, that was last year! This is the first day of your senior year! And who cares what those guys think?"

Shenita was enjoying the conversation. She hoped the bus driver wouldn't really get a blanking move on. This is what *girlfriends* do, she thought. Encourage. Soothe. Occasionally be plaintive and coy.

Stand by their man.

"Everybody cares what everybody else thinks," Robinson said, continuing to stare directly in front of him. "That's what makes this such a crap ride. Except Barry. He didn't care what anybody else thought. He even wanted to go to Country Day. Did you know that?"

Shenita knew that. She knew that.

"And what did he get for it? He said those rich white people at Country Day told your mom Barry could come if she paid fifty percent of the tuition. Five grand a year. Your mom told Barry and those rich white people she couldn't afford any five grand a year from cleaning houses, and those rich white people said well, we think everybody should pay what they can afford, and you can pay five grand a year and so can everybody else, so nobody pays less than five grand a year. Nobody. So your brother didn't go there and he stayed here and got called Obama ass every day. Until he lost it one day and hit one of those guys in the face and got popped for it. Suicide my ass." Robinson gripped the seat in front of him and rubbed the vinyl so hard that Shenita could hear the squeak over the rumble of the bus engine.

Shenita turned around to look at the guys in the back, then turned to face Robinson. "But Barry jumped off the Broad River Bridge," she whispered hoarsely. "He couldn't swim."

"*They* killed him."

"*Who?*"

"Those guys in the back."

"*Robinson.* How do you *know?*"

The bus pulled into the Lowcountry High School parking lot as Robinson fingered the seat in front of him one more time and then stood up.

"I gotta go to class. So do you, Shenita."

Shenita took her finger off of the spine of her spiral notebook and withdrew it from the hole in her backpack. She had only been posturing when she used Barry to talk to Robinson, but had not guessed that—

"Hey, *Obama* ass!"

The shout had come from the back. Robinson did not respond, as the bus rolled to a stop and the door unfolded again to present the students with a new day's, a new year's, opportunity.

"Obama ASS!"

Robinson stopped. Shenita stopped right behind him, just as she was about to enter the aisle.

Robinson turned to face the back of the bus. Shenita lowered her head and stared at her backpack. None of the students moved. The driver didn't move.

As Shenita stared at her backpack and the hole in it, the silence on the bus hurt her ears.

Shenita didn't look at Robinson when she asked the question.

"Did he pay attention to them, Robinson?" she whispered.

She felt Robinson staring at them. She felt them staring at Robinson. She felt Robinson paying attention to them. Her throat began to ache.

"Barry paid attention to them, Robinson," she whispered hoarsely. "He died because he paid attention to them, Robinson."

The ache in her throat was getting rounder, bigger.

Robinson turned to face Shenita. "What did you say?"

"You heard me." Shenita climbed up onto the seat, still clutching her backpack, still staring at the hole in the backpack. She drew a deep breath as tears began to well in the reservoir of her bottom eyelids. She did not look away from the hole in her backpack.

Robinson touched her elbow. "What are you doing? Get down, Shenita. Come on. Everybody's watching. Let's just--"

"Hey everybody! You hear them, everybody? You hear THEM? My brother died because he paid attention to THEM!"

For a moment it seemed as if the bus was crumpling, yellow and black like old newspaper, folding into itself, onto her, as Shenita began to cry.

"My brother DIED because he paid attention to them!"

She could hear the roof buckle.

"My BROTHER died because he paid attention to them!"

Someone took her arm and tried to pull her down off the seat. The grip was firm but gentle. It might have been Robinson.

She ripped her arm away, and both hands gripped the backpack as she continued to stare at the hole that lived there.

"My brother died because he paid ATTENTION to them!"

She could hear the bus driver yelling something. She could hear someone else yelling something, something, something about Michelle Obama Ass. She could hear someone else, another perceptible else (was it Mr. Swilling?), saying "That's enough now" and another perceptible else saying "Let me through" and the hole in the backpack was as big as a basketball and how could it be as big as a basketball and then—

"MY brother died because he paid attention to them!"

She felt herself being lifted up and then down and then her legs walking without weight on them and how could they do that and I can't fly and neither could my brother and I'm a good girlfriend Robinson and I'm a good sister Barry and I'm a good daughter Mama and this hole is too big it's too big I'm going to fix this hole with that singer machine grandmama used to use to fix my socks and my brother died because he paid attention to them and stop calling me michelle obama ass cause even white people don't call me michelle obama ass and barry just wanted them to stop he wanted them to stop and I said don't pay attention to them barry don't pay attention to them cause I can take care of myself and i can stop paying attention to them so you won't have to and you won't have to and i don't need the counselor's office why are we going in there when i just want to be a good *girlfriend*.

* * *

On the Thursday before Thanksgiving, Mama drove Shenita to school. After school she picked Shenita up and they cleaned the Armstrongs' house together. It was fun because the Armstrongs weren't home and they both got to listen to their i-Pods.

"Tomorrow we got the Trasks' house," said Mama on the way home. "We get to have as much Gatorade as we want, even if Miss Missy is at home, as long as we change the sheets. All on the same dime, Shenita. Don't much matter what the job is, cause it is."

"Better than nothing, right, Mama?" Shenita smiled into the question.

"Anything's better than nothing, child. That's some wisdom there, sure is."

At home, Shenita turned on the television, but it was three minutes before six, and three minutes before six meant three minutes of commercials, so she pulled her cell phone from her right front pocket and texted a message to one of her friends. She waited, focused on the little screen in her hand, eagerness moving her eyes in darts and flicks.

The response came quickly. She clicked to view it. Then she laughed, punched three buttons and then another to share her laughter, and got up to retrieve the last of last Friday's Gatorades from the door of the refrigerator.

AUTHOR BIOGRAPHIES

AARON BEYER

Aaron Beyer was raised on facts, on a farm in Nebraska. It was years before he saw his first fiction, and from that point on he loved the stuff. That love continues, and now he writes fiction in California's Bay Area.

D. G. BRACEY

D.G. Bracey is a shadow-chaser, sand-scribbler and freelance writer from the coast of South Carolina. Since graduating from the University of South Carolina with a degree in Journalism, D.G. has managed hotels, peddled retail and contributed columns to any publication with an audience larger than two. He is currently finishing his first novel and searching the shadows for inspiration because there is a whole lot of sand yet to be scribbled.

MARJORIE E. BRODY

Marjorie E. Brody was born in the City of Brotherly Love, traveled south to Panamá and settled in the heart of Texas, where she's become an avid Spurs fan. Her short stories, some of which have been adapted for the stage, enjoy recognition from Lorian Hemingway, the Santa Barbara Writers Conference, and the Vermont Studio Center. Her first novel was a finalist in the Writers' League of Texas mainstream category. Her current novel, *Twisted*, crackles with the reality of her experiences as a psychotherapist. Her short stories "It Was Said" and "In the Underside" were published by Short Story America last year, and are among the 56 short stories in the *Short Story America Anthology, Volume I.*

KATHERINE TANDY BROWN

Katherine Tandy Brown is a successful freelance travel writer and a writing coach. She resides in Beaufort SC, where she teaches in the Master Writers' Series at the Technical College of the Lowcountry. Currently, she is writing a memoir entitled *Anne, Queen of the Wingchair*.

LAWRENCE BUENTELLO

Lawrence Buentello's fiction and poetry have appeared in a variety of publications, including *The Wallace Stevens Journal, New Works Review,The Storyteller, Paradigm, The Writer's Journal* and many others. He is also the author of the novel *South of the Moon* and the short story collection *Ghosts of the American Dream*. His stories "Dog At The Gate" and "The Glass Mare" are among the 56 stories in the *Short Story America Anthology, Volume I*. He lives in San Antonio, Texas, with his wife, Susan.

RAY BUSLER

Ray Busler lives and writes in Trussville, Alabama. He became an addicted reader of the short story early on when a teacher exposed him to Saki, Isaac Asimov, John Cheever, and Ray Bradbury. Ray's first story was published in 1995 when he won a prize in a competition sponsored by the Alabama Writer's Conclave.

GREGG CUSICK

Gregg Cusick has supported his writing habit through work as a furniture mover, English teacher, paralegal, construction worker, and retail manager. He currently tutors literacy and bartends in Durham, NC, where he is a 2010 Emerging Artist Grant recipient. Recent stories won the 2010 Lorian Hemingway Short Story Contest and the *Florida Review* Editor's Prize.

SUSAN MARY DOWD

Susan Mary Dowd spent 20 tumultuous years as a copywriter in New York City ad agencies. She has also been a columnist for several B2B publications and feature writer for the magazines *East Coast Home and Design, Fairfield Magazine*, and *Backyard Solutions*. At present, she is a copywriter for a local university as well as doing free-lance copywriting for ads, brochures, web pages, and direct mail. "The Yard" is her first foray into fiction. It first appeared in *Notes* magazine, Issue 4, published by Grace Notes Books and Publishing.

LAURY A. EGAN

Laury A. Egan's stories "Fergus" and "Split" were published by *Short Story America* in 2010, and appear in *Short Story America, Volume I*. Her collection, *Fog and Other Stories*, is published by *StoneGarden.net*, and her psychological suspense novel, *Jenny Kidd*, is published by Vagabondage

Press. Her two poetry books, *Snow, Shadows, a Stranger* and *Beneath the Lion's Paw*, are available from FootHills Publishing or directly from her. In addition to writing fiction and poetry, Laury is a fine arts photographer.

ANDREW FLEMING

Andrew Fleming is a writer living in the North West of England. Since studying English at Oxford University, he has worked as a researcher, tutor, and verse-writer for Hallmark Cards. His work has been published in *Writing Magazine* and broadcast on BBC Radio. His story "Basket" will appear in a forthcoming anthology from Deserted by Dignity Publishing, *Standing in the Kitchen at Parties.*

FOUST

Foust is a writer and printmaker who lives in Richmond, Virginia with her lovely husband Melvyn and three spoiled dogs. Her stories have appeared in *Word Riot, Smokelong Quarterly, Minnetonka Review,* and *Flashquake,* to name a few. She received an MFA in creative writing from Spalding University and she sporadically maintains a web page at www.foustart.com. She prefers her tea black, with a little sugar.

HEATHER FOWLER

Heather Fowler received her M.A. in English and Creative Writing from Hollins University. She has taught composition, literature, and writing-related courses at UCSD, California State University at Stanislaus, and Modesto Junior College. Her fiction has been published online and in print in the U.S., England, Australia, and India, as well as recently nominated for both the *storySouth Million Writers Award* and *Sundress Publications Best of the Net*. She was Guest Editor for *Zoetrope All-Story Extra* in March and April of 2000. Her debut short story collection *Suspended Heart* was published by Aqueous Books in December 2010. Her poetry has been nominated for the Pushcart Prize; was recently featured at *MiPoesias, The Nervous Breakdown, poeticdiversity,* and *The Medulla Review;* and has been selected for a joint first place in the 2007 Faringdon Online Poetry Competition.

T. S. FRANK

Scott Frank is a playwright and storyteller. He is the chair of the Theatre and Communication Department at Washington & Jefferson College; Chair of KCACTF's National Playwriting Program for Region 2; a member of the Dramatists Guild; and a member of The M Night Fellowship, a consortium of writers and actors dedicated to the development of new plays. His play *Butter's Goat* has been performed in New York, London, and Pittsburgh; he has also directed for the stage in those cities as well. His plays *The Orchard* and *Carnival* have been staged by the W&J Student Theatre Company. His plays ELVES/BURN and *The Minotaur* have recently enjoyed readings by The Terra Nova Theatre Group.

LINDA GRIFFIN

Linda Griffin is a native of San Diego, California and has a BA in English from San Diego State University and an MLS from UCLA. She currently works as a volunteer in the Literature & Languages section of the San Diego Public Library and is a member of the Authors Guild. She has had work published in the San Diego University literary magazine, *The Phoenix*, and *Catholic Library World* as well as one novel, *Stonebridge*. "When Carol Left Me" was previously published in *San Diego Writer's Monthly*.

SUSAN GROTHOUSE

Susan Grothouse is currently pursuing her Bachelor's Degree in Writing from Franciscan University of Steubenville, where she parties in the spirit of St. Francis of Assisi. She hails from Warsaw, Indiana, the orthopaedic capital of the world, and has worked in the orthopaedic industry for a while. Miss Grothouse has also been published in *The Curbside Quotidian*. She wrote "Hollars" when she was a senior in high school.

JESS HARRIS

Jess Harris started writing fiction at a very early age. As editor of his high school paper, his motto was "All the news that might have happened if life in this town was just a bit more interesting." Any actual reporting was produced by others. A Bachelor's Degree in Music and Theater opened the gateway to a variety of exciting jobs, imparting invaluable skills such as basic home repair and car deal negotiations. He also became privy to more knowledge than any human should be allowed about where turkeys come from. While none of these noble professions turned into a career, they provided a lifetime's worth of scenes, situations and characters. Jess finally found his calling as an Army officer and writer, and is currently stationed at Fort Stewart, GA.

RICHARD HAWLEY

Richard Hawley is a lifelong teacher and writer. He is the retired headmaster of Cleveland's University School and the founding president of the International Boy's Schools Coalition (IBSC). He has published more than twenty works of fiction, non-fiction, and poetry. Among his novels, the critically-acclaimed *The Headmaster's Papers* won a number of literary prizes. John Irving devoted a chapter to the *The Headmaster's Papers* in Michael Ondaatje's anthology, *Lost Classics*. Other novel titles include *Paul and Juliana* and *The Headmaster's Wife*. Recent non-fiction works include *Boys Will Be Men, Beyond the Icarus Factor,* and the forthcoming *Reaching Boys/Teaching Boys*. Hawley's essays, stories and poems have appeared in dozens of publications, including *The Atlantic, Orion, The New York Times, Short Story America, The Christian Science Monitor, American Film, America, Commonweal, The New England Journal of Medicine,* as well as in many scholarly and literary journals. For ten years, he taught fiction and non-fiction writing at The Breadloaf Writers Conference, and has addressed schools, colleges and other audiences worldwide on the subject of child development and learning. His story, "For Love," has been adapted from a novel in progress, *The Life of Jonathon Force,* and appears in the *Short Story America Anthology, Volume 1*. Hawley and his wife, the artist Mary Hawley, live in Ripton, Vermont.

VANESSA HEMINGWAY

Vanessa Hemingway Blumberg is an occupational therapist and a writer. Her story "Elsa" is forthcoming in the spring issue of the *Southern California Review*. She lives in Santa Cruz, California with her husband and daughter.

MARK S. JACKSON

Mark S. Jackson currently works as the Director of Information Security for a Software Services firm in Texas. He graduated from the University of North Texas with a Bachelor's Degree, and currently resides in the suburbs of Dallas with his daughter and a part-time cat. His previous story, "Partaking", was published by Short Story America in 2010, and is in the inaugural first edition of the *Short Story America Anthology, Volume I.*

T. D. JOHNSTON

T. D. Johnston has taught English and Creative Writing at college-preparatory schools in Pittsburgh, Miami and Atlanta, and has served as Head of School at Beaufort Academy in the seaside community of Beaufort, South Carolina, where he lives with his wife and twin daughters. His stories have appeared or are forthcoming in *PineStraw Magazine, O.Henry, Hobart, Civil War Camp Chest*, and *Short Story America*, where he contributes four stories per year.

MYRA KING

Myra King is an Australian writer living on the coast of South Australia. She has written a number of prize winning short stories, including first prize in the UK-based Global Short Story Competition, and has a short story collection published by Ginninderra Press. In 2010 her short story, "The Black Horse," was shortlisted for the US Glass Woman Prize. "The Trousseau Box" was highly commended in the UK JBW short story competition in 2009. Among other publications her work has appeared in *The Pages, BuzzWords, Little Episodes, Orbis, Eclecticism, Meuse Press, Dark Prints Press, Battered Suitcase, Admit 2* and *Heron's Nest*. She has upcoming (or recent) work in *Boston Literary Magazine, Eclectic Flash, The Valley Review, Meat For Tea, eFiction, Red River Review, Fast Forward Press, Illya's Honey, The Fiction Shelf* and *The Foundling Review*.

GARY LAWRENCE

Gary Lawrence retired early after 30 years in aerospace technical writing management and earned an MFA from Vermont College. He lives in Mesa, Arizona with wife Linda and their Yorkie-Poo, Rocky, and teaches English at a local college.

SETH MARLIN

Seth S. Marlin holds a BA in English/Writing from Boise State University, and has recently been accepted into the Creative Writing MFA at Eastern Washington. He served four years in the U.S. Army before leaving to pursue his studies, and has been offered a fellowship by the Western Interstate Commission for Higher Education. His work has been published in *M-Brane* magazine and *Wit's End*. He lives with his wife in the Pacific Northwest.

CHRISTOPHER J. F. MARTIN

Christopher J. F. Martin is a Ph.D Candidate in Literature at the University of Washington. He holds a MFA in Fiction from the same institution. His work has appeared in *The Seattle Review.*

MARTIN McCAW

Martin McCaw dropped out of college to play poker professionally. He sold correspondence courses for seventeen years. While still selling, he returned to college, eventually earning an M. A. in psychology at Walla Walla University. In his mid-forties he began teaching college and basic education courses at the Washington State Penitentiary. Although riots and murders happened frequently during his early years at the prison, he was grateful that he could finally make a living by helping people instead of manipulating them. His story, "Light in the Window," first appeared in Short Story America in January 2011, and is in the *Short Story America Anthology, Volume I.* He presently lives with his wife and niece in Prescott, Washington, near the farm where he grew up, close to his favorite river. He is currently working on a novel.

B.F. McCUNE

B.F. McCune has been writing since age ten, when she submitted a poem to the *Saturday Evening Post* (it was immediately rejected). This interest facilitated her career in public relations and also in freelance news and features. But her true passion is fiction, and her pieces have won several awards. This short story, "The Desk," first appeared in *Alfie Dog* (www.alfiedog.com), an online collection. Her first novel, *A Saint Comes Stumbling In,* was published in 2012 by Inspired Romance Novels; and a novella, *Irish Episode,* is available at Amazon Kindle. Her other fiction credits include publications in *Infectiveink,* the women's anthology *Calliope, Overtime* chapbook series, *On the Premises,* and the website *Alfie Dog.* In fall 2012, one of her stories is to appear in *Best New Writing.* For reasons unknown (an unacknowledged optimism?), she believes that one person can make a difference in this world. McCune lives in Colorado. Visit her at www.BonnieMcCune.com

PAUL MICHEL

Paul Michel was born in Philadelphia and raised in Ohio. He has a B.A. from Kenyon College and an MFA from the Warren Wilson Program for Writers. His work has appeared in over two dozen journals including *Glimmer Train, Short Story, The Southern Indiana Review, Inkwell, New South* and many others, and has won several national awards. His first novel, *Houdini Pie,* was published in 2010 by Bennett & Hastings Publishing. Besides writing fiction he also plays the fiddle, mandolin and guitar. He lives with his family in Seattle.

JOHANNA MIKLÓS

Johanna Miklós is happy that her story is included here.

CRAIG MURRAY

Craig Murray lives in Canada, where his time is divided between writing fiction, prose and poetry, and working as the Architectural Designer for a Conservation Authority. A poetry anthology is due to be published this year by Willow Moon Publishers and his Novel *Forgotten Man* is due out next year. He has received Pushcart Prize nominations for both prose and fiction, a *Best of the Net* nomination in 2006 and his poetry and short fiction have been published in a number of print and online journals. He has written four novels, a screenplay and is working on his fifth novel. He says "I write, not because I want to, but because I must. The stories get stuck in my head and desperately need a release. These people and places are real to me and deserving of their own time to live."

GARY PERCESEPE

Gary Percesepe is Associate Editor at *BLIP Magazine* (formerly *Mississippi Review*) and serves on the Board of Advisors at *Fictionaut.* His short stories, poems, essays, reviews, and interviews have been widely published in *Mississippi Review, Antioch Review, Westchester Review, Rumpus, Pank, Word Riot, Necessary Fiction, Metazen, elimae, LitnImage, 971 Menu, Moon Milk Review,* and other places. He has a story in *Sex Scene: An Anthology,* and two other stories appear in anthologies by Red Hen Press. He is the author of four books in philosophy, numerous short stories and poems, and an epistolary novel with Susan Tepper titled *What May Have Been: Letters of Jackson Pollock and Dori G,* (Cervana Barva Press) which was recently entered for a Pulitzer Prize. He just completed his second novel, *Leaving Telluride,* set in Telluride, Colorado. His story "Go" appeared last year in *Short Story America, Volume I.*

TIM PLAEHN

Most of the writing Tim Plaehn has done over the last ten years has been at the bottom of student essays, but he has still found time to write short fiction and two full length plays. His short story "Please Read" was featured in Atlanta's *Creative Loafing*, and The Barefoot Theatre Company recently chose his play *West Asheville* for a staged reading at the Art of Acting Studio in Los Angeles. In his previous life as poet, Tim lived for a time on Inishmore off the coast of Ireland after he was awarded The Aran Islands Poetry Fellowship. Tim graduated from Northeastern University and holds master's degrees from both Harvard's School of Education and Middlebury's Bread Loaf School of English. He has been a teacher and coach for fifteen years and lives in Asheville with his wife Helen and their four children, Martha, Patrick, Flannery, and Henry.

ROLLI

Hailing from Southey, Saskatchewan, Canada, Rolli writes – and draws a little – for adults (*Rattle, SmokeLong Quarterly, New York Tyrant*) and children (*Ladybug, Spider, Highlights*). He's the author/illustrator of the tasty poetry/art book *Plum Stuff* (Montreal: 8th House Publishing). *God's Autobio*, his debut collection of short stories – a number of which first appeared in *Short Story America* - is now available from Now or Never Publishing.

MANUEL ROYAL

Steven Doyle (writing as Manuel Royal) was born, like Tristram Shandy, with a broken nose. Following a refreshing 30-year hiatus, he is making a second attempt at a writing career. He lives in Atlanta, Georgia.

BRIAN SANDERS

Brian Sanders is a writer of short stories and screenplays, often adapting the former into the latter. He recently optioned his science-fiction screenplay, *Mini Wars*, to Multivisionnaire Pictures. His screenplay, *Nostalgia*, won the 2010 QuickFilmBudget Short Film Contest and will premiere at the 2011 Bel Air Film Festival. After graduating from Cornell University in 2006, he packed his bags for Brooklyn, NY, where he currently resides. A love of fantasy, in all its shades, inspires him.

JONATHAN SAPERS

Jonathan Sapers is a freelance writer and editor in New York. "Under the Hood" is his eleventh published short story: others have appeared in *Confrontation, Northwest Review, Pank, Laurel Review, Concho River Review, RE:AL* and *Pacific Review*. He is currently seeking representation for his novel, *Ghost Road*, and is working on a collection of stories, to be titled, *Segues*. Sapers is also a contributing editor to Teachers College's alumni magazine, *TC Today*, and has published essays and non-fiction in a wide variety of publications, including *The New Yorker, Smithsonian, Newsday, The New York Times, U.S. News & World Report* and many others. For more information about Sapers, including links to other work, please visit www.sapersink.com

LINDSEY SIMMONS

Lindsey Simmons is native to the Philadelphia area of Pennsylvania. She is a recent graduate of Edinboro University of Pennsylvania with a BFA in Fine Art Photography, graduating summa cum laude. While attending Edinboro University, she had several pieces of her writing published in the annual campus literary and art magazine, *Chimera*.

WARREN SLESINGER

Warren Slesinger graduated from the Iowa Writers Workshop with an M.F.A., and has taught English and served as editor, marketing manager or sales manager at the university presses at the University of Chicago, University of Oregon, Penn, and the University of South Carolina. He received an Ingram Merrill grant for writing in 1971 and a South Carolina Poetry Fellowship in 2003. His fiction has been published in the *Alaska Quarterly Review* and *Short Story America*. His poetry has been published in *The American Poetry Review, The Antioch Review, The Beloit Poetry Journal, The Georgia Review, The Iowa Review, New Letters, The North American Review, Northwest Review, Poetry Daily, The Sewanee Review,* and *The South Carolina Review.* Over the years, he has been in residence at the Yaddo and MacDowell colonies for writers and the Sitka Center for Study of the Arts and Ecology. At present, he teaches in the English Department at the University of South Carolina-Beaufort.

JIM VALENTI

Jim Valenti is a professional engineer fixing New York City's iconic suspension bridges by day, and a married father of three longing to sail off to Margaritaville by night. Raised on a steady diet of *Twilight Zone* and *Unsolved Mysteries*, his wayward imagination has recently chewed his tremendously limited attention span into raw bits of life, some of which have eventually landed on the pages of *Alien Skin, 52 Stitches, Murky Depths, Bards and Sages Quarterly, Bete Noire* and *Short Story America*. He looks forward to continuing this trend as long as the hunger remains.

ERIC WITCHEY

Eric Witchey has made a living as a freelance writer and communication consultant for over 20 years. In addition to many non-fiction titles, he has sold more than 70 short stories and three novels. His stories have appeared in six genres on five continents, and he has received recognition from *New Century Writers, Writers of the Future, Writer's Digest, The Eric Hoffer Prose Award* program, and other organizations. His How-To articles have appeared in *The Writer Magazine, Writer's Digest Magazine,* and other print and online magazines. When not teaching or writing, he spends his time fly fishing or restoring antique, model locomotives.

JON ZECH

Jon Zech's short fiction has most recently appeared in *Mirror Dance* and *Splickety* magazines. His story, "The Tuesday War," earned an Honorable Mention in *Glimmer Train* and "A Good Short Ride" is scheduled for publication in *Echo Ink Review* later this year. His novel, *Buck and Tangee: Things that Happened,* is planned for release this spring through Woodward Press. He lives near Anchor Bay, Michigan with his wife, Rue, and various dachshunds.

Acknowledgements

Short Story America is deeply grateful for the excellent work of Steve Thompson of PC Web Services (Beaufort, South Carolina) for his excellent work at Short Story America's website, Nash Steele of the College of Charleston for her fine work as an editorial intern for Short Story America, Tim Devine and Bob Murr of Murr's Printing (Beaufort, South Carolina) for their superb assistance with the preparation of this book, the whole team at *Lowcountry Weekly* (a great arts and entertainment publication based in the South Carolina Lowcountry) for their support of the literary arts, author Alan Heathcock for his outstanding foreword to this book, and especially to Dr. Stacey Johnston for her incredible help and support for the mission of Short Story America.